An Approaching Storm

Other novels in this trilogy
by Sally Stockley Johnson

After Yesterday (2018)

The Land of the Living (2020)

An Approaching Storm

A Novel

Sally Stockley Johnson

Sally Stockley Johnson
Presbyterian Village, A-31
510 Brookside Drive
Little Rock, Arkansas 72205
501.313.7533
sallysjohns@comcast.net

ISBN: 978-1-7337964-9-1

Book and cover design: H. K. Stewart

Printed in the United States of America

To those who were present on that morning in December when the United States entered a war that was already threatening the whole world

And to all those around the world who fought for the democratic values they believed in and were willing to give their lives to defend and maintain

Part I

Excerpts from Ella's Journal: 1932–1936

Ella's Journal
1932

The first entry had been written when Ella realized she was pregnant after she and Jack had returned to Myrna from their two-week honeymoon in the MacPhersons' cabin on the Buffalo River. She had gone to see Dr. Jeffrey Anderson when she began to think she might have conceived while she and Jack had just been getting to know each other physically. She had been so sure she was already going through the change-of-life that she had told Jack they didn't need to use protection.

July 30, 1932

When Jeffrey examined me, he told me he thought I could be a few weeks into a pregnancy. He also told me I would need to be very careful because he was troubled by the way my uterus felt when he examined me. He said I should tell Jack I most likely was pregnant but might be facing some problems.

His words dismayed me, mainly because I really do not want to have a baby. After all, I have raised three children, well almost raised three since Dan is just 12, though he will soon be 13, and I am so looking forward to team-teaching 10th through 12th grade English and history that Jack and I have been planning for months and have actually received permission from the school board to try as an experiment during the coming year.

Women expecting a child are not allowed to teach, and actually, even women with young children are generally not hired as teachers. In fact, married women in general are not considered teacher material because they are supposed to stay home and take care of their families. Of course, since few male teachers make enough money to provide for a family these days, teaching is generally done by unmarried women and a very few men. Myrna, in the middle of this Great Depression, has become one town that has begun making exceptions to the rule.

My pregnancy provoked the first crisis in our newly married life as Jack seems overjoyed by my news, while I feel no joy at all. In fact, I feel guilty, like a spoilsport, because Jack is so pleased. He keeps saying how much he looks forward to being a "real father" and he plans to be a "hands-on daddy" and do all the things he'd failed to do in his first marriage after his daughter was born. He isn't going to let anything happen to this baby as it did when his and Charlotte's daughter, Carrie, died at age three from unknown causes.

I find myself resenting—not Jack's happiness exactly but the idea he doesn't accept my son Dan as his "real" child too. I know I am not being totally fair because Jack stepped in to be Dan's friend after my husband had been murdered. Dan was so filled with anger he wouldn't let me or our priest or anyone help him get over his fury at God and everybody around him. Jack had been brand new in Myrna as the pastor of the Presbyterian church at the time and had met Daniel only once before he was shot and killed instantly by an old drunk man, who turned out to be the husband of one of my closest friends.

On our honeymoon we promised each other we would be completely open and honest with each other about everything. And here we are, only a few weeks into the marriage, with me not able to share what I am really feeling about this pregnancy!

Several weeks later Ella had written:
If God and Nature had not stepped in, I'm not sure what would have happened to our relationship, but three weeks after I told Jack I was pregnant, I ended up back in Dr. Jeffrey Anderson's office and then in the hospital section, my pregnancy ending in a miscarriage.

Jeffrey told me on my first visit he feared I might not be able to carry this child to term because he'd found several things when examining me that caused him concern. In fact, he performed a hysterectomy on me, removing my uterus as well as the fetus. I felt so guilty—like I had somehow caused the miscarriage because I hadn't really wanted a baby. I cried a lot and felt like a bad person, also wondering what effect this would have on our marriage. Jeffrey had tried to assure me that once I healed from the surgery, it shouldn't make any difference in our marital relations and he would tell Jack that also.

Not long afterward Ella had written:

In one way, this entire event renewed our promises to each other to be able to talk through all our feelings in honest and open conversations. I shared my guilt with Jack because I had not really wanted this child since I'd already experienced motherhood and was looking forward to working with him as a partner and co-teacher rather than staying home taking care of a baby.

Jack confessed to having had mixed feelings about the baby too. In a way he'd wanted a child of his own and the opportunity to be a much more involved and attentive daddy to our baby than he had ever been with Carrie. But he'd also secretly feared that this child might interfere with our relationship and the closeness we had developed on our honeymoon because I might turn out to be as over-protective and over-involved with this baby as Charlotte, his first wife, had been with Carrie. So a part of him felt grief I had miscarried and another part of him felt relief.

When I talked about my fears that the hysterectomy might keep me from enjoying lovemaking even though Dr. Anderson had said that it shouldn't, Jack said we would cross that bridge after I healed from the surgery, but he assured me he loved me for myself, for who I was as his companion and partner, and not just for my body. Yet I confess we were both relieved when I did heal and we were able to re-start the intimate, physical part of our relationship, and found the hysterectomy had not damaged our enjoyment of our sexual life.

Ella paused and remembered how those first months after their honeymoon had also been a bit rocky due to the adjustment Jack and she had to make to having her three children in the same house with them as they grew accustomed to being "a family" of five.

Then they all had to deal with the pregnancy and her surgery, along with Ella's missing the first two weeks of school as her body recovered and her energy level returned to normal.

October 7, 1932

The Depression is still a major factor in all of our lives. The collapse of the stock market, while it didn't directly affect most people in Myrna, still made a difference in that it was causing the general public to lose confidence in the country's future. The wealthier folks in Myrna have cut down on their spending and in doing so have hurt the economy by not buying enough while the poorer people are simply getting poorer and can't afford to buy anything except the most basic necessities, and sometimes not even those. You can almost feel the fear these days as people's lives become more and more difficult. One economist, whose column Jack reads in the Sunday *Times*, describes it like a snowball effect because loss of confidence in the future leads to a decreasing demand for products, leading to cuts in production, and then to job losses.

Consequently, I'm really glad to be back teaching. I think what Jack and I are hoping to achieve this year, at least with the 10th graders (and with the juniors and seniors too, though in a less obvious way), is a realization of the hardships that most people faced when they first arrived in this country and then tried to create a new life of opportunities for a better future for themselves—and for their families as they married and settled down. We are emphasizing right now that this country was settled by strong, brave, and hard-working men and women. We come from hardy stock, and we will survive this Depression in spite of any difficulties we may encounter while it lasts.

Although school started two weeks late because of the Depression and the loss of money to pay teachers, and I was even later getting back than that, we are still off to a good beginning, I think, especially with the 10th graders, because our approach to

12

teaching history this year is completely new and is very family oriented. Our students have become really interested in trying to make contact with distant relatives and find out what they can about when, how, why, and where their first family members arrived and settled in this new land and then trace how and why their own families came and settled in or around Myrna.

Ella smiled as she continued reading because she was remembering how exciting it had been to move forward with their plans to integrate historical events and literature in ways that would help their students both understand and experience, even if vicariously, the times and situations they were studying. The year had progressed even better than they had hoped.

October 9, 1932

Our son Dan has given us new friends through a friendship he has formed with a young boy and his family who have moved here recently. Dan had mentioned him to me before school started, and I had said I would visit them, but I was so busy trying to get well and also prepare for the beginning of school, I didn't get around to it. But then Dan reminded me I'd said I would visit them soon, and soon was about to come to an end!

So yesterday afternoon Dan and I went calling on the Fredricks. I was expecting a blonde German beauty to answer the door when we knocked, but instead we were greeted by a dark-haired, petite woman with only a slight accent giving away her nationality. Her first name she informed us, after we had introduced ourselves, is Ruth. I already knew that her son, who has become Dan's good friend, is David. Her husband has recently become a member of the faculty at Arkansas State College in Jonesboro, and at some point they will probably move there. However David and his younger brother, Sam, have both made such good adjustments to the schools in Myrna, they hate to make them move again since their past few years have been full of many adjustments.

Ruth invited me in to have a cup of tea with her. Dan immediately followed David and Sam back outdoors to play with a football or something and left Ruth and me to visit in the parlor with our teacups. It was there she told me their story.

She and her husband Hans, who now goes by Hank, had met at a lecture in Munich in which a German professor was speaking against the policies of Adolph Hitler. Hitler had recently begun to move into a position of power in their country. Her own parents were very disturbed by the anti-Jewish language Hitler and his followers were using and the policies they had begun putting into place. They were alarmed because her family were well-to-do Jews. Hans was a Christian but totally against Hitler and what he was saying and the kind of hatred he was spreading against her people.

Hans was also a professor at the university in Munich. She had met him there, and they had fallen in love and married, somewhat against her parents' wishes although they had grown to accept and love him. Ruth was pregnant with David when Hans had come home from teaching one day and said they must leave Germany as soon as possible because it was becoming dangerous to be Jewish. He told her that several students had accosted him after his class one day and demanded to know if it was true he was married to a Jew. When Hans said it was not any of their business who his wife was, they had sneered at him and said that Herr Hitler thought otherwise and they would soon see that he was without a job, and then what would he do with his Jew?

Hans had gone to speak to the head of his department to file a complaint, but the old man, who had been the department head for many years, told him that he could do nothing about their threats because these "brown shirts" had more power and influence than he did.

Hans had some good friends in England who had been trying to convince him to come there and teach, promising that with his rep-utation and qualifications he could easily get a teaching job, and warning that Germany was gaining a reputation as a Fascist nation as Hitler's power increased. After this latest encounter with the

Brown Shirts, Hans talked with her parents, trying to convince them it was time for all of them to leave Germany and go to England.

But it wasn't just the anti-Semitism that impelled Hans to move his family out of Germany. Hans had also begun to make a name for himself as a research physicist in the area of atomic energy. He'd had at least two papers published on the subject that had attracted attention from some of the German scientists who were working in that field and were known to have received the attention of Adolf Hitler. These scientists had approached Hans about coming to work with them in their laboratory where they were exploring ways to create weapons to use atomic energy. That was the last thing Hans wanted to be involved in!

Ruth's parents weren't ready to leave their homeland yet but understood why Hans felt it necessary for him and Ruth to go. So the young couple moved to northeastern England and settled in Durham where Hans had been hired to teach at the university there. While David had been born in Germany, Sam had been born in Durham. He, at least, had British citizenship! But Hans, now Hank, had gained a reputation in the nuclear physics circles and was receiving some pressure from British scientists to join them in exploring how this new form of energy might be used as a weapon if war between Great Britain and Germany occurred. And war was looking more and more likely as Germany began re-arming and Hitler's popularity grew.

Hank had become friendly with some other doctors who had started a center for treating people who had been injured physically and/or emotionally during the war with Germany but were unable to be helped by usual medical procedures. Founded in the '20s, it was really more of a community where many patients, whose injuries disabled them in ways that made it difficult for them to be accepted by others, were provided with a place to live and work. She didn't really know much about it, but Hank had been very impressed with it, and not only with their work but also with their philosophy of healing that took place by living within this type of community.

I became more interested by the minute as Ruth talked and finally couldn't keep silent any longer. "I'm pretty sure I know this community you're talking about. It's the work of friends of my first husband, Daniel, who was a doctor and served in France during the war with Dr. Willingham. He actually started this wonderful place. Daniel and I visited St. Anthony's and met the staff and some of the patients there when we went to England in the summer of '25. I can't believe what a small world this is! But you still have to tell me how you all ended up in Myrna."

Ruth said Hank had become more and more nervous about the pressure he was getting to work with the British government's scientists to develop nuclear weaponry he felt *they* needed to move somewhere else. The Englishmen at the center, well actually one was a French doctor, who had recently been to the States and had visited in Arkansas, said this would be a good place to come because it was about as far away from England and Germany as you could want.

"That must have been Jean Marc LeCroix, a good friend of Daniel's and also of mine," I exclaimed.

Ruth didn't remember his name but said it could have been LeCroix. And, of course, it didn't matter. Ruth continued with her story. "My parents, to our surprise, knew of several German families living in New York City, and they had written one of them about the pressures Hank was feeling to work with these scientists. So our next move was to New York City.

"The Jewish community there was very tightknit in some ways, even though they had arrived from various countries—Russia, Poland, Germany, France, even Spain. We soon heard about these Jewish brothers who had moved to Arkansas, a state in the middle of this vast country, and they had become wealthy and among the leaders of the small town in which they lived. Hank, whose English had improved tremendously during our time in England, wrote to one of the brothers, Michael Lewis, who knew about this college in Jonesboro that was in its early stages of growth, and he said it was looking for a science professor. Hank sent them his resume, being very careful to mention nuclear physics as only one of his

16

various teaching fields. He stressed his emphasis on teaching the basics of chemistry, physics, and even biology—hoping they could use him in any one of these areas. And so he got the job and has been very happy there teaching the basic courses.

"The Lewises, especially Esther and Michael, took us under their wings, helped us find this house and the second-hand car Hank drives into Jonesboro every day. I've heard a good bit about you from Esther, and our sons have become good friends, so I already felt like I knew you fairly well before you came to see me."

I apologized for not getting by to meet her sooner, but she said she understood all that had been going on in my life. We became good friends that afternoon and look forward to getting Jack and Hank together, along with Michael and Esther.

October 30, 1932

One totally unexpected occurrence was the visit by the new minister of the Presbyterian Church last Sunday afternoon. He had just been installed as their pastor in early October. Neither Jack nor I had met him, though we had heard a good bit about him from our dear friend Molly Wainwright. She likes him and thought he might be able to heal the hard feelings which still existed among some of the younger church members who had not been happy with the way the church had treated Jack after learning about his divorce from Charlotte.

That morning Jack, Dan, and I had attended worship at the Episcopal Church where Dan and I still belonged. Dan was becoming increasingly bored with the lack of content in the youth group meetings. Jack and I were not impressed with the young pastor's sermons, which we thought were usually shallow, lacking not only in biblical content but in offering a relevant message of either challenge or comfort to the listeners.

We had just finished cleaning up the kitchen from Sunday dinner when we heard someone knocking on the front door. The unknown caller introduced himself as Greg Mitchell, the new pastor at First Presbyterian Church and offered Jack and me his hand. We were both surprised to see him but invited him in.

"I know you didn't expect to find me at your front door, but the truth is that I've heard a lot about both of you, and I wanted to meet you for myself. And actually, one of those who's talked about you the most is my son George. He is in your 10th-grade English and history classes and is more interested in both these courses than I ever remember him being before. He's been impatient for us to get everything unpacked so we can hunt for some old photos and letters from my grandfather, who came to this country from Scotland when he was just a lad, married my grandmother, and settled first in Georgia and then moved to Tennessee after the Civil War. Our son Grant is the same age as and is in the same class with your son Dan, and he likes him and hopes they will become good friends." Then he started laughing and said, "There I've given you some of my credentials and told you lots more than you probably cared about knowing."

Jack and I started laughing too, saying how much we were enjoying having George in our classes and what a good student he is. But he waved off the compliments and began talking again.

"I've got more I want to say. I've also gotten an earful from friends of yours like Molly Wainwright and the MacPhersons. They think the world of you both and feel like the church was unfair in its treatment of you, Jack. I understand that was before you two married. I've talked this over with my Session and they have backed me in what I'm about to do. I want to invite you both and your son Dan to visit the church and see if you feel welcomed and could forgive the church for the past and even join our membership if you experience God's leading you to do that. Would you be willing to at least come and visit us?"

Jack and I were amazed at this man's words, to say the least. But I could tell Jack was touched by the invitation and Rev. Mitchell's openness and friendliness. Jack had tried hard to feel at home at St. Mark's, but the truth was that both of us missed Father Banks's spiritual and intellectual leadership. We had hoped Father Brian Chandler would grow on us, but so far that had not happened.

I waited for Jack to speak. With a catch in his voice, he said, "Your coming here and saying these things to me have touched me more than I can say. I've felt I failed First Presbyterian in so many ways, some I had no power over and some were due to my inexperience. But I have found healing through my marriage to my wonderful wife and joy and fulfillment in co-teaching history and English with her. We will discuss your invitation together, but don't be surprised if we turn up at worship one Sunday. Ella, it's your turn to say something. I didn't mean to speak for both of us."

It was obvious how much Greg Mitchell's visit had meant to Jack. While both of us had heard about the new minister at First Presbyterian, neither of us had picked up on who George Mitchell was. The truth was that as teachers of all students in grades 10-12, we had so many students, many of them new to both of us, we had spent most of the first weeks of classes learning names and remembering which class each one was in!

I took my cue and said, "My husband has spoken for both of us. We will visit soon I'm sure. And forgive our manners—or lack of them, really. Won't you come in and have a glass of iced tea and tell us a bit about your family and why you answered the call to come to Myrna?"

He did come in and we had a good visit—found out he was a graduate of Union Seminary in Richmond, although he had grown up in Raleigh, North Carolina and was a graduate of the University of North Carolina where he'd met his wife Ginny. He had served churches in both West Virginia and Tennessee before receiving the call to Myrna. He and Ginny had both liked the members of the Search Committee and what they had heard about the church and the town.

The committee had been open and, they felt, honest about why Jack had resigned from his ministry there and then had left the ministry entirely They assured him that Jack had acted honorably and professionally while serving them, although a goodly number of members were upset and disturbed by his wife's actions and her refusal to come and join him in his ministry.

He understood that a very small group thought Jack's theology was heretical, but that group had calmed down since Elder Ezra MacGregor had died, and they knew on their own the Presbyterian Church and its seminaries, both northern and southern, were dealing with differences in biblical interpretations and understandings. He'd dealt with a bit of that in the church he had left.

I was especially impressed with what he said next. "I told the Search Committee I was one of those who believed the new ideas were one result of discovering ancient manuscripts and using modern scholarship as a tool to help us grow in our understanding of Jesus and the Christian faith. I told the committee if the congregation could not accept that about me, then I was not the right pastor for the church. They assured me that the elder who had been most disturbed by your beliefs had recently died, and his followers, who weren't many, had calmed down, though one couple had left the church even before Ezra's death.

"I came alone to visit the church because Ginny didn't feel she could leave all four of our children. Truth be told, I think the main reason they wanted to call me was that I had a wife and four children! Anyway, I liked Molly Wainwright, the MacPhersons who had me over to dinner, and the three other members of the Search Committee. So here I am and eager for you both to meet my wife Ginny and my other two children, Ginger, who's just turned 10, and Glen, who's eight."

Jack and I both looked at each other and smiled as he said these last words. "That was one of the major complaints against me," Jack said, laughing. "I didn't have a wife or any children. Your qualifications are certainly much better than mine were in that respect! I'm delighted you are here and cannot thank you enough for coming to see us!"

"One more question for you both before I go," Greg Mitchell said. "I've gotten to know Father John Banks a bit through Rotary Club meetings and really like him. I want to invite him and his wife to come to First Pres if you think they might be willing. We're a different sort as far as worship goes, but I understand they're not attending anywhere. I've also heard he leads a Bible study that is

20

totally ecumenical in its membership. I think that is amazing and wonderful, and I'd love for his group to include Ginny and me and any other members of our church who might be interested. And I'd be happy to get the Session to approve the group's meeting in our Fellowship Hall, if that would work for them. Do you suppose he'd think I was trying to take over if I invited them to worship with us, meet at our church, and even have some Presbyterians participate in his Bible study group?"

"I don't know that they will come to Presbyterian worship, though I suspect they might, but I'm pretty sure John would welcome you and your wife and any others to the Bible study. After all, he took me in!" Jack said with a smile.

"Well, I just think I'll go see them right now while I feel encouraged." He rose and said, "God bless you both in the good work you are doing in your teaching and continue to bless you in your marriage. It's been a real joy to meet you both and thank you, too, for how you are opening the world to the children you are teaching."

After he left, both Jack and I felt as if we had not only made a new friend but had also received a blessing from God!

In a later addition Ella had added:
Jack and I did visit and soon joined the church. Yes, Presbyterians worship a bit differently from Episcopalians, but since I grew up going to Quaker meetings, I had long ago decided God probably doesn't judge us by our manner of worship but how we live out the words of Jesus—"to love God with all our hearts and minds and strength, and to love others as we love ourselves." I felt that emphasis present in the First Presbyterian Church in Myrna, just as I had felt it at St. Mark's Episcopal under Father Banks's leadership and hope it will return as the young priest and his wife, who took his place, mature.

October 28, 1932
Well, Jack and I won't be the only family members to get married in 1932! Patrick Nolan brought Mary Beth home today

after finishing work at the clinic so that Patrick could ask Jack and me for permission to marry our daughter.

In some ways I was not surprised at the proposal because Mary Beth has had a crush on this man since the first time she saw him when he came to Myrna to meet Daniel and talk about coming to practice medicine at Daniel's clinic. But he's almost 15 years older than she. And I confess I would have had her fall in love with someone nearer her age. But since I'm six years older than Jack, I have to believe that age differences are not that important if the two parties are suited in other important ways.

Mary Beth had been helping/working at the clinic all summer. In August Jeffrey Anderson and Patrick offered her a real job as their assistant, with primary responsibility for women during pregnancy and childbirth. She would also be available to assist with surgeries if needed and invited to observe regardless. She had hoped to go to medical school, but the Depression had interfered, and she was content to learn from two doctors whose medical skills and knowledge she respected even as she continued to study textbooks on her own.

Patrick told us he'd been falling in love with Mary Beth for a long time but didn't want to admit it to himself because of their age difference. But finally he'd decided he'd risk having her laugh at him for thinking a beautiful woman like her would be interested in an 'old man' like him, not knowing she'd loved him for years.

They want a small wedding right after Christmas to be held in our living room with Father Banks performing the ceremony. Jack and Dan will give her away, and she wants Nellie and me to be her attendants. She's already told Nellie and received her promise not to leave for England before her wedding! We'll have a small reception here at the house afterwards—not too many people because who knows what the weather will be like after Christmas! It was obvious they had thought and talked through their plans, and it was left only to me as the mother of the bride and Jack as the stepfather to give our blessing. And of course, we did!

November 9, 1932

Ella had written with great excitement: We have a new president! Franklin Delano Roosevelt defeated Herbert Hoover to my great joy, and he will become our president on March 4. Many Americans, including Jack and me, can hardly wait because this man personifies hope, optimism, intelligence, ideas for the future, and courage!

Herbert Hoover as President had proved to be the disappointment many of us in Arkansas had expected since he'd failed to live up to the promises he made to us during the 1927 flood. Roosevelt, on the other hand, has demonstrated his courage by the way he faced and dealt with the effects of the polio that struck him down in 1921. Yet he has refused to become an invalid. In 1928 he was elected Governor of New York and re-elected in 1930.

Roosevelt was, and continues to be, an ardent conservationist, determined to save this country's magnificent natural forests from being carelessly over-harvested by the lumber industry or its mighty rivers polluted by manufacturing wastes. Like his cousin, Theodore Roosevelt, also a dedicated conservationist, he appreciates and relishes the beauty of the natural world and has made protecting it one of the key points of his politics.

But he is equally determined to preserve this country's human resources and improve our lives by creating opportunities for work, especially for the younger men who, since the Depression began, have had few or no opportunities to find jobs after graduating from high school. A good many of them, some older with wives and children, have become what we call "hoboes" because they leave their homes and families and ride the rails or hitch-hike, moving from town to town, seeking work of any kind or begging, if no work is available. What this does to a man's pride and feelings of self-worth is unimaginable for those of us whose menfolks still have jobs and income. Too many families have felt either the absence of sons and even husbands or the growing despair, embarrassment, and shame because there is so little opportunity to work and make enough money even to feed their families.

When the Democratic Party nominated him as their candidate for President at the National Convention in Chicago, Roosevelt had already gained the support of farmers, conservationists, western progressives, and women. He broke with tradition and flew to Chicago, showing up at the convention to accept the nomination in person, making all the papers and saying something like "You've nominated me and so I've come to thank you for that honor. I've broken with tradition, but let that symbolize how I will proceed. I promise you a 'new deal' for all the people in this country."

Al Smith, a former governor of New York, and John Nance Garner, Speaker of the House of Representatives, were his two opponents for the nomination. When Roosevelt offered to nominate Garner as his Vice President, Garner, who was running a distant third, accepted, giving Roosevelt the necessary votes to become the Democratic candidate. They did promise Americans "a new deal" and we are ready for one after Hoover! Roosevelt is not only decent and kindhearted, he is energetic and ready to try new remedies to cure the economic crisis that is crippling our country. As he knows firsthand what it means to be crippled, he is truly the right man for this job.

Fear of the future has prevailed since the stock market crashed. During the '20s, people's confidence in the economy and our government made Americans willing to spend beyond our incomes and even buy on installment plans. When the market crashed, the general public's hopes and dreams crashed with it. The wealthy cut down on their investments and spending, while the poor grew poorer and couldn't buy the basic things people need in order to live. The Depression began with the loss of demand for products, followed by cuts in production, and then by a loss of jobs. It had a snowball effect on the whole country.

I am not alone in my belief that this election is the most important step our country has taken in bringing a new feeling—no, a conviction that the tide of this Depression is about to turn in favor of the people of this land. God bless our new President! God bless America!

1933

January 1, 1933

Mary Beth married her long-time love, Dr. Patrick Nolan, on December 30. Although I wished (but said this only to Jack) that Patrick was not so much older than Mary Beth, I have nothing else against him, certainly no real reason to object to their marriage. He proposed to her early in October. She had been working with him and Jeffrey Anderson all summer. When Patrick sort of asked our permission to propose to her, he told us he'd been falling in love with her for a long time but didn't want to admit it to himself because of their age difference.

They married in our living room with Father Banks performing the ceremony, and Dan giving his sister away. We had a small reception afterwards for the few friends who had been present for the ceremony: Jeffrey and Helen Anderson, Sarah Banks, Michael and Esther Lewis, and Molly Wainwright. Mary Beth looked beautiful, a truly radiant bride!

They will be living in the little two-bedroom house Patrick bought the second year he moved to Myrna to join Daniel in his practice. He first lived in a rooming house and saved up money and looked for an affordable place to buy. This is a well-built little bungalow and will do nicely as a home for the two of them and even one or two babies, at least until they save enough to buy a bigger one. Both Jack and I want them to be as happy together as we are!

March 5, 1933

Franklin Delano Roosevelt was sworn in as this country's 32nd President on March 4. The country's enthusiasm and hope for a turn for the better in our fortunes is almost palpable. Jack, Dan, and I sat in Molly's living room with her and listened on her radio to his first inaugural address as he called for reform through a New Deal for the people of the United States. He was calling for a special session of Congress within days in which he will outline his plans to end the Depression. During the first minutes of his speech, the President spoke these words that I'm sure must have made the front page of every newspaper in our land, words that will go down in history. "This great Nation will endure as it has endured, will revive and will prosper. So, first of all, let me assert my firm belief that the only thing we have to fear is fear itself."

We stand in awe of this man who overcame polio and then had the will and the drive to seek the highest office in the land. He then won that election in a landslide victory and now is calling us to rise above our despondency over the financial difficulties the country has been struggling to deal with, overcome our fear of the future, and move forward with confidence in God, in him, and in ourselves! What a day this was for our children and for Molly, Jack, and me! May God bless this president and this country as we move into the future with faith and confidence!

May 30, 1933

As we come to the end of the school year, both Jack and I have been surprised and pleased by several outcomes from our experiment that we had not expected. The first was how interested so many of the parents became in helping their children make contacts with relatives in other parts of the United States and even in other countries. They made efforts to dig up old letters and mementos from the past, some from their countries of origin or from other parts of this country where their relatives had first settled or had then moved on.

We put up maps of the United States, as well as Canada and Mexico, and then of Europe and other parts of the world as our

26

students brought letters and pictures, even postcards, from distant places and shared them with their classmates on Fridays. As they learned about the different parts of the world and where their families had come from, Jack would talk about what their governments, customs, and problems had been like before they left to come to America and if or how they had changed now. He encouraged students to use the encyclopedias in the school library and even go to the town's library to see what else they could find. I searched both the school and town libraries for books that related to the students' stories of their families' experiences and had asked for suggestions and help from our friends. Before I knew it, all sorts of people in Myrna were offering me help and information!

Jack subscribed to the Little Rock *Gazette* and the Sunday edition of the *New York Times* and brought these papers to the school library after he had read, or at least had looked through, them. He made a point of sharing articles with our students about things they had been discussing in class, and then encouraging them to read further about current events in the newspapers in the library.

I combined grammar lessons with projects that had students writing their own accounts of the stories they were hearing about their ancestors. I also encouraged them to keep a journal of their thoughts and feelings about these relatives they were discovering, and even to write plays or imaginary conversations with these people or poems about them.

I have been amazed at the creativity our students display! Getting them to read aloud their poems, stories, and plays provided me with opportunities to talk about and have them practice oral communication—diction, oral expressiveness through voice control and volume, along with facial and body movement.

July 23, 1933

Perhaps the best thing that grew out of our approach to team-teaching 10th-grade history and English was the monthly get-togethers in the school's gymnasium on the third Saturday night of each month. We started small, with only 10 families who brought covered dishes, and then we would all eat together, sharing some information about what they had brought and why it was a special dish in their family. Then one or two families would share a bit of their history—where they were from originally and how they had ended up in Myrna. But friendships began to develop as they realized things they had in common.

New families came every month. At a time when money was scarce and little entertainment affordable, people looked forward to these dinners as a way of breaking the monotony of their lives, getting to know new people or know better a good many people they knew by name but really didn't know well at all. To my delight, quite a few of the students really enjoyed "performing" before an audience and were happy to repeat their performances at the monthly dinners attended by their families and others.

In fact, every dinner included as many as four or six students who shared something they had written about their family background. Jack or I had worked with all those who made oral presentations to help them feel at ease talking before an audience and to enunciate and speak loudly and clearly with expression so that their listeners not only could hear and understand their words but find them interesting and enjoyable.

One Saturday night in late March Jack invited some of the farmers he had lived and worked with that spring after he had been dismissed as pastor of the Presbyterian Church because of his divorce. Some of those who had children in the high school came, bringing their instruments and adding a little music to the festivities. They were such a hit that Jack encouraged everyone to invite others who played any instrument at all to bring theirs the next month and "join the band" so that every evening ended with people playing, singing, and even dancing to the music.

In October 1933, Ella had written:
Now town and country folks alike come to our monthly Saturday night get-togethers. They mingle and get to know and enjoy one another. I think soon we will open the group to anyone

who wants to come, as long as they bring a covered-dish and there is no alcohol or unpleasantness.

And in April 1935, she had written:
Our Saturday night pot-luck suppers continue to grow. A few adults without children have even begun attending and learning things about other people they had not known before. Jack and I are both overwhelmed and overjoyed with the success of the program.

The community spirit generated at these Saturday night gatherings are spilling over into the life of the town. The group voted to continue meeting during the summer and even caused like-minded people to join together on work projects, such as improving the city park, giving greater support to the town's library, and even putting on a city-wide celebration of the holiday on July 4th. Jack and I never initiated any of these projects because we have enough to do already. Even more, we wanted them to be the families' projects, not ours. Of course, we gave them our backing as long as it was something that might benefit all the people in the town, coloreds as well as whites.

There was a big discussion over whether colored people could get books from the town's library, and we were deeply pleased when the group voted overwhelmingly that Negroes should be able to check out books if they abided by the same rules as white people did. A committee from the group took their vote to the city council who, when they heard the number of people who had approved it, decided to pass it. Myrna became one of the few Arkansas towns to open our library to both races!

Ella smiled as she read these entries in her journal because neither she nor Jack had ever dreamed of all the benefits that would arise out of their plan, not only for their students but also for the town itself.

May 21, 1933
It's Sunday afternoon and I've finished grading all my final exams and putting grades on all the report cards, so I ought to be

too exhausted to write in my journal! But instead I feel an urge to write about our president and the new feeling of hope he has brought to our country. I believe his promise of a "New Deal" is already taking hold and making a difference. Perhaps some of it comes from the positive approach to life and its problems that this man personifies. He could have withdrawn into a shell, removing himself from politics and public life completely. Yet he has refused to become an invalid or a person to be pitied.

Instead it appears he has become more human and down-to-earth, more aware of the difficulties so many people are dealing with during this Depression, more deeply invested in finding solutions to the job losses and financial hardships so many of our people are facing.

What is really interesting to me is how many different kinds of people he has brought into the creative planning and the process of helping Americans find ways out of this challenging time. Yes, it's political, but there's a real human side to this man and to his wife, Eleanor.

When President Roosevelt took office he inspired hope in our paralyzed nation because, although he too had been paralyzed, he hadn't given up. Instead he found ways of dealing with his paralysis that filled people with hope for the rest of us. People were desperate for new leadership and wanted, actually were demanding, change. We were ready for the New Deal, even though we really didn't know what that meant or would entail. But since he appeared positive and cheerful, we dared to feel the same way.

I think a lot of that is because we feel he's on our side, the side of ordinary people. The New Deal he promises will emphasize cooperation rather than self-seeking, will benefit the ordinary people instead of the wealthy. He says that government must minister to all kinds of people with "honesty, ethics, and unselfish performance."

Mrs. Roosevelt shows her compassion for and interest in ordinary people as much as or even more than he does—maybe because she is a woman and has had more personal experience with everyday life. Whatever their reasons, the feeling that many of us get is that they not only care about people but are genuinely seeking ways to get our country out of this terrible time we are in right now.

I think everybody in this country who has a radio listens to his "fireside chats." Each chat deals with a particular problem the country is dealing with, and he talks to us, the people, in a calm, fatherly way—explaining the issue and the problems it causes and then what he and the government are proposing to do to solve the problem. He speaks using language ordinary people can understand and is very reassuring that we will come through these trying times.

One of the president's projects that both Jack and I are excited about is the Civilian Conservation Corps, which is referred to as the CCC. It has already put to work thousands of young, unmarried men, ages 18-23, housing them in camps, in state or national forests where they live together, are fed three meals a day, and learn to do such work as soil conservation and combatting soil erosion or developing parks with recreational and scenic areas.

They are provided uniforms, paid $1 a day with $22 to $25 of their pay mandated to be sent home, given training in battling fire, insects, tree and plant disease, or whatever other work they are assigned to do.

They also receive training in leadership and obedience. Unlike the army, there are no guard houses, drills, saluting, and so forth, although a good bit of attention is given to building morale. And besides being taught skills they will be able to use in ordinary life, they are being given self-esteem and self-confidence, along with hope for the future.

But that's not the only new program President Roosevelt has started. In fact, we are being so inundated with initials for these programs, I have a hard time remembering them and, even more, what the initials stand for. For example, there are FERA (the Federal Emergency Relief Administration) and the AAA (Agricultural Adjustment Act) and the NIRA (the National Industrial Recovery Act), to name a very few. So much is happening so fast that I can't keep up with it all, but the real news is there's a feeling of new life and hope, even excitement about the future that has been missing for such a long time in our country! Thanks be to God!

July 22, 1933

During this first year of our marriage the lives of our two daughters have undergone significant changes. Nellie worked for Molly and saved almost enough money to buy passage on a ship to England and then get to St. Anthony's, the hospital and recovery community Dr. Francis Willingham had created after the war. Jack had promised her he would give her the final fourth of the amount she had figured she would need to make the trip. That happened in mid-June.

Tears sprang to Ella's eyes as she remembered how hard it had been to put her first-born on the train to New York where she would board a ship and sail to England alone! But Nellie had welcomed the adventure and the freedom to be on her own.

We've received one long letter from Nellie, and it sounds as though she is already feeling at home at St. Anthony's. She's been staying with Frank and his family in the big house, but she thinks as soon as she finds a job she may be moving into one of the little houses and will have a roommate. She is happy and enjoying meeting the people there—both the patients and the staff/inhabitants. She is learning names and the faces that go with the names and even learning interesting facts about them. She sounds as happy as she can be! I'm delighted but also hope she's missing us at least a little bit. I'm certainly missing her!

1934

March 17, 1934

Mary Beth gave birth to a precious baby boy, born early this morning! Daniel Patrick Nolan, named for his grandfather and his daddy. I have no idea what they are going to call him. Nor can I believe I am a grandmother—and Jack a grandfather. I'm glad this baby is a boy because I think it will be easier for Jack to get used to having a little boy in his life and not feel Carrie's death every time he looks at him. I'm probably thinking what I would be feeling if I were Jack, and that may not have crossed his mind. Even though we are really good at sharing our thoughts and feelings with each other, I doubt we really do share everything, and that's all right as long as we don't keep too much of what we think and feel hidden inside.

July 20, 1934

Jack and I have been keeping up with President Roosevelt's "New Deal" plans and two in the past year have really pleased us— one I especially like and one that Jack does. Jack likes "The Federal Emergency Relief Act" which provides direct relief of $500 million to states, cities, towns, and counties for things like roads, school-houses, parks, sewers, airports…everything Harry Hopkins could think up that would benefit all sorts of people.

The one I am really pleased with is the WPA, the Works Project Administration that has set aside billions for planting trees where they have mostly been cut down, providing electricity in rural areas, sewage plants in towns, clearing slums and replacing them with new buildings and schools. But what excites me most is the starting of projects to employ artists to paint murals on buildings, writers and musicians and actors to create plays that are open to communities for free or a minimum fee.

Another of the president's projects that both Jack and I are excited about is the Civilian Conservation Corps, which is referred to as the CCC. It has already put to work thousands of young, unmarried men, ages 18-23, housing them in camps, in state or national forests where they live together, are fed three meals a day, and learn to do such work as soil conservation and combatting soil erosion or developing parks with recreational and scenic areas. They are given training in battling fire, insects, tree and plant disease, or whatever other work they are assigned to do, and they also receive training in leadership and obedience. And besides being taught skills they will be able to use in ordinary life, they gain self-esteem and self-confidence, along with hope for the future.

So much is happening so fast that I can't keep up with it all, but the real news is that there's a feeling of new life and hope, even excitement about the future that has been missing for such a long time in our country! Thanks be to God!

August 22, 1934

Nellie has been accepted into graduate school at the University of Durham this September and has received a small scholarship, which will pay her tuition. She has found a job in Durham as a live-in nanny for two school-aged children, and that will take care of her room and board, though how she will find time to study I have no idea!

September 11, 1934

I am loving being a grandmother. This little boy is as precious as Dan was and is full of smiles and changes every time I see him, though now that school has started it won't be as often as I would like. Mary Beth is a wonderful mother, as I knew she would be, and

Patrick is as doting a father as anyone would want. Of course, he grew up in a home with six siblings, four older and two younger; so he's perfectly at home with this little one.

They've had a bit of difficulty deciding what to call *Daniel Patrick*. Sometimes he's *Danny*, sometimes *Pat*, sometimes *Danny Pat*. Who knows what he'll end up choosing for himself someday? Whatever he's called, he is precious in this grandmother's sight!

October 10, 1934

Nellie appears to be thriving despite the load she is carrying—not only the history of England and two English literature courses she is taking but in the hours she spends caring for Jane and Michael, who are nine and seven. They sound like good children and their parents do not expect Nellie to do all the parenting work.

An interesting aside, Nellie has "changed" her name in a way. She has decided she wants to go by her "real" name, *Eleanor*, instead of "Nellie," which we have called her from birth. Actually, I'm pleased since that is my given name too, though I've never been called anything but "Ella" and I'm too old to change now.

1935

January 11, 1935

It's becoming fairly obvious from her letters to us that our Eleanor is falling in love with one of her literature professors, Dr. Ronald Douglass, who is eight years older than she is and has never been married. My daughters seem to go for older men while I'm delighted with my younger one!

February 23, 1935

Our beloved surrogate mother Molly Wainwright died in her sleep last night. Elsa Mae, her morning companion and caregiver, found her after she'd arrived and "Miss Molly" hadn't responded to her call or her knock on Molly's bedroom door. She looked completely peaceful with no expression of pain on her face when Jack and I went right over after Elsa Mae telephoned us. We were so glad it was on a Saturday when we were at home. Although we both stood looking at this woman who had become so dear to both of us, our arms around each other and tears streaming down our cheeks, Molly looked so peaceful, we would not have changed the manner of her death except for wishing we had been there with her or at least, had visited her yesterday afternoon.

We had to make the telephone calls to her children—her son, Jasper, and his wife, Lucille, in Little Rock and her daughter, Elizabeth, and her husband, Franklin, in Knoxville. Over a year ago Molly had sent her children directions that she wanted followed for her funeral and burial place and had given Jack and me a copy so we would not have to wait on Jasper and Elizabeth for decisions but could begin making the necessary arrangements.

Earlier Molly had told Jack and me she had already chosen a coffin and paid for it at Williams Funeral Home, and she had bought two gravesites when her husband had died. We notified Greg Mitchell and told him that we had just telephoned Molly's children. She had also given Greg a copy of her burial arrangements and the hymns and scriptures she wanted at her funeral.

Greg said he would call her children to see when they would arrive and the funeral could occur. We told him Elizabeth had wept during our call to her while Jasper had simply been silent except for thanking us for informing him. We hoped Greg, who had never met Molly's children would fare better and be able to find out when they might be arriving in Myrna.

Greg knew the church women would want to have food in the house when Molly's children arrived. He was fairly sure that some would be willing to offer them places to stay in their homes since Myrna's one hotel had closed soon after the Depression began. They would help in any way they could with the funeral itself and provide a meal after it for the family. Truthfully, while a few of the older members remembered Jasper and Lucille as children, Greg knew they had so rarely been in Myrna during their adult years he wondered who would recognize them other than Jack and Ella.

Jack felt he could not betray Molly's confiding in him by telling Greg his own opinions of Jasper and his relationship with his mother. Jack could not forget Jasper's failure to show any feelings of love toward his mother the Thanksgiving he and Lucille had driven up from Little Rock. Jack had been present for the dinner they had brought since at that time he was Molly's boarder.

Both Jack and I had encouraged Molly to reach out to her children and share some of her own feelings of failure as their mother, feelings that she had expressed to us, but neither of us knew whether Molly had done that or what kind of response she had received if she had. We were both so filled with grief over losing this woman who had become like a mother to us that we felt enough sorrow for everyone! We stayed with Molly's body until Williams Funeral Home sent Thomas and Max, two of their staff, to take Molly's body there. It brought back memories of Daniel's death to me, although I had not seen his body until after the morticians had done their work and made him look as much at peace as it was possible for someone who had been accosted unexpectedly and shot in the heart. At least Molly's death appeared to have been peaceful, as though she had simply ceased breathing in her sleep.

March 4, 1935

Elizabeth and Franklin and their children arrived first, even though they'd driven from Knoxville. They had made arrangements to stay in Jonesboro at the same inn where Jack and I had spent our first night. Jasper, his wife, and their two sons had immediately announced they would stay in Molly's house to keep an eye on it so that vandals wouldn't try to break in and steal any of Molly's antiques or do any damage to the building or yard. Neither Jack nor I had even given that possibility a thought since we had never known of anything like that happening in Myrna. Neither Jasper nor Elizabeth wanted to add or subtract any of Molly's requests for her service, and Jack and I were grateful for that. They even left the music in Greg's and our organist's hands.

Elsa Mae continued to come during those few days before the funeral to prepare breakfast for Jasper's family and for Elizabeth's also if they wanted it. She kept the house spotless, at least the part that callers saw, for many people from the church and also from the town came by to pay their respects. Molly had been highly regarded by many, especially the older people who had witnessed her development into one of the town's leading citizens in her own quiet way after her husband's death. In fact, I think her family, especially Jasper, were a bit surprised not only by the number of callers but also how well attended her service was on that Saturday at 10:00 a.m.

Our pastor, Greg Mitchell, insisted that Jack and I and our family members sit with Molly's family because Molly had put that

38

in her funeral instructions. We were touched but not really surprised since Molly had loved Jack as a son and, consequently, loved me and mine. It was obvious to us, though I hope not to others from the church and community, that Jasper and Lucille did not approve, although Elizabeth and her family seemed fine with it.

The truth was that Molly's service was very moving and true to who she was. I managed to keep my tears in check until we sang "Amazing Grace," which was Molly's favorite because she told me she thought it had been written for her.

The Women of the Church served lunch for the family afterwards, and I was glad to get to know Elizabeth and her family better without so many others around. I especially enjoyed visiting with her son and daughter and their spouses and getting the chance to know them a little bit. Jasper and Lucille spoke mostly to one another and their two sons who did manage to have some conversation with Jack, simply because he started asking the boys about what they were doing and what their interests were as neither was married. Jack was actually able to get them talking about their lives, one's girlfriend, their hopes for their futures, and then, to his amazement, they wanted to know how Jack had become a preacher and now a high school teacher.

All of Molly's family planned to head back to their homes early Sunday morning. The only reason they weren't starting that afternoon was that Molly's lawyer, Robert MacKay, had asked for a meeting with all of them at 2:00 that afternoon to go over Molly's will. He had also asked Jack and me to attend that meeting because Molly had included us in the will. We were both surprised because Molly had never mentioned her will to us, and we had certainly not expected to be given anything.

But we were! Molly had carefully remembered her children and grandchildren, along with the church, with gifts of money—actually percentages of what would remain of her fortune at the time of her death, and she had bequeathed jewelry, silverware, and dishes to the females, and any items of furniture, books, tools, or yard equipment to the males.

BUT she left Jack and me the house and the land it was on! She had included a letter to us that said we needed a house that had no memories of our previous lives. While Jack would remember living in the house with her for a short time, that would not hold any bad memories for him, she hoped, and the two of us could create our own future in this "new" place. She knew how handy Jack was with tools, and he would be free to remake the house in any way he and I wished, and we could decorate and furnish it to suit us both.

Both Jack and I were so surprised and most especially touched by Molly's thoughtfulness and generosity we were near tears and might have broken down if Jasper had not exploded in anger at his mother and her generosity to two persons who had no claim to her and her fortune. I don't know what would have happened if Mr. MacKay had not spoken up, saying, "Jasper, your mother, wise woman that she was, warned me that you might have this reaction. She loved you and while she felt she had not been as good a mother to you when you were growing up as she had wished, she had fairly recently sent you a long letter explaining why she had been unable to build a relationship with you. She asked for your forgiveness and understanding and begged you to give both of you the opportunity to get to know each other and become friends, or even better—a real family. She told me all of that when she drew up this will, and she also told me she had never heard a word from you. When she telephoned you one day, fearing the letter had never reached you, you told her that it was too late and you weren't interested in building any kind of relationship with her.

"She told me after that call she realized it really was too late and she had truly failed as a mother to you—but she had experienced what having a loving son could be like through her relationship with Jack and then with Ella and her children. Also, she and Elizabeth had made real progress in their relationship, and she was overjoyed with that, even though Knoxville was too far away for the kind of closeness she longed for, the kind of closeness that Ella and her children provided along with Jack.

"I swear to you in front of your family and everyone here that Jack and Ella had no knowledge of Molly's will and its provisions. She rewrote her will last summer because Jack and Ella had continued to spend time with her and include her in every family celebration. She found in their relationship what she had failed to give to or receive from her own children, and she would regret her failure for the rest of her days, even while she rejoiced in the progress she felt she and Elizabeth were making. And she set aside a special fund, separate from everything else, for her four grandchildren, and I was just about to get to that when you displayed your temper so inappropriately. So I will excuse all the adults and ask the grandchildren to stay while I go over the final terms of the will with you."

Jack and I were relieved to be dismissed. I hugged Elizabeth and said again how much we would miss Molly's presence in our lives. She had told me several times how grateful she was for Elizabeth's willingness to forgive her and give you both the chance to get to know each other as adults and make up for those lost years.

Elizabeth whispered to me that she was so pleased her mother had left us the house. While she and Jasper had grown up in that house, they had not ever thought about returning to Myrna to live after they had married and moved on with their lives. Jasper had already talked about selling it, even though it obviously needed some repairs and everyone knew the market for houses in small towns right now was poor to awful. Now there was no need to worry about that, and it gave her comfort and pleasure to think that Jack and I, who had had a loving relationship with Molly, might be living there and keeping her memory alive. We hugged each other again, and I told her I hoped she knew she would always be welcomed to come back for a visit and have a place to stay with us.

Jack and I said our good-byes to Elizabeth and Franklin and tried to speak to Jasper and Lucille, who turned their backs on us. Then with heavy hearts we drove home, where Dan met us, giving us each a big hug with tears in his own eyes. "Molly was like a real grandmother, wasn't she."

It was a statement and not a question, and I said, "Yes, Son, she was. And that was special because my mother had died before you were born, and you were really young when your dad's mother died. So it was nice that for these past few years you've been able to experience what grandmothers can be like."

In a later addition Ella had added:

Jack and I soon decided we wanted to make a few changes to the house before we moved into it. But since Molly died at the end of February, we knew we wouldn't have time to get anything done before summer; so we would spend what spare time we had making plans and getting estimates on what it would cost to make our plans happen. We immediately agreed on two major projects; the most important of them was to build a bathroom upstairs, using some of the space in one of the two rooms and then make what was left into a good-sized bedroom for Dan.

Our other plan was to enclose the back porch and make it a nice guest room with a bathroom and then add a bigger screened-in-porch all across the back. Jack intended to do a lot of the work himself with some help from Dan, who would be paid a minimum wage. The main expenses would be materials, wood and screen for the back porch, and especially for plumbing and fixtures for a lavatory, toilet, and shower for the upstairs and downstairs bathrooms.

We were both surprised when Robert MacKay came back a week after the service to tell us that Molly had left him an envelope with a check for his services whenever they would be needed but also an envelope for Jack to be given after everyone had gone. When we opened it after Mr. MacKay left, we found a beautiful letter she had written to both of us, telling us how much she had loved being an "adopted" member of our family, especially as a sort of grandmother to Dan and even to the girls. Enclosed in the letter were five $100 bills for us to use on repairs or needs for the house! Molly had thought of everything! I'm sure she realized what Jasper's response would be to her leaving us the house, not to mention what his reaction would have been to leaving Jack money on top of that. But that money gave us the freedom to put our plans in motion.

May 30, 1935

My first-born is now married, and I didn't get to witness it! I'm trying not to feel guilty OR sorry for myself. It wasn't a good time for us to go. They were eager to be married, and we had to finish our teaching responsibilities for the year. They had a small wedding in the Church of England that Ronald and his parents belong to in Durham. At least they married in a church with an Episcopal priest officiating at the service. They will have their honeymoon once the term is ended and have reservations at a hotel in the Lake District. I remember how beautiful the Lake District was when Daniel and I took Nellie, Mary Beth, and Danny on that wonderful tour of England. That seems so long ago now. Danny was only five going on six. Now he's in high school and will be graduating before I know it.

It is so hard to have my daughter so far away, leading her own life, now with a life-partner, and I have had so little part in this important time for her. Well, maybe next year we'll get to make that trip to England we keep talking about!

June 8, 1935

We have finally completely moved into Molly's house and spent our first night here last night, and we're already loving it! The money Molly left us, along with the house itself, enabled us to carry out almost all our plans for it, though there are a few finishing touches Jack and I can do ourselves, now that we are actually living here.

Dan is thrilled with his upstairs rooms—his large bedroom with its study space and good sized bathroom with his own shower, lavatory, and toilet. His bedroom has a double bed and a twin-sized one, so that he can have an overnight guest who has his own bed, and so that someday, when he has a home of his own, the upstairs bedroom can house guests, especially young children. See, we have been thinking ahead! After all, Dan will be a junior in high school this fall, and Jack and I are so pleased he will have his own bath and this big room to enjoy these last two years of high school. And when he leaves, we will then have room for grandchildren to come for sleepovers and even room for Eleanor and Ronald if they ever make it over here from England to see us!

We are already enjoying the new back porch, and the new guest bedroom downstairs is lovely. We have put in a medium-sized bathroom with a tub, set off by itself with a divider, and it will do nicely since we don't have many houseguests. After all, Mary Beth and Patrick will soon move into our old house. We were so glad we could give that to them, and they will soon need it with a second child on the way.

November 12, 1935

Mary Beth and Patrick now have a little girl, although Mary Beth had some problems with this delivery and gave us all a scare. The baby was breech, and I don't know exactly what Patrick did to reposition her and enable her to be born without damaging her or having to do surgery on Mary Beth, and I really don't even want to know. Jack and I had gone to the hospital as soon as school ended, not knowing that both she and the baby had been in some danger. I'm glad I didn't know or I couldn't have kept my mind on teaching and probably Jack wouldn't have been able to either. The truth is that "all's well that ends well" as the old saying goes, though Mary Beth is going to be sore for some time while she heals from the whole procedure. And actually, the baby looks pretty beaten up with a few bruises that Patrick assures me will soon fade. They've decided to give her my name, *Eleanor*, but since Nellie has started to call herself by her real name, Mary Beth and Patrick are thinking about calling this little one *Nora*, which I personally think is easier for a child to learn to say than *Eleanor*. Anyway, I'm pleased to have this little girl named after me—and my older daughter!

Later Patrick told me privately that this would be their last. He's getting too old and wants to be around to help raise his children, and he wouldn't chance putting Mary Beth through another breech birth for all the money in the world. He said he couldn't stand the thought of losing her or their child! I hugged him and told him I was relieved to know they wouldn't ever go through that again!

1936

July 16, 1936

A most unexpected event occurred two weeks ago when Jack and I had just come in from the garden in the back yard where we had been pulling up weeds and watering the plants with the hose. We were both hot and sweaty, for even though the sun had almost finished setting, the humidity was unusually high for mid-June. When we heard a voice calling Jack's name, he went to the front door, which actually was standing open so that the screen door would let in as much of the evening breeze as possible. He immediately called for me to please come.

I put down the rag I had been using to wipe off my hands and walked into the living room where Jack was standing with a pitiful, bedraggled, old woman who appeared to be on the verge of collapsing. Jack had taken her arm and was helping her sit in one of the armchairs near the door.

"Ella, my wife, this is Charlotte, whom you've heard me speak of. Charlotte, this is most unexpected. Why are you here? How did you find me?" Jack's voice was shaking with emotion from the shock of Charlotte's appearance, not just that she was in our living room but that she was almost totally unrecognizable from the woman he had last seen at their daughter's funeral.

"I didn't know where else to go. My French, so-called husband kicked me out of our house in Paris. I can't remember exactly when that was—weeks ago. I'm sick, but he gave me enough money to get passage on a ship back to the States and some to live on until

46

I could get to my parents. After I landed in New York, I rode the train to Richmond, but both my parents are dead. Your mother is dead. I didn't know where else to look for help.

"But then I remembered I had gotten a letter once from you in this place. It has taken me days to get to this god-forsaken little town in the middle of nowhere, but I made it. I don't know why I came here, but I think I'm here to die." Charlotte's words had been spoken haltingly, with her having to stop frequently to get enough breath to continue.

Truly, she looked and sounded like death had already claimed her. I could hardly believe this poor, haggard, dirty, sick human being was the Charlotte I had felt a bit of jealousy toward when Jack had told me all about their courtship and marriage during one of our in-depth sharing sessions on our honeymoon. All I could feel at that moment was pity.

Since I knew the guest bathroom did not have enough space for the three of us to move about in and that neither Jack nor I could handle Charlotte alone, I said, "Come, Charlotte, we are going to take you into our bathroom and give you a warm bath and get you into a clean nightgown. Then we will feed you something and let you get in the bed and have some sleep and much needed rest before we take you to see a doctor. Jack, help me get her into the bathroom."

I began filling the tub with warm water as Jack set her on the commode with its lid down and had her lean back on the tank. I began undoing and removing her clothes as gently as I could but had to ask Jack to help me get them off her body because in places they almost felt as though they'd been glued. There was no way to tell how long she'd been wearing them. The stench was almost more than either of us could bear.

When we finally got her completely undressed and the tub had enough warm water in it to cover her up to her waist if she sat up, Jack lifted her and put her in. She really didn't have the strength to sit up, so he scooted her back far enough so that she could lean on the back of the tub, and he kept her from keeling over while I washed her as gently and as thoroughly as I could. While I shampooed and rinsed her hair, Jack held a cloth over her face to cover her eyes and nose and keep the suds out. I was appalled at how dirty the water had become with a ring of scum left on the tub when Jack lifted her out and began drying her off. She truly was only skin and bones. It was hard to tell she had once been young and beautiful.

I had found an old nightgown of mine that I hoped wouldn't swallow her. It was soft cotton, and Charlotte actually sighed with pleasure as she felt it enfold her. In a hoarse voice she said, "This feels wonderful. I had almost forgotten what it feels like to be clean and to have on clean clothes. Thank you, Jack and—I don't know your name. I heard Jack say it, but I've forgotten what he said."

I replied, "It's Ella, and it doesn't matter if you don't remember. Jack is going to carry you into our guest bedroom, and that's where you'll sleep tonight. I hope you will rest well."

Charlotte was so exhausted she did not comment further but let Jack carry her and place her in the bed that I had made ready. She sank into the feather mattress and was asleep almost before we turned out the light.

Jack had followed me into the bathroom where I was looking at the drained tub with a dark ring of dirt around it at the level to which the water had risen. I found myself wishing we had built a larger guest bathroom so we wouldn't have had to use our tub because the receding water had left an ugly dirt sediment all over the bottom. He was looking at me like a lost puppy. "Oh, my Ella, I am so sorry to put you through this. I cannot believe she has come all this way and found me—found us and put us in this awkward and unwanted position of caring for her!"

I couldn't help feeling sorry for him and said, "Well, my husband, I know you didn't expect or want anything like this ever to happen, but it did, and now you can help me clean this bathtub or we'll never be able to use it again if we don't clean and sanitize it."

"Yes, ma'am. I am ready to do whatever you tell me," Jack said so meekly that I had to laugh in spite of myself.

48

We spent the next 45 minutes scrubbing that tub and the toilet seat with Bon Ami and Clorox water. Jack had put Charlotte's clothes in a paper bag and taken them out to the garbage can where he burned them. We didn't know what germs or insects might inhabit them. Then we used the shower that Jack had installed in the wall over the bathtub and each of us showered thoroughly, washing our hair and heads as well as our bodies. We then cleaned the bathtub again, just to make sure we hadn't contaminated it in any way because we had cleaned Charlotte.

Finally we were done—and exhausted. All I could think of was how glad I was that Dan had gone camping with a friend and had not been here and how glad I was to be finished with cleaning the bathroom!

Jack and I climbed into bed and talked. Jack apologized again because Charlotte had shown up at our house. I told him I felt nothing but compassion for her. She was obviously near death. We would take her in to see Jeffrey Anderson in the morning and put her in one of the hospital beds where one of his nurses could take care of her. We could go see her, but we didn't have to be totally responsible for her care, if he could agree to that.

He said, "Oh, Ella, I have been so shaken and upset by her arriving here in the shape she was in, I haven't been able to think straight. Of course, we'll take her to Jeffrey and put her in one of the hospital rooms, and I'll gladly pay to have a nurse with her. I would be relieved if I never had to look at her again and see this almost grotesque person she has become. She is truly pitiful, and I feel sorry for her, but I wish she had died before coming here."

I almost laughed. "Well, it's for sure if she'd died on the way, she wouldn't have made it here. Actually, in a way this has just drawn us closer, Jack. I will never again wonder what she was like. I will feel only compassion for her and the choices she made that brought her to this."

The next morning, after we had tried and failed to get Charlotte to eat a scrambled egg and drink some warm tea, we took her to Jeffrey's office, explained who she was, and asked him what we should do for her. Jeffrey examined her gently and then had a nurse take her to one of the patients' rooms and get her into bed. He was amazed when we told him how far she had come and how long it had taken her to make the trip from Paris to Myrna.

"She's not long for this world, as I'm sure you both have realized," he told Jack and me. I'll be surprised if she lasts 48 hours. Her heart is weak, barely beating, and her body is shutting down."

In fact, she didn't last the day. Jeffrey said it was sheer force of will that enabled her get to Myrna and Jack. He asked us what we planned to do with her body. Jack had gone to Williams' funeral home as soon as we left Jeffrey's office and picked out a casket. He and I would take her body in it to Richmond on the train and bury it in the same cemetery where their little girl was buried and as close to her grave as possible.

A week later Ella had written…

And that's what we did. Jack told me I didn't have to go with him, but there was no way I was going to let him go by himself. It was hard enough with both of us supporting each other. We were fortunate that the cemetery had an empty space, although there was not one near Carrie's grave. Jack's mother was also buried in that cemetery, and we found her grave and laid flowers on it too, just as we did on Charlotte's and finally Carrie's. Jack said a prayer at all three graves. His prayer at Carrie's had me in tears, though I managed to keep from sobbing.

Afterwards, we went back to our hotel room and just lay on the bed for a long time, not talking but just holding each other. After a while, Jack thanked me again for being there, for loving him and supporting him through this sad and unpleasant time. And truly, I am so glad I was able to be there with and for him. No one should have to deal with this kind of situation alone!

I realized I felt relief that Charlotte had come. I had met her and felt genuinely sorry for her, and she would no longer be a shadow, an unseen presence for me in our marriage. Not that Jack ever mentioned her after all he'd told me on our honeymoon, but

I always had a feeling, a fear, she would show up in our lives at some point. She had done so, and it was finally finished!

I did resent that we'd had to use the money we had been putting aside to go to England to pay for the casket, the train tickets, the cemetery plot and grave-digger's fee, plus the grave-stone he had ordered and paid to have delivered and put in place. He'd picked the simplest stone we could find and simply had her first and maiden names and the dates of her birth and death engraved on it, and since we never saw it, we simply have to trust it was completed and placed there.

Jack insisted we will use some of the money still in Michael's bank for us to go to England and see Nellie and her new husband next summer, and that will be our next big expense!

Life has gotten so busy for me, for all of us, I've decided to stop writing in my journal, as least until I'm old and retired from teaching and don't have so much else to do. I'll miss it, but I just don't have enough time to keep up with it the way I want to. I think Jack will be glad because I sense that sometimes he comes in while I'm writing in it, and while he's understanding and doesn't interrupt me, I get the feeling he really has something he wants to talk about, and I need to pay more attention to him. He's really and truly more important to me than what I put in my journal! So goodbye, Journal, at least for now.

Part II

Life in Myrna: 1936

Fall

1

September 7 was Labor Day, and while Myrna students wouldn't return to classrooms until September 14, their teachers would spend the rest of that week sitting in meetings, getting their classrooms and lesson plans ready for students, and making final preparations for the first few days of work. So this first Monday in September officially ended summer for all faculty members and staff, and even students who would return to schools across the state and the country.

Ella and Jack were two of those returnees. It was hard for Ella to accept that her son, her last child at home, was a senior and this would be his last year as a student in Myrna. She knew he was thinking about applying for college at the University of Arkansas, although he didn't sound very excited about going there. She suspected he was thinking about the U of A because he'd started dating Lilly Simpson, who had probably already put in her application since she'd been talking about being a "Razorback" for ages. She was a nice girl and a good student, but Ella hoped Dan wasn't ready to get serious about anyone just yet.

Within two weeks of classes starting, plans were already in the making for the Halloween Carnival that would be held on Saturday, October 31. This fall activity had become a school tradition even before the Depression began. It was supported by the entire town because it kept young people and children off the streets on Halloween night by providing all kinds of activities for them to participate in. The climax of the evening was usually a play but this year was to be a talent show comprised of students from all six grades and even a teacher or two if any were willing. It would be followed by the crowning of the Carnival King and Queen chosen from the boy and girl each class had selected by popular vote. However, the winner was decided by which boy and girl raised the most money to go into the school activity fund to support special events, which during the years before the carnival had been few and far between. The final event of the evening was always a dance honoring the royalty and open to everyone.

Dan had been elected as Senior High Prince and Lilly Simpson as Princess. They both made a pledge to each other to raise enough money that they could be crowned together because they had been dating since the summer and thought they were in love.

Jack and Ella had refused to give money to Dan because they were teachers and had tried really hard never to show any partiality toward their son. Even though he understood their position, Ella could tell Dan was a bit hurt that they wouldn't support him financially in his effort to become king. Actually they were hoping he wouldn't win because they worried some of the students and townspeople would think he'd made it because of who his parents were.

Ella and Jack had bent over backwards the past two years to avoid showing favoritism toward Dan, having explained to him how it was going to be as soon as he entered 10th grade, and in truth, as soon as he started seventh grade. Dan accepted their problem and lived with it, but still felt it was a bit unfair to punish him just because his parents were members of the faculty.

As Halloween drew nearer and the excitement about the school carnival increased, both Jack and Ella grew more eager for it to be over. The competition for both junior and senior high royalty heightened as the date approached. The faculty had decided several years earlier that the amount donated to each prince and princess would not be listed until the night of the carnival when both the junior and senior high King and Queen would be announced and crowned before the dance itself began.

On Halloween night, to Ella and Jack's relief, Bobby Edgerton, a junior, and Sissy Barber, a sophomore, were crowned senior high King and Queen. To their additional relief, both Dan and Lilly took their losses in stride and had a good time joking with the other losers.

The program, which began with the introduction of the royalty and the crowning of the junior high King and Queen, was followed by the senior highs in the same order. The junior and senior high royalty were led to their thrones by the Principal while the runners-up were taken to seats on each side.

For several years the music for the "coronation ceremony" had been provided by the town's local band, a group of nine men and women on a piano, a drum-set, two clarinets, a trombone, two saxophones, and two trumpets. After they were introduced and crowned, the royalty, including the runners-up, participated in the Grand March around the gymnasium with all the students and even teachers and other adults who wanted to take part joining in. The first dance was always a fox trot that had been taught in all the phys ed classes for the past two weeks so all the youth had had some practice. Jack and Ella joined other faculty members who danced, even Principal Adams and his wife, along with the students, while any who were shy quickly realized no one was watching, so they relaxed and just enjoyed being part of the festivities.

Ella had been concerned Dan might be disappointed by not having won the title of Halloween King, but he told her the next day that since his girlfriend didn't win either, he didn't care about being king if they couldn't "reign" together. He and Lilly just enjoyed the carnival and had fun dancing, and even became a bit sentimental because they realized this would be their last time as students at this event. He told Lilly he had filled out an application to the University of Arkansas and it was almost ready to mail.

So the Halloween Carnival ended on a pleasant note for the MacLean family with Ella and Jack relieved that Dan had not been crowned king. Dan himself had just had fun with his girl, allowing his ideas about his future to lie dormant for the moment.

The country was set to vote on Tuesday, November 3, to choose between Alf Landon, governor of Kansas, the Republican candidate, and Franklin Roosevelt, who was running for a second term as President of the country. Landon and many Republicans were saying that FDR had gone too far in his conservationist program by creating too many wildlife refuges and national parks. Landon, as a governor, approved some of the New Deal programs, ones that had created safety nets for the elderly and the poor. So he campaigned against Roosevelt by attacking his efforts to restore lands that had been deforested and over-farmed.

Roosevelt's election team had plenty of facts to use against Landon's leadership in Kansas. Kansas farmers had so badly over-harvested their land that the drought in the early 1930s left the state's farmers in bad shape. While on the one hand Landon spoke against the Civilian Conservation Corps and its work on conserving forests and replanting trees, he actually had complained to Robert Fechner, the director of the CCC, that Kansas wasn't getting its fair share of the CCC camps when Kansas had 27 camps while neighboring Nebraska had only 19. Across the country most farmers supported FDR because he and his government had come to the farmers' aid. In fact, one group of New Dealers had recently released a report entitled "The Future of the Great Plains" that praised Roosevelt's efforts to preserve the land.

Although the president's popularity had declined somewhat during 1934, he won back the support of most Americans by what many called "the Second New Deal" which included a works program, the social security act, and growth in wages. Both Ella and Dan expected the country to elect Franklin Delano Roosevelt for a second term, trusting that most people realized that while the country still had a long way to go before it would fully recover from the damage caused by the Depression and nature, most Americans would agree this president and his policies were making a difference and that he deserved four more years to finish the job. Their expectation proved to be right.

As one commentator expressed it, Franklin Roosevelt was more of a politician than an ideologist and so it was understandable that he turned toward the same direction as a majority of the people at the time—toward humanitarian and cooperative actions and values. He was re-elected in an overwhelming victory. And the possibility of a war in Europe was never mentioned during the campaign, much to Ella's delight.

3

Little did Ella know that while Dan did send an application for admission as a freshman to the University of Arkansas, what he really wanted was to go somewhere he could take flying lessons.

Dan was fairly certain the United States would end up supporting England and France if Germany started a war, and that possibility seemed more real all the time. He had seen some of the newsreels of Germany's troops and had read about what American participants in the 1936 Olympics had seen and experienced of the Germans' warlike spirit during the Olympics. If it came to war, he wanted to be in an airplane fighting the enemy from on high rather than on the ground. Of course, a part of him hoped it wouldn't come to that, but another part of him hoped it would and he could play a role in defeating the enemy. But he didn't dare speak of that to his mother and Papa Jack, having heard from them more than once about what war could do to people.

Yet Dan was not giving up his dream of becoming a pilot. In mid-October he read a long article in Jack's copy of the *New York Times* about the United States Naval Academy in Annapolis, Maryland. A paragraph about its addition of a program to train pilots to fly airplanes that could take off and land on ships in a time of war had caught his eye.

Dan did some research in the Myrna library on the Naval Academy and found out it had a high ranking among liberal arts colleges, there was no tuition, and to be accepted a young man had to have letters of recommendation. Those bits of information stirred Dan to start figuring out how he might attend the Academy.

Very casually, giving the impression he was doing research for a class project, Dan did some asking around and learned it wasn't enough for a teacher or the high school principal to write a recommendation about a young man. The recommendation from a senator or representative from his home state is what would made a difference. That information led him to write and re-write two letters about himself, lengthy letters telling a bit about his desire to fly airplanes in a war he feared was coming and would involve the United States, his being the youngest of three children with two older sisters, the murder of his father when he was 10, his mother's becoming a high school English teacher and her marriage to a high school history teacher, his growing up in the small town of Myrna, and his desire to attend the Naval Academy in Annapolis.

He included as references Mr. Doug Adams, Principal of Myrna High School; Mr. Michael Lewis, part-owner of Lewis' Department Store and sole owner of Farmers and Merchants Bank; and the Rev. Greg Mitchell, pastor of First Presbyterian Church. Before sending his letters he made a point of asking each reference if he would be willing to write a recommendation for him if it were requested by a college, and all three immediately had said *yes*.

In early November Dan mailed one letter to Senator Hattie Caraway and the other to Representative John McClellan. He mailed them from the post office, planning to mention a class project as the reason for his writing a United States Senator and a Representative if anyone asked why he was sending them letters, but no one did, to his relief.

Dan felt a bit guilty about not having talked this over with his parents, but he knew Ella was already concerned about his sister Eleanor and her family living in England and the threat of Hitler and Germany declaring war. More than likely, he thought, his letters to Mrs. Caraway and Mr. McClellan would never even be read or even if read, would end up in a trash can. Yet he felt satisfied, even a bit proud of himself, because he had made the decision to act on his belief a war was coming and that if he were going to fight in it, he wanted it to be on his terms—as a pilot and not some infantryman slogging through mud.

While he concentrated on putting his letters out of his mind, it was hard to do. To help him do so, he had gone along with Lilly's wishes that he apply to the University of Arkansas and sent his application in before Thanksgiving, with his mother and stepfather's approval. School and the approaching holidays helped Dan to concentrate on his everyday life so he was surprised when one day in early December he was summoned to the principal's office.

Dan could tell from Doug Adams' face something was bothering him when he asked Dan to have a seat and pulled a letter out from a stack of mail on his desk. He then asked, "Dan, do your parents know you've written a letter to Senator Caraway asking her to recommend you for the Naval Academy in Annapolis?"

Dan's face turned a bright red as he replied, "No, Sir. I have not told anyone I did that. Why do you ask?"

"Because I've received a letter from Senator Caraway asking a lot of questions about you—about your grades, your deportment and history as a student, and your reputation, your family—all because you want her to enable you to get into the Naval Academy. Dan, I know how your parents feel about you going to war, and I'm of the opinion we're heading that way eventually. So I will not reply to the Senator until I know you have confided your hopes for your future to your parents and received their approval to proceed with this."

"I understand, Sir, and I will talk with them tonight. I know my mother is not going to like the idea of my going to the Naval Academy, but if we are going to war at some point, I want to have some say about how I serve my country. And the Academy sounds like a really good school."

"Did you ask anyone else to recommend you? Should I be expecting another letter?" Doug Adams asked.

"Well, I did write Representative McClellan. So you may hear from him, or not. I don't have any control over that, I'm afraid."

"No, you don't, Dan, but I'll be on the lookout for a letter from him. Let me know what your parents say. You can tell them I will have to tell the truth about you when I write Senator Caraway or anyone else." Doug smiled as he said these last words.

"I wouldn't expect anything else from you, Sir. Thank you, Sir." Dan had risen to shake the hand the principal had extended and then left the office, already dreading the conversation he must have with Ella and Papa Jack.

4

As soon as they had finished the evening meal, washed the dishes, and placed them in the rack to dry, Dan said, "Mother, Papa Jack, I have to talk to both of you and confess something I've done that you're not going to be happy about. Can we sit down together in the living room, please?"

Both Ella and Jack looked at Dan in surprise. "Sure, Son," Jack said. "I can't imagine what you have to tell us, but we're game, aren't we, Ella?"

Ella had put down the dishcloth she'd been holding and stood looking at her son in amazement and disbelief. "Dan, are you in trouble? Have you done something wrong?"

"Not anything like you're thinking about, Mother. Let's go sit down and I will tell you everything."

They moved into the living room where Ella and Jack sat together on the sofa while Dan moved a chair a bit so he could sit facing both of them. "Mother and Papa Jack, I haven't said anything about this because I didn't think anything was likely to come of it, and it probably still won't, but I want to apply to go to the Naval Academy in Annapolis for college.

"I know I've already applied to the University of Arkansas and will go there if I don't get into the Academy, which I probably won't, but I did write letters to Senator Caraway and Representative McClellan asking them to nominate me for admittance to the Academy. And Senator Caraway has written Principal Adams to get information about me—my grades, activities, character, and I don't know what else. I'm hoping what she learns about me will encourage her to nominate me for acceptance into the Academy.

"Mr. Adams called me into his office and asked if I had talked this over with the two of you, and when I said I hadn't, he said I needed to do that immediately. And if you give me permission to pursue attending the Naval Academy, he will write Senator Caraway with his assessment of me as a person and as a student."

"Son, why in the world do you want to go the Naval Academy? I thought you were all set to attend the University in Fayetteville?" Ella said, her voice shaky.

"Mother, that's my fallback plan if I can't get into the Academy. But you see, I am fairly certain we're going to be dragged into a war with Germany and Italy. They're going to attack France and all the surrounding countries and then start bombing England after that. Hitler is after revenge for Germany's loss in the last war. It's going to happen! I really believe that.

"And I can't believe the United States will sit back and allow England or France to fall to the Germans. President Roosevelt won't let it happen. And when we enter, I don't want to be drafted. I want some choice on where and how I'm going to fight for the free world. I choose the Navy, and I want to be trained as an officer.

"So I've decided to apply to the Naval Academy, and I've done some research and learned I need to be nominated by somebody important in my state. If I get chosen, the four years will be free of charge, and I'll be graduated as an officer. I've also found out the Naval Academy is an excellent school academically, so I'll come out with a good education as well as a job for life." Dan took a deep breath and said, "That's my hope anyway. There's no certainty it will happen, but the letter from Senator Caraway is a start."

Jack looked at Dan, whom he first knew as an angry little boy, full of grief and fury over his father's murder, and now he saw, not a headstrong youth, but a determined young man who wanted to make something good of his life and was ready to accept a future that promised the real possibility of danger and death but also a life lived in service to his country in hope for a better world.

"So you have given this decision a good bit of thought, Son," Jack said. "I can tell this is not a spur-of-the-moment idea. Of course, you may not get accepted to the Naval Academy, and that will be a disappointment I'm sure, but you had to accept that as a possibility when you wrote Senator Caraway and Representative McClellan. I imagine you gave them some other possibilities for references besides Doug. Will you share with us who else you listed so we won't be taken by surprise?" Jack looked at Dan with pride and love.

Dan nodded and said, "Uncle Michael and Pastor Mitchell, and of course, Principal Adams. All of them know me pretty well and can give an honest assessment of my character, if they are contacted. If they are, you'll probably hear from the other two, so it won't come as a surprise. I'm sorry. I should have talked about this with both of you before I wrote those letters, but I was afraid you'd try to talk me out of doing this, and the truth is this is something I feel like I have to do. It's the right thing for me, and I'm asking you to trust me on this."

"Well, I'm sorry, but I'm going to pray this doesn't happen," Ella said with tears streaming down her face. "I didn't want your dad to go to war, but he went and came home damaged, had horrible nightmares for months afterwards. I don't want my son to be hurt in any way, much less killed."

Jack put his arm around her, saying, "Ella, darling, he's a man, truly a grown man, a fine man, and we have to let him be free to lead the life he wants as long as it is an honorable and good life. I don't like war. Truly, I'm against war! But Dan is right. If England is attacked, we will go in because we simply cannot stand by and let Germany's Hitler and Italy's Mussolini take over the world.

"As difficult as this may be, give your son your permission to do what he feels he needs to do, and we will both pray the war he is anticipating will never occur." Jack wiped Ella's tears away with his handkerchief and kissed her forehead. Ella gave Jack a hard look but then took a deep breath and said, "All right. Dan, I know you have thought about this, and it's not some boyish attempt to be a hero. I know you, my son, and I only want you to have a good life, a long life, and I can't stop my fear of the future from making me weep, but I will try to do better."

Ella stood up to go wash her face, but before she could leave, Dan rose, took his mother in his arms, and held her close. Now a good head taller than she was, he kissed her gently on the forehead and said, "Mother, I promise I will do my best to stay alive!" At that they all three laughed briefly, knowing full well that while Dan might promise, he did not have that kind of power.

Within the week, the principal had received a letter from Representative McClellan. Also both Michael Lewis and Greg Mitchell heard from both the senator and the representative, letting Ella and Jack know about these letters and how proud they were of Dan for wanting to attend the Naval Academy. Consequently, they felt compelled to write letters of praise about the fine young man Dan was and what a good family he came from.

Both men understood why Ella was not happy with Dan's choice, but they, as men, felt pride in his seeking admittance to such a prestigious institution. As far as they knew, no one from Myrna had ever attended either the Naval Academy or the Army's West Point. So Ella sought and received understanding and solace from her close friends Esther and Sarah and her daughter Mary Beth.

5

As Thanksgiving and Christmas followed quickly, filled with their customary activities, Ella concentrated on making these holidays more special than usual. She invited John and Sarah Banks to join her family for Thanksgiving dinner. The Presbyterians were having a special service in the morning, and Ella made a point of having her dinner preparations so far along that she could leave home for an hour knowing Doris, her Negro maid, would take good care that nothing overcooked or burned and would have the meal practically ready to serve when she and Jack returned after the service.

Ella slipped Doris a Thanksgiving bonus before Jack drove her to her house, and then returned home to find their guests had arrived: Mary Beth and Patrick with their young son, John and Sarah Banks, and Lilly, Dan's girlfriend. He would later go home with her for another Thanksgiving meal to be served to her family at 6:00. At both meals the families and guests stayed far away from the topic of war, giving thanks for a tradition held in memory of a long ago Thanksgiving feast celebrated by the Pilgrims and their Indian guests, eating together in peace.

Christmas came more slowly with lots of preparation needed to be ready for it. Since money still was not plentiful, many families, including Ella's, drew names and limited themselves to buying only one gift, being able to spend a maximum of $10 on that gift. However, they could give other kinds of gifts, gifts of love, that did not cost any money. Only Pat was exempt from giving unless a member of the family helped him make something. These "special gifts," as they were referred to, inspired them to all kinds of presents. Grandpa Jack gave Pat an hour of fishing in the pond. Ella gave son Dan a beautiful new jacket she made out of an old navy blue blanket. Mary Beth gave Dan a haircut for free. He was a little nervous about his sister trimming his hair, but was amazed when she did such a good job and said he'd never go to another barber. Dan drew Ella's name and gave her his senior picture in a silver frame he had found at a junk store. It had been almost black with tarnish, but he had spent several hours cleaning and shining it until it looked new. Nora gave Grandpa Jack a special kiss. All kinds of activities helped the days speed by so quickly that 1937 was upon them before they were ready to begin a new year.

Ella had tried to put the reality of Dan's graduation and entrance into college out of her mind and concentrated on making the holidays as joyful as possible. Yet the nagging fear of a war that would be fought in England where her daughter Eleanor lived with her husband, along with her son Dan's insistent desire to attend the U.S. Naval Academy in Maryland were never completely out of her mind.

Part III

Life beyond Myrna: 1937

1

In early April Dan had received a letter informing him that he had been accepted into the Naval College at Annapolis. His joy had been tainted a bit by his mother's unhappiness, but when Ella realized how excited he was about his acceptance and what an honor it was to be going there, she hid her concerns and let him see her pride, which was real, in his having been accepted.

Ella and Jack had already been planning a trip to England to see Eleanor and her family in June, and Dan would go with them as far as Annapolis where they would leave him to begin his summer of orientation at the Naval Academy. They would see as much of the Academy as tourists were allowed and then go on their way to New York to board the Queen Mary.

On May 6 all three of them were shocked by the newspaper's account and pictures of the horrible explosion of the Hindenburg, a strange kind of new airship built in Germany, that had occurred as it was attempting to land at the Lakehurst Naval Air Station in New Jersey. Ninety-seven passengers and crew members were on board when it exploded in flames. Amazingly of those on board, 62 survived, while 35 passengers and one ground crew member died. The fact that the plane had Hitler's symbol for Germany, the ugly Swastika, on the plane didn't even make Ella feel better about its crash. After all, these were human beings too, even if she didn't like what they stood for.

While Ella remembered that the Titanic had sunk with many lives lost, she told herself over and over that they were sailing in the summer when icebergs were unlikely to be a problem *and she was sure the Queen Mary would have plenty of lifeboats—and that they wouldn't need them.* Whatever went on in the minds of Jack and Dan, they didn't share it with Ella, and that was probably for the best!

2

Graduation Day, Friday, May 21, arrived. The ceremony had been set for 10:00 a.m. and would be outdoors under the trees. The junior class boys had arrived at 7:00 a.m. to help the custodian set up chairs, and then some had rushed back home to shower and dress to return and serve as ushers, handing out the mimeographed programs and helping parents and visitors find seats.

Everyone stood as the graduates, principal, and faculty members came through the doors leading outside and proceeded to the seats reserved for them. The city band that had performed at the Halloween Carnival was on hand to play the *March from Aida* as they made their way to their seats. Greg Mitchell, Pastor of First Presbyterian Church, whose son George was one of the graduates, gave the opening prayer.

Ella and Jack, as members of the high school faculty, sat in the section reserved for teachers and smiled and applauded as these eager young people accepted recognition for activities and sports in which they had participated and then walked forward to receive their diplomas and change the tassel on their mortarboards from one side to the other, a symbol of the life-changing event of high school graduation. Only a few of them would be attending college. Others would enroll in a trade school while most would be seeking work of any kind that would enable them to help support their families.

The boys whose parents were part of the co-op farming venture Michael Lewis supported through his bank, knew they had a place to live and work to do and were grateful. Only one of them planned to attend college in Jonesboro at Arkansas State. He had been awarded a scholarship.

Many of the girls would be getting married and helping their husbands by working at whatever they could find, hoping not to have babies until they had some financial stability but would shrug their shoulders and accept as best they could the pregnancies and childbirths when they came.

Ella sat and watched, quietly dabbing at the tears that kept forming in her eyes as she considered what the future might hold for these young people who had become dear to her and to Jack and to other faculty members. Of course, some of her tears were for Dan, who had received several honors and been recognized for his acceptance into the Naval Academy. But they were all so young with so much living ahead of them, she thought, and felt the tears forming as she prayed silently for a peaceful world and a good future for every one of them.

Jack sensed what she was feeling and reached over and took her hand in his, and the love that she felt between them made the tears flow faster. "These are good tears—of love and thanksgiving, my husband, but also some are fear for what the future holds," she whispered to him. Jack squeezed her hand gently and kept it in his, but covered both with the mimeographed graduation program, hoping that it wouldn't be obvious he was holding her hand and that the ink from the program wouldn't smear onto it.

The day was warm and the graduates were happy to shed the robes the school had rented for the occasion, thanks to the generosity of Michael Lewis and Farmers and Merchants Bank. The school secretary was busy counting the robes and making sure all had been folded and replaced in their paper bags. Little did the graduates and their families know these same robes would be worn the next day by the Negro graduates at Morton High.

The homeroom mothers had prepared punch and cookies for a simple reception outside under the trees in front of the building. Ella and Jack separated and spent time greeting the parents of the graduates and hearing them exchange the same comments over and over…"I can't believe my *son/daughter* is actually a high school graduate. It seems like yesterday when *he/she* started first grade."

Mothers were surreptitiously dabbing their eyes with their hand-kerchiefs while fathers were having problems with coughing and complaining about something in the air. It took all of Ella's will power not to let her own emotions show!

Finally the last parent and all the students had thanked the homeroom mothers for the refreshments and left the teachers to see that everything was put away. Even the faculty members were unusually quiet, feeling the ending of another school year and the goodbyes to another group of young men and women who were moving into a new dimension of their lives, one that in many ways was full of the unknown. This was the difficult but rewarding part of being a teacher—watching these young people, many of whom they had grown to care about deeply over the years, move into the future, not knowing what challenges they would be facing. These adults were hoping, even praying, that they had helped prepare them for whatever lay ahead, feeling confident about some and worried about how others would fare. But as of today they had to leave these young men and women in God's care.

3

Esther and Michael Lewis, Ruth and Hank Fredrick, and Sarah and John Banks gave a surprise *Bon Voyage* party for the MacLeans and Dan on May 28, the Friday after Dan's graduation. The party was at Esther and Michael's house, and Ella, Jack, and Dan couldn't believe how many people were there—Mary Beth and Patrick and their chil-dren Pat and Nora, the MacPhersons and their children, their pastor Greg Mitchell and his wife, Ginny, and their four children, Dr. Jeffrey Anderson and his wife, Helen, both the high school principal, Doug Adams and his wife and family, and the superintendent of schools, Alfred Wittington and his wife! Even Ella's maid, Doris, who was more her friend than a maid, her husband and two of their children were there too, helping in all kinds of ways. But it was good to see their children playing croquet and jumping rope with the white children. Michael had asked Dan to get games going for the children and, at Esther's request, to include the Negro children. Having been friends with Negro children most of his life, he had no problem getting them involved, with Daisy jumping rope immediately and Shep playing croquet after he'd watched a couple of games.

Every family had brought them a little gift to take on the trip "to remember them by," as if they could ever forget these friends. The hosts had gone in together and gave them a Kodak camera and several rolls of film to record their memories in print. Everybody had created or bought something small enough Ella and Jack could take with them or use or eat on the trip! Dan, who had already received gifts for graduation from most of the guests, was given a card that everyone had signed with congratulations and wishes for a great year at Annapolis.

Every woman had brought a dish for the supper so that the hosts did not have to prepare food for the 30 or so who were there. Ella and Jack then promised that after they returned home, they would have a similar party to share their adventures!

4

Ella and Jack spent the first days of June preparing for their trip. The three of them were taking the train to Memphis where they would spend the night at the Gayoso Hotel, and then on Friday morning take the train from Memphis to Washington, arriving that afternoon, which would be June 4, and their fourth wedding anniversary.

Since Dan had to report to the Naval Academy on Monday, June 7, by 10:00 a.m. as a fourth-class midshipman, Jack had made reservations for the three of them at a hotel in Annapolis for Friday, Saturday, and Sunday nights. Their train was supposed to arrive in Washington on Friday, and they would take a taxi to their hotel in Annapolis. They would have all day Saturday to explore the town of Annapolis, and then have Sunday to spend at the Academy.

Because Friday was their anniversary, Dan had his own room, and while the three of them ate dinner together, Dan had sense enough to go to his room alone and leave Jack and Ella to spend the evening together doing whatever they wished. Jack had assured both Dan and Ella that after the first night they would have the other two nights to enjoy time together.

Ella had bought a map of the campus and a guide book of the city at a bookstore near their hotel and found it a big help for their trip around the town on Saturday and their visit to the Academy on Sunday. Annapolis was rather what they had expected a university city to be like, although it was different in that so many of the young men they saw were dressed in Navy whites.

But the next day upon entering the grounds where Dan would spend the next four years of his life, both Ella and Jack were impressed with the beauty and the size of the campus as they walked around the grounds.

The building they were most awed by was Bancroft Hall which housed all the naval students along with the dining hall where the midshipmen were fed three meals each day. Ella simply couldn't imagine the size of the kitchen or the planning and collaboration needed to cook for that many hungry young men!

A young midshipman greeted them with a smile soon after they had entered the hall, saying, "Good morning. I am Midshipman Second Class Larry Coleman, and I would be pleased to show you around the Hall and answer any questions you might have about the Hall or the Academy itself."

Ella, Jack, and especially Dan were impressed with his appearance and manners and accepted his offer as their guide immediately, telling him how awed they were by the size and beauty of the hall, which they had entered through the central rotunda. Midshipman Coleman told them it had been designed in the Beaux-Arts style by architect Ernest Flagg. The original building had been built with a wing extending from each side and had taken over five years between 1901–06 for its completion. A second set of "wings" had been added in 1917, and the plans were to build a third set in 1939.

When Ella told Midshipman Coleman that Dan would be returning the next day to begin his life there as a "pleb" as all first year men were called, he broke into a huge grin and holding his right hand out to Dan, saying, "Congratulations, Midshipman 4th Class!" Then he asked where they were from, saying they sounded like his folks back home in Cape Girardeau, Missouri. When Ella said, "Myrna, Arkansas," Midshipman Coleman said he had actually considered attending college in Jonesboro before his acceptance at the Naval Academy. And he and Dan instantly became friends.

When Dan asked if first-year students were called "plebes" from the Latin word *plebeian*, Larry was impressed that he was familiar with the word and had had two years of Latin in high school. That led them into a long discussion about classes and then about what the summer induction would be like, in addition to information he gave them about the building where they were standing.

Larry told them Bancroft Hall also provided offices for the Commandant of Midshipmen, battalion officers and chaplains, company officers, a barber-shop, a bank, a small restaurant known as "Steerage," a textbook and general store for Midshipmen, and the USNA branch of the United States Postal Service. Visitors were only allowed into the Central Rotunda, where they found a map that listed all the stores and offices and medical clinics in the building, and in Memorial Hall.

A gorgeous central staircase led them upstairs to Memorial Hall which contained the honor roll of Naval Academy alumni who had died in military operations, their names listed by class year on the walls, and included non-graduates and midshipmen. Overhead was a beautiful skylight, and Larry said it contained 489 panes of glass. He also told them that if they wanted to see another magnificent building, though a much smaller one, they should visit the Navy Chapel.

Ella asked for his parents' address in Cape Girardeau so she could write them and tell them how much they had enjoyed meeting him. On the notepad she carried in her purse, Ella wrote down the information he gave her: *Mr. and Mrs. Lawrence Coleman, 111 Elm Street, Cape Girardeau, Missouri.*

They thanked Midshipman Larry Coleman for greeting them and showing them the parts of Bancroft Hall they were permitted to see. Midshipman Coleman said he would look Dan up and find him during his first week on campus. Ella, Jack, and Dan were laughing as they left that they had spent an hour and a half with their guide in that one building but were so grateful he had been present to give them the information about Bancroft Hall.

The Navy Chapel was a much smaller building but was so beautiful and worshipful inside that they sat down in one of the pews and had a quiet prayer of thanksgiving for being in this impressive place, meeting a young midshipmen who could have been Dan's older brother and who made Ella feel a good bit better about having her son become a Navy man, though she still wished he weren't going to be so far from Myrna, Arkansas!

The brochure they had picked up upon entering told them the chapel had been designed by the same architect, Ernest Flagg, who had designed and overseen the building of Bancroft Hall. The cornerstone had been laid by Admiral George Dewey in 1904 and the chapel itself dedicated on May 28, 1908. The two stained-glass windows facing the altar displayed symbols. One of Sir Galahad, holding his sheathed sword, portrayed the Navy's ideal of service. The other window signified the *Commission Invisible*, Christ pointing toward the flag, the beacon every new officer must follow. Other windows were memorials to Navy admirals and heroes.

While they were sitting reverently in the chapel, someone came in and began playing the 268-rank organ, and they sat there, each feeling God's presence as they thought about how the next few days would affect their lives.

Dan felt both excitement and trepidation as he realized anew that he had left the home and the life he knew and had enjoyed for almost 18 years in exchange for this new life which would present him with challenges, rewards, and possible suffering, all of which at this point he could barely imagine.

Ella prayed for her son who on the next day would enter a new phase of his life which would most likely eventually lead to encounters with danger as the threat of war seemed to be growing more real every day.

Jack's prayers were of thanksgiving that he and Ella would soon be on their way to England where they would meet Eleanor's husband and his family and also have some time at the medical/healing center established by Frank Willingham, one of the doctors who had served with Ella's first husband, Daniel Wood, in the war. He was a bit unsure how that would go since Daniel seemed to have been highly regarded by all.

When the organist ended his playing, the three of them rose from their own time of worship and went outside, leaving the Academy behind. They flagged a taxi to take them to downtown Annapolis where the driver, who had recommended a restaurant, let them out. There they enjoyed their last lunch together since the next morning Dan would turn his life over to the United States Navy, while Jack and Ella would take a train to New York and board the Queen Mary bound for England.

5

Ella, Jack, and Dan had breakfast together in the hotel and then all three piled suitcases and themselves into the taxi that first stopped to let Dan off at Bancroft Hall. Both Ella and Dan got out of the cab to tell him goodbye. Jack shook his hand while Ella hugged him briefly. She had taken advantage of the privacy of their room at the hotel to kiss and hug him as only a mother could who was turning her youngest child over to one of their country's armed services to educate and protect.

Both Jack and Dan were proud of her for not crying, though Jack had to hand her his handkerchief after they got back in the cab and were headed out the gates. Even the taxi driver, who had probably witnessed hundreds of parental farewells, was impressed that she had held back the tears until her son had turned away, headed for the line of young men who were waiting to be formally enrolled in the Naval Academy.

They had ridden for a while when the cab driver broke the silence. "Was this your first-born that we just left at the Academy, Ma'am?" he asked.

"No, my youngest. My first two were both girls, thank God, and won't ever have to be preparing to go to war. And truthfully, I pray my son won't be going to war either!"

"I understand, Ma'am. I fought in the last one, and that's one thing I don't want to do again and hope my sons won't either, though I have to say, it's looking more and more like war is going to come. I just hope we stay out of it."

"Were you in the Army?" Jack asked. "And if so, where were you located?"

"I was in the trenches in France, Sir. Were you in the service, Sir?"

"I was in France too, but I was hit by something during the second battle I was in, and that ended the fighting for me. I don't think I ever hurt anybody, though I fired my rifle enough. And I sure didn't see who hit me. It was a strange experience. I spent a lot more time getting trained to fight and then recuperating from fighting than I did in battle! What about you?"

"I felt like I spent more time digging trenches or trying to get the water out of the trenches we had dug than I did attacking the enemy. Of course, I'm exaggerating a bit, but, how I hated those trenches! And I hated just waiting for the enemy to attack again! I guess I was lucky 'cause I made it home alive and relatively unhurt. But it did something to my mind, because I've tried to get a decent job, but I can't seem to stay focused on anything. Driving a taxi is about all I seem to be good for."

"Well, we're certainly grateful you're good at that!" Ella said. "Do you mind telling us your name?"

"George Quincy, Ma'am."

"Well, I'm Ella and my husband is Jack, Jack MacLean."

"Pleased to make your acquaintance, Mr. and Mrs. MacLean. We're not too far from the harbor. What ship are you taking?"

"It's the Queen Mary, and we are headed to England to see our daughter and also some friends," Jack answered.

George became silent as he had to pay attention to the traffic and the turns he needed to make to drop Ella and Jack at the entrance to the building where they would check in and be able to turn their bags over to the men who would get them taken to their cabin on board.

When George had taken their luggage out of the taxi's trunk, Jack paid him and included a generous tip which George refused to accept, saying, "Thank you, Sir, but it's rare I drive folks as friendly and willing to talk to me as you were. I just hope you have a wonderful trip getting to visit your daughter and friends."

They thanked him again, telling him they were glad they had met him, and watched him drive off, acknowledging that the world was full of good people.

Part IV

England: 1937

1

The *Queen Mary* would dock in South Hampton in five days, then Ella and Jack planned to take the train into London where they would spend the night before boarding another train that would take them north to Durham.

Eleanor and Ronald had been married for almost two years now and had an apartment in Durham where both were teaching—Ronald in the literature department of the university while Eleanor held a position in a city college related to the university with hopes of moving up to the university level once she completed her PhD in literature.

Besides getting to see Eleanor and her husband and meet his family, at some point in early July the four of them planned to take another, more local train to do some traveling in the countryside and also see Ella's friends at St. Anthony's, the hospital compound that Dr. Frank Willingham had founded right after returning home from fighting in the war.

Ella looked forward to introducing Jack to Daniel's and her friends: Frank and Charlotte, Harry, Sarah and Geoff, and especially Cecile and Jason and their little children. Jack had met Jean Marc and his nephew Andre when they had come to Myrna after Daniel's death, but they really hadn't gotten to know each other. Yet what Ella was most excited about was first getting to meet Eleanor's husband and see for herself what her daughter's life was like!

When Jack had made reservations on the *Queen Mary* for him and Ella, he not only had wanted the trip on the ocean liner to be a kind of second honeymoon for them, he also wanted it to help his wife move past her concerns about Dan's new life at the Naval Academy. Ella understood Jack's purpose and had made up her mind that as difficult as it was going to be to leave her only son at the Academy, she would do her best to make this a special time with this man with whom she fell more deeply in love as each year passed.

Truly, their marriage had brought both of them so many pluses. One was the relief it had been to turn the family finances over to Jack! Every payday he put money in her household fund to cover their groceries and usually have some left over so that she had a little spending money for something she needed or wanted for herself or for one of her grandchildren.

Dan had been given an allowance in addition to any money he earned doing odd jobs for neighbors or other friends. Ella thought often how much easier life was to deal with when there were two of you to handle the problems and the ups-and-downs that inevitably come with living, especially with a son who insisted more and more on being treated as an adult.

Jack constantly thanked God for a wife who was a warm, funny, delightful partner and who enjoyed making love with him, letting him know he was loved and appreciated for every little thing he did for her and her children, who made him feel they were his family too.

On board the *Queen Mary*, Ella and Jack met a few couples whose company they enjoyed. One couple at their dining table was from Memphis and had a daughter who had been a student at Southwestern when Nellie and Mary Beth were there. While neither parent remembered names, just that link made conversation easy at first and a way to move on to other subjects. The time on board the ship enabled them to lie on deck and absorb the sun, explore and engage in any activities on deck that interested them, enjoy the shows and other entertainment at night, and have just enough time simply to act as newlyweds, though they had just celebrated their fourth anniversary!

"These days on board the Queen Mary were just what the doctor ordered!" Ella exclaimed as she and Jack stood looking at a spot on the horizon, gradually growing larger. "Thank you, Jack, for this trip—and this time together before we arrive—without lesson plans to make or papers to grade!"

Jack, who had his arm around her, pulled her closer and kissed her hair. He wanted to kiss her as he had that morning when they had made love, knowing that they likely would not have this much privacy during their time in England, but too many other people were crowded at the ship's rail watching as the ocean liner made its way into the harbor.

2

Since they had docked in South Hampton early that morning, they had taken a train into the city and then a taxi to the Piccadilly West End Hotel that was close to Piccadilly Circus, the heart of the city-center, so Jack said. They were able to check in and leave their luggage with the desk clerk, for even though it was nearing noon, their rooms would not be available until later. They were eager to walk and explore the area, ready to get their land-legs back after the slightly rolling movement of the ship. The Queen Mary had made it all the way across the Atlantic without encountering any bad weather or rough water, so it had not been a problem to adjust to the gentle movement of the ship. But after they disembarked, they had laughed at how different it felt to be back on solid ground with no movement at all!

The first thing Ella wanted to do was find a phone booth and call Eleanor to let her know they had disembarked and were in the heart of London, where they would spend one night before getting on the train the next morning to Durham. Eleanor had the train schedule and would meet them at the railway station at 2:30 the next afternoon and take them to their apartment. They would spend a few days getting to know their son-in-law and meeting his parents and other family members. Then the MacLeans and Ronald and Eleanor planned to go on vacation together since schools in England took the month of July for their summer holiday time.

England's red phone booths were easy to spot, and Ella had them stop at the first one they saw. She had a handful of British coins to use to make her call, almost dropping some of them in her eagerness to hear her daughter's voice. Eleanor sounded as eager to see her family as Ella was to see her daughter after four years.

Jack and Ella took brief turns speaking to Eleanor, and then commented on how much of a British accent Eleanor had acquired. She certainly didn't sound at all like the girl from Arkansas who had left them in the summer of 1933!

Jack, who had spent several months in London during the war getting surgery and the then therapy on his injured knee and leg, had finally been able to go outside the hospital enough to get a taste of the city.

He had learned his way around parts of London and felt comfortable taking the underground. Jack led Ella to a pub named "The Horses and Coach" he had discovered when he was recuperating, surprised it was still there. Proud of himself for remembering where it was, he hoped the food would be as good as it had been before the war ended. He and a couple of other recovering patients had often taken a taxi to Piccadilly where they had decided this pub was the best for the money.

Since it was near lunch time Jack ordered fish and chips with a mug of ale for him and root beer for Ella. He could not keep from exclaiming how good it was to see this part of London that had appeared dreary and sad was now filled with light and color and life. Back then, when he was able to leave the hospital, he had just been happy to get outside the walls, but he could not help seeing the damage to many of the buildings, the war-weariness on the faces of the civilians, and the number of those in uniforms who were on crutches or walked with canes or had arms in casts or slings.

Now there were no injured people in view, and no damaged buildings except those undergoing renovation, and despite the

Great Depression, London's inhabitants appeared to find life on the whole much more enjoyable than it had been in 1919!

Jack insisted they walk around the Circus to get a close-up view of the Shaftesbury Memorial Fountain with its statue of Eros reigning over the hustle and bustle of this famous section of London. Jack even quoted Oscar Wilde's statement he had recently read as they were preparing for their trip: "As I lounged in the Park, or strolled down Piccadilly, I used to look at everyone who passed me, and wonder, with mad curiosity, what sort of lives they led. Some of them fascinated me. Others filled me with terror." Ella was not familiar with Oscar Wilde, but Jack did not go into detail about him other than saying that Wilde had been a most interesting person. Changing the subject, he said they should be able to get into their room at the hotel and have time to freshen up a bit before they went out for dinner and more sightseeing.

Ella was pleased with their room and bath, although the room was not large. Having traveled in England before, she had realized that smaller rooms were common in places where space was often limited.

Ella and Jack spent an hour resting and freshening up before they were ready to sightsee some more. When they headed back out into the afternoon hustle and bustle, Ella wanted to know why the area was called "Piccadilly Circus" and was hoping Jack could answer. Even though she had read about the place in English novels, none had ever explained the reason for the name.

Jack did know—or remembered having read it when he had been hospitalized. "Piccadilly comes from the word *Picadils*, sometimes spelled with a *k* instead of a *c*. *Pikadils* were the stiff collars with scalloped edges and a broad lace or perforated border that were very fashionable in the early 1600s. You've at least seen portraits in books of men and women wearing them. I'm always grateful they went out of style several hundred years ago!

"Anyway, a man named Robert Baker made a fortune from making and selling them.. He bought land in this area now called Piccadilly and named his house Piccadilly Hall. He bought even more land with money he gained from a second marriage. I've seen a map published in 1658 that described the street as 'the way from Knightsbridge to Piccadilly Hall' and the word 'circus' really refers to the circle in the center where Albert Gilbert's stature of Eros stands.

"This part of London was once the center of fashion and culture and still is an amazing place. Tonight I've made reservations for us to have dinner at the Trocadero, an extraordinary and beautiful building that was constructed in the mid-18th century. The building itself is huge and has housed tennis courts, circuses, theater productions, horsemanship arenas, even boxing events and a mechanical waxworks exhibition. The Trocadero Restaurant we are going to was first opened in 1886 and continues to be known as one of the best in London. I can't wait for you to taste a bit of what fashionable London was like about a hundred years ago."

"Are we dressed appropriately for such a fancy place?" Ella's worried expression made Jack laugh.

"Yes, my love, you look quite elegant, and that is why I insisted you dress for an evening out. I imagine it's a bit more formal than it was the one time I ate there soon after the war ended, and people were still trying to recover from the hardships of those years. But I spoke with the desk clerk when I checked us in about appropriate night attire for the Trocadero, and he assured me that unless some special group had rented the building, ordinary evening dinner clothes would be appropriate in the restaurant itself, and that did not mean white tie and tails or long dresses. The Depression has hurt Merrie Ole' England just as it has the U.S.A."

They took a taxi to the Trocadero, and Ella was awed not only by the size but by the beauty of the building on the outside and even more so by the elegance of the décor on the inside. Their waiter was a delightful man who enjoyed telling his obviously American patrons a bit about the history of the building and the many restorations and up-datings it had received. He also rec-ommended several items on the menu he thought they would enjoy. Ella ordered steamed trout almandine and Jack the glazed porkchop. They were served appetizers, a soup, a salad, the main course with vegetables, a dessert, cheese and fruit. Jack had ordered wine with the main course and a dessert wine at the end. Although Ella was completely unaccustomed to having wine—period, Jack told her to sip slowly and not feel she had to empty the glass, much less the bottle.

After they had returned to their hotel, Ella said, "Jack, how are we affording all of this, especially the dinner tonight at the Trocadero? I know we had to get to England and our room on the Queen Mary was a necessity and this room also here in London. I know you told me we were drawing from some of the funds you had let Michael Lewis invest for you through his bank. But do we have enough for the kind of expense this evening must have cost when we have barely begun this trip?" Ella's voice expressed her concern.

Jack took his wife in his arms and kissed her tenderly. "Ella, you needn't worry about these extra expenses. Two days before we left I went by Michael's bank to get our Travelers' checks, and he called me into his office to give me this." And Jack pulled a letter out of a pocket inside his suitcase. "I want you to read it because it touched me so deeply when I read it I haven't been able to talk about it."

Ella read aloud:

Dear Mr. McLean,

This letter and the money that comes with it is an expression of our gratitude for all you have done for our children and our town during the years that you have been a coach and a teacher in our high school. Not only have you encouraged our young people to be interested in their family backgrounds and how their ancestors came to this country and why their families have come to live in this area of Arkansas, you and your wife have helped them learn to speak about their family histories with pride in who they were and what they accomplished in this new land.

Both you and your wife have also been an example of the kind of Christians we want our own children to become by demonstrating the love and forgiveness that we all ought to show when you took in your former wife who left you for another man but then came to seek your help when she had no other place to go. You and Mrs. MacLean have never said a single word about this in public to anyone, but it is hard to keep anything a secret in a town as small as Myrna. The fact that you ministered to her the night she arrived at your home, carried her to the hospital the next day and stayed with her until she died, then accompanied her body to Richmond, Virginia, where you buried her in the cemetery where your dead child's body lies—all of this at your own expense without ever saying a word against this woman who had wronged you— sets an example not only for our young people but for all of us.

So when we learned you and Mrs. MacLean were going to England to see your daughter who now lives there, many of us wanted to chip in with a "love gift" for the two of you that we hope will enable you to have a bit of spending money over and above what you have been saving up for this trip. So use it as you will and enjoy it with our love and appreciation for what you both do for us and our children!

All Your Friends in Myrna.

Ella could barely finish reading the letter out loud because her own emotions had been so touched by the words and actions of these people who had given anonymously so she and Jack could imagine the entire town had been part of their generosity. They stood holding each other silently until Jack finally said, "Now you know what I've been hiding from you, knowing that this would be as meaningful to you as it has been to me, even while I'm both a bit embarrassed by it because I don't feel what we did was anything that any other person wouldn't have done in that situation."

"But Jack, why did you wait so long to share this with me," Ella asked after she had wiped her eyes and blown her nose.

"I don't really know, my darling. My first impulse was to give it back to Michael, saying that we couldn't accept it, and at that time

I had no idea that it was over $200. Even before I realized how much it was, the idea that during this time when life is touch-and-go for so many of our folks, they had dug into their pockets and made a contribution to an expensive trip like our going to England made me uncomfortable.

"But when I said this to Michael, he silenced me, saying, 'Jack, this gesture comes from people who genuinely care about you and Ella and who recognize and appreciate what you have done and are doing for their children and for this town. You simply have to swallow your own pride and accept this graciously. When you come back home, you can share your gratitude and the experiences you have on this trip with the town in some way and let them know how much you appreciated not only the gift but the kindness behind it.'

"So, my Ella, this is what awaits us on our return. The truth is that I have been holding all this inside and really hadn't intended to tell you until we were headed back to the states. I didn't want this to bother you or get in the way of your enjoying this trip, and now I've done it. Will you forgive me?"

"Oh, Jack, of course! There's really nothing to forgive! I think this kind of thing bothers men more than it does women, though I don't know why it should. Maybe we're more accustomed to being on the receiving end of having nice things done for us or to us, and we're used to saying 'thank you' and meaning it without having our pride hurt or being embarrassed. And maybe some of that is because we are frequently the 'givers' as well as the 'receivers.' Oh, I don't know the reason! But I am as moved by the letter and the monetary gift as you are, and I certainly have no hesitancy about expressing these feelings to the people of Myrna. And I'm really glad we don't know the names of those who contributed because this way we can be grateful to everybody in town, and that's a really good feeling, isn't it?"

"Oh, Ella, I do love you so! You've set me straight and made it possible for me to just accept being grateful for the thoughtfulness and generosity of these people who have shown their feelings for us and what we have been trying to do! It's time for me to go to bed. The wine I drank has made me too emotional as well as sleepy. Finish in the bathroom and then come to bed so that I can take you in my arms and let you feel my love for you!"

The next morning they ate a late breakfast in the hotel dining room. Ella finished packing while Jack paid the hotel bill and asked the doorman to wait 15 minutes and then flag a taxi to take them to the station where they would board the train that would take them to Durham where Eleanor would meet them.

3

"Eleanor Douglass, you're expecting and you didn't let me know!" were Ella's first words to her daughter as they got off the train at the Durham Station that afternoon. "Can I hug you? You look as though you could have this child any minute. When are you due?"

"Yes, please hug me! I won't explode, though the truth is I am due any time now. I didn't tell you because I wanted it to be a surprise, and I was hoping you would be able to come, Mother, so that you might be here for the birth, but I didn't want to put any pressure on you about when to arrive. Now I'm fairly sure you will be present when this baby makes its appearance on English soil! The truth is I've been feeling rather like he or she is going to arrive soon. I hope so anyway. I'm feeling like an elephant, and standing up or sitting down is getting harder every day."

Eleanor had stopped talking long enough to hug her mother and then her stepfather, saying, "Papa Jack, I'd love for you to drive the car home. It's really difficult for me to get behind the steering wheel and shift gears. Ronald would have driven me here because he wanted to greet you and welcome you too and let you see for yourself who your daughter had married, but he had a meeting with his dean at 3:00 he couldn't miss."

While Eleanor chattered on, Jack had opened the "boot," proud that he'd remembered the British word for the trunk of the car, and loaded it with the suitcases, and the box that contained gifts for Eleanor, Ronald, and his parents, along with some small gifts for Frank and his family, Jean Marc and Andre, and Cecile, Jason, and their little children. Eleanor sat in front with Jack to give him directions to their apartment and provide commentary on landmarks as they drove by.

Ella remembered the impressive towers of the Norman Cathedral that dominated the woods along the River Wear. The older part of the city of Durham perches precariously on a narrow bit of land below the castle's north wall. Equally impressive was the castle itself with its first buildings erected in the second century. One was circular with two floors with small openings for windows that allowed the inhabitants to keep watch over any approaching enemy and shoot arrows at them if they came close enough. The castle had been added onto over the centuries so that it had become a walled city by the Middle Ages.

Ella, who was sitting in the back seat alone and whose memory was being teased by the view, broke in between Eleanor's directions and said, "Jack, do you know the story of St. Cuthbert who is buried in the Cathedral here."

Jack, who was concentrating on driving on what he considered to be the wrong side of the road, said, "No, I don't. I'd like to hear it but not right now while I'm doing my best to stay in the right lane and listen to Eleanor."

Ella knew better than to press the issue but decided that she would get him to the Cathedral and let him hear the truly interesting story of St. Cuthbert. Ella had hardly finished her thought when Eleanor said, "We're here! Our apartment is in this building on the second floor. We'll let Papa Jack bring your luggage up because there is no elevator, and I'm in no shape to carry anything heavy up a staircase.

"This was a beautiful old home until the turn of this century when it was converted into four apartments. Mother, you'll appreciated the crown molding around the high ceilings and the long windows. We're actually more grateful it has electricity, fairly new plumbing, gas heat, and an updated kitchen. And even the rooms are larger than they are in some of the more modern apartment buildings."

Eleanor chatted on about the apartment until they entered and faced the main staircase leading upwards from the large entryway, and then she stopped, saying that the stairs at this point in her pregnancy took much of her breath to climb. Ella understood and hoped she could handle the climb herself and especially that Jack could also as he was carrying their large suitcase while she had a smaller one containing gifts she had brought for Eleanor's new family.

All three of them were glad when they arrived at the landing and hallway where Eleanor and Ronald's apartment door was a welcomed sight. The apartment itself was truly charming. It opened onto a living room with a fireplace and windows on both sides, a sofa facing the fireplace and an armchair on each side of it. A dining area opened off the living area and contained a round table with six chairs around it, a sideboard with some pieces of china decorating it, and a door leading into the kitchen. The kitchen had a gas stove, a sink set in a counter with cabinets above and below, and a gas refrigerator. There was room for a small work table. A door on one side of the kitchen led into a narrow hallway with three doors, two of which opened into one large bedroom and one smaller bedroom. The middle room was the bathroom with a bathtub and shower, a lavatory with a small cabinet above it, and a water-closet, or toilet in American terminology. The master bedroom contained a large double bed, a bassinet already prepared for the soon-to-come arrival, a closet, and a large dresser with lots of drawers. Each bedroom had a large window facing a garden.

Ella "oohed and aahed" over how comfortable the apartment was and how attractive and homey Eleanor had made it, asking where they had gotten all the furniture, pictures, kitchen dishes and pans, and so forth. Eleanor said that she and Ronald had shopped at used furniture and second-hand shops, delighted when they found something they liked and could afford to add to their first home. Ronald's parents had also helped, giving them a few items they had saved for when he married, though they had already given some of their own things to their oldest, a daughter who lived in York, and to their son who also lived and worked in Durham.

"You will all have the opportunity to meet Ronald's parents and his brother and wife when they come here for dinner tomorrow night. We figured that tonight we could just eat here and give you two and Ronald a chance to get to know each other. Tomorrow night Mrs. Douglass and Vicky, Regie's wife, are bringing food so that I won't have to do so much cooking. They are delightful people, Mother, and I think you all will enjoy getting to know one another."

"I'm sure we will. I look forward to meeting all of them." And Jack added his assurance. "Eleanor, what do you call your in-laws?" Ella asked.

"I called them Mr. and Mrs. Douglass for a time. I was waiting for them to ask me to call them something more familiar, and they soon did."

They had hardly finished seeing the apartment when the door opened and Ronald Douglass entered, giving Ella and Jack their first in-person introduction to their son-in-law.

"I'm so sorry I wasn't able to meet you at the train station and then help you unload your luggage and carry it up to the apartment! But I'm really delighted to meet you at last. Eleanor has told me so much about you and talked about you almost non-stop during these past two days! Seeing you, Mrs. MacLean, I know where Eleanor gets her beauty! It's a pleasure to meet you, Mr. MacLean."

Ronald had taken each one's hand as he spoke to each personally, and they were touched by his warmth and friendliness. Ella immediately said, "You are exactly what I had expected from Eleanor's description of you in her letters, Ronald. It is so good to meet you in person at last and to welcome you as part of our family. I just wish Dan, Mary Beth, and her family had been able to come with us too!"

The evening continued to be easy and delightful as they sat around the dining table together, eating the dinner that Eleanor had prepared earlier, sharing memories. Ella wanted to hear all about how Ronald and Eleanor had met and fallen in love. Eleanor had already written to them her side of the story, but she wanted to hear Ronald's account of their first meeting and how it had slowly become a love affair.

"I had already noticed Eleanor and thought she was beautiful even before she took my Romantic poetry class. To be honest, her beauty had actually prejudiced me a bit against her—that and the fact that she was from the middle of the United States, actually from a state I had barely known existed, and I simply couldn't imagine why she had come to England to study and how she had ended up in one of my classes. I have to admit that my fairly new PhD in literature had made me a bit pompous and overly sure of my intelligence and knowledge.

"But the first paper I read by your daughter was incredibly well-written and insightful. The assignment was an essay on any poem by Wordsworth that the writer selected. They were not to use any sources or commentaries but to write what they heard the selected poem saying to their own heart and mind. Eleanor had chosen 'Lines Composed a Few Miles above Tintern Abbey' for her assignment. Her understanding of and feelings about the poem were so in tune with the poet's words and so clearly and beautifully expressed, I thought this young woman from Arkansas could not have possibly written this paper on her own. And I accused her of getting help.

"Well, I wasn't at all prepared for her reaction. I expected her to confess, ask to re-write it and beg me not to hold it against her. Instead her eyes flashed with anger as she said, in a voice she tried hard to control but didn't quite succeed in doing, that she had suspected I wouldn't be able to understand that she had long loved Wordsworth's poetry and that this particular poem had spoken to her personally, even though it had been several years since she read it for the first time in high school. Yet at this later reading, she had been able to grasp even more the underlying sorrow and beauty of the poet's feelings and his ability to express them.

"If I thought she had cheated by relying on someone else's insight into the poem and the poet who had written it, then she would be perfectly willing to defend herself before a committee of professors and speak without notes. By the time she finished with me, I was apologizing to her like an imbecile and practically begging her to give me another chance as her professor."

Ronald had told his story so well, almost acting it out with his voice and facial expressions, that he had his audience smiling and then laughing out loud by the time he finished.

Eleanor was laughing so hard she had tears in her eyes. "You all do know he's exaggerating, I hope. But he did question me, rather gently, about my sources for the paper, and when I told him I had not used any but had written from my own understanding and feelings for the poet, he did act a bit as though he couldn't believe I was capable of that. Then I did get a bit huffy and said, 'I suppose you think I'm just a hillbilly from Arkansas who is incapable of understanding an English poet's writing.' So that's when he began back-tracking! And just see how that ended!" Eleanor said, putting her hand on her stomach.

They ended up sitting at the table, talking and laughing, until Eleanor stood up, saying she had to go to the powder room or embarrass herself. At that they all rose, and Ronald, Ella, and Jack began to clear the table, taking everything to the kitchen. Ronald said he would wash, Jack offered to dry, and Ella said she would put the dishes away but might need help in putting them in their accustomed places. They had made a good beginning by the time Eleanor returned, only to be told to go sit down and put her feet up while they finished in the kitchen. After all, since she had prepared the meal, they could at least do the clean-up—and because there were three of them working, it would be done quickly.

After all the dinner dishes were put away, Jack, Ella, and Ronald joined Eleanor in the living room where they began talking politics. Ronald wanted to know their opinion of President Roosevelt and how he was handling the Depression and how Arkansas was being affected by it.

Ella spoke up, saying, "I like so much about President Roosevelt, but I do feel he needs to be doing more to help the economy. He's all into protecting and improving the land and building dams, but poor people are still just getting poorer and we don't seem to be coming out of the Depression. He's not speaking much about what's going on in Europe, but I can't believe he's not paying attention and that we won't step up to help England and France if it comes to that."

Jack, who was much more interested in how England was feeling about what was going on in Germany and the prospects of war, asked Ronald what the feeling was in England about Germany.

Ronald replied, "I'm aware of a lot of war talk going on at the University because of what has been happening in Germany under Herr Hitler. His popularity with the German people seems to be growing daily, but I do not like him. I think he is dangerous. I really don't like what is happening in Germany to the Jewish people, and also I fear Hitler's ambition to spread his Third Reich politics into surrounding countries. We've been very concerned that Germany and Italy seem to have become partners in their desires to take over weaker countries, or parts of countries like the Rhineland. And then Italy under Mussolini conquered Ethiopia, and its ruler is in exile.

"Our Prime Minister, Mr. Chamberlain, seems to think Britain can get along with Herr Hitler without becoming involved in what he is doing in gaining power over other countries. But we have serious doubts about England's ability to remain uninvolved in European politics. We have too many memories of what life was like in this part of the world during the last war. Yet we can't imagine Great Britain will be able to remain neutral and sit by and watch if countries like France, Holland, Belgium, and Poland are taken over by Germany.

"But what are people saying in the States? President Roosevelt is respected over here because of what he has done with conservation efforts, but his foreign policy has been unknown until fairly recently when some of your senators and other politicians have made a few comments about what is happening in Germany. Our press has picked them up, but we haven't heard much from the President himself, at least not that I'm aware of. I thought he might speak more about what's happening in Europe after he was re-elected, but in his inauguration speech in March he never mentioned what Germany under Hitler and Italy under Mussolini are doing."

Ella spoke up, "We have a German family living in Myrna now. They moved there after living a few years here in England. The husband teaches mathematics at Arkansas State College in Jonesboro. The mother is Jewish and therefore their children are too, and that's why they left Germany and came to England. I don't remember why they ended up in the U.S.A., especially how they came to Myrna, but we've become friends.

"And they are really worried about what's going on in Germany because Ruth's parents still live there. Ruth has been trying to get them to come to the States for several years, but now the situation is so bad they are sort of under house arrest—can't go out without wearing a big 'Star of David' on their clothing to identify them as Jews, and often they are even afraid to leave their house. It sounds awful!"

"We've read and heard about that sort of thing happening there too," Eleanor said. "I'm just so glad we live on a big island that is not really part of Europe. Our prime minister is determined to keep us out of war, should it come to that. I hope he can, though Ronald and I don't agree on that. He thinks if Germany starts taking over the countries right across the channel from us, we will have to go to their defense because it will just be a matter of time before Hitler comes after us. Let's don't talk about this any longer. I get scared just thinking about it. It's almost my bedtime, and I can't imagine that the rest of you aren't ready to call it a day!"

With that, the evening wound down, and Ella and Jack went to the guest bedroom to prepare for bed.

"Well, my love, are you satisfied that your eldest made a good choice of a husband?" Jack asked as they pulled up the sheet and light blanket.

"Oh, Jack, I really like him and think he's great for Eleanor. I could tell you approved of him and found him as delightful as I did. He's got a great sense of humor and is really good for her. I am both relieved because I truly like him and I am so happy for her— actually, for both of them—because he obviously adores her. But let's stop talking and hope we sleep as soundly as we did in London where there was a lot more traffic noise than there is here!"

She snuggled into his arms and they soon were both sleeping so soundly neither one woke up when Jack removed his numbed arm.

4

The next day after Ronald had left to go teach his summer school classes at the University, Eleanor and her mother had time for a good long talk. Eleanor wanted to know her opinion of Ronald, and Ella was able to say honestly that both she and Jack were delighted with him—his personality and sense of humor, his intelligence, and his obvious love for his wife. They looked forward to meeting and getting to know other members of his family at dinner that night. Eleanor said she hoped they weren't too disappointed that it was obvious she and Ronald would not be able to go with them on the trip around England. Ella assured her that being present when this child arrived would be far more enjoyable than seeing the English countryside. They would find time to go to see their friends at St. Anthony's hospital and living facility. She wanted Jack to meet these friends of hers and them to meet Jack.

Eleanor then said she wanted to take them to get a close-up look at the University of Durham and maybe have lunch with Ronald there. Ella told her that Jack should see the cathedral, and Eleanor said they would certainly have time to do that since it truly was worth a visit.

While Jack was driving them to the university in Eleanor's little car and with her directions, Eleanor also suggested Ella and Jack might want to attend Evensong at the cathedral, noted for its organ and the acoustics. Different boys' choirs from around the country and sometimes even from the Continent came during the summer months to sing during the service. It was always a beautiful service and lasted about an hour. She would go with them if she weren't so full of baby that even sitting in a pew was uncomfortable, while kneeling was really impossible. But she was so glad that she had grown up Episcopalian because it had been easy for her to fit into the worship and life of the Church of England!

Ella said that she thought attending an evensong service would be lovely even though Jack was a Presbyterian from birth, and now the whole family had moved their membership to First Presbyterian. Even Mary Beth and Patrick, who had grown up Catholic, had joined First Presbyterian because St. Mark's was so different without Father Banks.

Relieved when they had arrived at the University, Jack let Eleanor and Ella out in front of the entrance to wait there for him while he found the carpark, which didn't take long since it was summer and fewer students were on campus. Eleanor proudly showed them where her office and classroom had been before she took a leave-of-absence to have this baby. She hoped she and Ronald would be able to afford for her to stay on leave for at least the first two years after the baby came. She wanted to be a "stay-at-home mother" for as long as possible, although at some point she wanted to return to the classroom.

Ella smiled to herself as she remembered how eager Eleanor had been to finish her Master's Degree, and now she was willing to put that aside to be a stay-at-home mother, at least for a few years or as long as they could afford for her to do so.

The classroom building was old but in good repair. Portraits of former professors and students who had made a name for themselves after their graduation lined the halls and the faculty lounge. Jack was impressed with the obvious age and history, not only of the building itself but in looking at the portraits of the people who had been associated with it.

They peeked in on Ronald as he was finishing his class on British and Scottish literature, and then all four of them went to the dining room for an early and light lunch. Ronald had a meeting with the Dean after lunch and Eleanor begged off going to the cathedral with them, saying that she had been there several times and would enjoy sitting on a bench in one of the gardens and reading a book she had brought with her while they took the tour.

Jack, who really was interested in English history and as a former pastor himself, said, "We'll try not to be long, but I would like to see the cathedral because of the little I know about St. Cuthbert."

After seeing where Eleanor would be waiting for them, Ella and Jack, walked over to the Cathedral where they encountered a docent standing alone and obviously delighted to see two people he could talk to about the magnificent structure whose towers rose above the trees on the outside and about the beauty and history of its interior as well.

The words of the docent rang true as he called it "a triumph of engineering, a creation of faith, a parable of God." Then he added, "But there would have been no Cathedral had it not been for Cuthbert of Lindisfarne, the best loved saint of the northeast of England. His mortal remains found their last resting place here in Durham, and they now lie under a plain marble slab behind the high altar. Although the richly ornamented medieval shrine was destroyed, his spirit is alive, and people still gather at his tomb to join their prayers with his. Would you like to know more about St. Cuthbert?" the docent asked. When Jack said he would, the docent continued.

"The legend was that when Cuthbert was just a shepherd boy, he saw in a vision the soul of St. Aidan being carried to heaven by angels. This vision inspired him to become a monk. He wanted to be a hermit, but his reputation for holiness and learning was so great that the people insisted he be made a bishop. He was consecrated Bishop of Lindisfarne, the Holy Island, in A.D. 685, where he died two years later. When his coffin was opened 10 years after his death so that his body could be placed in a shrine above ground, it was found to be without any signs of decay.

"It rested in the shrine for 200 years until Danish raids threatened the area, making the monks on Lindisfarne decide to seek a safer place for it. When the monks opened the shrine after those 200 years, to their amazement and awe St. Cuthbert's body still appeared to be as free of decay as on the day it was buried. The monks enclosed the body in a wooden coffin and wandered for 10 years looking for a safe place for his burial."

"Is that possible? I mean for a dead body not to decay?" Ella asked.

"I wasn't there, Madam, but I have to trust that the good monks at Lindisfarne would not lie about such a thing. But there is more to the story.

"Those devout men wandered for 10 years, looking for a safe resting place for their saint. In 995 they came to this rocky piece of land that was almost completely surrounded by the River Wear. They sheltered the Saint's body for a time in a little church they made of tree boughs. Then they built a shrine they named "the White Church" until it was pulled down in 1092 to start building this Cathedral where the White Church had been.

"The body was protected in a temporary burial place until the shrine behind the High Altar in the cathedral was completed in 1104. The monks had prepared everything for the removal of the precious bones and all was ready except for taking down the heavy timbers supporting the vault over the new tomb. The timbers were so huge and heavy that taking them down would not be easy, but the morning they were to be removed the workers entered to find all of them lying on the ground with no harm done to anything. The story was told that St. Cuthbert himself had taken care of the problem!

"Cuthbert's shrine was for hundreds of years the Cathedral's great glory and a center of pilgrimages, not just for common people but also for kings and prelates who brought their offerings along with their prayers. Men only, no women, were allowed to approach the shrine. Women were allowed to come only as far as that black marble line in front of the font.

"One story is that in 1333 when Queen Philippa, the wife of King Edward III was staying in the Prior's lodging, she was awakened in the middle of the night, told of Cuthbert's dislike for women, and offered a bed in the castle. In reverence for the saint, she didn't take the direct way through the cathedral but instead went through the great gate of the monastery along Dun Cow Lane to the castle, begging the saint to forgive her for a deed she had done in ignorance."

"I was quite taken with St. Cuthbert until I heard this last story," said Ella with a smile.

Jack spoke up. "I think I'll change the subject and ask about the Venerable Bede. I think my wife has some interest in him, don't you, Ella?"

"Yes, I did read about him in one of my books on English history because he was an early historian of this remarkable country. What can you tell us about him?" Ella asked, her voice communicating her genuine interest.

The docent was eager to oblige because few foreigners knew anything about Bede. "He was probably born near Durham sometime in A.D. 673, although nothing is known of his family background except that at age seven he was given into the care of Benedict Biscop, who had founded the monastery of St. Peter at Wearmouth around A.D. 680. We do know that in 682 Bede moved to the monastery at Jarrow, where he lived for the rest of his life, surviving a plague that struck in 686 and killed most of the population. He became a deacon at age 19 and then a priest at 30.

"Although he lived at the monastery, he is known to have visited the archbishop of York and the king of Northumbria along with stops at several abbeys and monasteries across Britain. He was a noted scholar, teacher, and author. His writings included a number of Biblical commentaries with his most famous work being the Ecclesiastical History of the English People."

Ella smiled and said, "Yes, I did read a bit about that one."

"Did you know that another area of his study was the science of calculating calendar dates? For example, one of the most important dates he worked on was Easter, which was mired in controversy between different branches of the Church in those days. Actually it still is since parts of Christianity celebrate Easter at different times.

"Bede also helped popularize the practice of dating events forward from the time of the birth of Christ. In Latin, the common scholarly language of those days, Bede helped spread the custom of using the words Anno Domini, "in the year of the Lord" referring to Christ's birth, throughout Europe, and it's still used all over the Christian world today, though usually written just A.D."

"That's something I did not know, and that is interesting because few of us ever think about how or when we started using B.C. and A.D." Ella looked at Jack. "Did your history courses ever mention that?" And when Jack shook his head, Ella said, "Neither did mine."

The docent smiled. "I am not surprised. Our British young people don't usually learn that in school either. Another fact about Bede is that he was a skilled linguist and translator and his knowledge of Latin and Greek made the writings of the early Church Fathers available and accessible to his Anglo-Saxon brothers in the faith. He died in his cell at the monastery at Jarrow in 735.

"Many historians consider Bede to be the most important scholar of the Early Middle Ages, that period between the death of Pope Gregory I in 604 and the coronation of Charlemagne in 800. In 1899 Pope Leo XIII declared Bede a 'Doctor of the Church,' the only native of Great Britain to achieve this honor. That's about all I have to tell you, but I appreciate your interest. You were good listeners! And you're Americans!"

Ella laughed. "You say that like you don't expect Americans to be interested or good listeners!"

"No, no, that's not what I intended at all! It's just that we don't get that many American tourists in this part of the country. And you don't sound like the visitors from your country that we do get? What part of the States are you from and what brings you to Durham, if you don't mind my curiosity?"

"We're from Arkansas, a state that's in the middle of the country but in the southern part, and we're here visiting family, our daughter and her husband," Ella said smiling. Her husband is part of the university faculty."

"Now I can guess who you are!" the docent said with a big smile. "My name is Gerald Sutherland, and before I retired and became a docent, I was a member of the history department. You are the in-laws of Ronald Douglass, who was one of my students years ago, and the family of his charming wife Eleanor. We've all been looking forward to your visit, though I wasn't quite sure when you were to arrive. But you've arrived before the birth—and that is wonderful!"

"We are so happy to be here for this miracle which my daughter had not even told me was going to happen because she wanted it to be a surprise. And it certainly was—though a lovely one! Now we are just waiting—although I don't think it can be much longer! But how nice to have one of their friends share his knowledge with us about this remarkable and beautiful place, Mr. Sutherland! My name is Ella MacLean, and this is husband Jack."

After shaking hands with them, Mr. Sutherland said to Jack, "I understand you are a high school history teacher. So do you teach any English history, Mr. MacLean?"

"Mostly my students learn about English history when it relates to America. I do teach a world history course for seniors and they learn more about England during that final year of high school, and I have to admit that most American textbooks for world history classes concentrate more on western countries than on the eastern ones, especially from the Middle Ages on. Yet with Japan on the rise, we may wish we had paid a bit more attention to the East."

"I'm afraid I agree with you there, though we here in England have enough to worry about with Herr Hitler and Germany and lately Mussolini and Italy and what their plans are. It's a trouble-some time. Did you have any part in the last war, Mr. MacLean?"

"A very small part. My leg was injured pretty badly on my second day of combat, and I spent the remainder of the war recovering in a hospital near London and then at a desk job in London itself until the Armistice. Actually I was with some of the last Americans to head home. I must say, I came to admire and love the spirit of the British people—still do. At some point, sooner than I want to think, we're all going to be at war again. The last one didn't redress all the issues, and Germany and Italy are looking for an opportunity to get back at us. And maybe I need to include Japan in that too."

"I hate to think you are correct in your assessment of our world today, Mr. MacLean, but I fear you speak the truth. Will America join us?"

"To be truthful, I do not know. There is a huge number of our citizens who do not want any part of another war. We are still recovering from the terrible effects of the Depression. People are just now seeing the progress the country is making under President Roosevelt. They don't want to get involved in a war if they don't see a real reason for it."

"Yes, I understand, though we Brits were a bit surprised when the President, in his second inaugural speech, didn't even mention what was going on in Europe with the Nazis and the Italians."

"I have to say I was too, but this president is an astute politician. We as a country are not ready to think about getting into another war as horrible as the last one, much less hear about it from a man who, while extremely popular, has lost some of his following. And also, there are some folks who follow British and European politics who don't think much of Mr. Chamberlain, though others think he's doing exactly the right thing in trying to work with Hitler and Mussolini. What's your opinion?"

"I'm caught in the middle. I have two sons who will most certainly be called into service if we have to go to war with Germany and Italy, and I fear that as horrible as the last war was, this one will be worse. I don't want my sons to have to fight this war, but they will. Part of me wants to appease Herr Hitler and Signor Mussolini as long as possible. However, I don't think that's going to work in the long term."

"Jack, the topic of this conversation ceased to be enjoyable some moments ago. I think it's time for us to thank Mr. Sutherland again for being such an excellent guide, and truly it has been a pleasure, but we need to go find our daughter and hope that she has not gone into labor!" Ella smiled, but tugged on Jack's arm to pull him in the direction of where they had left Eleanor.

Jack apologized to Gerald Sutherland for getting into such a deep discussion about the prospects of war and then took Ella's hand as they headed toward the bench where Eleanor sat reading her book.

5

Since her in-laws were bringing dinner that night, all Eleanor and her family needed to do to prepare for the dinner that evening was to add the leaf to the table that they kept in the coat closet. Unfortunately they had only four dining room chairs. While they were able to set places for eight, they decided that the four, more comfortable chairs would go to Eleanor because she was pregnant, and to Ella, and Mrs. Douglass, whose first name was Margaret, according to Eleanor, and to her sister-in-law Vicky. The men would sit in the kitchen chairs.

"Mother, the British are a good bit more formal than Arkansans. It's all right I think, if you invite Ronald's family to call you and Jack by your first names, but don't be surprised if they don't reciprocate, although I think they will. It's just a bit of a different culture and way of doing things. Actually, I addressed them as 'Mr. and Mrs. Douglass' until they invited me to call them 'Margaret' and 'Reg' or whatever I wanted to call them."

"So how do you address them?" Ella asked.

"If it's just family and even with close friends, I call them by the same words Ronald uses—Mother and Father. Though as I've grown closer to the whole family, I sometimes use Mama and Papa.

"British English sounds very different from Arkansas. I confess I've blundered at times because of my way of expressing myself and some of the Southern expressions I've used, although now I.ve begun to feel quite British. Yet it's a little like the States in that people in this part of Britain don't sound or speak exactly like those in the southwestern parts of the island, not to mention the Irish and the Welsh. Actually, there are all sorts of different dialects all over the place, just like there are at home."

"Yes, we already ran into a bit of that in London and then on the train coming here. I rather like the variety," Ella said with a smile, "even when I don't understand and have to ask for a repeat or an explanation."

"But at least it is English, even if a bit different from what we're used to in Arkansas!" Jack said. "Travel is always interesting and the more different the cultures and people are, the more interesting it is, not necessarily more comfortable for us, but certainly more interesting and challenging."

"Eleanor, do you remember how we used to try to get your daddy to tell us stories about his encounters with French people, like some of the nurses who worked with them at St. Antoine's during the Great War. He would attempt to imitate their speech, especially that of the cooks and other helpers. He would have us in stitches describing how hard it was at times to understand or be understood and all the different gestures they used to communicate with one another. Language and dialects and commonplace expressions in one language that don't mean the same in another certainly make communication a challenge," Ella said, and Jack agreed as he added some of his early experiences in the hospital in London.

"Every country, I imagine, has different expressions and sayings and even pronunciations in different areas of it. But I think with the invention of radio and more travel among the different parts of a country, people will lose some of their uniqueness, and that's probably too bad."

"Why do you say that, Jack? Why wouldn't it be better for mutual understanding if we all spoke the same language in the same way?" Ella asked.

"Perhaps it would be better, but it certainly would be less interesting. Personally, I don't think we'll ever all be exactly the same in language or in any other way. Genuine communication and understanding will always require respect and real efforts to understand how and why others think and speak and act as they do. There! I'm off my soap-box—and that's just one example of a phrase that might confuse somebody."

Jack had barely completed his sentence when they heard footsteps on the stairs and then knocks on the door. Eleanor hurried to open it for her in-laws and welcomed them into the living room to meet her parents.

Margaret and Reginald Douglass, along with their older son and daughter-in-law Ralph and Vicky, entered so loaded down with bags and trays of food for the evening that Eleanor immediately led them into the kitchen where they quickly unloaded the food and then returned to the living room to meet her family.

Mrs. Douglass immediately held out her hand to Ella, saying "It is such a pleasure to meet you at last, and I do hope you will call me Margaret. We all loved Eleanor immediately and can hardly wait for this little one to arrive."

Ella, still holding Margaret's hand and smiling, replied, "Of course, you must call me 'Ella' and my husband 'Jack' because we are family. Eleanor surprised us, not writing that she is expecting— and at any moment—but what a wonderful surprise! And we loved Ronald practically from the first minute we met him in person. As glowing as Eleanor's letters have been about her 'wonderful husband' we realized quickly they had simply told the truth. We couldn't be happier about everything, could we, Jack?"

Jack, Reginald, and Ralph, who had been standing a bit to the side while their wives introduced themselves to each other, stepped forward, smiling and agreeing that they were happy. Reginald added that he'd be happier if they called him "Reg with a j" or "Regie" because he'd never liked his name, thought it sounded a bit snobbish. That comment further broke the ice and they immediately began talking like old friends. The Douglasses asked about the trip over and what they had done in London and were interested in Jack's impression of how London had changed since his time there toward the end of "The War." They were impressed that Jack had taken Ella to walk around Piccadilly Circus and that they had dined at the *Trocadero*.

Ronald, Ralph, Regie, and Jack went into the kitchen to pour sherry for the ladies and something stronger for themselves. The women were enjoying getting to know one another as Eleanor took them into the bedroom to see the bassinet that she had prepared for this baby they were all eager to arrive, and to "ooh and ahh" over the baby gifts Eleanor had received at a shower the faculty at the university had given for her and Ronald.

Dinner around the table was delightful with the American guests finding the food different from Southern cooking but delicious. Vicky had made Stilton soup and a green leafy salad while Margaret had made steak and kidney pie for the main dish and a strawberry trifle for dessert. "We thought you might enjoy trying some of our main dishes that might be a bit different from Arkansas cooking but not too different," Margaret said, after she had described what it was they were eating.

Jack had remembered once having steak and kidney pie when he was 13 and visiting his father who had come from Scotland and lived in Massachusetts. "I liked it all right, but this is much tastier than I remember it being then. The cook obviously makes a huge difference!"

Ella asked if they would share the recipes for all three dishes, while Jack said he hoped she would make a trifle as soon as they got back to Arkansas, especially when Margaret assured him that one could substitute other berries if strawberries were out of season.

Dinner lasted for more than an hour as they chatted and enjoyed one another's company. Then the ladies shooed the men out of the dining room while they cleared the table and both Regie and Ralph went outside to smoke cigars. Ronald had quit smoking when he started dating Eleanor because she did not like the odor on his clothes or person or in their living quarters. Neither did Margaret, but she had learned to live with it. The women made a quick end to the kitchen duty with Vicky washing, Margaret drying, and Ella putting things away as directed by Eleanor, who was told to sit in a chair and put her feet up on a stool that Ronald carried into the kitchen for her. Ronald and Jack made themselves useful in other ways—putting the good plates and glasses on the top shelf of the cabinet, taking the extra leaf out of the table and putting it away.

After everyone returned from either cleaning or smoking and were seated comfortably in the living room, the conversation turned more serious as they began discussing the political situation in England and Europe. "What are Americans thinking about the possibilities of another war?" Reg asked, looking at Jack for an answer.

"To be honest, while there are some conversations and concerns about the Italians taking over Ethiopia, the United States is still struggling to return to some kind of normalcy from the Great Depression. Ella, do you want to add anything to what I've said?" Jack looked at his wife, hoping for some additional comment.

"No, Jack, you've pretty well summed up what I know or think about the future. I know I'm hoping there won't be another war, and that's a pretty common hope I imagine of most people who have any memory of the last one. We met Gerald Sutherland today at the Cathedral, and he certainly isn't eager for another war. He has two sons who would surely be drafted if they don't join up on their own."

Ronald nodded. "I'd forgotten he's been working as one of the docents at the cathedral since his retirement. He fought in the first war and knows only too well what war is like. He was a good professor. I had him for history when I was a student at the university."

"War gets personal in a hurry when you know the people who are going to be most affected by it. I have a feeling that all of us on this island are going to be even more in touch with its reality than we were in the last one," Margaret said with a catch in her voice.

"Why do you say that, Margaret?" Ella asked.

"Because of the airplanes. They are so much bigger and more powerful than they were 15 years ago, and they were scary then.

114

They seem to come out of nowhere and wreak death and destruction below." Margaret shuddered as she said the words. "The last war was horrible. The next one will be worse, much worse, I fear."

"Your Mr. Chamberlain seems determined to find ways to keep England out of war," Jack commented.

"Yes, he is doing his best to keep us from getting involved," Ralph said. "But some of us feel he's going too far, willing to make too many concessions, giving away too much. We don't like Herr Hitler. He is truly a cruel and greedy man. His treatment of the Jews in Germany is getting worse every month. At some point we are going to have to do something about him. My fear is that the longer we wait the more powerful he and his Nazis become."

"Oh, Ralph, you know how you scare me when you talk that way. I don't want you to go to war. We have two young children who I want to grow up with their daddy being present in their lives, not off fighting in some faraway place or even here at home!" Vicky sounded as though this subject had been broached before.

"No same person wants to go to war," Ralph replied. "But neither does any sane person want Herr Hitler ruling one's country. He has Germany under his thumb except for those who oppose him, and they are under house arrest or being sent to prison."

Eleanor interrupted, saying "This conversation has become far too painful for me. I can feel this baby kicking like crazy. So I think he or she feels the tension that is building up inside me. Or maybe I'm just getting close to going into labor. Whichever it is, can we please talk about something else." She looked as though she might burst into tears.

"Of course, Eleanor, my love. Forgive us all for getting so worked up over something we have so little control over, especially tonight when your family has come all the way from the States to be with you," Ronald said as he put his arm around his wife and pulled her closer to him. "Do you really think you might be ready to have this baby?"

"I don't know. I've never had a baby before. It's just that I feel different and am having some pain. If it doesn't get better in a little while, I think we may need to call the doctor." Eleanor voice was shaking as she leaned into Ronald's embrace.

"Do you feel like you are having contractions, Eleanor?" Ella asked.

"I don't know what contractions feel like, Mother. If they feel like something's clinching me inside my stomach, I have had a couple of those. They didn't really hurt too badly and they happened fairly far apart. Oh…there goes another one. Ohh, this one was a bit harder."

"You're in labor, daughter!" Ella and Margaret said simultaneously. "Call your doctor," Ella said to Ronald. "You know where we are to take her, don't you?"

Ronald had already gone to the phone and was giving the operator the doctor's number, his eyes never leaving Eleanor's face. "He will meet us at the hospital in 20 minutes. Eleanor, you do have your bag already packed, I hope?" Ronald asked anxiously, still holding Eleanor's hand.

"It's on the floor on my side of the closet—only needs my toothbrush and toothpaste," Eleanor said, and then gasped as another pain rolled through her.

"You two go on and we will follow after we gather up the dishes we are taking home. Vicky and Ralph, you take your car because you may need to leave and we'll drive Ella and Jack." Margaret efficiently gave out instructions while Ronald carried Ella's bag in one hand and had his other hand clasping her arm, supporting her as she carefully made her way down the stairs

6

After 10:00 when they arrived at the hospital, it was a long night for the Douglasses and the MacLeans, but especially for Eleanor and Ronald. Family members sat in the hospital waiting room, occasionally being allowed to go in to see Eleanor when she was between contractions. Even Ronald was sent out when the labor pains began occurring only two minutes apart. Shortly after 4:00 in the morning a nurse came into the waiting area and announced that Mrs. Douglass had given birth to a fine eight-pound boy and that the father might come in to see his wife and the baby before he was taken to the nursery.

Breathing a sigh of relief and inwardly thanking God that the birth had occurred and mother and child were doing well, the two sets of parents were prepared to go home and get a few hours of sleep. Ralph and Vicky had left after the first hour at the hospital, since they had a sitter with their children at home, and both had to work the next day. Regie also had to be back at his job in the morning and had been napping as best he could while the others waited. Ronald had telephoned his dean and told him that Eleanor was in labor and was told that the dean himself would see that his two classes for that morning were cancelled. Only Ella and Jack had no responsibilities for the next day and did not have to worry about getting enough sleep.

Ronald went in to see his wife and soon came back to the waiting room to invite all the family to come and look at his son in the nursery where a nurse was cleaning him and getting ready to put him in his bed. Both mothers teared up as they gazed at their grandson, unabashed at shedding tears of joy while the fathers turned their heads to keep from being seen dabbing their own eyes with their handkerchiefs.

By the time they went into Eleanor's room she had been able to wash her face, brush her hair, and put on a gown with the nurse's help. Eager to see the faces of her family, Eleanor's eyes filled with tears of joy when they walked into the room raving about how beautiful this baby was and how proud they were of her. Ronald stood holding her hand and looking down at her adoringly, as if she had just performed the most amazing feat in the world, giving birth to a healthy and beautiful child. And she had!

They stood around Eleanor for a while but then Ella, realizing that her daughter was exhausted from the labor of giving birth, said that it was time for her and Jack to go back to the apartment.

It had been a long day for them. Regie said it was time for him and Margaret to go home also. They left Ronald with Eleanor so that the two could have a bit of time alone and spent the time in the car driving back to Ronald and Eleanor's apartment sharing compliments and saying how fortunate they were to have such fine children and now a new addition to the family. Finally Regie said he wondered if all grandparents sounded like them, causing all four to laugh, saying "probably" or "only if they are as fortunate to have children like Eleanor and Ronald and Baby Douglass!"

7

Hospital rules were that neither Ella nor Jack would be able to have personal time with the baby until Ronald brought both mother and child home after a week, provided both were over the birthing and in good health. Consequently, they decided this was a good time for them to take the train to York and use the week visiting St. Anthony's Clinic, Hospital, and Rehabilitation Center. Dr. Francis Willingham had founded this clinic on land his father owned and gave him after the war.

Francis had adopted "Frank" as his 'nickname' after the Americans had entered the war and a young 'Yank' made fun of a 'sissy' name like 'Francis' for a man. He had formed close friendships with Daniel Wood and Jean Marc LaCroix, while working together as surgeons on the battle front in France. Jean Marc had joined the staff of the Center a few years after the war's end. Daniel had turned down Frank's offer to work with him on mending the bodies, spirits, and minds of veterans and of any man who had experienced a life-altering injury and needed both physical, mental, emotional, and even spiritual healing. Daniel's commitment had been to return to Arkansas and open a clinic that would treat both white and black people with equal care and courtesy, something that was not often done in the South.

In early May Ella had written Frank and his wife Charlotte that she and her husband would be in England for a month to visit

Eleanor and meet her new husband. They would arrive in mid-June and stay until mid-July and would love to spend some time with friends at the Center. Charlotte had written immediately that they would be welcomed whenever they could come, and Frank had added a sentence to emphasize how good it would be to see her and meet Jack.

Ella telephoned the day after the baby's birth to see if it would be convenient for them to arrive the next day or the day after and was told that "their house" was ready and waiting for them. Frank said for them to come on the next day and that the train from Durham to York left Durham at 11:00 a.m. and arrived in York at noon. He and Charlotte would be at the station in York to greet them and drive them to the Center, 20 minutes away.

Both Frank and Charlotte were a little nervous about meeting Jack, wondering if they could accept this man who had taken the place of their 'brother in wartime.' Jean Marc had actually met Jack when he and his nephew Andre had made their trip to America and visited Ella in Myrna, but he really hadn't been in Jack's presence but once and had paid scant attention to him. After hugs and handshakes, they loaded the luggage into the Center's bus. Jack sat in the front with Frank, while Charlotte and Ella sat behind them with the luggage.

Charlotte, who had grown to love Eleanor during the months she had lived and worked at the Center before entering graduate school, wanted to know if Ella had any inkling that Eleanor was "expecting." Charlotte explained she had not written a word of the pregnancy to Ella because Eleanor wanted to surprise her mother and had sworn Charlotte to secrecy.

"Well, it was certainly a surprise! I could hardly believe that this woman with a very protruding stomach was my daughter! But I am so pleased and happy that we were here for the birth of their son, though I don't know yet what his name is. I am supposed to get a call here through you, Charlotte, when and if they decide on a name," Eleanor said laughing. "I know his name is important, but the truth is that once I saw that he was healthy and Eleanor was fine, I didn't really care what they call him! Am I a terrible grandmother?"

"Heavens no! You are a mother who has been through birth and knows that once the pain is over, all you really care about is a healthy, normal baby—boy or girl! But actually, I did get the call from Eleanor this morning, and I can tell you what they're naming him—unless you really don't care what name they're giving him," Charlotte said with a grin, knowing that Ella really did want to know.

"Tell me, Charlotte! You're just having fun with me, I understand. But don't keep me in suspense, please."

"Well, his first name is 'Ronald' for his father, but his middle name is sort of for his grandfather, for Daniel. They've named his 'Ronald 'Lee' although Eleanor knows Daniel's middle name was Leighton. But Eleanor and Ronald both thought Leighton sounds and looks too different, especially since they intend to call him Lee. Ronald has never been crazy about his name and likes 'Lee' Douglass, if they spell it this way. So what do you think? Do you mind if they didn't name him Leighton?"

"I don't mind a bit. Daniel never used his middle name— always just said it was an old family name on his mother's side. I don't even remember, if I ever knew, exactly where it came from. But I'm pleased Eleanor and Ronald have remembered her father that way. She was his firstborn and she adored him, although they were not particularly close. Mary Beth was closer to him because she was so interested in medicine and even as a little girl wanted to become a doctor.

"Anyway, Charlotte, thanks for helping take care of Eleanor as a sort of surrogate for me. Truth is, Eleanor had more in common with me because we both love literature and history. Jack and I share both those interests too and that is one reason we were drawn together. I know how much all of you here loved Daniel. But I hope you'll both like and even grow to love Jack."

"We'll certainly approach it with an open mind, just glad for you that after Daniel's tragic death you have found someone to spend the rest of your life with. We've all been both curious, and eager to meet him, especially after Eleanor had good things to say about him.

"Of course, Jean Marc and Andre both met him when they went to the States and visited you in Myrna, but they didn't spend much time with him and barely remember him. Truthfully, he didn't make that much of an impression on either of them. So we were all a bit surprised when we received your letter about the wedding."

"To be honest, it surprised both of us. We were working together on plans for a new approach to teaching literature and history that would include writing and speaking skills. The longer we worked together the more we enjoyed sharing ideas and plans for the courses. Both of us had been hurt by a previous relationship—me and my children by the suddenness and unexpectedness of Daniel's murder and the prospect of facing life without husband and father.

"And Jack's hurt came from a disastrous marriage to a woman who married him thinking he was wealthy and who had no interest at all in becoming the wife of a seminary student who would become a young Presbyterian pastor with a church. She resented his having a congregation that looked to him for help with faith questions and personal problems and tragedies.

"I don't think either of us expected to marry again—until we each realized that feelings of love had begun to grow inside us, and we didn't know what to do with those feelings until one night they sort of exploded. We had never even held hands when Jack told me he was in love with me. And I told him I had deep feelings for him too. Even now it's hard to believe we've been married for four years, but they have been good years overall, with a few difficult times like most marriages have. Goodness, I didn't expect to go on so long!"

"I am so glad you did. You've written us a bit about some of this, but it's not the same as talking about it face to face. We're both so glad you are here. I have to say, we were both surprised when you wrote that Dan had been accepted at Annapolis. I know how hard that must have been for you to accept. I'm terrified we are headed toward another war, and I'm grateful I don't have a son to worry about. And Frank is too old, thank God.

"My girls were both hoping to see Dan now that he's all grown up and were disappointed when they learned he won't be here, but they are going to be so impressed he's going to be a career Navy officer!

"And here we are. You are going to be so surprised at all the changes Frank and Jean Marc have made to our place! And I know how eager Cecile, Harry McGregor, and the Abbots are to see you."

"And I them! It's been 12 years, and that's too long to go without seeing people you care about!" Ella smiled as she looked out the truck window at the driveway leading up to the main building of St. Anthony's Medical Center. "At least I recognize the house!"

"The outside looks the same except for some fresh paint, but you'll be surprised at the changes on the inside," Charlotte said.

Frank, who had been giving Jack a description of the Center and its grounds, explaining to him what he and the staff were trying to accomplish there, said, "My wife is right, Ella. We no longer live in that house, but in a smaller one we built on the grounds. The girls are off to college during the school year, and while we want them to be able to come home whenever they want to, we simply do not need that much space. You will be staying in rooms in the Big House that I think you will find convenient and comfortable. And here we are!"

8

While Ella and Jack were unloading their luggage, and Ella was hoping to run into Harry McGregor or Geoff and Sarah Abbot or Cecile and Jason Bates, the first person they saw walking toward them was Jean Marc LeCroix, who approached them smiling and calling their names.

Ella had told Jack about Jean Marc's profession of love for her in a letter she had received from him soon after his and his nephew's trip to the States and Arkansas a year after Daniel's death. It had been followed quickly by another letter that had actually been a plea for someone to listen to his terrible story of being raped many times by the priest of the Catholic church in his village when he was only a boy.

Ella had written Jean Marc a long, understanding, and sympathetic letter after receiving his in which he'd told he didn't deserve to be loved by any decent woman and why. She had both dreaded and looked forward to seeing him again, hoping what she'd heard about the woman psychiatrist who had begun treating him and then had married him, truly helping him accept and love himself, was true.

The Jean Marc who practically ran to them, kissing each on both cheeks in the French way of greeting old friends, was so totally different from what Ella and Jack expected that they both started laughing and saying how good it was to see him. Jack had really only been around Jean Marc once during his trip to Myrna and barely remembered him. He had been invited to Ella's house for dinner to meet him on one occasion because she had invited all the members of the Bible study group that Father Banks led, but even that night he had spent part of the time playing croquet with Danny.

As a former pastor, Jack had felt deeply distressed by Jean Marc's horrible experience as a boy when Ella told him what had happened to him. It was hard to believe that a man of God had done such a thing, but then they had to wonder what, if anything, had been done to the priest that would enable him to commit such a criminal act on innocent boys.

Both Ella and Jack greeted Jean Marc warmly, who immediately said, "You must come with me and meet my wife Marie. We just finished lunch and she has a patient in half-an-hour, but I've told her so much about you, Ella, and about what happened to Daniel and what good friends we had been, I can't wait for you to meet her and for her to meet you and your husband."

Jean Marc was so eager and insistent that Ella and Jack followed him to one of the newer buildings, which Jean Marc said housed the offices of the six doctors who were now part of the Center's staff.

"Charlotte had written me that St. Anthony's had added quite a bit of staff, but I didn't know how many. Do you all get that many patients even though there is no war going on?" Ella asked.

"Actually, we do," Jean Marc said. "We have a couple of orthopedists who have been doing some amazing work on all kinds of injuries to backs, spines, legs, knees, hands, and feet. We have three psycho-therapists who work with patients with brain damage, psychotic illnesses, personality disorders, or crippling life experiences that have left them dysfunctional or addicted to drugs and/or alcohol. My Marie is one of the those. She has saved my life.

"And we have one general practitioner who takes care of the staff and our children. Actually, that's me, and that kind of medicine is the only one I want to do these days."

"Wow!" Jack exclaimed. "I am truly impressed. I'm a bit surprised that you need more psychiatrists than orthopedists. Are there that many people with mental or emotional problems?"

"More than you'd think. But part of the reason is that it usually takes a lot longer to get people mentally or emotionally healthy than to heal physically," Jean Marc said. "But also, people who have undergone a traumatic injury, like losing an arm or a leg in an accident, frequently need some psychological, emotional, and even spiritual help in dealing with and adjusting to a new way of living."

"That certainly makes sense. I've never had that kind of injury, but I certainly could have used some emotional and spiritual help a couple of times in my life. It's really amazing and wonderful what you all are doing here," Jack said.

And it was Jack's praise for the Center and those doing the work to keep it going that gained Jean Marc's friendship.

Dr. Marie Smithson LeCroix was as warm and friendly as Jean Marc had made her out to be, and she and Ella immediately liked each other. When they were able to have a few minutes alone, Marie told Ella how much difference the letter she had written to Jean Marc had made to him, and that her letter had been one of his motivations for seeking Marie's help. "You would make a wonderful counselor, Ella, if you ever want to get a bit more training to go that route."

"I'm flattered, Marie, but honestly, I love working with young people, introducing them to good literature and helping them learn grammar, writing and speaking skills. And actually at times I even feel like I'm a counselor because some of them come to me to talk about problems at home or with a girl or boy friend. I become so proud of most of my students that I love them like they are my own children, and in a little way, they are!"

"Then you are certainly doing the work you were called to do. Would that all children had teachers like you! I hate to end our conversation, but I have a patient arriving in 10 minutes and I need to review my last session with him. We'll have more time to visit tonight," Marie said, and as Ella stood, they clasped hands, and Ella left.

Ella and Jack wandered around the grounds, Ella exclaiming over the new buildings while Jack was impressed with the entire village of staff and patient houses, a dormitory, a gymnasium with an indoor and an outdoor swimming pool, an exercise or workout building, tennis and basketball courts, a picnic area and refreshment stand, the hospital off to itself away from the activity area, and the chapel where Harry McGregor was standing in the doorway looking for them.

"I heard you had arrived, and I've been looking for you. Then I heard Jean Marc had corralled you and taken you to meet Marie." Almost without taking a breath, Harry continued. "Ella, you are as beautiful as ever, and you, of course, are Jack. It's a pleasure to meet you, though I've read so much about you in Ella's letters that I feel like I already know you."

"My letters? Did they become a 'round robin' affair?" Ella asked, laughing.

"They most certainly did. Whenever you wrote to Cecile or Charlotte, they posted your letters on the bulletin board in the House, and everybody who met you and remembered your visit would read them. So don't think all of us who met you in 1925 haven't kept up with you. Daniel's death was a shock to all of us."

"Yes, it truly was. I appreciated your sweet letter, Harry. I knew you understood my loss better than anyone, but everybody here has suffered losses of one kind or another. You are a blessing to all of them I know," Ella said as she hugged him. "I've told Jack your story. We've all experienced loss and grief. But I understand you have some good news to share."

"Charlotte told you then that I have met a woman who has said 'yes' to my proposal of marriage. I want you to meet her while you are here. I never thought I would fall in love again."

"When will we get to meet Jennifer? I'm so happy for you both."

"Tonight at dinner. She lives in York and is a widow. Her husband died of cancer four years ago. She has two children—a daughter who is 12 and a 10-year-old son. They are good children. They will all be here for dinner tonight.

"Now even though I already feel I know Jack from your letters, I want to meet him formally," Harry said, giving Ella another hug and turning to Jack with a big smile.

The three had barely started talking together when Cecile appeared with two children and ran straight to Ella to give her a big hug. "I can't believe I'm actually seeing you in person, Miss Ella," Cecile said. "It's been way too long, and I still can't believe what happened to Dr. Daniel."

"I know Cecile. I wasn't sure I'd ever get over his death, especially the way it happened. But thanks to my children and this other wonderful man I've married, I've been able to get past it," Ella said. "And it's certainly time for you to call me 'Ella' and forget the 'Miss.' Also I want to formally meet these two beautiful children."

"Cara and Andy, this is Miss Ella who brought me to England with her family so that I could meet your daddy, get married to him, and give birth to the two of you. So in one sense, she's a big reason why you are alive."

"Well, that's only a tiny reason you two are alive, Andy and Cara," Ella broke in. "The real reason is that your mother and daddy fell in love with each other while we were visiting here and then had the love and patience to wait for over a year..."

"Writing letters to each other because they didn't really know each other and wanted to make sure they loved each other enough

126

for Mama to come back to England to live," Cara said, obviously having heard the story many times from her mother an daddy.

"You are so right, Cara!" Ella said and asked, 'Do you mind if I give you a hug too?" And Ella hugged her close when the girl nodded and moved into Ella's arms. "Andy, I don't know if boys here mind being hugged by women they hardly know, but I'd love to hug you too."

Andy looked a bit doubtful but said he guessed it would be okay if Ella hugged him. So she did, but not too long, and then said, "I can tell you're going to be a good man, just like your daddy. I'm looking forward to seeing him too!'

"Will you hug him too?" Andy asked?

"If he'll let me, I certainly will!" And when Jason appeared shortly, he let Ella hug him and hugged her back.

Jack had stood watching his wife greet all these people he had heard so much about and now could understand why. He had been told by his father the English were a bit cold and aloof, but that certainly was not the case with those he had met who knew and loved Ella because she had kept the friendship alive with her letters over the years.

"Well, I've now greeted everybody but Geoff and Sarah. Where are they?" she asked.

"They're waiting for you in the dining room in the big house. Wait till you see what they've done with the house!" Jason smiled and added, "It's a little past time for lunch, but we're all waiting for you."

"We apologize for holding everyone up! We should have gone straight to the house," Jack said, "but ..."

"I kept running into people and couldn't keep from stopping and talking to them," Ella said, laughing, but a bit embarrassed by letting the time get away from her. "I'm really sorry."

Harry, Jason, Cecile, Cara, Andy, Ella, Jack, and Dan had been walking toward the Big House as they apologized for holding up lunch. "Please don't worry about that," Harry assured them. "I'm sure that those who have appointments or need to be somewhere by 1:00 will have already started eating. They just want to see and meet you because they've heard so much about you and read parts of your letters, Ella, when Charlotte or Cecile thought they would be interested in something you had to say. You're an excellent letter writer, and I confess we've all enjoyed whatever we've read. We were excited about Jack and loved your letters about the wedding and honeymoon. So, Jack, just realize that we feel like we know you too and thoroughly approve of this match."

"Ella, I had no idea you'd been writing about me to your friends, but it's too late for me to worry or be bothered by that now," Jack said, laughing. "I guess I'm relieved you all 'approve' of our marriage since I've heard so much about how deep was the friendship Daniel had with Frank and Jean Marc. Actually, I've often wished I had known Daniel too."

9

By this time they had arrived at the Big House and entered the entry hall and the dining room. The first people Ella saw were Geoff and Sarah, who rushed forward to embrace her. "It's so good to see you again," Sarah said as Geoff nodded in agreement. We were terribly grieved over what happened to Daniel. We couldn't believe that he came through the Great War, only to be murdered by a crazed old man. The shock must have been awful!" Sarah continued. "But you've obviously come through it intact. And I'm guessing that this handsome man had a lot to do with that!" And she smiled as she and Geoff shook hands with Jack.

"Jack, I've heard so many good things about you, and I'm happy for Ella that she has you in her life." Geoff asked.

"I've certainly heard a lot of good things about both you and Sarah. I'm glad to meet you in person," Jack responded.

"Well, a face like mine is hard to forget," said Geoff with a grin on the half of his face that was not covered by his mask. "It's all right. I learned a long time ago to accept and live with my disfigurement and even to joke about it, thanks to this woman who brought healing to me in so many ways!" And Geoff looked at Sarah with so much love that Ella's eyes filled with tears.

"You both are part of what I loved about this place when Daniel and I came here to see it. And it seems to me, even in the brief time we've been here, that it just keeps getting better and better! And the building and program additions are amazing and wonderful," Ella added.

"Both Sarah and I love it here—love the people we work with and almost all the patients who have come to us for help with their physical and emotional needs for healing," Geoff said.

"Have some of the ones who've come been a problem?" Jack asked.

"Only a very few. After the war all the men and the few women who came were great. I don't mean they were in good shape physically and even mentally, but they were glad to be alive in a place where they were treated with kindness and love and were receiving the kind of treatment that helped them physically and emotionally. Not all of them were able to return to 'normal' life, what we call 'life in the real world,' but some of those who couldn't, opted to stay here. Eventually most of those did go 'home,' wherever that happened to be. A lot of that depended on their families and how able and willing they were to take them in.

"The few we've had real problems with have almost all come from wealthy families and never had to obey rules or actually take care of their own personal needs. Some of them left us dissatisfied with the amount of healing or the treatment they received here. Occasionally we've had someone with such deep psychological problems in addition to his physical needs that we really couldn't help him. But those cases have been few and far-between, thank God! Forgive me, I didn't mean to get off on that track."

"Actually, that was my fault because I asked the question," Jack said. "I spent several months in a London hospital after I was wounded, and I am well aware of the variety of injuries, both physical, emotional, and mental, that men came out of the war having to deal with. I have nothing but admiration for the work you are doing here and the kind of healing atmosphere and lifestyle you have created. Frank, I give you the credit for being the man behind what I am seeing and feeling here. I am deeply impressed!' Jack said, and then added, "I really don't want to hold up lunch for those of you who have to get back to work."

Frank escorted Ella and Jack to the main table at the front where Charlotte and Jean Marc awaited them. Frank invited them to sit as soon as he introduced them to the staff and the other guests, who were in fact residents or live-in patients at the Rehabilitation Center. Both Ella and Jack spoke briefly, telling the group how glad they were to be there and how impressed they were by everything they had seen, and Ella commented on how it had grown with the changes and buildings added since 1925.

Lunch consisted of a choice of either fruit or vegetable salads, ham-and-cheese sandwiches, and either chocolate pie or pound cake with lemon sauce. Ella and Jack were both complimentary of the food. Ella was amazed at how beautiful and modern everything appeared from what it had been like in 1925. The round tables, they were told, had all been made from oak lumber in the area. Some of the residents at St. Anthony's had hand crafted, stained, and polished the wood into the tables that the diners were eating on. The individual skills and artistry of each builder who created a table made each one just a little different from the others. Every table could seat eight comfortably. Charlotte said that it had taken almost nine years to make enough tables and chairs for the entire dining room. Some of the residents who were artists had painted murals on the walls, scenes of the countryside with its fields, forests, villages, and even of the Big House as seen from the drive leading to it.

Several of the staff who needed to get back to work stopped by their table to welcome them personally, saying how much they had heard about Ella and her family and how much they had liked and enjoyed Eleanor the summer she spent there and how delighted they were to hear of the birth of her son. Of course the compliments on her daughter touched Ella.

After lunch Charlotte took them on a tour of the building, delighted to show off the changes that had been made. Across from the dining room, the wall between two large parlors had been removed and at the far end a stage had been built surrounded by chairs that could be easily set in place. Behind the stage, doors led to dressing rooms for women and men. Restrooms for women and men and a large, modern kitchen with a storage room in the rear completed the first floor, except that an elevator ('lift' in England) had been installed to take people up to the second and third floors. Bedrooms with their own baths had been built, six on the second floor, four on the third, with storage space left where two bedrooms might have been. Each bedroom and bath was beautifully decorated and different from the others.

"Who was your decorator?" Ella asked.

"I was!" Charlotte said. "I had so much fun picking out colors and fabrics and hunting for used furniture that we could refinish or paint. It took me four years to get everything the way I wanted it, but now I'm so pleased with it I love showing it off. I know Jack is probably bored stiff, but this is where you will be staying. You get to choose your room, though I suggest you stay on the second floor. The rooms are cooler there. The third floor rooms can be warm in late June through August, though they are fine the rest of the year.

"Right now only one of the rooms on the second is occupied. One of our donors and his wife are spending a couple of nights with us. He likes to come and visit with the staff and get to know some of our new patients and also visit with the long-term ones he's already met. He is one of our larger donors. He had a son who was badly injured in the war and who spent four years here before he felt strong enough physically and emotionally to face life in the real world. The son eventually married and he and his wife have two daughters. We don't see the son and his family that often, but his father continues to donate generously to the upkeep of this place. We're certainly grateful for that!"

Jack and Ella chose the blue bedroom with two large windows facing north covered by blue-and-white striped curtains and the bed covered by a spread of the same fabric. "I'll have all the suitcases brought to your room, Jack and Ella."

"Charlotte, it's great what you all have done to this place, not just the Big House but all the new buildings you've added since Daniel and I were here," Ella said—and then added, "not to ignore all that you all have done to help patients recover from not only the damage to their bodies but to their minds and spirits also."

"Well, it's true that we encourage our patients to become as self-sufficient as they can as soon as they can. It makes them feel better about themselves. Pity, especially self-pity, is truly destructive to anyone's self-esteem and personality," Charlotte said. "I've really witnessed that since Frank opened the hospital here. Some of the patients who come here are from very wealthy families, and often they've been injured in some accident while skiing or mountain climbing or even an automobile crash that maybe they caused themselves. Those who wallow in feeling sorry for themselves or even feeling guilty because they acted irresponsibly but still want to be waited on hand-and-foot are the slowest to heal."

"So how did you change that? What did you do to get people over feeling sorry for themselves?" Jack asked.

"Well, when Frank soon realized that attitudes can hamper healing from taking place, he started looking for psychiatrists and counselors who were interested in the kind of therapy that helped people see themselves as they were and become willing to be honest about facing their own demons and learning new ways of coping with reality. He hired two people, one of whom is still with us. He was very young when he started here, but he has such a warm, friendly personality as well as skills as a therapist that we hope he'll stay until he gets too old to work. Actually with him, I doubt that will ever happen. You'll get to meet him tonight," Charlotte added. "And actually, by just being here as a man of many talents and jobs, Geoff is a living example of a man who shows no self-pity."

"I heard his story and saw the miracle he has become, thanks greatly to God and Sarah, when we were here in '25," Ella said.

"Yes, Geoff is a living example of what love and good care can do for a man. But what about the second doctor?" Dan asked.

"Well, she's is a woman, and Frank had real reservations about bringing a female on board. You see, most of our patients are men. It seems more men are injured in accidents or by life choices than women, though we do get some women here. Interestingly, many of the men find it easier to admit their weaknesses and receive help from a woman than from another man. You may have already met her, since she is the person who really brought Jean Marc back to real life from his alcoholism and the trauma from his childhood," Charlotte added.

"Yes, we did meet Marie before lunch this morning. And I'm so happy for Jean Marc. He is a fine man and a fine doctor," Ella said. "It was wonderful to see him and Andre when they came to Arkansas four years ago and now to meet his wife, who has made such a difference in his life. She obviously is what he needed."

"We are proud of our staff. I look forward to your meeting the rest of the staff tonight at dinner," Charlotte said. "I'll leave you alone for a bit to get unpacked and settled, but come down to the entry when you are ready. I have some bookkeeping to do, but I want to take you and show you our house," Charlotte smiled.

"Yes, I wondered where you all were living," Ella said, "when I realized that you had turned the rest of the house into guest lodging."

"Well, we decided that as the girls were getting older and might soon be leaving home for college, careers, or marriage, we ought to think about a smaller place. So we built a smaller place with three bedrooms and two baths, ours on the first floor and the girls on the upper level. We have a somewhat formal living and dining area for entertaining special guests, a kitchen and breakfast area, and a good-sized family room for more relaxing company. It's really tempting to eat most meals at the Big House because the food is so good here. But it's also nice to have our own home when we need a break from staff and company," Charlotte said and then added, "We'll have at least one dinner there while you are here, so that we can have a more relaxing evening together. I know Frank wants some special time with just the two of you."

Ella and Jack smilingly nodded agreement with that plan. Charlotte left them to unpack and make the space 'theirs,' which did not take long.

"Jack, I can understand that this part of our trip may be difficult for you, since so much of it deals with people who were Daniel's close friends? As glad as I am to see Charlotte, Frank, and even Jean Marc again, I don't want that to be a problem for you."

"Thank you, my love, for even thinking about my feelings at being here, but if I were ever 'jealous' of Daniel, I got over it a long time ago. After all, his reputation and the affection and admiration so many people in Myrna felt for him have been part of my life almost from my arrival in Myrna. The more I've learned about him, the more I have respected the man that he was. And the more gratitude I feel for having you in my life. How could I be envious of a man whose death made it possible for you to marry me?"

Jack took her in his arms and kissed her long and hard and then said, "We'd better go downstairs and find Charlotte or I will make love to you right here and right now!"

And Ella giggled as Jack led her into the hall, where they headed downstairs to find Charlotte's office.

10

"Charlotte, I hope we're not interrupting your bookkeeping," Ella said as they entered the room where Charlotte was leaning over an opened book. When Charlotte said she was done, Ella asked, "What kind of entertainment or programs do you all have in the auditorium? It's really a nice space, actually better than the auditorium at the college my girls attended."

"Well, occasionally we get a local theater group to come out and perform for our residents and staff and pay them a small fee. Every once in a while, we luck into a professional performer who is willing to come here in between appearances in York or even

Durham when he or she realizes that the audiences are composed of injured people, some of whom may never completely recover.

"But some of our best entertainment is provided by staff members and even some of the patients themselves, and it can be anything from juggling to dramatic readings. It's really interesting, but the patients generally enjoy seeing a different side of their doctors and caregivers. We don't have theater seats in here because we want the space to be open for wheelchairs and moveable chairs. We've even had one member of the audience come in his own bed, thanks to staff members he paid to bring his bed here."

"That's really amazing!, Jack said. "I hope we'll get to enjoy some of this 'entertainment' while we're here."

"Oh, the entertainment committee couldn't wait to start planning as soon as they heard you all were coming. It's scheduled for Thursday night. Don't ask me what it's going to be. They refuse to tell me, so there is no telling what they will come up with," Charlotte said, shrugging her shoulders and smiling.

Frank walked up just as Charlotte finished speaking and clapped Jack on the back. "Do you have a sec? I'd like to speak to you alone if you've got the time."

Jack looked a bit surprised but replied, "Sure. Do you mean right now?"

"If you don't mind. Let's walk outside." Frank looked at Ella. "Is it all right with you if I take you husband with me for a minute?"

Ella laughed. "He's his own boss. Just bring him back when you're done. I like having him around!" But she couldn't help wondering what was going on. Frank and Jack left the Big House and started walking toward the hospital.

Frank said, "I'm sure you're wondering what this is about, and I didn't want to bring this up in front of Ella. But the fact is, I've noticed that you favor your right leg a bit at times when you walk. What's going on? Have you hurt it lately or is this an old injury? And is this something you're trying to hide from Ella or does she know?"

"She knows and has known since our honeymoon. It's an old war injury—and I'm rather embarrassed about it, so I try to hide it. It was the second day of my first time in battle. The truth is I barely remember what happened. A bomb exploded near me and set off a land-mine, and shrapnel sort of tore up my knee and leg. I was knocked out, and the next thing I remember is being carried by two guys who said I'd been hit and needed a doctor. I blacked out again and didn't recover consciousness until I was in a tent with a lot of other wounded soldiers and heard one of the orderlies say, 'This soldier needs his leg attended to, but I think he can wait till you get your patient's chest closed. I sure hope your patient's going to make it.' I wasn't sure he wasn't talking about me, and I don't remember anything else until they had finished tending to my knee and leg. I waked up in a tent full of injured men, some of whom were moaning in pain. At least I knew they were alive.

"I ended up in a hospital in London and stayed there until the war ended almost a year later. As I recovered and could get about in a wheel chair and then on crutches, I was put to work in an office and that's what I did until Armistice Day on November 11. Actually, I was there another six weeks before I could get on a ship headed back to the States. That's probably a lot more than you wanted to know, but it's my story although it's not much of one."

"Well, a bit more information than I needed for what I wanted to talk to you about, but as one of the doctors who could have been working on you in the tent, I was glad to hear what you had to say. It was bloody awful over there whenever there was a battle. You really could have been one of my patients because often there would be so many injured we couldn't take time to find out names or anything. We just tried to patch them up as best we could and send them to a field hospital until they could get back home in France or to England if they were British or American.

"But what I wanted to talk to you about is that I'd like to have one of our docs examine your knee. Medicine has made a lot of progress since the war and I think another surgery might help you. We try here to keep up with new procedures from all over the world, and recently I read about an orthopedist at Walter Reed Hospital in Washington, D.C., who has been doing some remarkable work with scar tissue removal surgery and a new knee along with a physical therapy program. I didn't know whether you'd be interested in finding more out about that, and I didn't want to bring anything up in front of Ella until I knew where you were about whatever is going on with your knee. What do you think?"

"I'm all for it! Ella will be too. She notices when I tend to limp a bit more than usual and she worries about me when she can tell I'm in pain. I have to confess that it interferes at times with our lovemaking, and neither one of us is happy about that. I look forward to talking with your orthopedist, and Ella will want to be in on that conversation, and I certainly want her there with me."

"I was hoping you'd say that. Let me set it up, maybe for late this afternoon or this evening, if that's okay with you and Ella."

"I'm sure it will be. Did you know that Ella is a pacifist—doesn't like the thought of another war at all? She grew up Quaker, more or less. Did Daniel ever mention that?" Jack paused.

"You know, I think Daniel did say that once. He was trying to explain why she had been so against his serving as a doctor during the war. He loved her dearly and hated making her unhappy because he enlisted, but it was something he felt he had to do. He and I spent time together at a restaurant the night before his ship sailed. We didn't talk much about what peace was going to be like and what we'd be facing when we got home.

"But I remember Daniel saying something about his daughter asking him about what comes after yesterday and Daniel telling her 'Today, today comes after yesterday.' And then he said something I'll never forget. He said, 'Well, it's today, Frank. And I have to admit I'm a bit afraid of today. I'm not the same man I was when I left Myrna. And I'm not ever going to be the same. Ella's not going to be the same either. But it's not yesterday, never will be, and she and I, you and I, have to deal with it!'"

"Frank, thank you for sharing that with me. I find myself often wishing I had known Daniel. But I'm so grateful to have Ella in my life! I truly hate the thought of another war. Yet I know deep down that we're headed in that direction. It almost did Ella in when Dan applied to the Naval Academy without our knowing and then was accepted. On our way to New York to the ship, we stopped off in Annapolis at the Naval Academy to leave Dan, who had to be present for summer camp, really three months of preparation for life in the Academy. We were able to see a bit of the place for ourselves with Dan. He had to sign in on Monday and won't be able to come home until maybe Christmas or even next summer. We realize that Dan and Eleanor's husband Ronald and so many others will be the ones to fight this next war, and that makes me sadder than I can say.

"But, yes, I do want to speak with your orthopedist, and perhaps next summer will be the time for me to see if another surgery will help my knee. Thank you, Frank, not only for noticing my limp but also for accepting me not only as Ella's husband but as a friend, a man, in my own right." Jack's voice broke a bit as he said these last words, and when he held out his hand, Frank grasped it and said, "Daniel was a good friend, and I grieved over his death. But he would be glad that his beloved Ella has found a good husband, and she has that in you, Jack. All of us who loved him are happy for both of you!

"And I do want you to see about getting something else done to your knee. I know Ella would like to have you around for a long time, especially if you could walk without pain. And I think I can say an 'Amen' to that for the rest of us here. If you can't get anything done at Walter Reed, come back over here for two months next summer, and I can pretty well guarantee we'll send you home walking like a young man!" Frank held out his hand and Jack shook it.

"Thank you, Frank. I won't forget this, and if nobody at Walter Reed wants to have a go at fixing my knee, I'll come back here for you all to do it!" Jack was smiling but had tears in his eyes. "I have to confess, though, that I had no idea how you all would receive me, having heard from Ella how close you, Jean Marc, and Daniel had been in France. The three of you obviously made a huge dif-ference to the men you treated and the nurses who worked with you, judging by what I've heard from Geoff and Sarah. I'm really grateful I'm having a chance to meet and get to know you a bit.

"Getting to spend a little time with Eleanor's new husband and some of his family, being here for the birth of our grandson, and now meeting and getting to know the St. Anthony folks makes this entire trip more than worthwhile, truly a memory we'll cherish."

Frank nodded his assent and then added, "But the fact is, life just goes on—at least for some of us, doesn't it? Daniel's death was so unfair to so many—his wife and children, his patients, even to those of us who knew him during the war. But we have to go on living, doing whatever we can to make the world where we are a better place. I know Daniel was doing that, and knowing that makes his murder even harder to understand and accept.

"Yet, Jack, what good does it do anybody to become bitter and angry and refuse to go on with life? We've all dealt with loss and sadness, but at the same time we have much to be grateful for. Life does goes on, taking us with it, usually, unless we're too damaged to move forward. Here where we are we see it as partially our responsibility to make sure that doesn't happen. That's why we not only have some really excellent doctors to care for bodies and minds but why Pastor Harry and nurses like Sarah and even handymen like Geoff are so important to the staff."

Looking at his watch and shaking his head, Frank said with a smile, "Now it's time for me to get off my soapbox and go do some paperwork. We'll see you and Ella tonight at dinner. Afterwards we're going to our house and some of the staff will be coming by to visit with you. One of them will be the orthopedist who wants to look at your knee, Jack. You'll be interested in hearing his opinion, I think."

The two men shook hands and parted, Frank heading toward his office and Jack going back to look for Ella. Both men felt better about each other, finding a common bond of respect and liking for each other. Jack was eager to tell Ella about his conversation with Frank, knowing that she had been hoping the two of them would hit it off. Now he had only Jean Paul to win over, but he didn't think that would be a problem since Jean Paul had fallen in love with his therapist and married her!

11

Dinner in the dining room at the Big House was somewhat of a more formal affair than Ella and Jack had expected, though they had dressed as though they would be dining at a nice restaurant and were glad they had changed clothes from their daytime wear. When Frank and Charlotte had told them they would be formally introduced to everyone during dinner, they had expected they would simply stand up, smile, and say another 'thank you' and 'how glad they were to be here' or something on that order. But Frank gave a much longer introduction about Jack, alluding first to his own army doctor friendship with Daniel, and how much grief Daniel's murder by a drunken old man had caused both him and Jean Marc. Frank went on to say that as he was getting to know Jack, he had realized he could accept Jack as his friend and as Ella's husband and he knew the rest of the staff, especially those who had known Daniel, would also like and appreciate Jack for himself.

Jack realized as Frank spoke that he had to say more than 'thank you,' and called on his preaching and teaching skills to give a short but eloquent speech about having both looked forward to and sort of dreaded coming to St. Anthony's because he was well aware of how much Daniel had been loved and respected by those who had known him during the war as well as by those who met him during the week he and his family had spent at Saint Anthony's. He now was delighted to be here and get a firsthand look at the work they were doing and was as impressed as Ella had told him he would be. He looked forward to meeting more of the staff and residents and learning about all they were doing at St. Anthony's, and he hoped that when any of them saw him and had a bit of time, they would stop him and tell him about themselves and what their part was at this remarkable center for healing.

The applause when Jack stopped talking was genuinely enthusiastic. And after Charlotte introduced Ella by saying she really needed no introduction except to those who had not been at St. Anthony's in 1925 when she and her family had spent an entire week visiting there, Ella shook her head and began to speak. "I truly did not expect to be speaking except to say how happy I am to be back at this amazing place and to see all of the updates that have occurred since I was here last, from the changes at the Big House to the new buildings that have been added. I'm looking forward to a more in-depth sight-seeing tour during our too short a time to be here. Even more I want time to visit with old friends and to make new ones.

"Daniel was so impressed with what Frank and Charlotte were doing here, and he would have been thrilled that Jean Marc, his other wartime friend, has added his medical skills to St. Anthony's. I'm so glad for Jack to get to meet, and I hope become friends with, those of you I loved getting to know when my family was here in '25. And both of us expect to go home with new friends we meet here now. So thanks to all of you for your hospitality and friendliness."

Ella received an equal amount of clapping and one voice that shouted, "You're just as beautiful as you were 12 years ago, and we're glad to see Jack is making you happy!" She recognized that it came from Geoff and an "Amen" added by Harry.

12

It took a while for them to break away from the many staff members and even some of the patients who were able to come to the Big House to eat. But eventually they made their way to Frank and Charlotte's new home where some of the guests had already gathered, sitting out on the big screened in porch at the back of the house.

Ella was pleased that those present were old friends and their new "spouses" like Harry McGregor and his fiancée Jennifer, Geoff and Sarah Abbot, and Cecile and Jason and their children, along with Jennifer's two, whom Frank and Charlotte's daughters, at their mother's request, had agreed reluctantly to entertain.

As their guests settled into the comfortable porch chairs, Frank poured glasses of wine or beer for those who wanted it and Charlotte served fruit punch to those who preferred something non-alcoholic. They chit-chatted about life in general, asking about Eleanor and her life with Ronald and now the new baby, what plans Ella and Jack had after leaving St. Anthony's until finally Geoff brought up a subject that was nearly always on the minds of those who lived and worked at St. Anthony's.

"We're sitting on a powder keg here on our island because we know that Herr Hitler is preparing Germany for war. While England most likely won't be the first country attacked, we will have to fight, and we are nowhere near ready," Geoff grimaced and shrugged. "We've just recently more-or-less recovered from the war all of us remember and are not eager to engage in another. Jack, what about the States? What's the talk over there?"

"It's pretty quiet, Geoff. We're still struggling to get the nation back on its feet economically. The Great Depression has really hurt a huge portion of our country, especially the lower middle class and the poor. While the President has come up with many attempts to help those who have been hurt the most get back on their feet, we aren't there yet. At least, too many of them aren't. We definitely don't want to get into a war at this point.

"From what I read in *The New York Times* I'd say your Prime Minister Mr. Chamberlain is doing his best to keep you out of it too, but that may not work because you're too close to the continent," Jack added.

"That's a big worry on the minds and hearts of lots of us— probably the great majority of us," Geoff said. "We've also been struggling to recover from the Depression as well as from the effects of the war. We've just raised a new generation of young men and no one wants to send them to the war to be killed or come back looking like me." Geoff's voice broke slightly during this last sentence.

"What about Mr. Chamberlain?" Ella asked, surprising the other women and some of the men by joining the conversation since women generally sat and listened, speaking only when they were asked for their opinion about something. "As your Prime Minister, do you think he has the power or the ability to keep England out of a war if Germany continues to show its strength and desire to acquire more territory and power?"

"He still has a fairly large following, a good number of veterans of the last war who know how brutal and awful war it. Some who are younger and a few of the stalwarts, however, would prefer Mr. Churchill's leadership. He is seen as a strong man who will not let Germany and Italy take over parts of the world that belong to the British Empire, much less invade our island. To be honest, I personally like Mr. Churchill," Jason said.

"He has quite a following, according to some of the columns we see in the *The New York Times*," Jack said. "I've read that President Roosevelt and Mr. Churchill have a strong relationship, even though our president seems intent on keeping us neutral, certainly for the time being. He still realizes there's a good bit of improvement to our economy that needs to happen before we'll be anywhere close to being ready to get involved in another war."

Jean Marc spoke up. "I'm afraid we won't be in a position to wait around for your country to get prepared to fight Hitler and Mussolini. I'm just waiting to see who in Europe they attack first. Surely it won't be France, but the Huns hate us for being on the winning side in the last war, so I guess I wouldn't be surprised if they strike France first. I'm afraid my country would not be able to put up much of a fight if that happened," Jean Marc said with a sigh.

"Well, at least France has De Gaulle," Jason said. "He's a strong leader, so I understand."

"Maybe so, but does he have a real fighting machine to lead? I don't think he has, at least not one that can face the Germans. I'm afraid the Allies made a big mistake by taking or destroying all the Germans' fighting equipment at the end of the war," Jean Marc said.

"Why do you say that?" Frank asked.

"Because the Germans have had to rebuild their war machine from scratch, and they've taxed the people and pulled in expert scientists and builders and started over. But now they've got state-of-the-art equipment, and they've been recruiting and training their young men, building a war machine to conquer anybody they want to while we've been trying to build 'the good life' for people," Jean Marc paused and took a big gulp of his fruit punch.

"From what I hear from friends in France who live near the German border, life is hard there for ordinary people because the government is spending so much money on preparing for another war. Here and in France we've concentrated on peace and making ordinary life livable, even enjoyable. I fear we will see sooner rather than later who has made the better choice."

"Do you think that another war is that close to happening?" Jack asked.

"I really hate to say this, but yes, I do," Jean Marc said. "But it's time to change the topic of conversation. I didn't intend to get us started on the subject of another war, not tonight anyway, and I apologize."

"Well, you've given us Americans something to think about anyway. I worry that because we are somewhat protected by having oceans on both sides of us we feel we are safe," Jack said. "And yet I know as airplanes continue to be improved and can fly greater and greater distances, we are not as safe as we like to think we are."

"Before we leave politics and war, we Brits would like to know what you think of your Mr. Roosevelt." Frank spoke up. "Ella, I suggest you go first."

"I have to admit I was really excited over his first election and so impressed with what he promised to do, but after his first two years it felt like he backed off. It seemed like his wealthy friends took charge, and the help that Mr. Roosevelt had promised to give the struggling lower middle class and the really poor seemed to be disappearing. The economy and their lives were growing worse instead of better. It looked like Mr. Roosevelt might be a one-term president.

A lot of us were disappointed in him. But then…Jack, you take over from here….” Ella looked at Jack, who nodded his okay.

“Ella’s right. Those of us who had voted for him wondered where the bold president who had seemed so determined not to let the Depression get the better of us had disappeared. And some bad movements with charismatic leaders had risen among the ranks of ordinary people. One was a Catholic priest named Charles Coughlin out in Michigan who began preaching on the radio in 1929. He attacked Communists and became so popular he turned on bankers, charging that Mr. Roosevelt was the bankers’ friend who protected Wall Street.

“By this time FDR had realized Coughlin presented a real challenge because millions of people were listening to him and his anti-capitalism rants. Father Coughlin at first had supported Roosevelt, but by the fall of 1935 his position and his peaching made it clear that ‘the New Deal’ was the antithesis of Coughlin’s support of and belief in ‘social justice.’ Coughlin, for a while, posed quite a threat to Roosevelt’s re-election in 1936. But he wasn’t the only one.”

“You know, I do remember reading about him in the London Times. He had a huge following in the States. He was quite a preacher!” Geoff spoke up. “Were there more like him?”

“Well, not exactly like him, but two other men played parts in saving FDR’s second term. If you all aren’t bored, I’ll try to summarize their part in our recent history.” Jack waited to see if anyone would speak up, and all the men did, saying they had had so much history being made in their own country they had obviously not paid attention to their younger relatives in the States.

So Jack continued. “There was Dr. Francis Townsend, a retired physician who was sure he’d discovered a cure for our economic ailments. His plan was for the government to pay every citizen over the age of 60 $200 every month, IF he or she had never been convicted of a crime, agreed to give up all other income, and promised to spend the entire amount by the end of every month.”

“That’s the craziest thing I’ve ever heard!” Frank was laughing.

"Well, Dr. Townsend's belief was that his plan would end the Depression and benefit old and young because the old would no longer have to compete with the young for jobs, and spending by the old would benefit the economy, and everyone would benefit. But there was one catch."

"What was it? Though I'm thinking there's something here that doesn't make sense," Frank said, squinting his eyes in thought.

"You're right. Somebody has to pay to make the $200 available for everyone over 60. He proposed a 2% 'transaction tax' the doctor said would be fair because everybody would be taxed alike. But that was the problem. The tax would be extremely regressive. The over-60 folks make up one-eleventh of the population while their money would not be coming mostly from the rich but from the struggling middle class and the poor. Townsend's plan would help one poor group, old people, but only at the expense of the working-class folks who were struggling to survive. All the really rich would be unharmed by a 2% tax while the economy wouldn't have been helped at all.

"So it was opposed by all kinds of groups—Socialists, Communists, the American Federation of Labor. The only ones who liked it were the senior citizens, but there weren't enough of them to get it through Congress. However, the Townsend Plan demonstrated how discontented many middle class people had become by 1935. And it was based on the idea in the Plan that there was enough wealth in our country to provide everyone a decent, even comfortable living.

"Yet there was one more threat to FDR's recovery plan and it was the most serious of all."

"You can't stop now. What was it?" Several voices said at once.

"This is better than a suspense radio program," Jean Marc said laughing.

"This one came from one of the Senators, a man from a large, poor family in the hill country of Louisiana, as poverty stricken a state as are most in the South. Huey Long was elected governor in 1928 after running and losing in 1924. He was different in two important ways from most southern politicians who campaigned on the side of the poor. One was that he did not sell out to the wealthy and powerful once he was elected. The second was even more unusual. He had almost no racist feelings toward black people, and that is fairly amazing in white people in the South. He did more to help the underprivileged in Louisiana than any governor in the state's history by improving education, taxation, roads, medical care, and public services.

"Huey Long had supported FDR in his first election in 1932 but had deserted him by 1934 because he saw the 'New Deal' as a failure. He was quoted as saying in a speech to the Senate, 'Unless we provide for redistribution of wealth in this country, the country is doomed.'

"By 1934 Long was supporting a program called 'Share Our Wealth' that promised to limit the size of fortunes controlled by the wealthy so the poor could have decent livelihoods. His goal was a comfortable living for everybody. His popularity among the middle class and poor was growing by the minute.

"When it became obvious how fast Long's popularity was growing after a 1935 poll by the Democrats showed that between three and four million people might vote for Long and wealth-sharing, FDR began rethinking his campaign, and thus was born 'The Second New Deal.'

"Roosevelt had little respect for Long's politics, seeing him as more of a dictator than a democratic leader because Long ignored the democratic process, openly telling state legislators which bills were to be passed and which, rejected. Long, whose real ambition was thought by many to be elected President at some point, was shot by a young man with a pistol as he stood in a hallway talking to his aides in the state capitol in Baton Rouge in September of 1935.

"But there's little doubt the populist forces that encouraged and supported the ambitions of these three men had much influence on Franklin Roosevelt's re-election and so dedicating his second term to a Second New Deal, one that would be aimed more at improving the lives of the common man than of the already wealthy and powerful."

"Is it working?" Jean Marc asked. "Would you call the 'Second New Deal' a success? Is the economy and life for the average family improving?"

"A bit better, but with still more improvement needed." Jack said. "Those of us who had some savings or inheritances and still have jobs that are able to pay our salaries are doing all right. Thus, Ella and I were able to make this trip to England. But we are having to spend little on lodging and food and entertainment, so we are fortunate."

Ella spoke up, "My husband reads the Sunday edition of the *New York Times* faithfully if you're wondering where he gets his information. But I have one interesting bit of information about Senator Long involving Arkansas that Jack didn't mention.

"When Arkansas' Senator Thaddeus Caraway died unexpectedly in late 1931, his widow Hattie ran to fill out the 11 months of his term, but once she was in office she decided she liked the job and on the last day before the filing deadline, she put her name in the pot for the six-year term. This time she had formidable competition. When it looked like she couldn't win, Senator Huey Long who had sat next to her in the Senate and grown to admire her pluckiness, announced he was coming from Louisiana to help her campaign.

"He literally roared into Arkansas bringing the first sound trucks Arkansans had ever heard, campaigned with her throughout the state attracting huge crowds, and Mrs. Caraway received 44.7 percent of the vote, which included several other 'want-to-be's,' enough to make her victorious and become the first American woman elected to a full six-year term in the Senate. So Senator Long had his good side because there's little doubt Mrs. Caraway would have lost had not he come to help her with his sound trucks and entertainment.

"Speaking of entertainment and a needed change in our conversation since we've talked politics and serious topics long enough, what is the staff planning for its big production to

148

entertain us?" And with Ella's question the conversation took a different turn, with the subjects of war and politics being laid to rest for the remainder of the evening, though many of the comments that had been made lodged themselves in the memories of those who had been present.

13

The other happening that evening was that as people began to leave, Frank pulled Jack to the side and said, "Can you stay a minute. The orthopedist I mentioned to you earlier wants to have a look at your knee."

Jack replied, "Of course, but let me tell Ella. Is it okay for her to stay and hear whatever the doctor says?"

"Sure. I know Paul Masterson would expect that. As soon as a few more people have left, I'll take you into the library where, if he wants you to, you can take off your pants so that he can examine your knee, in fact probably punch around on your entire leg."

As soon as Jack and Ella said "goodnight" to those who were the last to leave, Frank ushered them into the library where the doctor had pulled up three chairs with two facing each other and one placed sideways in between the two. He then asked Jack to sit in one, roll up his pants legs on both legs and put both legs on the middle chair. He said, "This won't be comfortable, and I won't ask you to stay that way for long, Jack, but I want to examine and compare both knees. That way I'll have a better understanding of the damage to the bad knee and how much it has deteriorated."

"That makes sense," Jack said. "After all, you didn't know me when I had two good knees."

"And I'm not taking X-rays, though I'll have a good idea of what the damage is and whether the doctor at Walter Reed I'm thinking about recommending can help you or not."

Jack tried to sit immobile while Paul pressed and pushed on both knees, sometimes flinching when he was pressing on parts of the damaged knee. After he had pressed and pushed for several minutes on both knees, Paul Masterson said, "Well, Jack, you've obviously been faithful about exercising and trying to take care of your bad knee, and it's in better shape than I expected it to be. How do you exercise it?"

"Riding my bicycle back and forth to the school where I teach, weather permitting and then going on long rides with our son on weekends and holidays. I'm guessing I ride 15 or 20 miles a week during the school year and at least that much or more during summers, though I have to admit it's becoming more painful every year," Jack replied.

"I can vouch for him on both accounts," Ella said. "He's started putting an ice bag on his knee after a long ride. He says that helps."

"Good work, Jack," Paul Masterson said. "What you have done has kept you mobile, but it is time you have another surgery on this knee. I can feel the inflammation around the knee cap, and I going to guess you've got a crack in there that is going to give you real problems if that knee cap doesn't get replaced fairly soon." He stopped talking and wrote something on his notepad and handed it to Ella. "Here is the name of a fine doctor at Walter Reed Hospital in Washington, D.C.

"I met him when my wife and I had made a trip to the States to see what orthopedic doctors were doing there. I had spent several days at Presbyterian Hospital in New York City when one of their doctors said I ought to look in on Dr. Jonathan Mackinley at Walter Reed in Washington. He was testing some new procedures and products especially for knees. So we made the trip down to Washington by train and met him, and I was really impressed with his work. He was so open and willing to share his learnings with me that I highly recommend him. You won't have any problem finding him because Walter Reed Hospital is so well known in the medical community for its work with service men and veterans."

"Thank you so much, Paul," Jack said as he pulled his trousers up. "I plan for us to stop in Washington on the way back to Arkansas, provided I can get in to see him. If not, Frank told me if

I don't have any luck or don't like him, I can come back here next summer and you all will take care of my problem. But I'm counting on my knee holding out for the next 11 months or so."

"Well, if you don't get to see Dr. Mackinley or he's isn't willing to take you on, we'll be here," Paul Masterson said as he shook Jack's hand and then Ella's.

After the doctor had left, Jack turned to Frank and said, "God bless you, Frank, for getting this good doctor to examine me and then recommend a doctor in the States. As much as we have loved being here, it's a long way from home."

"Frank, I have to say that I'm all for Walter Reed because by then Dan should be able to spend some time with us, at least on the weekends, I hope," Ella broke in, smiling. "It'll be a lot easier for me to deal with Jack's pain if I get to see our son every so often!"

And Jack added, "That will help me too because I'll know Ella will have someone to take her mind off me." And he hugged his wife.

Frank laughed and said he was delighted to be of help!

14

The rest of Ella and Jack's time at St. Anthony Medical Center passed quickly and pleasantly. Ella was able to spend some special time with Cecile, Jason, and their two children, visiting with them for a couple of hours at their home and seeing it for herself. She was proud of the homemaker, decorator, and housekeeper Cecile had become, but she was even more pleased with how Cecile had been able to combine teaching with being a wife and mother. She could feel the love between Cecile and Jason as well as their enjoyment of and delight in their two children.

She stored her time with them in her memory so that she could tell Lee Jones, Cecile's uncle, all about them, knowing he would be equally glad to hear how settled and happy his niece was in this country that was not her own but had accepted her as though it were.

When Ella was telling Jack about her time with Cecile and her family, she ended by saying, "How sad it is that Cecile and Jason would not have found that same acceptance if they had tried to live in Arkansas or anywhere in the South or maybe even anywhere in the United States for that matter!" Jack could only nod in agreement knowing she had spoken the truth.

Jack and Ella had both enjoyed spending bits of time at lunch or after dinner with the couples like Geoff and Sarah and their children, Jean Marc and his wife Marie, and others whom they enjoyed meeting and getting to know.

Jack and Frank found lots to talk about since Jack was truly interested in the treatments of different injuries at the Center. Having spent many months in the hospital in London recovering from his own war wound, Jack had started asking questions and even reading up on different procedures the doctors were using there as his health improved. So it was not surprising he was especially impressed with the kind of treatments and the nature of the care men were receiving from the doctors at Frank's hospital.

Ella and Charlotte had the most time to visit and bring each other up-to-date on what had been happening in each other's lives. One afternoon on Charlotte's porch, Charlotte asked Ella if it would be too painful for her to share the details of Daniel's murder, and Ella said enough time had passed that she thought she could relate all of it without tears, but if she cried she knew Charlotte would understand. Ella talked and Charlotte was a sympathetic listener, so that at one point they both had tears in their eyes.

They shared with each other how difficult it had been to be with their husbands when they first returned home from the war—that they had felt almost as if these men were strangers. And in a way they were because they had lived through so much bloodshed and death that they weren't the same men who had gone to war.

And neither were she and Charlotte the same women because they had been forced to assume responsibilities for their children and for life itself that they had not been prepared for. Ella talked about dealing with the Spanish flu when her children both had it and then its weeks of isolation at home with just her and the girls.

Charlotte had had that same experience, except she was the one who was ill and had to turn to her mother-in-law for care both for herself and her children. She was thankful Frank's family was wealthy and could afford maids and nurses and everything they needed, but it was still a very difficult time.

For Charlotte the only bright spot had been that while she slowly recovered, she and Mrs. Willingham had finally become good friends. But her mother-in-law did not want to be called Mrs. or Mother or Grandmother by Charlotte or her daughters. Eventually they settled that Charlotte would call her by her name Marjorie or even just M, since that's what she preferred her granddaughters call her.

Charlotte wanted to hear details about how Jack had come into Ella's life, and Ella enjoyed telling her all about it, so by the time she had finished, Jack and Frank were approaching the house, and the two couples drank iced tea and laughed together about the strange wonders of life!

15

That evening in the Big House those of the staff who enjoyed theatrics performed a variety show built around a visit by citizens from a strange, foreign country called *Amerikana*. These strangers from a distant land were *Jorge Washerman*, *Rosy-felt*, and *Polkahontas*. The rest of the cast consisted of residents of *Engleland* who were as strange in their own ways as those from *Amerikana*. They included *Gloriana* and her daughter *Victoriana*, *Lady Wallis* and *King David Simpson*, *Shake-a-spear*, *Lord Tenny's son Alfred*, *P.M. Chamber Pot*, and *Winnie the Church Lion*.

The actors were in costumes and makeup that were supposed to clue the audience in on the characters they were playing. Ella recognized immediately that she was Pocahontas, but Jack couldn't decide whether he was George Washington or Pres. Roosevelt. Jack finally decided he must be Roosevelt because he had a bum knee!

The entire cast was in rare form, cracking jokes about the political situation in both countries which kept their audience laughing, but also singing both popular and patriotic songs from each country and with the audience invited to join in, using song sheets that had been printed in the program.

The performance lasted more than an hour, with curtain calls and a few requests for some more songs, and all of it was followed by refreshments in the dining room where the cast and the audience mixed and mingled, getting to know one another and giving Ella and Jack a chance to praise the cast. The two Americans actually weren't the only guests present since the cast members had invited friends and family members from York and some of the smaller towns near St. Anthony's Medical Center.

Later after Jack and Ella had returned to their room for the night, they were both laughing and talking about the evening. "I don't know why some Americans think the English are stiff and proper and boring. They must not know any English people like those we saw tonight. They have such a wacky but great sense of humor," Jack said.

"I know," Ella said adding, "I don't know when I've laughed this much. Some of those on stage I would have sworn were professional actors if I hadn't known what their day jobs are here at St. Anthony's. I read somewhere that 'laughter is the best medicine,' and I believe it. It's wonderful that St. Anthony's offers opportunities for the patients and staff to mix with people who live around here and find commonality in laughing and singing together."

"I agree completely, my Ella. You know, it reminds me a bit of our monthly dinners with students and parents where in a way our students perform and then anybody who can play an instrument and is willing to get together to practice occasionally comes forward, and we all join together to sing and even dance, if anyone wants to."

"You're right, Jack. You were a genius to come up with the idea of getting parents and students together, those from town and a good many from out in the country so that they have gotten to know and like one another and actually appreciate their differences! If people take the time to be around one another and get to know each other a bit, all sorts of good things can come from that. We've seen it happen.

"But now I am really ready to fall asleep in my husband's arms. Will you please turn out the light and come to bed?"

And he did.

16

On their final day at St. Anthony's Ella and Jack spent the first half with Harry McGregor, who drove them out to the Holy Isle of Lindisfarne. Ella, who had become really fond of Harry in the week she and Daniel and the children had spent there in 1925, was delighted to have some special time with him. She had liked Jennifer, the widow he was planning to marry in the fall, but she was actually pleased when Jennifer was unable to get away on that particular day because she wanted Jack and Harry to have some real time together and promised herself she would do her best to speak less and simply encourage them to share their stories with each other. Since both had lost their wives, though in very different ways, she hoped they would talk about their losses and how they had gotten through their grief and found love in someone else.

Jack had been a pastor whose little daughter had died suddenly and whose wife had left him after that and then wanted a divorce. Harry had almost completely lost his faith in God when his wife and young son were killed in a freak automobile accident when he was driving.

Jack had left the ministry when the church he was serving asked him to leave, and he knew it would be almost impossible to receive another call to pastor a church and that he would never be able to marry again. Harry, who had also been badly injured in the wreck, was taken to St. Anthony's where he had met Geoff and heard his story. Both men had gone through crises of faith.

Jack had found strength and comfort through his friendship with Episcopal priest John Banks and Molly Wainwright, a member of his church who had supported him in his ministry.

Harry had been touched by Geoff's story and getting to know him and also Frank while he was a patient at St. Anthony's after the terrible car wreck in which his wife and young son had died. Then Harry, who had been a Presbyterian minister, had a mystical experience of God's presence, as he was reading the 11th chapter of John's Gospel. As Harry continued to heal and grow in his new relationship with God, Frank had then invited him to stay at St. Anthony's as its chaplain.

Ella encouraged each of them to share his story with the other. Harry, who was accustomed to talking about his experience with other damaged men who needed to hear of someone who had felt God's presence healing his grief, offered to share first.

When he finished, Jack said softly, "Wow! My experience of God's presence in my life hasn't been that dramatic, nothing that mystical. I would say it has been real to me, but my healing from the death of our daughter, my wife's leaving me and then divorcing me, and then the church's voting to terminate my ministry along with the Presbytery's rule that if I wanted to marry again I must renounce my ordination—all of that has been a long series of very painful events."

"That's a lot of blows coming one on top of the other. So what happened to help you get through all of that?" Harry asked.

"I have a Jewish friend, who's actually as Christlike as any human I know. He invited me to go out to visit some farmers he supported in forming a co-operative venture. This was in early spring soon after the church voted to ask me to leave. Michael suggested it might be good for me to get away from town and do some different kind of work, outdoors, where I didn't have to worry about anything but doing the job, whatever it might be. He told me he'd often found nature, just being out in it, could be a source of healing.

"I started out behind a horse-pulled plow, but my knee gave me so much pain I was switched to driving a tractor. And that I could do, and I ended up loving doing it. I found peace being with these men who worked hard 10 or more hours a day but who could laugh and joke and then go home to their wives, eat supper, go to bed, and start fresh in the morning. I lived in a couple of rooms at the back of one of their houses, ate meals with the family, experienced family life without the complications of my first wife's personality.

"I enjoyed Saturday nights when the community would set up long tables and every wife would bring out whatever food she'd prepared and we'd all eat together. And then somebody would start strumming a banjo or a guitar or some instruments I didn't know anything about, like a zither or a dulcimer, and people would start clapping and singing and even dancing. It brought healing to my soul and my body too.

"Then in mid-summer, Michael came out and told me the high school was looking for a history teacher, and he thought I'd be great for the job. I told him I'd never had any training to be a teacher and doubted any school would hire me, though I was interested and had always loved history. But Michael was on the school board and had enough clout that they hired me. That's how Ella and I began working together, gradually getting to know each other, and then falling in love, realizing God has been at work through all of it."

Harry laughed and said, "Life is really strange and wonderful, isn't it? And the best part is there is this God of love and strength and mercy and power who is with us even when we are completely unaware or worse, convinced there is no God. I'm so glad we've had this chance to be together. I liked Daniel immensely when he and Ella were here before. Ella knows that, don't you, Ella?" And when she nodded her assent, he continued, "I grieved over his death and hoped and prayed she would not have to live the rest of her life without a partner. I now know I no longer have that worry, Jack. You two have so much in common, and your faith is a major part of that. I thank God for your love for each other."

Ella said, "Harry, I am equally happy you have found Jennifer or that she found you—or maybe I would be more on target if I said God was just waiting for enough time for you both to get past your grief to bring you together." And with that all three of them laughed together at the wonderful way God can work in humans' lives.

The three of them explored the part of Lindisfarne where the monks had lived before and after Cuthbert's death until raids by the Danes threatened and forced them to leave and look for a safe place elsewhere. Then they had dug up Cuthbert's remains and taken then to the mainland to be buried in Durham.

Harry had brought mead and bread, and sitting on the rocks where they had celebrated Holy Communion when Ella had been there with Daniel, on this new day she, Jack, and Harry ate and drank the Lord's bread and wine together. Ella took Jack's hand after they had celebrated the Eucharist in this holy place, and Jack kissed her hand and whispered, "I thank God for you, my love," bringing tears to Ella's eyes.

17

Ella wanted to return to Eleanor and Ronald's apartment before they brought the baby home because she planned to make sure that everything was ready for the arrival of this new member of the family. She wanted Eleanor's bed to have fresh linens on it and flowers to be on the bedside table. She intended to see that the bathroom was sparkling clean and the baby bed ready for Lee Douglass. She had even decided what she would prepare for the family's first meal at home with its new occupant. Unfortunately, the best-laid plans often go awry!

When the taxi delivered them to the apartment at 2:00 the next afternoon, Ronald had already brought Eleanor and Baby Lee home from the hospital. In fact, they had arrived before noon the previous day, well before Ella had expected them. Eleanor was even up and dressed, sitting in the rocking chair in their bedroom trying to breast feed the baby when they knocked on the apartment door and were greeted by Ronald, who looked a bit harassed as he welcomed them back from their trip to St. Anthony's.

"I meant to call and find out what time the train from York arrived and then forgot to do so. I intended to meet you at the station, but it's been a bit hectic around here because Lee doesn't seem to want to take the nipple today. He's upsetting his mother terribly and, as a consequence of upsetting her, his father is a nervous wreck." Ronald laughed a bit as he said these last words, but then added, "Of course, I am exaggerating. But we're not used to his being fussy about feeding. Or at least, Eleanor says he learned quickly what to do to get milk from her breast and by the third day was acting like a pro. Now, all of sudden, he doesn't want it, and we don't know what to do!"

Ronald, who had seemed to be extremely calm and at ease with Eleanor's pregnancy and labor, at least as far as Ella and Jack could tell, was obviously at a loss about what to do to help his wife or their son. "But do, please, come in and forgive me for babbling. Ella, if you have any idea what to do to help your daughter and grandson, please go in the bedroom. Jack and I will put your bags in the guest room."

Ella didn't wait to be asked twice but instead put her purse on the nearby table and hurried into the bedroom where Eleanor was shaking her head in frustration as she tried to get Lee to suck. Ella said, "Oh, precious boy, help your mother by taking the nipple she is offering you," but then had to smile and say, "I'm afraid he has a mind of his own, daughter," as she watched him purse his lips together in refusal as Eleanor tried to tempt him to open his mouth.

"Mother, what am I doing wrong? He hasn't acted this way a single time that I've tried to nurse him. Why now? And I wanted to show you how well we've been doing together."

"It doesn't look to me like you are doing anything wrong. It may be he has a little gas he may need to get rid of. Turn him over and lay him on his stomach; then pat his back gently to see if he burps," Ella suggested.

Eleanor gently turned the baby on his stomach and began rubbing and patting Lee's back. In a few minutes he not only burped, he spit up a little milk. Then in another minute it was obvious that he had messed in his diaper. But after all that he made a soft happy noise, sighed, and went to sleep.

"Well, no wonder he wouldn't eat. He needed to get rid of some things first," Ella said with a smile. "It's amazing, but even babies can let you know what they need or want. This one certainly did, anyway!"

"Oh, Mother, I'm so glad you came when you did. I thought I was doing something wrong. There's just so much I don't know about babies, and I've read the books the doctor suggested or other mothers have given me."

"Eleanor, he's barely a week old, and I doubt you had him with you much of the time in the hospital. You will get to know him, be able to tell when he's uncomfortable or hurting and what to do to help him. And he'll make you happy much of the time and worry you and even irritate you some of the time, but whatever he does, you'll love him more than you ever thought you could love anybody that demands as much of you as he will.

"Being a mother is so different from being a wife, especially if you have a good husband, and you do. A husband and wife are partners, I hope equal partners who work together to raise good children who will be good adults. You won't always agree on how to do that, but if you love each other and love your children you will learn how to be good parents, wise parents."

"Mother, you and Daddy were good parents, especially you—because Daddy was working and sometimes didn't get home, especially when he had patients who were really sick. How did you do it? We seem to have turned out all right, don't you think?" Eleanor asked.

"Yes, all three of you have—well, Dan's not quite there yet—though I have a feeling the Naval Academy will force him to mature even more than he already has. But even good parents, even if you're a good mother, you will have times when your children assert their own wills and disobey you or disagree and argue with you. They will demand to be their own persons and sometimes they will make mistakes and disappoint you and even make you angry. Those are the times it will be difficult to be a good parent because you have feelings of your own and hopes for your children's lives too. But you and Ronald will be wonderful parents through it all, and I look forward to knowing your children, loving them, watching them grow up!"

"Mother, I haven't even asked you how your time at St. Anthony's was. How was everyone? And did you find the place much changed?"

"Everybody was fine. We were able to spend some time with Cecile, Jason and their children, and we met Jean Marc's new wife—well not so new, really, but new to us, and we liked her very much. She is just what he needed. And we also met Harry's fiancée and she's lovely. I'm so happy for him and so glad he has found a good woman—and one with children! Have you met her?" Ella asked.

"No, but I've heard about her. Charlotte calls me every so often and fills me in on what's going on. I met Charlotte for lunch in York one Saturday well over a year ago when she was shopping for fabric and getting ideas for redoing the Big House. Harry had just recently met Jennifer but had brought her out to St. Anthony's to see the place and meet Frank and Charlotte and some of the staff. Everybody liked her and was hoping the relationship would flourish and I'm so glad it has. He is such a dear man and deserves happiness, though I suppose most of us do!"

Ella could tell that her daughter was in need of some rest herself, and after giving Eleanor a kiss on the forehead, she left her to sleep a bit while the baby slept.

18

The days passed quickly with the parents getting used to a new routine of sleeping and waking, feeding and changing diapers, and very little time for each other and the two guests in their home.

Ella took advantage of the quiet times to write to Dan and Mary Beth and even sent notes to Esther and Sarah, air-mailing them, hoping they would arrive before she and Jack were back in Myrna.

Jack and sometimes Ella would go for a walk or take a tram down to the town part of Durham and sightsee to let Eleanor and Ronald have some time alone with their son when he was awake or just with each other when he was asleep. And they also babysat one evening while the couple went for a walk by themselves so that Eleanor could get some exercise and they could have a bit of time alone outside the apartment. Ronald's parents came by twice for brief visits, but they were thoughtful and did not stay very long when they came. They realized that Ella's time with her grandson and her daughter would be brief, while they would be there long after she and Jack had returned to Myrna.

Before it seemed possible that three weeks had gone by, the day came for them to take the train back to London and then to Halifax to board the ship for their return to the States. Ella had vowed she was not going to cry when she held her precious grandson and hugged her daughter for the last time, at least for now, and she held the tears back for the most part, though a few fell on Jack's shirt as he sat with his arm around her in the taxi that took them to the train station. Jack had no idea how difficult it had been for her to get her emotions under control before they arrived at the station. But Ella had been taught by her Quaker mother to practice calming herself when her emotions were too strong to contain, and she had called on that teaching as they drove away from Eleanor, Ronald, and Baby Lee and was glad it had come to her aid!

The train ride to London was uneventful. Both Ella and Jack were tired because no one had had a full night's sleep during those last three weeks. Ella and Jack's room was close enough to hear the baby's cries when he awoke during the night, and at their age it was often harder to fall back asleep.

They had one night reserved in the same hotel they had stayed in when they first arrived in London, and they truly looked

162

forward to the privacy and hoped for silence, even though the sounds of the bustling city would be outside their windows. And they hoped their staterooms onboard the ship home would provide more peace and quiet.

That final hope became even more important because their night at the Piccadilly West End Hotel was interrupted by a fire in a building across the street from their side of the hotel They were awakened about 1:00 a.m. by the sirens of fire trucks and police cars and all the noise of firemen getting their hoses ready to spray water on the flames that were visible from their bedroom windows.

Ambulances with nurses had come to take anyone who had been a victim of the fire to a hospital. Police were cordoning off all entrances to the burning building and making sure anyone who was just an onlooker was obeying them. Some of the police and the nurses were trying to tend to those who were coming out of the building, most of whom were in robes or pajamas.

It appeared that while the bottom floors were offices, there were a few apartments that had occupants on the fourth floor. Newspaper reporters were trying to talk to anyone who looked as if he or she could give them any kind of information they could use in their write-ups. At different times when it looked as though sparks from the fire might be blowing in the direction of their hotel, a fireman might direct his hose toward the Piccadilly and the sound of forced water might strike their building, startling them with its impact and noise.

Obviously it was going to be impossible to sleep with all the commotion going on so near their building. The Americans stayed watching until the fire appeared to be out and the ambulances, police cars, fire trucks, reporters, and watchers had gone. The people who lived in the apartments were taken somewhere, and Ella and Jack hoped their belongings in their apartments had been spared, but there was no way for them to know that—and they never found out what the outcome was. Yet it was difficult to get back to sleep; and when they finally did, morning came far too soon!

As exhausted as they were, they were relieved the voyage home on the Queen Mary was quiet and uneventful. They didn't even meet any couples they wanted to get to know, finding it restful just to be alone with each other, something they had had little time to do in England. In fact, they had missed their time together and took advantage of that part of the ocean voyage on the way home, enjoying catching up with each other's thoughts and feelings about their trip. They both realized that once back in Myrna, other people and activities would claim their attention.

One afternoon while they were stretched out in their deck chairs enjoying the breeze while staying out of the direct sunlight, Ella said, "You know, Jack, everybody at St. Anthony's seems to feel that another war with Germany is inevitable. It's more a question of 'when' than 'if' and that's pretty worrisome to everybody there because they know England's not ready for another war. Nobody wants war if it can be avoided. But the men believe that Hitler will make that impossible. What do you think, Jack? You talked to a lot more people than I did during our time at St. Anthony's."

"I agree Hitler is not going to allow Great Britain to be neutral. He wants revenge on England and France for winning the last war. From what I heard from the staff at St. Anthony's, they think Hitler is building a war machine that will destroy western Europe, including Great Britain. And after that happens, who knows where he'll stop.

"And that's the real problem, Ella. Hitler won't stop. He's got some kind of madness, I fear, that makes him want to conquer the whole civilized world, and I fear he believes he can do it. And at some point the United States will be forced to deal with him, and I'd just as soon that not happen."

Part V

Back in the States: 1937

1

The taxi had dropped them at their hotel, a clean but modest brownstone in Brooklyn not too far from the station where they would take the train to Washington and then board another train headed southwest to Memphis. Finally they would take one final train to Jonesboro that would make a brief stop in Myrna. They planned to telephone Michael as soon as they arrived in Memphis because he had said he would pick them up at the station when the train stopped in Myrna.

Jack was glad they hadn't set an absolute day and time for Michael to be prepared to meet them because he had been pondering whether they might take advantage of being in D.C. to visit Walter Reed Hospital and talk with the doctor Frank had recommended he see about surgery on his knee. He had raised that possibility with Ella on the ship, and she thought it was worth a try.

They had been told when they had reserved a room in their hotel that it did not come with a telephone but there were several pay telephones in the lobby. Jack had the number for Dr. Jonathan Mackinley Frank had given him, hoping he had taken it down correctly and would provide him with access to the doctor with one try. Naturally, one try didn't connect him with Dr. Mackinley, but the woman who took his call was able to transfer him to the correct office. Dr. Mackinley's secretary took his call, listened to Jack's request, and asked him to wait while she passed his request to the doctor. Jack had just about decided she was not coming back when she returned to the phone, thanked him for waiting, and said she was transferring him to Dr. Mackinley.

Ella was standing near enough to hear Jack's words but not the doctor's. Jack explained he and his wife had just returned from England where they had spent almost a week at St. Anthony's Treatment and Rehabilitation Center where Dr. Frank Willingham and one of his staff doctors, Paul Masterson, had examined his knee damaged by a battle injury in 1918. As the war was still raging, Jack had been transferred to a hospital in London for surgery and had spent the remainder of the war there, but that had been almost 20 years ago.

Doctors Willingham and Masterson had told him scar tissue and some inflammation were causing him problems with pain, and his limp, that had become increasingly troublesome over the years, was only going to get worse if he didn't have another surgery on his knee.

They had recommended Dr. Jonathan Mackinley, a knee surgeon, whom Dr. Masterson had met during a trip to the States at Walter Reed Hospital. Dr. Masterson had also kept in touch with Dr. Mackinley over the years, and was well aware of the success he was having with knee surgery there..

Jack explained they had just disembarked in New York Harbor and were spending the night in a hotel but would be on their way home to Arkansas the next day. However, he felt it wouldn't hurt to make a phone call to see if there was any possibility of speaking with Dr. Mackinley, just to ask if he might be able to see him and then perhaps even be willing to take him on as a patient.

The doctor told Jack he had great respect for the work St. Anthony's was doing and he remembered Dr. Masterson well from his visit to Walter Reed. If Jack could be at his office by 7:30 the next morning, he would examine his knee to see if he thought he could do anything to help it. He realized 7:30 was early, but he had a surgery scheduled for 8:30, and unless Jack was able to be at his office at 6:00 that same afternoon, 7:30 was it.

Jack explained they had just left the ship that had brought them home from England and had hotel reservations in Brooklyn for the night but could be on a train to Washington the next morning. Ella, who had been listening intently, whispered it would help if they had an address for the hospital and then try to get a hotel room fairly near the hospital so they could easily be there for a 6:00 p.m. visit.

Dr. Mackinley told Jack he would transfer them back to his office assistant who could help them with the address of the hospital and even get the reservation for them since the hospital had an arrangement with a nearby hotel that offered rates by the week for hospital patients. They might be interested in checking it out in case Jack needed surgery. Then they would already have a place where he and his wife could stay if he needed rehab on his knee.

The hotel where they spent the night in Brooklyn was clean and quiet, and knowing they had to be out by 8:00 in the next morning in order to catch the commuter train to Silver Springs where Walter Reed was located gave them a reason to go to bed early. By now they were looking forward to returning to Myrna and their own home and bed. Consequently, they found a nearby restaurant that served plain food at a reasonable price and had a leisurely dinner, making an early night of it.

Jack and Ella lay awake awhile discussing what they might learn at the meeting with Dr. Mackinley the next evening. "Jack, I rarely ever hear you complain about your knee. Tell me the truth, how much pain does it give you? Does it hurt all the time?" Ella asked, her concern showing in her voice.

"No, not all the time. If I stand too long or put my weight on it for too long or when I turn a certain way, it hurts. The problem is I am noticing it more and more, and Frank told me that was only going to get worse over time. The longer I go without getting something done about it, the less improvement I will get from any treatment on it. He said if I am careful and try not to overdo walking or standing on it, giving it a rest every hour or so, and if I keep cold packs on it when it gets really painful and sore, I can last a year or two without limping worse than I'm doing now."

"Jack, I hardly notice you limping. You hide it well. Or maybe I've gotten so used to you favoring that knee I don't pay attention until I see you wince when you stand or even when you are walking sometimes. But you never complain, don't even mention it most of the time. I am so glad we are actually going to see a specialist about it. Thank God for Frank's noticing it and getting Dr. Masterson to examine it and tell you about this doctor here!"

"I'm also grateful Frank sort of took charge of getting me to let Paul examine it. They offered to do the surgery at St. Anthony's for me free of charge, but I figured it would cost less to do it in this country and not have to pay for the trip to England.

"But, Ella, it wasn't just the cost. It's that I really am afraid England could be at war with Germany and Italy within a year and travel to England might not be possible." Jack had pulled her closer to him as he saw the expression of horror on her face. "I don't want to frighten you, my darling, and I truly hope I'm wrong, but Germany wants revenge on England and France for winning the last war, and Hitler wants to lead the conquest. I know this frightens you for Eleanor and Ronald and Baby Lee."

"Yes, of course it does, but my fear is not just for them. The idea of another war scares me for everybody who will get hurt by it, who will suffer because of it, who will die a horrible death from its bombs and bullets and poison gas, the way they did in the last one. You are one of those who was injured and is still paying for your service in it. And you're one of the lucky ones because you survived, even though you live with pain. I think of Dan and all the young men whose lives will be changed forever, even if they survive, and we can't even imagine how horrible this one will be." Ella had tears streaming down her face as she struggled to speak, her voice breaking with emotion.

"Oh, my Ella, I'm sorry I brought this up tonight, but it has been on my mind ever since we were at St. Anthony's. Most of those who work there were in the last war and some still bear the scars—not as noticeably as Geoff, but they're there—on Jean Marc, Frank, Harry, and others. They don't go around displaying their scars, but when I was with only men, I could feel them, hear them, their concerns about what they think is coming. These are people who have dedicated their lives to bringing healing to those who've been hurt physically and/or psychologically by war or by life experiences.

"But war is the worst because the pain is delivered intentionally, deliberately, with conquest of the other as the goal, the reward being the damage done to the 'enemy.' If I were God, I would make it so there would never be another war, but obviously I'm not God, nor do I understand all of God's ways. So I stew about it and upset my wife, whose heart is tender and loving."

"Jack, do you think we'll get in it if England does?"

"Yes, my love, I don't think we'll be able to remain neutral. I don't know what the tipping point will be, what will force us to get involved, but something will do it. We are such a large country, I doubt we'll actually feel the attack in Arkansas, but that won't matter. We as a country will respond wherever it comes, and maybe will get involved as soon as England does because they're the 'mother country' and I can't see us letting them be invaded by Herr Hitler's forces.

"But that's enough war talk for tonight. I want to hold you close and kiss your tears away and make you feel safe in my arms even while I'm wishing I could make all of us safe forever."

And that's what he tried to do as best he could, succeeding in some ways, but both of them accepting how limited his power was to keep the world at peace!

2

Jack and Ella, had no trouble getting a taxi from the station the next day before noon when their commuter train arrived in Silver Springs at 1:00 p.m. The cabbie was very familiar with the hotel, appropriately named Healing House, near Walter Reed Hospital, and dropped them off so that they had plenty of time to check in, have lunch, and even explore the area around the hospital and rest a bit before making the short walk to the building where Dr. Mackinley had his office. Since his office assistant had left for the day, they entered and made themselves comfortable because they could hear the murmur of voices in a nearby room and realized the doctor was still with a patient. Dr. Mackinley appeared shortly, walking with another man and nodding to them as they sat in the waiting room while he escorted his patient to the door.

After he'd left, the doctor locked the door and turned back to them, holding out his hand, saying "Mr. and Mrs. MacLean, I hope I haven't kept you waiting too long."

"No, of course not. After all, we appreciate so much your willingness to see me at all," Jack said. "It just seemed ridiculous to be so near and then go back to Arkansas without attempting to meet you and get your opinion about my knee."

"I'm glad you did. I had received a telegram from Frank Willingham telling me he had recommended to you that you get some additional treatment for your war injury since it was nearly 20 years ago that you were injured. Let's go into my office and let me examine your knee and get some pictures of it, and then I'll have a better idea if or what we might do to make it better. Mrs. MacLean, if you want to watch you may follow us or you can stay here, whatever you prefer."

Ella willingly followed him into his examination room where the doctor indicated two straight back chairs where they could sit and where Jack was told to remove his trousers and lie down on the table. "I want to be able to examine both knees and see how the damaged knee differs in appearance from the good knee. And I plan to take some X-rays of both knees. I wish I could have seen this when it was first injured, or soon thereafter, because it has obviously been a long time since you were injured and had surgery on it. But we will do the best we can with what we have." Dr. Mackinley had kept speaking as he helped Jack position his legs on the table with a rolled pillow under the knees.

The doctor then donned a pair of huge glasses he said acted as magnifying lenses so he could better examine the knee and the areas around it. He gently but firmly used his fingers to press and move the kneecap and the cartilage surrounding it, nodding his head when Jack grimaced in pain. He stopped and wrote some notes on a pad he had placed on a nearby table. "I can feel the swelling and the edema in several places. You know where they are because you showed discomfort when I pressed or rubbed them. You do not want to go too long without surgery to clean those areas of infection there. Now let's get those X-rays taken."

As Dr. Mackinley positioned the X-ray machine for the area he wanted pictured, he said, "I am going to recommend, Mrs. MacLean that you move into the other room because we just don't know how powerful or damaging to the human anatomy X-rays may be or how far they may travel. I wear a shield myself when I take them."

Ella had already risen, saying, "I hope I can come back in to hear what the X-rays show, Doctor."

"Of course. I will call you back when I finish and can show you the X-rays themselves."

It seemed to Ella that she waited for hours in the waiting room whose name suited it as far as she was concerned. Actually it was only a half-hour for the pictures to be taken and then developed. Dr. Mackinley came to the door and invited her back into the room where Jack was now sitting at the end of the table where the doctor had laid the X-rays.

Dr. Mackinley began talking as he held each X-ray up for Jack and then Ella to view. He began by showing them the pictures of both knees and pointing out the differences. "See these darkened areas around the knee cap; these are areas where some infection has begun to build up. These other areas that are not so dark indicate the beginnings of infection. Wherever there is infection, Jack is aware of pain. Some of these areas have been present for a long time. Others indicate that infection has begun. I would like to perform surgery on you within the next month, but you have told me that your teaching job will begin in a very few weeks; so that will not be possible."

"Dr. Mackinley, how much time will he need for healing after he has this surgery?" Ella asked, her voice expressing her concern.

"I would want him to spend at least a month under my care after he has the surgery. I would have him go through some intensive rehabilitative exercise and treatments during that time and I would want him here so I can oversee his care and his improvement. I understand this is impossible at this time. But would it be possible for you to come as soon as the school year ends next year, and do you know when that will be?" Dr. Mackinley asked.

"This year we ended school in the middle of May because of a lack of funds. I suspect it will be the same next year, but I cannot swear to that. However, I can be certain we will be done by the end of May, and we both could be here by the first of June." Jack said, looking at Ella to corroborate his statement.

"Will that work?" Ella asked. "Or will the infection have spread and gotten worse before then?"

"I am going to give him a prescription for a new medication I expect to slow down the infection and also one for the pain. They will help your husband somewhat and give you both the time you need to fulfill your obligation as teachers."

Opening his work calendar for the next year, Dr. Mackinley said, "Mr. MacLean, I am going to put you on my surgery schedule for Monday, June 6, and expect you both to be here, ready for a painful and difficult month. I'll have Mrs. Rogers make a month's reservation for you both at the Healing House where you are spending tonight. They have suites that provide you with not only a bedroom but a small sitting room and your own bathroom. They have a dining room that serves three meals a day and can provide room service for those who are recovering from surgery.

"I expect you will be in the hospital for the first week, Mr. MacLean, but will then move to Healing House for the next three weeks. By then I believe you'll be able to return to your home in

174

Arkansas. You will still be on a fairly strict exercise regimen to strengthen your knee. Do you ride a bicycle, Mr. MacLean?"

"Yes. Truly that has been my main form of exercise because I can ride it with very little pain, some days with no pain at all."

"Good. I will want you to walk as much as possible, but riding a bicycle will also be good exercise because your knee will be moving when you pedal. Do either of you have any questions?" Dr. Mackinley looked at both of them, somewhat expectantly.

"Will my knee be as good as new?" Jack asked, thinking he knew the answer but hoping he didn't.

"It depends on what you mean by new," Dr. Mackinley answered. "If you mean you will have the knee you had before you went to war, the answer is 'no.' If you mean you will have a healthy, workable knee like a 45- or 50-year-old man who has taken care of himself, the answer is 'yes.' You will always need to be a bit careful and not take any unnecessary risks climbing rocks or jumping off cliffs, but you should be able to live a life of normal activity for many years yet, and that's the best I can offer," Dr. Mackinley smiled as he finished talking. "Any more questions?"

"No, but thank you, Doctor. You've given me hope I can go on living and not become an invalid, at least not for a good many years. You have relieved my fears, and I am grateful. And, God willing, you will see my wife and me next June! I'll certainly be in touch with you before then, letting your secretary know our date of arrival. Thank you so much for seeing me, even though it meant you would be late going home to your family! I mean it, Doctor, thank you!"

"It has been a pleasure to meet you and your wife. I look forward to seeing you in 11 months. And if you have any problems or questions, you have my phone number. My secretary always knows how to reach me."

With that, Jack stood, as did Ella, and both shook Dr. Mackinley's hand and left, feeling as though they had taken an important step toward Jack's future.

They enjoyed a good meal together in a small, quiet restaurant, with Ella wishing they had known they were coming so close to

Annapolis and had with them the phone number at which they might have reached Dan and been able to talk to him. Somehow it felt unfair to be so near him, even for such a brief time, and yet not know how to get in touch with him. Jack promised they would call him as soon as they got home and thought they had a chance of reaching him. But even without contact with Dan, it felt good to be back in the States. They were ready to return to Myrna and their own lives.

Part VI

Home Again: 1937

1

When Michael met their train in Jonesboro he told Ella not to say a word to anyone other than Mary Beth about Eleanor's baby until she could tell Esther all about him, and they both wanted to hear about their time in England. Since Esther had not yet received the letter Ella had written her about the baby, Ella must save her description of Eleanor's baby for Esther who would want to hear all the details and see the photographs as soon as Ella had them developed.

When they asked him what had happened in Myrna during the month they had been away, he said the town had been pretty quiet except that Lee Jones had proposed to a black high school teacher he had met at a meeting and wanted Ella and Jack to meet her.

Both Jack and especially Ella immediately wanted to know all about her, and Michael said, "Well, Esther approves and that was important because you know how much we both have grown to love Lee. He's become like the son we never had, and it truly touched us both when he came by and told us about her, that he'd asked her to marry him, and she'd said 'yes.'

"We Jews know what it's like to be ostracized and looked down upon by some people, and the Negroes here in Arkansas and elsewhere in the South and even in New York City when I was coming of age there have experienced more than their share of prejudice against them. Ella, I know you don't have those prejudices against people because of their color or their religion because we've talked about it, and Jack, I've never been aware of any of those feelings in you. So I hope you will come to dinner this Saturday night and meet the wife-to-be."

"We'd love to, Michael. Jack, I didn't mean to accept for both of us, but you don't have other plans, do you?" Ella looked at her husband expectantly.

"No, ma'am. I will be most happy to escort you, ma'am." Jack was grinning, as Ella retorted, "Oh, quit teasing me. I'm too excited about Lee's news for you to bother me. Michael, you've told us the news but you really haven't given me any information about this woman. What's she like?"

"Well, she's five years younger than Lee, grew up in eastern Arkansas out in the country near Brinkley. She was a bright little girl. and this will interest you, Jack. About the time the Civil War ended, the Northern Presbyterian Church began founding schools across the South for Negroes; and they started a co-educational boarding school in Cotton Plant, Arkansas! Now I've heard of Cotton Plant though I have never been there, but the Cotton Plant Academy is located on the outskirts of the little town. Yet Suzanna not only lived at the Academy as a girl, but went back to teach there after she had graduated from college. She's amazingly well educated." Michael said, and then added, "Did that sound as superior and snobbish to you as it did to my own ears?"

"Michael, I interpreted it as surprise because so few of our colored people have the opportunity to get that much education. Lee more or less educated himself until you gave him the opportunity to attend college at Philander Smith. So I can't wait to meet her," Ella said.

Jack, whose mind had gone in a different direction, chimed in, "You know, now that I think of it, I do remember hearing about these schools that had been built in the South by Northern Presbyterians—Christian boarding schools for Negro children. I might have even heard about the one here in Arkansas, but at that time I barely knew anything about the state, much less suspected one day I'd be living here. But the church in Myrna is part of the Southern Presbyterian Church, and the school in Cotton Plant has never been mentioned. Of course, now I understand why," Jack shook his head. "That's really sad."

"I've never paid attention to the fact that the Presbyterian Church in Myrna is different from other Presbyterian churches. Why is that, Jack?" Michael asked, and Ella added that she hadn't realized there were different kinds of Presbyterian churches either.

"It was the war, the Civil War, that caused the division. By the time I went to seminary there was already talk about reunion between the two branches. The seminary in Princeton was part of the Northern church and that's where I began to realize the differences, since the seminary in Richmond where I grew up was Southern. Yet both seminaries were struggling to find commonalities in the hopes that someday they would reunite into one church.

"By the time I entered seminary, the divisions were still there but were more doctrinal than political, though there were still those, especially over the treatment of Negroes."

"What were the doctrinal differences about?" Ella asked.

"Over whether some parts of the Bible should be taken literally or not—like the creation story in Genesis as opposed to Darwin's and other scientists' theories about the beginnings of the earth, and the idea of the evolution of humans and other living species. Scientists and doctors and even artists and inventors had begun asking questions as far back as the beginning of the Renaissance, even back to the Greeks, looking for knowledge about life and the world with its tremendous variety of creatures and natural resources. And they weren't satisfied with the answers that religion so often provided." Jack shook his head in uncertainty. "I've gone on too long. I hope I haven't told you more than you wanted to know."

"No, but you've given me a lot to think about," Ella said. "I'm one who hasn't really questioned the Genesis version of creation, and yet I don't know what to do with it because I don't really believe in it. So what do I do? I am a Christian. At least I want to be. I try to be."

"What about you, Michael? What do you believe about the Bible and creation? As a Jew, the Old Testament is your Bible. Do you read it literally, every word in it coming straight from God?" Jack asked.

"No. I do not read the creation story literally, but I do read it as a gift from God who was the creator, the mind and the heart behind the universe, regardless of how it actually came into being—whether over millions of years or in six days. I do believe there is a Power, a Divine Being, behind it. I have found the Bible studies that Father Banks leads tremendously provocative, meaningful, and helpful in the expansion of my own beliefs.

"And you also, Jack, you are a thinker and a teacher. It is sad your denomination refused to let you continue as a pastor simply because you had married a woman whose faith was so shallow and weak she couldn't be a wife to you—or, as you found out when she appeared at your door one night, she couldn't be a wife to anyone. Regrettably, she had no understanding of herself, of anyone else, least of all of God."

"Thank you, Michael, for your kind words of understanding about my life. I am grateful for people like you, Father Banks, and most of all, for this woman who has shown me what a real marriage is like." And Jack, who was sitting with Michael in the front seat of the car, turned and gave Ella such a look of pure love it brought tears to her eyes and she mouthed "I also love you—so much!"

"We've sort of strayed from the subject of Lee and—did you say her name is Suzanna?" Ella asked. "What does she teach, Michael?"

"Eleventh and 12th grade English and also serves as a counselor for students with problems during the other parts of the day when she is not teaching. She graduated from LeMoyne College in Tennessee, where she had some training in counseling. Her strength, Lee says, is in her ability to listen and to relate to the students. Also, her common sense and kindness. He's so in love it's almost comical because he's never even really dated anyone, much less wanted to marry them. I'm so glad you can come to dinner on Saturday night."

"We are looking forward to it. I'll call Esther and see if there's anything I can do to help," Ella said.

As they pulled up to their house, Ella and Jack were looking at the town, wondering what if anything had changed in the almost six weeks they had been away. However, it looked very much the same, but since it was "home," they both felt a bit relieved and at the same time eager to go inside.

2

Esther called as soon as Michael arrived at home and told her he had helped Jack unload their suitcases and had seen them safely into their house. She told Ella she was going to run by with a casserole she had prepared for them, along with some fresh tomatoes and lettuce from their garden. She knew Ella would need to go to the grocery store but maybe having food brought in would give her time to unpack and call Mary Beth to let her know they were home. She also invited them to dinner on Saturday night to meet Lee's fiancée Suzanna. And she could hardly wait to hear Ella's accounts of leaving Dan at Annapolis and being present for the birth of Eleanor's baby.

Ella accepted immediately, asking what she could bring or do to help with the dinner and was told if she would bring a salad to go with fried chicken, mashed potatoes, and green beans, that would be a big help.

Esther promised she wouldn't stay long but could hardly wait to hear all about their trip. She had received a couple of postcards Ella had sent soon after they arrived, but realized how slow the mail was when the cards had been written, one on the ship on the way over and the second had been mailed on the day after they arrived. Ella said she had finally realized it took two weeks or longer for the mail to get from northern England to New York and a few days more to make it to Myrna, Arkansas, and so she might-just-as well keep a sort of diary and share their experiences once they arrived home.

Ella had just finished talking to Mary Beth when Esther arrived. She had asked her daughter if she and Jack could come by to see them right after supper, promising they wouldn't linger because they were tired from the trip, but she wanted to see her grandchildren as well as Mary Beth and Patrick.

Pat, as Daniel Patrick had become, was three-and-a-half, red-headed, stubborn, and smart as he could be, having started talking in complete sentences by the age of two. Nora was as beautiful as her mother, with dark curly hair and a pixie face, but she was taking her time talking, letting Pat be the center of attention, which he most definitely enjoyed! Nora's vocabulary consisted of Mama, Daddy, Pat, Amma, Papa and a few other words to get something she wanted, but she wasn't making long sentences with them yet. However, she was so cute and beguiling, she was not missing out on anything, though Mary Beth was working to get her to learn to put her words together in long, complete sentences. Nora, however, had a mind of her own, and would hold her chubby arms up to her mother and say, 'Nora kiss Mama," when she could tell her mother was getting impatient with her for her lack of language skills! Mary Beth never could refuse a kiss from this little girl, who would start speaking in long sentences when she was ready, as Ella would reassure her mother.

Ella had not had much time to shop but had picked up a British flag and an emblem of the British Empire that would stick on a book just to let the children know she had been thinking about them. She wisely asked them to choose which they wanted, letting Pat go first as the older. Nora, who adored her brother, was so accustomed to Pat's being 'first' that she never fussed about it. Ella had expected him to choose the flag, but he chose the emblem to her surprise, saying he was going to stick it on the back of his tricycle as his license plate. Nora, who had actually wanted the flag to wave around, was delighted with her gift, saying "Nora kiss Gamma" to Ella's joy.

Ella and Mary Beth moved to the kitchen because the men had begun talking politics and Mary Beth wanted to hear all about her sister, the new baby, their apartment and then about their visit with Cecile, Jason, and the other people at St. Anthony's.

184

Mary Beth also wanted to hear all about Annapolis, although Ella had written a little about it in a letter. "I haven't the slightest idea how time passes so quickly, but it does," she said. "I still have trouble believing my youngest is a student at the Naval Academy. He was so excited about everything we saw and especially over the nice young midshipman who showed us around a bit and filled us full of information about Bancroft Hall and the Navy chapel and a bit about life as a student there.

"But the other thing I want you to know is that we stopped in Washington on the way home for Jack to see this doctor at Walter Reed that Frank knows of and recommended, and Dr. Mackinley wants to do surgery on Jack's bad knee next summer. We've already set the date for early June and made a reservation in the place where patients' families can stay."

"Patrick will be pleased," Mary Beth said. "He's told me a couple of times he's noticed Jack's limp is getting worse. And he doesn't really know any doctors in Arkansas he'd recommend to do this type of surgery right now. I'm really glad too, Mother. Jack is not my real father, but I certainly love and respect him as if he were. I'm so glad you married him, and I know Eleanor is too!" With those words, she hugged her mother and Ella hugged her back, grateful the girls had long since moved passed their initial antagonism to their father's replacement.

Ella sat holding Nora on her lap and said, "I can't get over how much Pat and Nora have changed in the few weeks we've been gone." Ella paused and then said, "I am so grateful you and Patrick live here and I will get to watch these children grow up! It was so hard to leave Eleanor and her son and Ronald also. He is a dear man and a good father."

"We're equally glad you and Jack live her too, Mother. I really missed you both while you were away."

Jack called out, "Are you ready to go home, Ella? This old man is looking forward to sleeping in his own bed."

She was, and after kissing her daughter, grandchildren, and even Patrick, they left, glad to be home.

Ella and Jack knocked on the Lewis' door the next evening at a few minutes before 7:00, wanting to arrive before Lee and Suzanna. Ella had brought an elaborate salad of lettuce and vegetables with two choices of salad dressings and wanted to deliver it before the honored guests came. If they had been five minutes later the two couples would have arrived at the same time.

As it was, Ella and Jack were standing just behind Esther and Michael to greet Lee and Suzanna. Ella was always delighted to see Lee because their friendship went back many years to his first encounter with Daniel. Ella had always accepted Lee without reservations while Daniel had struggled with it once he learned that the two men of different colored skin were kin through the relationship his grandfather had had with a servant.

Ella was immediately taken with Lee's fiancée, who was almost as tall as Lee, with skin only slightly lighter than his. She was smiling, showing beautiful white teeth, with her hair pulled back from her face into a bun that had green ribbons woven through it. She was wearing a flowered dress with a green jacket and green sandals that matched the green of the leaves on her dress. Lee looked handsome in a blue sports coat, a lighter blue shirt, and gray pants. His grin proclaimed how proud he was to be able to introduce his fiancée to his friends.

There was so much food that Esther had put all the food dishes on the breakfast room table, along with six plates and had invited everyone to gather around the serving table and hold hands while Michael said a Jewish blessing, first in Hebrew and then in English. Lee and Suzanna, as the guests of honor, led the way, filling their plates, and then carrying them to the dining room table where they sat sat-by-side. Following their lead, Ella and Jack filled their plates and then sat across the dining room table from Lee and Suzanna. Michael and Esther followed, taking the chairs at each end.

Conversation for the first few minutes centered on the food as they began eating. But soon, Ella, who was dying of curiosity, began asking Suzanna about the Cotton Plant Academy, amazed that a private boarding school for Negroes existed in Arkansas. She wanted to know how and when it was started, what it was like, how many students attend there, how Suzanna had known about it and become a teacher there, what she was teaching, and how she and Jack had met.

After Ella finished listing all the questions she had, Suzanna started laughing as did everyone else.

"Goodness, Ella, you'll have me talking all night. I'm going to try to give you the information you've asked for, but in an abbreviated form so y'all won't get bored. At least, you can be enjoying this wonderful meal, and I'm going to be as brief as possible so I can enjoy it too."

"Now I'm embarrassed and I apologize, Suzanna," said Ella. "You don't have to answer everything that I listed right now. I don't want your supper to get cold."

"Well, maybe I'll just start with a few sentences, and Lee can tell you how we met, and I'll eat while he's talking. First, the Cotton Plant Academy was founded soon after the end of the Civil War by the Northern Presbyterian Church Board of Missions. These Northern Presbyterians founded schools all across the South. The first schools began opening in the early 1860s, but the board didn't open any in Arkansas until the '80s after a new northern Presbytery was organized in the state when a good many African Americans from eastern states began moving here to start new lives. The only academies organized here in Arkansas were the one outside Cotton Plant and one near Arkadelphia.

"Since that time the Academy in Cotton Plant has undergone many changes and growth in new buildings. By 1895 it had almost 200 students and five teachers with living quarters for teachers and female students and started adding rooms for males.

"My family sharecropped on a farm north of Brinkley. My parents knew about the academy and were determined that my sister and I would go there. We had a brother too, but Daddy said he was needed to help work the land. My sister Clemmie and I moved into one of the dorm rooms there in 1926 and loved the school. I graduated in 1930. I had done well and received a full scholarship to LeMoyne College in Tennessee. It had just become a four-year college that year. When I received my degree in English and teaching in 1934, I was offered a position as an English teacher back at the Academy and have been there ever since. They have been good years for me.

"Now I'll let Lee take over and tell you how we met and what our plans are while I enjoy some of this wonderful meal!"

Lee looked at Suzanna with both pride and love as he smiled and said, "You can see why I am a lucky man. I never thought I'd be loved by such a woman! We met at a Negro teachers' conference in Little Rock at Horace Mann School on a Saturday in mid-October not a year ago. We actually sat next to each other in the meeting, and I wish I could tell you all that the speakers said, but I was so taken by this beautiful, intelligent woman that I couldn't stay focused."

Suzanna broke in, "You didn't miss much! I was really disappointed in two of them who spoke about what we already knew—that black schools in general were lagging far behind because they were poorly staffed and supported with inadequate funding. I knew my school was one of the more fortunate because it received a decent amount of money every year from the Northern Presbyterian Church and didn't have to depend entirely on the state."

"She's right about that! We'd be in bad shape here in Myrna if Michael weren't president of the school board and kept them honest in giving us a decent share of the funds allotted to the schools in Craig Country. Of course, I suspect Michal adds a bit from his own pocket, though he won't own up to doing so," Lee said with a smile.

Michael laughed and said, "Now, Lee, you've gone to meddlin' in my private business. Finish telling us how you've gotten this beautiful woman to agree to marry you."

"Well, I have to brag and tell you it wasn't too hard, at least not as hard as I thought it was going to be. You see, I asked her to marry me on our first date, and she laughed and told me I was ridiculous, that we didn't know each other at all. I had driven over from Myrna, and we had gone to a Negro club outside of Brinkley for dinner and dancing. We'd had a good evening together, and I refused to be discouraged.

"We started writing letters to each other almost every day. Also I drove over to see her at least once or twice a month, even slept in my car a couple of times so that we could spend time together on both Saturday and Sunday.

"And we had some real quality time together over the Christmas holidays because I went with her to meet her family in Brinkley and spent a week there. I proposed to her again, and this time she said she was thinking about it. And she said 'yes' in April and agreed to move to Myrna because we had a teaching vacancy at the high school. Mrs. Adams was retiring and we needed an English teacher. That's when Michael met her for the first time." Lee looked at Michael and grinned. "I knew you'd be you impressed!"

"And you were right about that!" Michael replied.

"So when's the wedding going to be? What are you waiting on? The summer is more than half gone," Jack asked with a chuckle.

"We've set the date, four weeks from today at the Cotton Plant Academy Chapel. The truth is we were waiting on you and Ella to get home from Europe. 'Miss' Ella knows we couldn't get married without her. She's been in my corner ever since I first met her. She's my family, along with Michael and Esther—and now you, Jack. The four of you are the only guests on my list. We're not spreading the word around here about when the wedding is going to be. In fact, hardly anyone but you four know the date. The reason I'm not telling anyone here is that the chapel only seats about 30 people, and Suzanna wants all her family and the faculty who live at the school to be there."

"Oh, Lee and Suzanna, I am so happy for you. This is wonderful!" Ella had tears of joy running down her cheeks and was wiping them away with her napkin. "Did you two already know about this?" Ella asked, looking at Esther and Michael.

"Of course," Michael replied. "Lee told us about Suzanna right after he first met her at the teachers' conference. He came by to see us that Sunday afternoon and said, 'I've just met a woman I want as my wife—if I can convince her to marry me. And I'm not going to give up on her until I do!'"

Michael and Esther were both laughing as they looked at Lee lovingly. "We've been keeping up with this relationship as best we could from its beginning, trying to be patient and letting Lee tell us how it was going when he wanted to do so," Esther said, shaking her head and then adding, "but that was hard on me because I wanted to ask him every time we saw him. Yet I had promised Michael I'd hold my tongue and let him tell us when he wanted to. He brought Suzanna by to see us one weekend in March when she had come to see what Myrna was like, and we got to meet her."

"I really liked what I saw," Suzanna said with a big smile, "and I was completely taken with Esther and Michael. I could tell how much they cared about Lee, and that pleased me tremendously. It's so rare to find white people who are completely open to and accepting of black people as equals. These two people are! And Lee assured me that you were too, Ella, and I think that must be true of you also, Jack, or I can't imagine how you would all be such good friends."

Jack spoke up, "I was a Northern Presbyterian before I was called to the church in Myrna. I'm glad to know they sponsored schools in the South for Negroes after the Civil War.

"My father immigrated to this country from Scotland, and his prejudice was against the British, not people of color. My mother was a snob—more about money and social position, but also about race. She had almost no influence on my thinking because I was raised more by my nanny, who was white but poor and had no prejudices against anybody that I was aware of, except maybe against rich snobs like my mother, though she never said a word against her in my presence."

Ella, who definitely had a practical side to her, broke in. "So where are you going to live? Have you found a place or a house yet?"

"Actually, Lee is building us a house in his 'spare time' on a piece of land he bought years ago when he first came home from the war." Suzanna said, smiling. "He owns 10 acres between Myrna and Jonesboro that has a beautiful grove of trees on it, and he's designed a modest home for us with a large kitchen and breakfast area, a living/dining room, two bedrooms, and a bathroom. It's going to have a screened porch that will go around the side and across the back with doors into the kitchen and the dining area. This man I'm marrying is a genius, if you all didn't already know that!"

"Well, we've known he was smart because he graduated from Philander Smith in less than two years, but I didn't know he was an architect!" Ella said. "Lee, have you started building this house?"

"The truth is I started building on it right after I met Suzanna. Of course, I have to do it in when I can make the time, which you teachers know is hard to carve out, especially when you're traveling to see your lady friend every other week or so! But I've got the foundation laid, the scaffolding for the whole house up with siding and a roof, and the kitchen, one bedroom, and the bathroom are finished and livable. The living/dining room and the other bedroom have walls and the underflooring and are unfinished but soon will be. I've had to hire a few friends to help me get it ready enough for us to move into as soon as we're married. I have to say I've been working really hard in what spare time I've had and will be really glad to have it done!"

Suzanna said with a smile and a catch in her voice, "I've never known a man like this one! It really didn't take me long to realize what an exceptional man he is. I've been trying to find ways to help him with this house. He's let me choose flooring and paint colors and kitchen appliances. Also, I've been saving some money over the years because I didn't know whether I'd ever marry, and so I've been able to help out with the building costs a little. It makes me feel that it really is our house. I'm excited because I never thought I would ever live in a new house, a really nice house that I am part-owner of!"

"Well, Lee, I've got some free time these next few weeks before school starts again, and I'll be glad to lend a hand," Jack spoke up. "That can be my wedding gift to you."

"I want to help too—not with the building, of course, but with cleaning and also shopping for things that you need for the kitchen. We should get Sarah involved, Esther. She has all sorts of great ideas and can get things from the store at bargain prices." Ella's eyes were sparkling with excitement. Few things get women more excited than weddings and houses, except maybe babies, and Ella was fairly sure they weren't thinking about that yet.

Suzanna was just about to respond to Ella's enthusiasm when Esther said, her voice trembling, "Something's on fire outside. I see flames and torches outside the living room window. What's happening?"

4

Ella and Jack, who could also see one of the living room windows from their side of the dining room table, now joined in. "It's people with torches! And they're in costumes!" Ella exclaimed.

"That's not a costume. It's Klan members! What is going on?" Jack's voice was more angry than fearful.

"I don't know," Michael said, "but whatever it is, I don't like it. I'm going out to see."

"We'll go with you," Jack and Lee both said at the same time.

"No, I'll go alone." Michael said, "Lee, I have a feeling your being here may have something to do with our uninvited 'company' (and then thinking two might be better than one, added) "Jack, if you want to come with me, I'd be glad to have two of us."

Jack rose and he and Michael went to the front door while Esther went to the phone to call the chief of police. Lee had taken Suzanna's hand, while Ella sat frozen to her chair, afraid of what might happen next.

Michael opened the front door, and he and Jack walked out on the porch as though it was customary for a group of men in white with their faces covered by pointed white hats with openings for eyes and holes for the nostrils and mouth to be standing before them holding flaming torches.

Michael spoke calmly, as though he were greeting friends. "Good evening, Gentlemen. May I ask why you have gathered in front of my house?"

One of the Klansmen spoke up. "We heard you got a nigger inside your house, Mr. Lewis, and we don't have no use for niggers who act uppity like they's somebody. We don't like you having niggers sittin' at your dinner table with you."

"Well, I am afraid you are mistaken, Eddie Carnes, because I don't have any 'niggers' here. I do have as my guests four school teachers whom I am proud to call my friends, and two of them happen to be Negroes. So, Eddie Carnes, I would appreciate it if you and your friends, whose names I am fairly sure I can guess, and who don't have anything else to do here, would leave and allow us to finish our supper together."

The costumed and masked speaker said almost plaintively, "How come you knowed it was me, Mr. Lewis? We don't mean no harm. We's just having a bit of fun."

"I recognized your voice, Eddie. I've known you for a long time, and I know who your friends are. The Chief of Police will soon be paying a call on you. Oh, look, I think that may be his car coming down the street now. I imagine my wife called him as soon as I got up to come see who our visitors were. The Chief doesn't have a very good sense of humor, and I doubt he'll find this 'bit of fun' as you put it, something to laugh about."

While Michael was speaking, he had noticed that several members of the group had begun taking their Klan outfits off and were trying to slip into the shadows so that only three of the seven or eight remained. "Billy Jacobs, I'm guessing you're one of the two remaining, and I'd wager the other is Mick Malloy. Am I right?"

Neither one answered but instead took off running, leaving Eddie Carnes standing there alone. "Eddie, I afraid you don't have very loyal friends. I imagine the Chief is going to want to have a visit with you and your friends who were with you tonight.

"You know, Eddie, I don't think at heart you're really a bad boy, but you sure do some bad things, dumb things. My guess is that the Chief will lock you up for a month or two to let you think about your mistakes—that is unless I speak up on your behalf and ask him to give you one more chance to straighten up and stay out of trouble for a good long while, in fact forever. What do you think about that?"

Eddie Carnes didn't have time to answer because Chief Phillips had pulled up in front of the house, gotten out of the car, and was approaching Eddie with a pair of handcuffs dangling from his arm.

"Evening, Mr. Lewis. Looks like you and Mr. MacLean have the situation well under control. Now, Eddie, I wish I could say I'm surprised to see you, but I'm not. Pulling out your Klan outfit to spread a little terror, huh? Well, it's not Halloween, Eddie. You'll just have to be satisfied finding your excitement spending some time in the jail. Maybe you can scare Ole' Man Haney, who'll be in the cell with you, sleeping it off."

"Mr. Lewis, Mr. Lewis," Eddie called out as he was being pushed into the police car. "You said you'd try to get me out of trouble if I promise to do right!"

"I'll be by the station sometime tomorrow to see you, Eddie. One night in the jail won't hurt you—just maybe give you some time to think about what you really want to do with your life."

Michael turned and he and Jack walked back to the house.

"Are you really going down tomorrow to try to get him out?" Jack asked.

"Yes, I'll go, later in the afternoon to give him time to think about what it will be like if I don't come. Eddie grew up in a really bad family situation. His dad was a mean alcoholic who beat his wife and all his kids when he was drunk. His mother was one too, slept around with anyone who'd have her, which wasn't many. Eddie's had a chip on his shoulder forever. But he's not really

194

stupid. I have this feeling there's something good in him if somebody could help him find it and cultivate it.

"So I'll go and see if I can glimpse the good in him and tempt him to work at bringing it up to the surface and let others see it too. It may not happen, but I feel I've got to give him one more chance." Michael shrugged his shoulders in frustration to express his mere glimmer of hope for Eddie's future as a changed man.

"Michael, you are a better minister than I ever was. I never was faced with a 'down-and-outer' like Eddie."

"Maybe not, Jack, but I've seen what you and Ella have been able to do to challenge and encourage young people to want to improve their lives, to accomplish things they had never thought about before. And maybe, if Eddie had had a couple of teachers like you two, he wouldn't have ended up envious of, jealous of, a Negro man and woman who have achieved, in spite of prejudice and few opportunities, what Lee and Suzanna have made and are continuing to make, of their lives. Everybody deserves a chance, and too many need help that they never receive.

"Jack, I decided a long time ago that if I made money, and I have, I didn't want just to make more money by investing in the stock market or my business. I wanted to invest in people, in helping people have better lives, and that takes money sometimes, but it's so much more than money. It's helping them to like and respect themselves, giving them opportunities and reasons to reach out to others in need of help and providing that help without demeaning those who need it. We all need help at one time or another. You needed it when your church fired you, when your Presbytery didn't support you enough."

"Yes, I did need help. And you were there for me, Michael, taking me out to the co-op farm, and then later, making it possible for me to be hired as a teacher, even though I didn't have a teaching degree. I know I've never thanked you enough!"

"It's not your thanks I want, my friend. My payback is witnessing the difference you've made, both you and Ella, in the school and in the town.

"And that's the way I feel about Lee. I saw excellence in him that had had little opportunity to grow and express itself. I could feel the goodness in him. And he has earned every good thing he has, but my joy comes from the fact that Esther and I have made a small investment that has paid enormous dividends in the relationship we have with him and now Suzanna.

"When we learned that Esther could not have children, it was a huge blow. Lee and now Suzanna have become for us the children we would never have had. And they are investors in people, just as you and Ella are.

"But we need to go back in the house or Lee, Suzanna, Ella, and especially my wife will be worried, wondering what we've been talking about."

Michael took Jack's arm and together the two men walked to the door and went into the house to give a full account of what had happened outside.

5

Michael made his way to the jail the next afternoon shortly after his bank closed its doors to the outside world at 3:00 p.m. His staff remained at work counting money and adding figures and notations to the account books, while the custodian swept floors, emptied trash cans and spittoons, and wiped down counters, window panes, and ledges to prepare the bank for the next day.

Chief Phillips was expecting Michael because he had telephoned the jail in mid-morning to see how Eddie Carnes had comported himself during the night and early morning, and Michael had been pleased to hear that he had been quiet, courteous to his cellmate in spite of his snoring, and to the night staff, and was obviously hoping Michael would act on his word and come by to see him—and maybe get him out.

"Paul, I'm glad the boy has enough sense, and I hope character, to know how to behave when he's gotten himself into trouble.

What I really want from him is the desire to become a decent human being and not get himself into trouble!" Michael looked at the Chief, hoping he might give him some insight into Eddie.

"Well, Michael, I wish I had something really positive to say about this boy, but the truth is I don't know him well enough. He sure comes out of a bad family. I can't tell you how many times we've picked up old man Carnes and let him sleep it off in one of our cells. His wife's no better. We've had to go to their shack and stop him from beating her a couple of times for sleeping around, though it's hard to blame her, he's such a mean drunk. She's tried to leave him at least twice, so I hear, but he always goes and drags her back and hits her as punishment or a sick kind of love, though I'd sure find it hard to call it love!

"The three older children left home as quick as they could find some place to go. You'd think one of 'em might have come and rescued their younger brother, but as far as I know, none of 'em have come back from wherever they ended up. He's goin' to get himself in some real trouble if he doesn't get help."

"I have to say you're not very reassuring, Paul. I may be crazy, but there's something about him that makes me think there's something inside him that is begging to get out and make something of himself, something inside him that knows he can't do that alone and needs help. And I'm not sure why, but I want to give him that opportunity to make something positive out of his life. Would you be willing to release him into my custody and see if I can do anything with him?"

"Michael, what I'm not sure about is that you know what you're doing, what you may be lettin' yourself and your wife in for, but I do know how much you've done for some of our needy folks in Myrna. You and your missus are carin' people, good people. And if you want to take on Eddie Carnes, I'm willin' to take that risk along with you. Do you want him released to you this afternoon?"

"I don't think I do, Paul. I have a notion he may need to spend a couple of more nights in a jail cell. It also might be helpful if he appears in court before a judge, who then turns him over to my custody so it will seem to him that I have some real authority over him. That may give him some real motivation to respect my wife and me and the rules we lay down for him. What do you think?"

"That makes sense to me. I suppose you'll take this up with the city judge. I've heard you and Judge Moore are good friends."

"We've been friends a long time. I'll give him a visit and clue him in to what we've been talking about. If he approves of our plan, I'll let you know. But right now I need to see Eddie and let him know I'm keeping my word to him about visiting him. Depending on how Eddie responds to me, I'll tell him I'm looking into what the city may do about his case and get back to him with what I learn. His behavior through all of this will give me some more information about the kind of boy he may be or want to be!"

"I'll take you back there. Mr. Haney's daughter came and got him out this morning. He's not a mean drunk, just a noisy one. I'm pretty sure Eddie was glad to see him go because he's a smelly drunk too."

Eddie's face lighted up when the Chief and Michael appeared and the Chief unlocked the door so that Michael could visit with Eddie. He then left them alone, with Eddie sitting on his bed which he had made and Michael on the one chair in the room, relieved he didn't have to sit on Mr. Haney's bunk which had not been stripped of its sheet and blanket.

Eddie spoke immediately saying, "I'm so glad to see you, Mr. Lewis. I was gettin' afraid you weren't going to show up."

"Well, Eddie, I have a bank to run, and I can't always just get up and leave whenever I want to. But I'm glad to see you look better than you did last night and that you've even made your bed. So obviously you're doing pretty well. Have you heard anything from your mother or father? Are they getting a lawyer for you?" Michael knew that neither of those had occurred and weren't likely to.

"No, Sir, Mr. Lewis. My folks don't care nothing, I mean anything, about me. I could be dead, and they wouldn't mind. It'd probably just be a relief."

"I'm sorry to hear that, Eddie."

"It don't, doesn't bother me much anymore, Mr. Lewis. They're not very good people."

"Do you care about whether you are a 'good' person or not, Eddie?"

"Sometimes I do. But most of the time, I don't give it much thought because I don't really see what difference it would make. My family don't seem to care one way or the other. Truth is, I just don't really know what a good person is like or how to go about becoming one."

"You know, Eddie, I can see you need a little time to think about the kind of man you want to be, and jail is not a bad place to do that kind of thinking. I'll drop back by tomorrow to see you because I'd really like to hear what you may have to say. What if I told you that I glimpse a good man inside you? What would I be seeing? And what would you or could you do about that? Anyway, I've got to get back to the bank and make sure everything is all right there. I'll see you tomorrow afternoon about this same time."

"Mr. Lewis, I really appreciate you keeping your word and coming to see me today. That don't, doesn't happen to me often. Thank you, Sir!"

"You're very welcome, Eddie. See you tomorrow." And Michael left, feeling that his hunch about the person who was covered up inside Eddie really existed. He'd been polite. He was smarter than he let on—certainly had a better knowledge of grammar than his speech had demonstrated last night. It was obvious there was a different person hiding under that tough-boy façade.

Michael stopped at the bank on his way home to make sure everything had been put away and locked up as he had taught his staff to do, and seeing that all was well, he didn't linger but eagerly headed home to share his idea with his wife.

Esther was in the kitchen preparing their dinner when Michael arrived. They had been married long enough for Michael to know that trying to have an important conversation with his wife while she was cooking was a waste of time. She had asked him too many times not to talk to her while she was making dinner because she couldn't keep her mind focused on what she was doing and what he was telling her without confusing or forgetting one of the other.

His job was to set the table, fill the water glasses when it was time to eat, and otherwise sit in a chair, go through the mail if there was any, read it or any magazine that had come, and just relax until she had the meal ready to serve. His wife asked so little of him that he readily accepted her requests when they were made, and they had lived together for nearly 30 years with only rare moments of irritation, much less anger.

Once they were seated at the table in the kitchen with their supper before them and Esther had told him about her day, which had been pleasant with little activity, Michael felt it was a good time to tell her about his visit with Eddie at the jail. Michael, who knew his wife well and loved her dearly, had learned to approach something he wanted to do slowly, carefully, and thoroughly.

So he started by talking about Eddie Carnes and his poor background, his father and mother and his brothers and sisters and how none of them had succeeded in accomplishing much with their lives. So it looked like Eddie was headed that same way unless something happened to change him. He'd been the ringleader in getting the group of boys to put together Klan wear, make torches with rags tied around sticks, and come to their house to scare their dinner guests, especially Lee and Suzanna.

The Chief of Police had arrested Eddie and put him in jail, and Michael praised Esther again for immediately telephoning Chief Phillips. "Well, I doubt time in the jail did much to help that boy. His family is a total disgrace, and it's obvious Eddie is headed in the same direction." Esther made her statement as fact, nodding her head as emphasis as she said the words.

"Well, my love, I may have to disagree with you a little bit right there. When I went into his cell, he immediately stood up and greeted me. He thanked me for keeping my word and coming to see him, though he'd begun to think I might not. He'd made his bed and had been sitting in the only chair in the cell when I arrived. He offered me the chair and sat on his bed. I told him I was a man of my word. I asked him if he'd heard from his father or mother and if they were getting a lawyer to get him out of jail.

"He told me he hadn't heard a word from them and didn't expect to because they don't care anything about him. He caught himself making some grammatical errors with verbs and corrected himself several times while we were talking, which surprised me, but pleased me too, because it showed he'd been paying attention in school and knew the correct way of speaking but didn't have much practice using correct grammar because he wasn't around people who used it.

"He actually said he didn't know what good people were like because he hadn't spent much time with 'good' people. He thought he'd like a be a good person, but he didn't really know what that meant or how to be one. I told him I could see the beginnings of a good person inside him and that I hoped he'd spend some time in jail thinking about what it would take for him to become a 'good' person. I told him I'd be back to see him tomorrow and we'd talk then about what that might or could mean for him."

"Michael, did you really see some possibility in him of becoming a 'good person' as you put it?"

"Esther, I truly did. I think he's hungry to be a good person, but he hasn't received much help. And that's what I want to talk over with you."

"Oh, Michael, my dear, good husband, this obviously involves me in some way. Go ahead and tell me what ideas you have to 'save' Eddie Carnes."

"You make me sound like some kind of 'revivalist preacher' but yes, I do have a kind of plan that involves you—us. After he's spent another couple of nights in jail, I want to bring him here to stay with us for two or three weeks and let him get a taste of what a good life can be like."

"Just two or three weeks? Are you sure we won't be taking him on for life?" Esther asked, her reluctance displaying itself in her tone as well as her words.

"Yes, I'm sure, because I want to get him into the CCC, the Civilian Conservation Corps, in case you'd forgotten what the CCC is," Michael said, realizing Esther needed information about this New Deal program. "This is one of FDR's programs to help young, single men find something constructive and healthy to do with themselves when they can't find jobs in their home towns. The CCC takes any single man who is willing to work at improving or creating national parks by planting trees or building roads or structures for offices or housing or lodges. Every man gets a place to live and work along with clothing to wear, and he is paid a dollar a day. It's a little bit like the military in that respect. But they don't follow the whole military regimen and practices. Instead, the men keep a little money to spend at the canteen store and send the rest of the 25-plus dollars home to their mothers to help pay the family bills.

"I have a couple of friends in Washington I plan to call and ask about how to get Eddie enrolled, provided he's willing. I don't want him to get used to staying here and thinking he's found an easy life. But I really don't think that's who he is deep down. Would you be willing to let him live with us for a couple of weeks?" Michael's voice relayed his genuine concern for the boy and his hope for Esther's agreement to give his plan a try.

"I will, if, and this is an important if, you can get hold of your 'friends' and find out how plausible your plan is, that is—can you tell me honestly that we could get Eddie into the CCC and that he will give it his honest effort to make it work?" Esther looked at him, her concern showing in her eyes and facial expression.

"I will try to telephone one of my friends right now—or as soon as we finish our dinner—and see what I can find out about how to get him into the CCC. I can say only that I have a genuine feeling, actually a belief, that Eddie will take this opportunity to do something constructive with his life, and if he doesn't, we won't allow him to stay here, and I will leave him to be master of his own fate. How's that?" And he waited for his wife's answer, fairly sure he knew what it would be.

Esther took a deep breath and let it out slowly. "All right, my love. Make your phone call after supper."

7

To his surprise he was able to get a phone call through to Senator Hattie Caraway that same evening. She was always willing to talk to her constituents in Arkansas and was most interested in hearing what Michael had to say about wanting to help Eddie Carnes get away from his family and background and start a new life through something like the CCC. She promised to get Michael the information about CCC projects in North Carolina and east Tennessee, both of which would be far enough away from Arkansas to offer him a way of escaping the poverty and life style of his parents.

Esther had to admit that she was impressed he had actually been able to talk with Senator Caraway and that she was interested in helping him help Eddie. She was even more impressed when Senator Caraway called again the following night to give Michael the information he needed about both camps.

Michael visited Eddie the next day and told him he had talked with the Chief of Police and Myrna's city judge about releasing Eddie to his care for the next few weeks. He had received Judge Morrison's and the Chief's permission to take Eddie to stay with him and Mrs. Lewis while they tried to make some arrangements about his future. But Michael told Eddie that all of this was Eddie's to decide whether he was willing to be under the care of Michael and his wife instead of remaining in prison.

Eddie looked at Michael in disbelief. "You've gotten permission to get me out of prison and take me to stay in your home if I'm willing? That's for real?"

"Yes, Eddie. That's for real. But you need to know that if you come to stay with Mrs. Lewis and me, you have to live by our rules. They're not hard rules, but they are rules. You have to stay at home. That means you can't go out carousing with your friends at all. You have to make your bed and keep your room picked up and clean. You have to help Mrs. Lewis with any chores around the house whenever she asks, and that won't be hard because she is used to doing all her own work. And you have to answer 'yes, sir' or 'yes, ma'am' when we ask you to do something reasonable. When we have guests, you are to show them the same respect that you show us. That's about all. Do you have any questions?"

"No, Sir." Eddie answered quickly.

"Can you obey our rules if you come to stay with us?" Michael asked, his voice stern.

"Yes, Sir. Thank you, Mr. Lewis, thank you. And tell your wife I'm really grateful for this opportunity," Eddie said, his voice quivering with emotion.

"You'll be able to tell her that yourself, Eddie, and I hope you will. And I hope you will see us both as caring adults. I don't think you've had a lot of experience with adults who really were interested in your well-being. Well, Esther and I are, but what happens with that is really up to you. You have one last night here to think about what you are agreeing to and to change your mind if you want to. But I'll be by tomorrow afternoon to take you home with me if you're still willing. I'm looking forward to that. I hope you are too." Michael wanted to hug the boy before he left, but he refrained and instead patted his shoulder and smiled.

Eddie, who had stood during Michael's last speech, sat down on his cot, feeling the iron springs through the thin mattress and tried to imagine what it would be like to sleep in a real bed in a house where people might actually care about him. It seemed too good to be true. In his almost 18 years of living it was something he had never experienced firsthand, though he had glimpsed it from a distance in the lives of others his age. He made up his mind to do whatever was asked of him and prove he was worthy of their interest in him, not daring to believe they could really care about—or better still—actually love him someday!

The Lewises' time with Eddie turned out better than any of them expected. The boy was so eager to obey and please that Esther eventually told him to quit worrying about whether he was doing everything she wanted him to and working so hard to be perfect. It was obvious even to her that under his "smart alec" façade there was a good boy, even a sweet one.

Michael and Esther took him with them to Lee and Suzanna's wedding in Cotton Plant. It was the first time Eddie had been around educated black people, and he was both surprised and impressed with the behavior of those at the wedding and the reception afterwards. The Lewises and Eddie along with Jack and Ella MacLean were the only white people at the wedding, but no one seemed to mind or notice, least of all the bride and groom or the black guests. Michael had told Lee about his and Esther's decision to give Eddie a chance to become a good man and asked for permission to bring him to their wedding. He also wanted them to come to dinner as soon as possible once they had returned from their honeymoon and give them a chance to know Eddie and vice versa.

Lee, who knew how much both Esther's and Michael's friendship had benefitted him, immediately said that he and Suzanna would be delighted to come to dinner any time after August 6 when they were officially moving into their new home. While they remembered Eddie as being the leader of the group of boys who had appeared dressed as Klansmen and carrying torches the night they had come to dinner at Michael and Esther's, they understood that the Lewises were trying to make a difference in this young man's life. Since that is what he and Suzanna always hoped to do as teachers, they'd come and do their best to give Eddie a glimpse of who they were because of and in spite of the color of their skin. They had done that and found Eddie to be so different from what they understood he had been that Lee offered him a job helping finish the building of their house. Eddie actually had some carpentry skills that he hadn't known he had.

Because Eddie's only means of transportation to and from their house was Michael's car with Michael as his chauffeur, Lee and Suzanna invited him to stay with them in their newly finished second bedroom. With Michael and Esther's okay, he did so and his help enabled Lee and Suzanna to get the entire house finished a week earlier than they had expected to, a real bonus for them because it was nearing the end of August and school would soon be starting.

The best outcome from Eddie's time with Lee and Suzanna was that they accepted Eddie as a younger brother and Eddie ceased even to notice that their skin was darker than his!

After Michael had gotten all the information about the CCC and the work it was doing in the Blue Ridge Mountains of North Carolina, he and Esther drove Eddie to the camp and had a difficult time leaving him there because they had become accustomed to having him around and had grown to love this young man who promised to become someone they would be proud to claim as their son. He had ended staying with them six weeks instead of two, though one of those weeks he had been at Lee and Suzanna's.

Both Michael and Esther had told Eddie they didn't need the part of his one-dollar-a-day salary that would be sent home every month and were moved to tears when he said he wanted Lee and Suzanna to get the money, and they watched him write Mr. and Mrs. Lee Jones and their address on the paper he signed to make that happen.

8

Jack and Ella had not forgotten their intention of thanking the people of Myrna for the generous gift of money they had given them to use during their trip to England. The problem was they had no idea who or even how many had contributed to the fund. After talking it over with each other for days, they decided the best thing they could do was to invite everybody in town, both white and black, to a picnic in the city park. Jack took their idea to the town's mayor who thought it was a great idea, and they set the date for the last Sunday afternoon in August starting at 5:00 in the afternoon, hoping the late time would make the summer heat more bearable.

Jack and Ella worked on an invitation that they would buy space for as an ad in *The Myrna Courier*, hoping it would attract enough attention that everyone, especially those who had given money for their trip but even those who hadn't would understand they were welcomed to join the fun. Knowing there was no way they would be able to provide food for everyone, they decided that they would make a number of cakes and buy the fixings for ice cream and then ask those who had an ice cream freezer to bring it to the park and help make enough ice cream for everybody to have some. They decided to call it an "End of Vacation" pot-luck picnic and not even mention the monetary gift they had received, not wanting to embarrass anyone who had not contributed. The newspaper editor offered to run the "ad" for free since the picnic was open to the entire town.

Jack would make a couple of remarks about their trip and how much they had enjoyed their time in England but how good it was to be back home with friends. Jack would also talk a little about the Naval Academy where they had left their son Dan to begin his first year as a Fourth Class Midshipman. And Ella would bring greetings from their daughter Nellie, who now went by her birth name of Eleanor and who had given birth to a son while they were there. She would be happy to display her photographs of Eleanor and the baby but also of some of the other pictures she had taken while they were in England.

When they shared their ideas with their close friends like John and Sarah Banks, Michael and Esther Lewis, and their daughter Mary Beth and her husband Dr. Patrick Nolan, who in turn told his partner Jeffrey Anderson and his wife Helen, they all offered to bring their ice-cream makers and also make cakes.

The town had gotten accustomed to monthly "get togethers" at the school during the year, pot-luck suppers with programs featuring their students and often ending with music, singing and even dancing led by musicians from both town and country who just liked to "jam" and had started their own bands or combos. The ad in the newspaper invited anybody who had an instrument and wanted to play to bring it and provide music from the town's bandstand in the park. A group of men in the town had built it during the last summer and now it was used for speeches, awards, and other events during the year when people could enjoy gathering outside for programs open to the entire community.

Some of their friends worried about how the town might act if Negroes were included as guests, but Jack and Ella assured them that they couldn't imagine anyone would start anything. But just to make certain, Jack informed the Chief of Police that they expected some Negroes to attend, faculty members from the Negro school, some staff of the white/Negro clinic that Ella's first husband had founded and that was still going strong, and farmers and other folks whom Michael Lewis' bank had helped. Jack also passed the word out to their white friends to reach out to and welcome any black folks who came to the picnic.

The day arrived and the picnic turned out to be a great success. Michael and Esther had brought Suzanna and Lee Jones with them. Soon they were in the middle of a group of whites: retired pastor John Banks and his wife Sarah, the Rev. and Mrs. Greg Mitchell from First Presbyterian Church and their four children, Hank and Ruth Fredrick and their two sons, along with Ella and Jack's daughter Mary Beth with Patrick, her doctor- husband, and their two children. So much laughter was coming from them as they all took turns turning the handle on the ice cream maker or played horseshoes that others joined them.

And even better, the families that had brought along some of their Negro servants to help with children, seeing that there were whites and blacks who were talking and laughing and playing games together, loosened up and became part of an integrated afternoon—one that was still predominantly white but in which blacks and whites for a few hours laughed, played, and ate together more as equals than as servant and master.

Even a few of Morton School's Negro teachers came with their children to meet Lee's new wife. Michael, who was a long-time member of the school board took Esther over to meet them and tell them how glad they were to see them there. Jack and Ella, as the hosts, did the same.

In fact, Jack and Ella were so totally delighted with the outcome of the picnic and its interracial overtones that they wondered if this is what life in Myrna could be like some day, perhaps in the not too distant future. They hoped it might be so.

Part VII

Studies and Surgery: 1937–1938

Fall 1937

1

The last few days of summer passed quickly. Dan had continued to write long letters home every week, and Ella learned from Lilly, Dan's high school girlfriend, she was hearing from him, too. She and Dan had agreed she should date when she went to the university, and she had already been on a couple of dates, but so far she had not been out with anybody who really interested her. She wanted to hear from Ella all they had learned about the Naval Academy. Dan had written her mostly about what life was like as a lowly Midshipman 4th class. Ella was happy to share her and Jack's impressions of the Academy and told her about the young Midshipman 2nd class who had shown them around and who was from Cape Girardeau.

Lilly had signed up for rush at the University of Arkansas and was looking forward to meeting the girls in three sororities that had heard about her and had sent her letters with invitations to their rush parties to be held the week before classes actually began. She was a bit nervous about having to meet and make a good impression on the girls in Pi Phi, Chi Omega, and Zeta Tau Alpha, but she was going with an open mind and would see which, if any, of these she would like to join, or even be invited to join.

Ella and Jack missed Dan's presence in the house and in their lives but slowly began to get used to the quietness of no loud music being played on his radio upstairs that seemed to echo throughout the house and no feet bounding up the stairs two at a time.

Before it seemed possible, the new school year began with new students' names for Jack and Ella to learn. The 10th-grade classes were always a bit of a challenge because Jack and Ella had not previously taught these young people. Of course, some of them were siblings of older students or had already made a name for themselves through school activities of some kind, and their names were easier to remember or learn quickly.

Most helpful was that the students had already been in the school for grades seven, eight, and nine and had heard so much about Jack and Ella's teaching methods that they not only knew a lot about what to expect but were excited about being in their classes. Consequently, Ella and Jack spent hours every summer trying to come up with different ideas and planning what they could do to make each "beginning" just a little bit different.

2

The first Bible study group meeting after its summer break gathered in the fellowship hall of the Presbyterian church. Father John Banks, who had led the group for many years, was pleased to see they had not lost any of their members over the summer. In fact, the group now included both Presbyterians and Episcopalians along with its Jewish members, Michael and Esther Lewis, who had been faithful members now for almost 20 years. Tonight the study group was welcoming a new couple, one of whom was Jewish. Ruth and Hank Fredrick had been invited to attend by Michael and Esther. The Fredricks had emigrated from Germany by way of England and New York City where they had been welcomed by the Jewish community there and learned about Myrna from Michael and Esther's families. It had sounded like a good place to settle, far enough from Germany that Hank would be safe from Nazi scientists who had wanted him to work with them on developing atomic energy as a weapon of war, and where his wife and children would be safe from Hitler's soldiers who were arresting Jews.

Thanks to Michael's contacts, Hank had easily found a job as a math professor at Arkansas State College, a fairly new college but one that was growing larger every year.

Father John Banks, who had brought Michael and Esther into the group years before, now welcomed Ruth and Hank, saying it gave him joy to have the Lord's chosen people studying and discussing biblical passages together. He gave both Hank and Ruth time to tell a little bit about themselves for those in the group who had not met them previously to get to know some facts about them.

Hank began by saying, "We are obviously Germans who have left our country because it has been taken over by Nazis under the rule of Adolph Hitler. We both needed to get out, I because I have some scientific knowledge that the Nazis wanted me to use to help them create horrible weapons. I obviously chose to leave my country rather than do so. I'll let my wife speak for herself."

Ruth said, "I am so grateful to be here as a practicing Jew and yet am not afraid of being arrested and put in some kind of prison. I thank you that as Christians you have welcomed us here to study your Holy Book.

"What is happening to the Jewish people in my country is horrible, and I grieve over it. My parents wouldn't leave when we did. Now I doubt they could leave regardless of how badly they might want to do so. I am glad my sons are growing up in a free nation, and I pray they will always live in freedom. That's enough from me."

"Thank you, Hank and Ruth for sharing a bit of your history with us. We're delighted to have you join our discussions," Father Banks said.

"Tonight I want us to explore First Corinthians, chapter 13," and he read it to them aloud, having them follow the reading in their Bibles. He then asked them to share with the group any feelings or thoughts they had about faith, hope, and charity as the three highest virtues, with the greatest of them being charity. His question surprised his class because while all of them were familiar with the passage, except for Michael, Esther, and Ruth, they had not given these words much thought.

"I suppose charity requires us to be generous with those who have less than we do, those who are in need of food or clothing or even lodging," Frank Simpson spoke up.

"I have to say I find it interesting charity is considered the most important because I would have thought it would be faith, though to be honest I hadn't thought about it at all until you asked the question, Father Banks," Paul Henderson added.

"What does charity mean to all of you who are sitting here thinking about this question I've posed? What does a charitable person do? How does he or she relate to someone who might need charity?" Father Banks looked at his class members expectantly.

"It means we need to be aware of those around us who are in need of help—money, clothing, food, the necessities of life, even friendship." Esther spoke up. "We Jews have charity toward others as one of our responsibilities also."

"Yes, you do, and I must say the Jews I have known are very generous with their charitable acts." Father Banks smiled at Esther.

"Well, I was thinking charity might involve more than the giving of material things," Ella said hesitantly. "We should also be charitable in the way we think about and act toward people who are not necessarily like us, haven't had the advantages we've had. It's kind of like giving people who are 'different' the benefit of the doubt rather than treating them as 'less than' we are."

"That's an interesting thought, Ella." Michael said. "It's a whole different way of thinking about charity, isn't it? It's more about understanding and acceptance and being willing to offer people our caring about them instead of looking down on them as not being as worthy or as important as we are."

"That's not how I look at or think about charity at all," Fred Benson broke in. "I see it as a kind of civic or even a religious responsibility to work within organizations and churches to recognize needs within the community and join together as people who have so much to try to help those in need. We certainly do that here in Myrna. We have the Rotary Club and other groups and our churches who do those things." Fred, who was the current president of the Rotary Club, nodded his head for emphasis as he spoke the last sentence.

Father Banks smiled and said quietly, "Most of the things that have been mentioned mesh with our understandings of what charity is and what it asks of us. But what if I told you that the Greek word that is used in First Corinthians 13 is *agape*, a word that really means love, the highest and best kind of love, the kind of love God has for us? I'm sure those of you who have been to seminary know this but remained silent to give others time to begin sorting through their own understandings of charity.

"I have to say Ella, Michael, and Esther came closest to thinking about charity as providing something more than, other than, material goods. What would it do to your understanding and thinking if we translate the word charity as love? Esther, would you please read this chapter out loud, substituting the world love for charity? I ask you to think about what difference the word love makes in the way you understand this passage and to ask yourselves about what Paul's words mean, or might mean, to us today?"

Though I speak with the tongues of men and of angels, and have not love, I am become as sounding brass, or a tinkling cymbal. And though I have the gift of prophecy, and understand all mysteries, and all knowledge; and though I have all faith, so that I could remove mountains, and have not love, I am nothing. And though I bestow all my goods to feed the poor, and though I give my body to be burned, and have not love, it profits me nothing. Love suffers long, and is kind; love envies not; love vaunts not itself, is not puffed up, does not behave itself unseemly, seeks not her own, is not easily provoked, thinks no evil; rejoices not in iniquity, but rejoices in the truth; bears all things, believes all things, hopes all things, endures all things.

Love never fails: but whether there be prophecies, they shall fail; whether there be tongues, they shall cease; whether there be knowledge, it shall vanish away.

For we know in part, and we prophesy in part. But when that which is perfect is come, then that which is in part shall be done away. When I was a child, I spoke as a child, I understood as a child, I thought as a child; but when I became a man, I put away childish things.

For now we see through a glass, darkly; but then face to face: now I know in part; but then shall I know even as also I am known. And now abide faith, hope, and love, these three; but the greatest of these is love.

"It makes all the difference in my understanding of this passage," Justin Wall spoke up.

"Okay, Justin, but can you describe the way it makes a difference to you?" Father Banks pushed him to go further.

"I have to admit that charity to me is doing something to help somebody who is in need, somebody who is poor or down and out. And if I give that person some money, I am being kind, helpful, and it's not bad, but I'm generally doing it out of pity and maybe a bit of guilt because I can afford to help him out a little bit and doing so relieves me of my guilt and makes *me* feel good about what a fine person I am.

"But if I do it out of love for 'my brother, my friend' or even out of my love for Jesus, I have a completely different motivation and feeling about it. I'm not explaining this very well, but I can feel the difference the two words make in my motivation," Justin said haltingly but with genuine feeling. "At least, I don't think I'd have any feelings of being 'better than' or 'superior' to the person. I would be acting out of genuine caring and love for the person and not to make me feel good about myself."

"I think Justin is right on target," Milton Brown chimed in. "I was trying to think how to clarify the difference between charity and love, and Justin did it for me. When we really do something out of love for another person, it's not self-serving, not to make ourselves feel good, not even just out of pity. Using the word love instead of charity really does make a difference in the way I feel and think when I read this passage."

Almost everyone spoke up or nodded in agreement. Father Banks had noted that Fred and his wife had remained silent, so he said, "Fred, I think something about changing the wording is bothering you. Would you be willing to share whatever it is with us?"

"It's not so much that it's bothering me, but it is concerning to my wife. Edith believes that the Bible is the very word of God and when we start changing those words, we are sinning against God. So if the Bible says *charity*, we humans ought not substitute *love* for it."

"I know there are many people who feel that same way about the Bible," Father Banks said. "The problem is that the Bible all of us grew up reading and thinking of as the Word of God is not God's original word. It's a translation. The first part of the Bible that we call the Old Testament was written in Hebrew and was copied on scrolls and then translated into Greek and into Latin and other languages, including English. The part we call the New Testament was first written down in the Greek the ordinary people spoke, not in the classical Greek of some of Greek literature. This *koine* Greek was later translated into Latin and other languages including English.

"The Bible most of us grew up hearing read in church and have a copy of at home is the King James Version. It was translated into English in the early 1600s at the command of King James I of England. There were other translations into other languages, including English, before then, but this version became known as the Authorized Version because it was done by scholars on order by the authority of the British King, James I.

"So what we've been reading as God's Word to us for the past 300 years is actually a translation by learned men who have taken the Hebrew language of the First or Old Testament and the Greek words of the New Testament and put them into English as best they could with the knowledge they had of Hebrew and Greek."

"So why do we read this book and believe that what it says is God's Word?" Fred asked. It was obvious from his voice that he was upset.

"Because even though it was written down by human beings in whatever language they could speak and write, the writers believed, trusted, God was speaking to them, using these words to communicate with us humans," Jack said. "Even though we can't read God's message in its original language, we believe God opens our hearts and minds to what He's saying to us, first through the life and teachings of His Son Jesus and through the gift of the Holy Ghost, who helps us understand."

"But what about the Jews who don't accept Jesus as God's Son or believe in the Holy Ghost?" Fred asked. "They only read the Torah. I think that's what it's called."

Michael spoke up. "Some of us Jews are more willing to explore other beliefs and even admit Christians have some understandings of God we can find helpful as we try to live as God's people on earth at this time. I've even read that several groups of scholars are working on new translations of your present Bible, updating the language so people in today's world can read and understand its message better. We Jews are still using the original Hebrew."

"So the scriptures you read are all in Hebrew?" Fred asked.

"Well, yes and no. I need to explain. The original Hebrew Bible had no vowels. So sometimes it was difficult to figure out what a word really was, what it meant. Then sometime around the 11th century I think it was, a group of Hebrew scholars created the vowels, which are really symbols more than letters, and added them to the scrolls. And those symbols are still used today. So even the Jewish faith has updated its Hebrew language, though that happened almost a thousand years ago, a few centuries earlier than the time the King James English Version was written,"

Father Banks smiled. "I do give our Jewish brethren credit for still relying on learning the original language and being able to read and speak it. Many pastors study Hebrew and Greek in seminary, and while we are grateful for our King James translation, we also look forward to the new scholarship we trust will help our under-standing of God's Word to us in Holy Scripture."

"We've kind of gotten off track from First Corinthians 13," Jack said. "I'd like to hear from some of the rest of you about your preference for charity or love in this passage."

220

Frances Brooks said, "That's a hard question. We were taught early on in my home that charitable giving was part of a Christian's responsibility as a follower of Jesus. We are to help those in need. I think we still should be aware of those who are needy."

"I was also thinking along those lines," Marjory Schmidt chimed in. When I was growing up, we had an alms box at the entry to the church. Worshipers were encouraged to put a few coins in it every time we entered the sanctuary. We children called it the 'poor box' because the money was supposed to go to help poor people. These people had no faces for me. I dropped the money in because my mother or daddy handed it to me, and they would say, 'Doesn't that made you feel good? You've helped somebody. That pleases God.' But I don't think it made me feel that good. And I realize I did it to please my parents, not God."

"Agape, or real love, truly caring about another person, asks more of us than dropping a few coins in an offering plate, don't you think?" Jim Schmidt spoke up. "I know that this Depression has made me aware of the really hard times many people in our town have been going through. I've gotten to know and visit with a few of the families because they shop at my grocery store.

"And I've grown to care about them because my family lived in Germany during the war. Although I was a child when we came to this country, I remember the stories Daddy told me about being hungry. I look at these families who are suffering because of the Depression, and I feel a kind of relationship to them. When I give them food, I tell them it's not charity but a way of remembering my dad and what life was like in Germany during the war years. And I feel a kind of love inside." Jimmy's voice broke as he finished his story.

"You are right on target, Jimmy," Father Banks said softly. "That is *agape* sharing, not charity bestowing. I believe that many, maybe most, of us frequently experience that kind of love for others but don't know how to name it because love in our culture so often means romantic or sexual love except when we are speaking of our love for our children and family members. We accept our *agape* love for them as being normal, but rarely think of its being appropriate to feel for others or for our country or city and the people who inhabit it."

"Wonder what life would be like here in Myrna or Arkansas or our country or the world if we, or at least most of us, felt and acknowledged the kind of love you're talking about, Father Banks," Susan Todd said. "You've made me start thinking about my motivation for giving. Is it from a kind of guilty conscience because my family and I have been blessed with more than somebody else? I have to admit, I think that's part of it, maybe most of it. Do I even see the people I'm giving to as my friends, as someone I care about, or am I doing it simply to make me feel better about who I am so I won't feel guilty because I've been blessed?"

"Why don't we all give that idea some thought over the next couple of weeks and perhaps we can share our thinking with one another the next time we meet," Father Banks said. When most of the group nodded in agreement, he asked them to join hands as he closed them with prayer.

3

Two weeks later when the Bible study group gathered again in the basement of First Presbyterian Church, it was immediately obvious that Fred and Edith Benson were missing. When Father Banks asked if anyone knew the reason they were not there, Susan Todd spoke up. "I do. Edith is a good friend of mine, and she was shocked by the idea that the King James Bible she and her mother read from together every day is *not* the very Word of God. She thinks we are being heretics when we do not accept our Bible as the literal Word of God. They have started attending a different church, the new one that's out off the highway to Jonesboro."

"I'm truly sorry to hear that, Susan, but thank you for telling us. I do know a little about that church because I called on the pastor soon after he moved to Myrna to lead a group that believes every word in the King James Bible is literally from God. Their faith even calls for them to handle poisonous snakes in order to demonstrate their trust in God's power. He was not at all interested in joining the Ministerial Alliance because he very frankly said we were not true Christians if we did not accept every word in the Bible as God's actual message to us. It is truly sad when servants of the LORD cannot accept one another if our beliefs are not all exactly the same."

"What about you, Father Banks. Do you think every word in the Bible comes from God's mouth or mind or whatever?" Susan asked.

"That's a difficult question to answer, Susan, because so many people have very different understandings of what 'the word of God' actually means. For many people the words in the Bible were literally spoken by God or were divinely given to human beings to speak for God, in place of God. While we Anglicans and Presbyterians believe divine inspiration is behind the words of the Bible, many of us question that every word in the Bible comes straight from God's mouth or mind or heart. Some are human interpretations or understandings of what we think God is saying to us. Some may be just what we humans want to hear from God. Or we reject them because we don't want to hear the message.

"For many of us, being a follower of Jesus and a believer in God, the Father of Jesus, means we have to study the words of the Bible and seek to grasp the true message God has for us in the words of this Holy Book. Yet we do not always read or understand a passage the same way when we study it or try to hear its message to us in a certain way.

"Maybe the truth is that God can speak to us in different ways at different times, depending on what the situation is and what kind of help or leading we need from the One who knows all.

"Does any of what I've just said help you at all? For me it means being open to the presence of God, to what we sometimes refer to as the Holy Ghost, though personally I prefer the word Spirit instead of Ghost." Father Banks sounded a bit doubtful that his words were communicating his deep thoughts about his faith.

It was Hank Fredrick, who rarely said a word during a Bible study, who spoke first. "You've made a point, Father Banks, I think is crucial in studying Scripture. And that point is God speaks to us in different ways at different times. Understanding Scripture is not just about what the words say. That is certainly an important part.

"But what makes a difference is how open our hearts and minds are to hearing—feeling—understanding—what God is saying to us in a particular time or situation. And that may happen to each of us when something in life has thrown something at us we weren't expecting and don't know how to deal with but at the same time opens us to hear, think about, grasp what God is telling us to do or feel or think at this particular moment.

"I know I'm not expressing myself very well. It's just I've at times felt God's leading me, even pushing me to go in a direction I hadn't considered taking. Being here in Arkansas is certainly one of those times, and I am so grateful for God's leading us, and my family and I were willing to be led."

Without thinking, Michael and Esther said at the same time, "We understand hearing God's voice that way and are here because of it."

Father Banks smiled and said, "My brothers and sisters, I have no doubt all of you here have had that same experience of being surprised by doing something you hadn't expected to do. You just didn't think about it as being a 'God inspired action.' One of the weaknesses of our churches is we are not practiced in recognizing God at work in our lives. It is my prayer that coming together to study and discuss God's Word will help us develop and grow in this kind of awareness." And with no prompting, the entire group said as one, "Amen!"

Summer 1938

Jack's Surgery

1

It wasn't just Dan's future Ella worried about. While the United States remained neutral, President Roosevelt had managed to get the government at least to put money and materials into providing aid to the British, should war come, as it was looking more and more likely to happen. As loath as Americans were to fighting another war, it was obvious that if they didn't help the English and the French stand up against Germany, Hitler would take over and spread his prejudices against Jews and people of color, and who knew how far he might go in his desire to conquer other nations and spread his hatred. Ella continually worried about her daughter Eleanor and her family in northern England.

Hitler had already shown his intentions of moving into eastern Europe by invading Austria in February of '38 and then assuming control of the Austrian government in March, having called for a popular vote that favored unification with Nazi Germany, an act many saw as forced by the Nazis and was simply naked aggression.

Yet many Americans were split in their opinions of Adolf Hitler's actions. Charles Lindberg, a famous American airplane pilot, openly supported Nazi Germany and pro-Nazi groups in the United States. And for several years Spain had been involved in a brutal civil war between Republican forces, backed by Russia, fighting against the Spanish Nationalists, who had support from Hitler's Nazi Germany and Mussolini's Fascist Italy. And it was the support the Nationalists received from the Nazis that won out and took over Spain with General Francisco Franco as head of the government.

Although President Roosevelt had been speaking of the possibilities and dangers of war for over a year, Americans did not seem to be taking the war threat seriously. Ella and Jack, along with Michael Lewis and Hank Fredrick, were among the few people in Myrna who were keeping up with what was going on in Europe. But nobody in Myrna was paying much attention to what was happening in the Far East, where the Japanese had been moving into China and taking control of large areas.

2

As the school year neared its end Jack and Ella's thoughts were occupied by Jack's upcoming knee surgery at Walter Reed Hospital in Silver Springs, Maryland, scheduled for June 6. Their train tickets had delivered them to Washington on June 5 where they then took a bus to Silver Springs, and a taxi to Healing House. They were grateful their trip had been without problems.

As soon as they had checked in to their two-room apartment, Ella had telephoned Chaplain Mark McGinnis at the Naval Academy to tell him who she was and that she and her husband had arrived at Healing House where they would spend the night and then be at Walter Reed Hospital early the next morning for Jack's surgery, and she asked if he would please get that message to Midshipman 3rd Class Dan Wood. The Chaplain, who had become very familiar with the MacLeans through their son who had made a good impression on him and was doing well at the Academy, assured her he would let Dan know that very evening so that he might call if he could get to a pay phone. Ella thanked him and gave him their room number as well as the phone number for Healing House. He told her he would keep both Mr. MacLean and her in his prayers and hoped to visit with them at Walter Reed when it would be convenient.

Ella was overjoyed when Dan managed to call before 9:00 even though he couldn't talk long, but said he would ask for permission to leave the Academy to come to Walter Reed to see Jack and her late Monday afternoon.

The sun was just peeking through some clouds early the next morning when Jack and Ella got into the taxi they had asked the desk clerk to call for them and told the driver to take them to Walter Reed Hospital. Dr. Mackinley had written Jack to check in by 6:00 a.m. where he would be taken to the surgical waiting room to be examined by an intern and have all his vital signs checked and recorded.

As soon as the intern was done, another young doctor appeared to take several additional X-rays of Jack's knee. He told Jack and Ella Dr. Mackinley would be in to talk to both of them and go through the surgery he planned to perform on Jack after he'd had time to study the newest X-rays and compare them with the ones he had taken of Jack's knee the previous summer.

They didn't have to wait long before Jonathan Mackinley appeared, smiling and saying he was pleased that although the X-rays showed some additional deterioration and infection around the kneecap, it was not as much as he had feared it might be since almost a year had gone by from when the original pictures were taken. He then proceeded to draw a diagram of Jack's knee on a chalk board and show them the areas of infection he intended to clean out, the new kneecap he intended to use to replace the old one, and how this one would be able to bend and move to allow Jack to walk and sit and even to dance if he didn't go too wild with his movements. Both Jack and Ella laughed and assured him there was no reason for worry there!

When Ella asked how long this kind of surgery usually took, Dr. Mackinley said Jack should be done and be back in his room in three or four hours after the orderly came to take him to surgery. The orderly would show Ella where the waiting room was, and Dr. Mackinley would see her after the surgery to tell her how it had gone and even take her into recovery to see Jack for herself. Usually the patient stayed in recovery until he regained more-or-less full consciousness. Dr. Mackinley then would call an orderly to take Jack and Ella to the hospital room where Jack would be staying for the next week.

This hospital was so much larger than any Ella had ever been in she had to make herself pay attention to where they were going and how they arrived at Jack's room so she would be able to get back there on her own.

Jack was so preoccupied with concern about his wife being all alone during this operation and during his recovery time he paid little attention to where they were taking him, feeling sure he would soon get familiar enough with the hospital he would be able to get around. After all, he'd been in a big hospital in London where, despite sometimes having difficulty understanding what nurses or aides were saying to him because of their various English accents, he had not only survived but even thrived. He was much more concerned about leaving Ella on her own for the week he would be in the hospital.

Ella barely had time to get Jack's clothes placed in drawers or hung in the closet before an young orderly came to take him to surgery. She followed them to the door leading into a waiting room where he told her to sit and the doctor would come out to see her as soon as he finished with her husband. Ella then kissed Jack, told him she loved him and would be waiting for him in his room or wherever the doctor told her to be, and kept the tears from filling her eyes as best she could. Jack assured her he would be fine and was just glad to be able to get this done and get rid of the pain his knee was causing him. He would be able to take better care of her when his knee was fixed, and he winked at her as he said this so that she almost giggled, understanding what he meant. She just barely managed to say, "I certainly hope so," and kissed him again.

Then she sat down in the waiting room, closed her eyes and prayed another prayer God would be with Jack and Dr. Mackinley and the nurses and make this operation a success so this man she grew to love more every day would be completely healed and able to walk and ride his bicycle and even run without pain!

Within an hour a nurse came in and asked, "Are you Mrs. MacLean?" and when Ella said that she was, the nurse continued, saying, "Dr.Mackinley asked me to let you know Mr. MacLean is doing fine, but the doctor has about another hour or more of work to do on rebuilding Mr. MacLean's knee. He will be out to tell you himself once he is done. Do you have any questions?"

Ella had taken a deep breath, relieved to know this much. "No, I don't even know what to ask now that you've told me my husband is doing okay. Thank you, and thank Dr. Mackinley for sending you out to tell me what's going on."

A little more than an hour later, Jonathan Mackinley himself walked in and sat down beside her. "He did fine, Mrs. MacLean. He's going to be in a good bit of pain for the next few days because I did a lot of work on his knee, cleaning out the infection, and then I removed the damaged parts and essentially put in some pieces out of a new material that will function like a new knee as soon as he gets used to it and heals from all the work we did on him.

"He'll need to stay in the hospital for a full week, and if all goes well and no infection shows up, he can move to Healing House with you, and you can get him over here every day where he'll be having physical therapy to help him learn how to use and take care of this new knee. It will be difficult and painful at first, but I expect each week will demonstrate enough progress he'll feel encouraged and realize this part of the process was worth every bit of the pain he'll be experiencing for the next week or so. Do you have questions for me?"

"Only when will I be able to see him?" Ella looked relieved, though her voice betrayed her anxiousness.

"He's in recovery right now, but you can come back and see he's alive. He's a bit out of it at the moment, but the anesthetic is wearing off and he may or may not realize you are there. So just speak to him and tell him he did fine and you are happy or proud or whatever positive remark you feel like making. He's probably not going to remember anything you say anyway." Dr. Mackinley patted her shoulder and then said, "Come on, follow me, and I'll take you to him."

Ella was on her feet instantly, saying "Oh, thank you! I feel so relieved and grateful, Dr. Mackinley."

"Just doing my job," he replied. "But the truth is I'm glad your British friends told him about me. His knee needed this surgery, and I'm glad I was the one to do it for him—and for you. I'm pretty certain he's going to be able to tell a huge difference by the time you all are ready to go back to Arkansas."

"That will truly be wonderful because I've been aware for a good while his knee has been bothering him more and more. Both of us will thank you more than we can express!"

By the end of Ella's speech they had arrived at the room where Jack was waking up from the anesthetic and was trying to say something but was not making sense. Ella went to him and kissed him on the forehead and saying softly, "It's over, my darling. The surgery is done and you have a knee that's as good as new, so your doctor tells me. You don't have to talk right now," Ella said softly. "Give the drug that put you to sleep time to wear off."

Whether Jack understood her words or was just soothed by the sound of her voice, he quieted down, closed his eyes, and went back to sleep. Dr. Mackinley said, "He'll wake up again shortly and may not even remember you were here. So why don't you sit in this chair, so you'll be the first thing he sees when he wakes up again. It shouldn't be long because the anesthetic is wearing off. I'll be back in a bit to check on him before we send him back to his room. Then I'll see you both before you leave to go back to your hotel."

It really wasn't long before Jack woke up again, this time recognizing Ella and calling her by name. "Have you been here long, my Ella?" he asked, slurring his words just a little.

230

"As long as you have, my love. I was sitting in the waiting room while Dr. Mackinley was operating on your knee. He seems pleased with the outcome and says you'll be able to tell a huge difference after a few weeks of exercises and therapy."

"I'm counting on that, but right now I feel the need to take a little nap," and he had gone back to sleep before Ella could reply.

3

Jack woke up again surprised he had been asleep for almost an hour, but he obviously was a lot more alert and himself. This time the orderly rolled him back upstairs to his room and Ella followed, glad she didn't have to remember how to get there. Jack fell asleep again as soon as the orderly and the nurse rolled him onto his bed. After they left, Ella ate the sandwich and drank the tea that had been brought in and left on his rolling tray, waiting for Jack to wake up once more and hoping he would stay awake for a while when he did so.

This time when he opened his eyes and smiled at her, he eagerly tackled what was left of his lunch, teasing Ella for taking advantage of his napping and eating the food he needed to regain his strength. She told him to hush and she was going to get him another sandwich as soon as she found someone who could tell her where to find one!

Ella had hardly gotten the words out of her mouth before a nurse came in to check on Jack, who immediately said to her, "Nurse Williams, what do you think of a woman who ate her sick husband's sandwich while he lay here helpless in the bed?"

"I think she had probably been up since early this morning and had eaten so little for breakfast she figured any loving husband would have gladly shared his sandwich with her," Amy Williams said with a laugh. "And you needn't think you're going to starve. I ordered a second lunch for you before I came in. It should be here shortly. And Mrs. MacLean, if you want something more to eat, just tell me. We try to take care of spouses at times when we know they don't want to leave the hospital."

"That is truly thoughtful," Ella said, thinking again how glad she was they had been able to come to this hospital!

It was mid-afternoon before Ella was willing to leave Jack while she went to find a telephone from which she could call the name Dan had given her. Dan thought the world of Chaplain Mark McGinnis and knew if she called him he would get the message to him. When the chaplain answered, identifying himself by name, and she told him who she was and why she was calling, he immediately recognized her and asked how Mr. MacLean was doing after the surgery. She then told him that it had gone well. She told him her husband was back in his room, and asked him please to get word to their son he was doing fine.

The Chaplain sounded truly happy to hear her news and said he would personally deliver the message to Dan. He said he had really enjoyed getting to know their son and if she ever needed to get in touch with Dan in an emergency, to call his office and he would take care of getting the word to Dan, and if necessary, make it possible for him to call home. Ella felt much better about putting her son in the hands of the Naval Academy after talking with Chaplain McGinnis.

When Ella returned to Jack she was happy to be able to tell him she not only had spoken with the Chaplain but also had liked him and was feeling much more comfortable about having their son at the Naval Academy. Knowing full well how reluctant Ella had been about Dan's signing on with the Navy after being been accepted into the Academy, Jack smiled, saying how glad he was to hear her words.

Ella sighed, but also said, "Well, I am relieved to have had some contact, even if only a phone call, with someone who is part of the establishment. But how are you feeling, my love? Are you having any pain now that the anesthetic is beginning to wear off?"

"Some," Jack said, "but I'm so used to feeling pain in that part of my body, it's not too bad, I'm glad to say. But let's don't talk

232

about me. How are you going to sleep without me?" He grinned as he asked the question.

"Oh, you know me. I'm a good sleeper, especially when there's no one around to bother me," Ella replied teasingly.

"Well, I must say you really know how to hurt a fellow's ego," and he put on his long, sad face.

"You know I'm just giving you back some sass. I dread going to sleep in this strange place without being able to cuddle up against you. But since you're supposed to be out of here in a week, even if you have to come for physical therapy every day, I think I can deal with an empty place in my bed for that long. Seriously, Jack, I hate it you're here and having to go through all of this, but if it works and you come out of it free of pain, it will have been worth it for both of us."

"You are truly right, my love, and while I dread the initial pain for the next few weeks, if this does what Jonathan Mackinley says it will, I can manage going through a few hard days.

"But I'm just so grateful you're here with me, and I'm not doing this all alone. I remember how lonely I felt in the hospital in London after I was wounded in the war, especially during those first weeks before I began to realize I was going to survive and started making friends with some of the guys in my ward, many of whom were in much worse shape than I was."

"Oh, Jack, I can only imagine what that must have been like. I do remember how alone I felt at home during the Spanish flu epidemic with only my daughters for company, and they were too young to be of much help, except they did keep me busy tending to them and then trying to think of ways to entertain them once they started feeling better. At least, I'm thinking you will be easier and more enjoyable to be with than Mary Beth and Eleanor were!"

"I promise I will try," Jack said as he took her hand he'd been holding and pressed it to his lips.

He had barely put their clasped hands back on the spread when Dr. Mackinley entered the room to check on how his patient was recovering from the anesthetic and the surgery.

"Well, you look pretty alert for a man who spent several hours this morning knocked out while we did some rather intricate work on your knee. But you did fine, Jack. We cleaned out a lot of scar tissue and some infection around your knee cap, and we put in some new parts that once you get used to them will make life a lot more pleasant for you.

"You're going to feel 10 years younger by the time you leave here if you do all the physical training we're going to demand of you. It's going to hurt like hell the first couple of weeks, but I promise you if you stick with us, it will get better and better so that you will feel like a different man by the time you go home. You've made a good start. Do you have any questions for me?"

"So when does the really hard stuff begin?" Jack asked.

"We're going to take you downstairs in a little while and introduce you to the folks who'll be working with you. I want you to meet them this afternoon because they'll be coming for you soon after breakfast in the morning.

"Mrs. MacLean, you may as well stay at Healing House until about 11:00 and then come over to have lunch with Jack, who may or may not be very hungry. He'll go back down for some more physical therapy about 3:00 tomorrow afternoon for an hour or so, and you can stay here or wander around outdoors until 4:30 or so when he should be back in his room.

"Jack may want to rest or even sleep for a bit after each session because these first few days will exhaust him. BUT it will get easier on him. And I'm fairly sure he will be ready to go back to Healing House with you by Sunday evening.

"For a week or two he may need a taxi, or maybe Healing House still has a driver, who can bring him back to the hospital for P.T. during the day. We'll set that schedule up at the end of the week when we see what kind of progress you're making, Jack. Do you two have any questions?"

"I'd like for you to call me Ella, and may I come with you this afternoon when you take Jack down to meet the P.T. staff?" Ella asked.

234

"Of course," Dr. Mackinley replied. "It's really important that you meet them and get to know them a bit, Ella, because they're going to play a major role in getting Jack back to normal during these next few weeks. He's going to see a lot more of them than he will of me, though I'll be checking on him every day to see how much progress he's making." He smiled, shook both Jack's and Ella's hands, and left.

4

That afternoon Ella and Jack both were impressed by the men and women who were members of the Physical Therapy team at Walter Reed. They looked so young, not much older than Dan. Their genuine concern for helping people regain their strength and mobility in whatever part of the body that needed it, their obvious liking for people in general, and their own vitality and energy along with the confidence they had in the benefits of their work gave assurance to Jack and Ella they had come to the right place for him to get help.

Ella and Jack had barely gotten back to Jack's room when Dan walked in. Ella hugged him and said she might not have known who he was if he hadn't been wearing his Navy whites because he didn't look like a boy any longer but a man. He grinned, saying "You look pretty young and sassy yourself to be my mother," then picked Ella up and swung her around. Then he leaned down and took Jack's hand and said, "You look better than I expected you to, Papa Jack. How are you feeling?"

"Not as good as I was feeling this morning when I had all that knockout medicine in me, but the nurse promised she'd give me something to help me sleep tonight. And I suspect I going to need it. But, Son, you're a sight for sore eyes. You've become a man. When I look at you I can't believe it's been almost two years since we last saw you. You look good!"

Dan pulled a straight chair from against the wall and sat down between Jack's bed and Ella's arm chair, and answered their questions about his life at the Academy. Ella, who had read and re-read every letter he had written her until she practically could quote them verbatim, now asked him by name about people who were part of his life. While Jack had not read them as often as Ella had, he did remember from the letters most of those Dan talked about, and told him how proud he was Dan was a Midshipman in the Navy.

Both Ella and Dan realized Jack was getting tired and needed to sleep or at least rest. Ella kissed Jack goodnight and was sur-prised and touched when Dan stooped down and kissed him on the forehead, saying "Sleep well, Papa Jack. I love you and I am glad the surgery is done."

"I love you too, Son, and you, my Ella." But Jack's voice was begin-ning to fade and his words to slur. So they tiptoed out of his room.

Dan had to return to campus because he had a meeting he had to attend that night, though he was vague about what kind of meeting it was when Ella asked him. He had borrowed a car to get to Walter Reed and dropped her off at Healing House, although she had assured him it was so close she could walk. Still it felt nice to have her grown-up son chauffer her there. He told her it would be a couple of days before he could make it back to see them because he had things going on at school that would take up his free time, but since Ella had not expected to see a whole lot of him because he was in classes, she told him she would be grateful for whatever amount of time he had to give them. She kissed him good-bye, thanking him for coming to see them, and watched him drive away, realizing again her little boy had become a man, and a strong, fine man at that!

5

Ella ate supper in the Healing House dining room which served home-cooked meals with three choices of entrees along with side dishes and a dessert, and she sat with an older couple who were there to see their son, a navy pilot and instructor, who had been injured in an airplane crash. He was going to recover, but his flying days were over. Ella had listened to them talk about the son and his injuries, grateful Dan was not into flying. She told the Ellisons she would keep their son, Walter, in her prayers, and she meant it.

She went back to her room, replaying in her mind the short time Dan had been with them in Jack's room. She had only spoken with her son seven times during the full year he had been at the Naval Academy, but just the memory of his voice helped her through those times when he seemed so far away. After all, she would tell herself, two of her "chickens" had flown far from their nest.

She missed Eleanor and her precious new grandson. She thought about Eleanor's voice, now with its British accent and was happy for her in her marriage to Ronald and now with the presence of baby Lee in her life. Ella was so grateful she at least had Mary Beth and her husband Patrick and their two precious children Pat and Nora. And with that thought she took her coin purse, went to the pay phone in the hall, and gave the operator their telephone number in Myrna, Arkansas. It helped her to remember they would be there when she and Jack returned home.

Mary Beth was glad to hear the surgery had gone well and Dan had come by the hospital to see them. Mary Beth promised to pass the word around that Jack was doing fine, and Ella was sure soon everyone in Myrna who cared would be talking about it. She would send a telegram to Eleanor and Ronald the next day since she was obviously going to have a good bit of "alone time" for a while.

Ella was glad she had brought a notebook along since she realized she was going to have more time to write than she often had at home. Even though she didn't really feel in the mood to write, she made herself sit down at the desk in the sitting room and put pen to paper. Before she knew it she had begun describing everything she and Jack had done since getting there, including the details of Jack's surgery, or at least what she knew of them.

She listened to some music on the radio in her room after she had put on her nightgown and gotten in the bed, and then said her prayers, leaving God in charge of all those she loved, and fell asleep.

Some days Dan was able to come see them late in the afternoon when he had finished classes, meetings, or drills. Since Jack had physical therapy both mornings and afternoons, when Dan would arrive sometime after 4:00 Jack would be tired but alert and glad to see him. He rarely stayed longer than 30 minutes because he had to be back on campus for the evening meal at 5:30.

On Sundays though, after attending chapel and eating lunch on the campus, Dan would come and spend an hour or more with them at Healing House, talking about his classes, his activities, his friends, and giving Ella a chance to get a real feel for what his life was like. The only thing he did not mention was that he was taking flying lessons and loved flying.

6

On what they were sure would be their last day at the hospital before Jack would move into Healing House, Larry Coleman came with Dan and both Jack and Ella were delighted to see him. He was looking forward to graduation at the end of this school year and hoping that as a Navy pilot, he would be located somewhere like Pearl Harbor. Ella had to ask where Pearl Harbor was and Larry told that it was in one of the most beautiful places on earth, if the photographs he had seen could be believed. The Hawaiian Islands were in the middle of the Pacific Ocean below the equator so the seasons of the year were reversed, although Hawaii was so centrally located the weather there was warm all year long. While it sounded like Paradise from Larry's description, Ella still hoped Dan would be stationed somewhere nearer home after he graduated.

Both she and Jack were glad to get to visit with Larry a bit. Ella asked how his parents were doing, though Larry knew from his mother's letters she and Ella wrote to each other every so often. Ella asked how his parents felt about his flying and probably becoming a pilot. He said his dad thought it was great, and his mother had sighed and said she guessed it was about as safe as being on the ground when war was raging all around you. She had told him to learn to be the best pilot he could be and hoped that would help keep him safe up in the air!

Jack shook his hand and Ella hugged him when he and Dan left to be back in time for "mess" as they referred to this meal, or maybe all their meals. Ella told herself she needed to ask Dan about that the next time he came. In the meantime, she wrote a long letter to Larry's parents to tell them how much Jack and she had enjoyed their son's visit and what a fine young man he was.

During one of Dan's visits he told Ella and Jack he and Lilly were still corresponding and he felt they might be getting serious about each other. She was leaving the University of Arkansas after her first year with plans to enter nursing school in Little Rock in the fall. While she had enjoyed college and being a member of Pi Phi, she didn't feel like it was preparing her for anything real.

She had begun to think about nursing when her mother had become really ill the previous summer. She had gone home to help care for her and soon realized this was something she really wanted to learn how to do as an actual career, at least until she married and had children of her own. Even then the skills and knowledge she would gain from nursing school would be useful.

Ella had been impressed, realizing there was a lot more to Lilly than a pretty face and a good figure! She told Dan she was glad Lilly had ambitions beyond being a sorority girl or even a college graduate.

All in all Ella treasured these days she had with her son and her husband, one at the beginning of adulthood and the other going through pain in hopes of a less painful aging process. She felt she had accepted she had little or no control over what the future might have in store for her or for any of those she loved, and so she allowed herself to hold on to the joys of each day she had with her son and to the gratitude she felt with each step of Jack's progress.

For the first week Jack was at the hotel he either called a taxi or was able to get a ride from the hotel to the Physical Therapy Department at Walter Reed. But by the middle of the third week, he and Ella would walk to the hospital together. Jack was a bit slow at first, but Ella could see the progress he was making while Jack could feel it because the pain was decreasing substantially with each week they were there.

Ella and Jack called Mary Beth every Friday to report on how Jack was doing, share news from Dan's visits, and catch up with what was going on in Myrna. Ella also wrote weekly letters to Eleanor and Ronald she sent by Air-Mail, which cost a bit more but made her letters arrive so much faster she felt it was worth every penny. Eleanor did not write her quite as frequently as she would have liked, but when her letters arrived, they were so full of details about the baby's growth and what their lives were like she was willing to wait for them. Actually, Ella was somewhat glad Eleanor did not use Air-Mail because her letters were a lot longer with much more description than she could have ever gotten on the thin Air-Mail paper the sender was required to use. She treasured the two letters she received from Eleanor while she was at Healing House and saved them to take home for Mary Beth to read.

7

On Thursday night of what they were pretty sure would be their final week of treatment at Walter Reed, Ella and Jack decided to go to a movie. There was a very nice theater not too far from Healing House, and they asked Mrs. Stone at the front desk who had become a friend, if they were allowed to miss a meal and go to a movie and perhaps even eat in a restaurant. Mrs. Stone said that of course they could do both, and in fact there was a movie playing in a nearby theater she and her husband had gone to see the past weekend and it was delightful. *It's a Wonderful World* starred Jimmy Stewart and Claudette Colbert. While it was a bit complicated with a lot of characters, she and her husband had finally gotten everybody straight and laughed all the way through it. Jack and Eleanor could easily walk to the theater, and there was a nice restaurant near it, though they might want to flag a taxi home. While the streets were generally pretty safe in this part of town, it would probably be safer to come by cab.

Jack had been given a cane to use when he needed it walking, and he took it with them on Thursday evening. They left Healing House at 5:00 and made the walk to the *Café Francais* in half an hour, arriving before the evening crowd and so getting a choice of tables near one of the large windows. Jack ordered them a glass of sherry and an *aperitif* while they decided what to have for dinner. Their waiter, who was very American but did not have a Southern accent, asked if they minded telling him what state they were from because he did not recognize their accent. When they told him Arkansas, he said, "Ah, yes, across from Tennessee on the western side."

Both Jack and Ella were impressed with his knowledge of geography, and he said it was a hobby of his. He liked living near Washington because the area attracted people from everywhere. He enjoyed meeting people from all over, not only the USA but the world. Ella and Jack said although they had not traveled widely, they also enjoyed meeting people from different places.

Jack then asked him if he minded being addressed by his name, which according to the name plate he was wearing, was George, and then added that he was Jack and his wife, Ella. When George said to call him by his name was fine, Jack asked him what items on the menu he particularly liked and would recommend for their dinner. George then said this restaurant had a large menu and served excellent food, but he would show them on the menu which dishes he especially liked and thought might please them.

Pointing to a line on the menu, he said, "For the lady, I recommend *Fillets de Tuitte Amandine*, which is sweet, tender trout poached in whole milk and butter, topped with toasted almonds and served with russet potatoes and butter along with French-style green beans.

"For the gentleman I think the *Pot Au Feu* would not only be tasty but filling. The French words literally mean "pot in the fire" which refers to a traditional recipe in which a beef roast or a

241

chicken is stewed in its own broth with herbs, spices, and fresh vegetables. When it is done, the meat, which in this case is beef, and the vegetables come separately from the broth, which is served steaming hot as a first course. I hesitate to say this to you, Sir, but you appear to have lost a bit of weight lately, and I think you not only would find this dinner tasty but it would not hurt if you gained a pound or two."

Jack broke into laughter at that, and said he indeed had lost a pound or two from recently having had surgery on his knee that had been injured years ago in the war. For some reason his appetite seemed to have been affected, but perhaps that was because the food he had been served in the hospital was not as tasty as what he was accustomed to getting at home from his wife who was an excellent cook.

George nodded and said, "I understand. So it is good you are recovering and the two of you are out for an evening of pleasure. So Mr. Jack and Mrs. Ella, if you are both willing to accept my choices for you, I will take your order to our chef, and leave you to enjoy your sherry. If you should want anything else, just place this flag in its stand, and I will be right with you. Your food should be ready shortly." He smiled and bowed, then headed toward the kitchen.

George, who had kept a close eye on their enjoyment of their meal, came to clear their plates, saying he had a special dessert for them as a gift from the kitchen. He returned with two bowls of Creamy Custard Sauce mixed with strawberries and blueberries. Both Ella and Jack said they had never tasted a custard this good! And they asked George to please thank the cooks because George had told them the kitchen staff had peeked through the kitchen door at them after George had told the chef a bit about them.

Jack added a generous tip to the bill when he paid it with cash he had brought with him. After all, he told himself, he had spent almost no money since he and Ella had been in Washington, and he didn't expect movie tickets to be a whole lot more than they were in Myrna.

The movie theater was one street down and east of the restaurant, an easy walk for Jack, who so far had not used his cane at all and was wondering why he had brought it with them. The movie tickets were twice what they would have cost in Myrna, but the theater itself was four times bigger and more decorative than the one in Myrna, so Jack thought the tickets were quite reasonable. They were a little early for the next showing but took the time to read a flyer with information about the movie which starred Jimmy Stewart as a private detective named Guy Johnson and Claudette Colbert as Edwina Corday, who would be his love interest.

The plot was complicated because Jimmy Stewart had been hired to watch over and protect Willie Heyward, a wealthy man with a drinking problem that gets him into trouble. After his ex-girlfriend Dolores Gonzalez has made a public scene over their relationship, a drunk Heyward goes to see her, not realizing it's a set-up. Dolores is being held at gunpoint by a man who kills her when Heyward enters, exits, and makes it look like Heyward has murdered her. The only clue is half of a dime, made into a piece of jewelry, Miss Gonzalez had been able to snatch from her assailant. Detective Johnson, whom Heyward had the sense to telephone, hurries to the scene intending to hide his client until he can catch the real killer. Instead both of them are nabbed by the police and end up being tried, convicted and sentenced: Guy to prison for one year and Heyward to be executed.

The audience soon learns that Heyward's new wife Vivian and her lover are behind the whole murder plot because she inherits Heyward's millions when he dies. Vivian's former husband, whom she thought was dead, arrives from Australia, learns what has been going on, and starts blackmailing her.

On the way to spend his year in prison, Guy picks up a newspaper and reads an ad in the Personal section from "Half a Dime" asking the owner of the other half to contact him at a certain place. Guy, realizing this is the evidence that can save him from jail and Heyward from death, jumps from the moving train into a river, taking with him the bumbling policeman handcuffed to him .

Claudette Colbert plays the part of Edwina Corday, who just happens to be strolling near the river and witnesses Guy's actions. Guy has no choice but to kidnap Edwina to keep her from alerting the law, and after convincing her (as only Jimmy Stewart's sincerity could do) she insists on sticking with him and helping him solve the case. Actually, he is annoyed by this because he has a low opinion of women's intelligence.

The movie only gets more complicated when Guy gets hired as an actor to try to figure out who knows about the half dine. He calls in his associate but Edwina thinks he's a policeman and knocks him out. Some more nutty things happen including Guy being arrested again, but Edwina saves the day and they catch Vivian and her lover in the process of escaping. Guy has fallen in love with Edwina and the movie ends with them embracing.

They caught a bus back to Healing House, and Ella said, "I have to admit I had a hard time keeping up with who was guilty of what! That is truly one of the craziest movies I've ever seen, though I loved Jimmy Stewart and Claudette Colbert."

Jack laughed, saying, "It was a challenge to keep up with all the characters and the plot, I admit. I feel kind of exhausted myself just trying to keep straight who the bad guys were. I wasn't even sure about Jimmy Stewart for a while. Why did he ever get involved with Willie Heyward anyway?"

"Because Heyward was paying him lots of money to watch his back. But, I'm certainly glad you are a school teacher and not a private detective, Jack MacLean!

"What I enjoyed most about the movie was being in a place where nobody knew us and I could feel at ease having my husband hold hands with me and then put his arm around my shoulders. Those are things we've never really been able to do in a movie theater in Myrna because some student would have seen us and then told other students including Dan that he'd we'd been making out during whatever movie we were in when all we could possibly have been doing was holding hands. And we quit doing that so we wouldn't have to worry that some student would see us and then make us a topic of gossip."

"I enjoyed that too, my love, and will demonstrate my love even more when we get back to Healing House and our room."

And for the first time since their marriage Jack was able to take the upper position and not experience any pain anywhere at any time. That made the whole trip worth the time, the effort, the pain, and the money.

8

Actually, the total cost of the surgery turned out to be much, much less than they expected because Jack was a veteran and Walter Reed was a hospital that treated veterans at a discounted rate. Even Dr. Jonathan Mackinley's fees were discounted.

Jack had his last appointment with Dr. Mackinley on Monday morning at 8:00. He took new X-rays of Jack's knee and was able to show both Jack and Ella the difference between these X-rays and the ones he'd taken right before the surgery. Seeing his new 'kneecap' without all the infection around it and the kneecap itself looking whole and new made Jack smile and say, "I can't believe I'm looking at the same knee. Well, actually I guess I'm not looking at the same knee but a new one in place of the old one! And this one doesn't hurt and I can walk and sit without pain. I don't know how to thank you enough, Dr. Mackinley!"

"And neither do I!" Ella said with a huge smile.

"I was just doing my job," Jonathan Mackinley said, and then said, "Actually I'm really happy with how it has turned out, Jack and Ella. Now that you are no longer my patient, Jack, I'd like to think of you both as friends and call you by your first names—if you'll call me Jonathan.

"You had told me you all weren't leaving until tomorrow so that you can say goodbye to Dan this afternoon, but I would like it if you two could join my wife and me for dinner tonight. I really would be glad for the opportunity to get to know both of you better and for my wife to meet you too. Would that be possible for you?"

Jack and Ella looked at each other, both nodding yes, and Ella said, "Dan has to be back at the Academy by 5:30 for dinner, and we don't have anything on our schedule after telling him goodbye. Actually, it would be really great to have dinner with friends somewhere other than at Healing House, as a nice way to end these five weeks we've been here."

"Good. That will work! We don't live very far from my office, and I will come by in my car and get you a little after 6:00 and take you to our home. We will probably go out to eat somewhere that is not too crowded so we can get to know each other better and so my wife won't be tied up with cooking and getting food on the table. My mother is living with us at this time, so she will be there to see to our two children while we go and have a pleasant dinner somewhere nearby. I doubt you have been here long enough to have preferences for restaurants; so I hope you'll trust us to choose a place."

Jack spoke up, "That really sounds like a wonderful way to spend our last evening here, doesn't it, Ella?" And she nodded agreement, saying "Dr. Mackinley, I mean Jonathan, this is so thoughtful of you, and I do look forward to meeting your wife. We'll certainly be ready by 6:00."

"Well, I have a patient waiting. So until 6:00 this evening," Jonathan Mackinley said as all three rose and he walked Ella and Jack to a door leading into the hall.

Ella and Jack's last visit with Dan was a bit strained at times because all three were aware of how long it would be before they would be together again. Dan had begun to feel guilty because he had never told them about his flying lessons and that while he had passed his first course easily, he was now learning to fly fighter planes designed for air battles and dropping bombs on targets. These were larger planes with crews trained to fire guns and artillery installed in the plane itself so that crew members prepared for this kind of combat could protect the plane while other crew members unleashed bombs to land on targets. He was going to be sent to a Naval Air Base for a few weeks to get some real practice in these bombers. He found himself wanting to tell them but not wanting to end their time together with this kind of news.

Ella just wanted to hug him, hold him in her arms the way she had when he was a little boy, but not daring to do that to this grown man sitting beside her on the small sofa in their two-room apartment.

Jack kept looking at the grown man Dan had become and hoping that this possible war that was becoming more of a threat every month would not call on his service, and if it did, as deep down he felt it was going to, it would not demand the ultimate sacrifice.

Ella tried her best to make small talk—wondering how much Eleanor's son had grown, chattering about how much he must have changed since they had been in England last year. She could hardly believe Lee was already a year old, and how she wished they didn't live across the ocean.

Jack tried to change the subject, saying to Dan how glad he was that Dan would have enough of a Christmas break to come home to Myrna for the holidays. Dan took the cue and started saying how good it would be to see everybody and asked a few questions about what Ella was planning for Christmas activities. Ella was relieved to have a new topic of conversation, and they spent the last minutes of Dan's visit talking about what he'd like to take place during the holidays. And before they knew it, it was 5:00 and Dan had to get back to the Academy for the dinner hour. He hugged his mother and told her he loved her and then hugged Jack and told him once again how glad he was to have him as part of the family. And before it seemed possible the 90-minute visit had passed, and Dan had headed back to what had become his life.

Jack had enough time to hold Ella in his arms, let her shed a few tears, and then have few minutes to wipe the tears away and powder her face, before the front desk called to tell them that a Jonathan Mackinley was downstairs calling for them and would be out front in his car, a dark green Chevrolet, waiting for them.

Jonathan had opened the car door on the passenger side for them, saying the front seat was wide enough for all three of them to sit together. Ella was in the middle, delighted she was getting to sit up front with both men when at home she was usually sitting in the back behind them, often by herself. She didn't mind being in the back seat if another woman was with her and they could chat while the men carried on their own conversation in the front. It was an unusual treat to be up front in between two men.

This time she was especially glad to be in on what they had to say because Jonathan began the conversation, saying, "Jack and Ella, I'm sure you were a bit surprised by this invitation, and I do have to tell you it is not usual for me to invite former patients for dinner with me and my wife. But I've had two telephone calls from friends of yours wanting to know how the surgery went and how you were doing—one all the way from England and one from your banker friend in Myrna. I imagine you probably have guessed who these calls were from."

Ella was smiling while Jack replied, "The call from Myrna was from our close friend Michael Lewis and from England, Frank Willingham. Frank is the one who recommended you, Jonathan. Michael's call does surprise me a bit, though he's not just our banker. He and his wife are our good friends, but I wouldn't have expected him to call."

"I have to say," Jonathan continued, "I have sometimes received telephone calls from a patient's family members, but rarely from their friends. and these two men are very definitely your and Ella's friends. Frank's call was more about the medical side of your surgery and whether it was going to make a difference or had you waited too long to get it. I was able to assure him you hadn't waited too long, I was pleased with its outcome, and I could speak for you also, and I assume Ella too.

"But Dr. Willingham did go on to tell me briefly about what close friends he had been with your first husband, Ella, how they had worked together with one other doctor taking care of the wounded on the front lines in France. He said he and Daniel had been so close he wasn't sure how he would feel about you, Jack, but he had liked you immediately upon meeting you because you

248

respected Daniel's memory and the important part he'd played in your life, Ella. Dr. Willingham said he was glad he had met you, Jack, and that you and Ella had fallen in love with each other."

Ella had tears in her eyes that she wiped away with her handkerchief. "Daniel and I had taken our three children to England to see this medical colony Frank had begun. Daniel had developed such a close friendship with Frank and Jean Marc as doctors in the army I didn't know how they would receive Jack last summer. We went primarily to see my daughter who had married an Englishman and just given birth to their first child, but the five days we spent with Frank and the others at St. Anthony's couldn't have gone better." Jack nodded his agreement.

"Well, the one who called just to let me know about you both and how much your town thinks of you, Michael Lewis, is not just your banker but your dear friend and cheerleader. He praised you both to the skies. Jack, he told me you had come to Myrna as pastor of the Presbyterian Church, but not long before you accepted the call to the church your little three-year-old daughter had died suddenly, with no warning, while you were at a hospital in Richmond with parents from your church whose son had been in a terrible car accident and was dying from the injuries. When you got home that night your wife was so full of anger over your little girl's death and you not being there when she needed you she never got over it. Instead she left you, went to France, moved in with a man, and wrote you to ask you to divorce her since that was what she needed to do in order to get her divorce in France.

"My wife and I are Presbyterians, and we know that divorced preachers cannot be called to another church and rarely are allowed to stay in the one they are serving at the time. Anyway, he filled me in on your resignation from the church and how you found healing by working on a kind of group farm. Since he was also President of the School Board, he had the clout to get you hired to teach history even though you had no training in teaching, and that's how you and Ella became friends as you worked on a way to combine literature, grammar, and history.

"And Ella, he thinks just as highly of you as he does of Jack. Your doctor husband was shot in the heart by a crazed, drunk old man when he had driven out into the country to make a house call. He left you with three children, one I've met—your son here at Annapolis, and two older daughters who went to college at Southwestern at Memphis, a fine Presbyterian liberal arts college. Both of them are married. One, you've already mentioned, lives in England and the other in Myrna. Mr. Lewis couldn't have spoken more highly of both of you than he did. I told my wife all he said about you, and she has her own connection with you I'll let her tell you herself, because here we are at my house."

Jonathan Mackinley had pulled into his driveway as he finished speaking. Jack and Ella followed him to the front door which he opened and called out, "Catherine, I'm home with our guests."

"Come on in. I'm in the kitchen getting the boys' supper ready to put on the table." Catherine replied. She finished filling two serving bowls, one with sliced tomatoes and the other with black-eyed peas and then put slices of ham on a platter and somehow carried all three into the breakfast room at the same time, placing them on a table set for three. She picked up a small silver bell and rang it three times, then saying, "So sorry not to greet you properly, but I needed to get this done first."

At that moment two boys burst into the breakfast room followed by their grandmother saying, "Slow down, boys. Guests are here, and the food's not going away until you sit down properly, are introduced to our guests, and then we bless the food. Then show you have some manners by passing the food to each other and serve yourself. Just leave some for me!"

Jonathan's mother asked the boys to introduce themselves to Jack and Ella, said a brief prayer thanking God for the meal set before them, and then smiled at Ella and Jack saying, "I'm Margery Mackinley. Please excuse our table manners, but I know the four of you have reservations for 6:30 and need to get on your way. If it's not too late when you finish your dinner, I hope to really meet you and visit a bit, that is if you have time."

As the four of them seated themselves in Jonathan's car, Catherine said laughing, "Well, you just got a glimpse of family life in the Mackinley household! Our boys are 11 and 13, and they can be well-behaved and sweet sometimes, but when we have company, sometimes their manners need improving."

Ella laughed, "Although my son is almost 20, I still have vivid memories of what he could be like when he was your sons' ages. Actually, they're just being boys!"

"Ella, I know you have a son at the Naval Academy. Do you have other sons or other children, I should say?" Catherine asked.

"Yes, I have two older daughters. Dan was a later 'gift' after my first husband came home from the war. He was pretty spoiled until his father was killed when he was nine, and then he had a hard year or so getting over that.

"But Jack entered his life and became a kind of surrogate father to him, and that made a real difference. Both my daughters are married. My older daughter decided after college to go to England to live, and there she met the man she married, a professor of literature at the University of Durham. She gave birth to a son while we were there visiting last summer; so we did get to see him for a bit after his birth, but now I have to rely on photos and letters. Our other daughter, Mary Beth, lives in Myrna near us, is married to a doctor, and they have two children, a son who is almost five and a daughter who just recently turned two. I'm really glad to have them around, what with Eleanor in northern England and Dan here at the Naval Academy."

Jonathan had just pulled into a parking place at the restaurant where they were having dinner, and they waited to continue their conversation until they were inside and had been shown to the table Catherine had reserved for them.

They had been seated and were studying the menus the waiter had handed them, when Catherine said, "I have a kind of connection with you all that is going to surprise you, and I'll tell you as soon as we order."

Jonathan laughed and said, "Well, I'm sure you've made it harder, at least for Ella, to concentrate on selecting what she wants to eat, Catherine. Ella and Jack, do take your time."

Jack smiled and said, "Everything looks so good. Do you have a recommendation?"

Jonathan said, "Well, I'm getting my usual, the Porterhouse steak, baked potato and salad. It's my favorite."

"That sounds good to me," Jack said, thinking to himself, "I'm glad he's a doctor and can afford to treat me to this kind of dinner, especially as he heard Ella order fillet mignon, following Catherine's order of the same.

As soon as the waiter had left, Catherine said, "My mother lives in Cape Girardeau and is a good friend of Larry Coleman's mother, with whom you have become letter writing friends. She thinks you are a great correspondent, Ella, and had mentioned several times she hopes to meet you one day, although her son Larry will graduate next year while your son will still have two more years. She hopes you continue to write each other, because even though she hasn't met your son while you have met her Larry, she sort of feels like she knows you, and Dan and Jack too and your daughters, because you write long, newsy letters she can hardly wait to read when they arrive."

Ella was listening and almost laughing when Catherine finished, by saying, "Mother was telling me all this on the telephone last week, and I couldn't believe it when Jonathan came home a few days ago and said he wanted to invite the two of you to dinner because he'd had two phone calls from friends of both of you. Now tell me, is this a small world or not?"

They all agreed that the coincidences were amazing. And the four continued to find much to talk about and share as they ate their dinner together. They sat talking for so long after they had finished eating they had established a friendship they intended to maintain, although neither couple had any idea of ever seeing each other again. But as Jack said, "Only God knows what is going to happen to us and to our world."

252

Then leaving the future in God's hands, they left the restaurant with Jack and Ella deciding they really needed to get back to Healing House because they should be at the train station by 8:00 in the morning with a long day ahead of them. Catherine rode with Jonathan to drop them at Healing House, and she and Jonathan both got out of the car, the women to hug each other and the men to grasp hands to shake that ended in a tentative embrace. All of them promised to stay in touch.

Ella and Jack couldn't stop talking about the evening as they went to their room to finish packing, stopping at the front desk to ask for a 6:00 a.m. wake up call. They had had two special nights out, and while they had really enjoyed the dinner at Café Francais and the movie, they decided this evening had topped that one because they had formed an unexpected friendship, one they hoped would be a lasting one despite the distance between them.

9

Their train to Memphis left Silver Springs on time, exactly at 8:30 a.m. and arrived on time at 6:30 p.m. They had made reservations at the Gayoso in Memphis for that night, and at 10:00 the next morning boarded the Delta Eagle from Memphis to Jonesboro , making a brief stop in Myrna where Michael Lewis met them, helped load their luggage into the car trunk, and then drove them home.

They were more than happy to get back to their own house. Jack had looked forward to making love to Ella in their own bed and did so, giving joy to both. In the first few days after being back home, he tested his knee by climbing the stairs to Dan's room, walking the mile to the high school and back home, and riding his bicycle, which had been his knee-saver for years. When walking, climbing stairs, riding his bicycle, and driving the car gave him no pain, he knew the surgery had truly worked and he was really as good as new—or as good as new as any man his age could be!

Ella was delighted to see her grandchildren and have a chance to tell Mary Beth in detail about Jack's surgery, since Mary Beth's goal was to become a doctor herself as soon as Pat and Nora were old enough to be in school.

The rest of the summer passed quickly. Dan continued to write long letters home every week. To Ella's surprise Dan's high school girlfriend, Lilly, came by one afternoon just to visit. She told Ella they had corresponded all during the past year, although both she and Dan had agreed she should date when she went to the University. And she had dated a few boys during the year but so far had not been out with anybody who really interested her. Lilly had joined Pi Phi after going through rush at the beginning of her first year, and while she enjoyed being a part of a sorority, she wanted to spend her time doing something more meaningful. She and Ella began a friendship on an adult level, with Ella as her older friend and advisor.

While Ella and Jack still missed Dan's presence in the house and in their lives, they had also gotten used to the quietness of no loud music being played on his radio upstairs that had always seemed to echo throughout the house and no feet bounding up the stairs two at a time.

They spent time together going over their lesson plans for 10th, 11th, and 12th grade English and history, making some changes after having been in the Washington area for over a month. Healing House subscribed to *The Washington Post* and several other newspapers and magazines, and Ella had had time to read much of the *Post* every day before she went to the hospital to be with Jack. She had liked the *Post* so much because of the depth of its news about the President that Jack subscribed to the Sunday edition as his gift to her for taking such good care of him while he was in the hospital. She said no gift was necessary, but they both enjoyed reading the Sunday edition because its news of the country and the world was much more current and detailed than that in the state papers.

Part VIII

The War Begins in Europe: 1939

1

In April of 1939 when both the British and French governments feared Germany would invade Poland at any moment, they had guaranteed the Polish government if the Nazis attacked, the Poles would receive "all the support in the power of the Allies to give."

During the months between April and September, Hitler, who had publicly avowed his detest of Bolshevism, in a surprise move sent his Foreign Minister to Moscow to negotiate with Stalin's new Foreign Minister, Molotov, with whom he formed an alliance. This new "friendship" added armed forces to Hitler's army that had already conquered and now included Czechoslovakia and Austria, along with the forces of his new ally Russia.

On September 1, 1939, the German air force and infantry attacked Poland on the ground and in the air from the south and east while Russian forces invaded from the west. The Poles had neither adequate air nor ground troops to defend themselves against Germany's strength. Although the Poles fought valiantly to protect their homeland, their freedom, and their way of life, they were no match for the Wehrmacht, Germany's "war machine" or armed forces. Within a month, Germany had gained total control of Poland.

The British and French, despite their pledge to defend Poland, did not come to the aid of the Poles. As valiantly as the Poles fought to save their country, they were no match for the Germans and the Russians. Blitzkrieg or "lightning war" was the term the Germans used to describe their defeat of the Poles in less than a month. The Polish army was decimated except for those who managed to escape and make their way to Britain where they formed Europe's largest army in exile.

The one amazing contribution the Poles made during the battle for their country was that Polish mathematicians were able to break the code of the "Enigma machine," which the Germans used to "encipher" their military communications. After the Poles deciphered the mathematics behind the "Enigma" they turned the information over to the British, who in turn were able to provide valuable information to the Allies as the war progressed.

The defeat and surrender of Poland was followed by a six-month period of "peace" that became known as the Phony War. The British and French people were lulled into thinking perhaps there would not be a major war after all.

2

People in the United States followed the war in the newspapers and on the radio but seemed more relieved they were not involved in it than concerned about what the British and the French would likely face when Germany decided to move onward.

While Poland was being conquered by the Germans, life in Myrna was continuing as usual with the beginning of the school year, and as always, feelings were mixed. Parents in general were delighted their children would return to classrooms where teachers would be responsible for their behavior as well as their learning. For the most part, the majority of children were glad to return to school because many of them had begun to grow bored with playing, while they really liked school and its activities. Others felt safer and more taken care of by teachers and better fed in the school lunch room than they did at home. Even when study was involved, many were simply glad to be back with their friends and to make new ones.

In mid-summer the high school principal Doug Adams had been promoted to Superintendent of the Myrna School System, including the Negro elementary and high school. After the former superintendent had announced his retirement at the beginning of summer and Doug had accepted the position, Ella and Jack, and all the high school teachers were concerned about who their new principal would be. Almost everybody had liked and respected Doug, and that was important because principals generally have a much closer relationship with the teachers, students, and even parents than superintendents do.

The position as principal had been hard to fill, mainly because so many schools were having difficulty paying its personnel due to the Depression. It was the end of August and school was scheduled to start the second Monday of September when Charles Maynard Clifton accepted the position and moved to Myrna from Monette, Missouri, where he had spent 10 years as the assistant to the principal of the high school there. He had recently earned a graduate degree in school administration from the University of Michigan and was, as he put it, "raring to go" as the new principal of Myrna High.

While his enthusiasm for his new position was evident, the new principal's ability to work with his staff was not, primarily because he began with plans to make a lot of changes in the class schedules and teaching responsibilities. From his first day on the job he made it clear he did not approve of Ella and Jack's combined English and history classes nor of the way they had rearranged the courses so that 10th graders were no longer studying world history as was customary in many schools.

Mr. Clifton paid no attention to Jack's and Ella's attempts to assure him that 10th graders were getting introduced to world history through learning about where their ancestors had come from originally and what their reasons were for leaving their native lands to move to a different continent.

Nor did he approve of their reasons for reworking the 11th grade course to focus on the settling and creation of the United States of America so that by their senior year their students would understand why and how it had become such a different country from where their original families had lived. American history would prepare them to delve deeper into world history, using the information they had gained about the different countries, cultures, and difficulties that had made their families leave their native lands and immigrate to the United States, even before it became a nation on its own.

However, as soon as the word had gotten out that the new Principal was returning the English and history high school classes to the old way of organizing and teaching them, the students and their parents began to make their feelings known, not so much to the Principal but mostly to Superintendent Adams. Doug Adams as Principal had been respected and well-liked. He hoped to continue to be so as Superintendent, although the rumor mill was operating at full force throughout Myrna over the situation.

At first Superintendent Adams had kept his thoughts to himself about the changes the new principal was making, but after the first two weeks of classes, the rearranged 10th–12th grade class schedules were returned to what Jack and Ella had set up three years prior.

What Superintendent Adams said to Principal Charles Clifton was never reported, but Principal Clifton withdrew his objections, and the history/English classes were once more united.However, Principal Clifton made no effort to keep silent about his own feelings of having been treated unfairly, so that the high school and its principal were still a major topic of conversation and that was damaging the atmosphere within the school itself.

Michael Lewis, as President of the five-member school board, called a special meeting of the board to seek a solution to the growing problems within the high school. Michael presided over the called meeting and listened to each member give his assessment of the situation and what should or could be done to improve it.

The only solution any of the four suggested that received approval from the others was to fire the new Principal and ask Doug Adams to return as to his old job, though no one thought he would give up the salary increase and prestige he had received by becoming Superintendent.

Finally, after listening to all of their opinions, Michael said, "Well, why not give Doug the increase, or at least most of it. You see, I think it's possible that Doug applied for the superintendent's job because he needed the extra money since he has three children, two of whom will be going to college in a couple of years. We actually owe him a bit more salary if he comes back as Principal. Or it may be that he really wants to be the superintendent. Why don't we at least invite him to a meeting and talk with him about it?"

Michael's suggestion drew some questions and discussion from the four but all agreed that it was worth acting on. Michael telephoned Doug and asked him to meet with the board the next evening if he was free, and he was.

At the called meeting the following night Michael thanked Doug for agreeing to meet with them and then said, "Mr. Superintendent, I know you are aware that Principal Clifton stirred up a hornet's nest with his disapproval of the high school curriculum for history and English classes and the way they were being taught, and now there's his anger over being made to return them to the way they were before he became Principal.

"You were Principal when the school board met with both teachers of those classes and voted to try out their proposal to change the order of the history courses and to allow the English and history teachers to work together to incorporate both subjects so the English classes learned literature and wrote papers about what the history students were studying. Parents have been really pleased with the way these two teachers merged their subjects so their children are more interested in these classes than they ever remember their older children being. You solved the problem with Principal Clifton by making him return them to the way they were when he arrived, but he is not happy about the solution and has been letting his feelings be known."

Doug spoke up. "I was and am very much aware of all of this because I received a good number of parental complaints. As Superintendent I take responsibility because I hired Charles Clifton, and I felt pretty quickly that I'd made a mistake. The trouble was that I hadn't had any success in my search for a new principal. He had just received a degree that gave him the credentials he needed for the job, and he seemed bright and eager for the position. I should have done more investigating of his previous positions, but time was running out, and I brought him before you, the board, without having vetted him carefully enough. You all seemed impressed by him. We hired him, and now we have to find a solution to our problem."

"As President of the School Board, I have done some checking on my own," Michael said. "I called the University of Michigan that supposedly granted him his latest degree and learned they had never heard of him, had no record of his ever having attended there," Michael said and waited for their reaction. There were gasps and "That's hard to believe!" And one said, "He showed me his new degree all printed out and framed."

"He showed me his degree, also," said Superintendent Doug Adams, "and I believed it was real. I should have been more careful about checking the references he gave me. I've let the whole town down and hurt this school and our students. I don't need to be anybody's superintendent!"

"Doug, don't be too hard on yourself. You are an educator, not a detective. You were new to your position and were feeling the pressure to have a high school principal by the time school began." Michael said gently.

"But you checked on him, Michael, and found out he had misled me and others about his qualifications. How did you know to do that?" Doug's earnestness was evident from the tone of his voice.

"Because I'm a businessman and a banker. I learned early on to be suspicious enough to check out what people claim about themselves. Very few have ever lied about their past history to me, but some have, and I've had to confront them with their lies. It's not something I enjoy doing, but it has to be done. I don't look forward to confronting Mr. Clifton, but I will do it and ask one or perhaps all of you to be with me to witness to what is said and done. In fact, I think it would be best if all of you, including Doug, be present.

262

"So, Gentlemen, I think we have a case we can bring against this charlatan that will free us from having to pay him anything except for the short time he's been here. We obviously cannot give him any kind of recommendation, but we can agree not to bring charges against him if he releases us from our contract with him and leaves quietly.

"But, of course, that means we will be without a principal. Doug, we were hoping you might be willing to step down from your position as superintendent and return as the principal of the high school. The whole town has missed you. I think the board is willing to give you a well-deserved raise as our principal if you're willing to do that, aren't we, board members."

The four men were looking at Michael as though he had just pulled a rabbit out of a hat and wasted no time giving their 'ayes' of approval along with "Please, Doug." and "The whole town wants you back!"

Doug was smiling as he said, "I'll have to talk this over with my wife. She was so proud of me for becoming the Superintendent of Myrna schools. But when I tell her everything that has gone on and that you want me back with a raise, she'll understand. She knows how much I've missed the students and the faculty, and she'll be okay with it. Just don't make any announcement of this until I've told her."

"We can't say anything to anybody," Michael said, "until we've met with Mr. Clifton, but I'll set that up for tomorrow night, if that's all right with everyone."

"The sooner the better!" Ed Matthews said. "It can't be too soon for me," Henry Peterson added as both Franklin Pearce and Jason Wall nodded. "Good job, Michael!" Jason added, "And we're glad to have you back, Doug."

"We really are, Doug," Michael said. "But let's remember, we're still in the middle of the Depression and we still have to find a superintendent!"

And at that, they all groaned, bade each other 'good night' and went home, promising not to tell anyone anything until Michael and they had met with Charles Clifton.

The meeting with Charles Maynard Clifton went better than anyone had expected. Mr. Clifton realized he was in trouble as soon as Michael began questioning him about his courses at the University of Michigan. He ended up apologizing for his lies, agreed to resign, effective immediately, and said he would be leaving town for his home in Missouri by the end of the week.

3

As soon as the word went out Mr. Clifton had resigned as principal of the high school and Doug Adams had agreed to assume his position, it seemed as though the entire town breathed a sigh of relief.

While Ella and Jack had been as delighted as the students and their parents to return to co-teaching 10th through 12th grade classes, it was a relief not to have to listen to Mr. Clifton's comments about the changes. Jack and Ella had become so accustomed to planning their classes together and getting to know their students together they had felt as much joy and relief as the young people did at the return to the former schedule. Even though all the English and history classes were now two weeks behind schedule, Jack and Ella spent hours planning what could be omitted and how to make up the lost time.

It was easiest done with the 10th graders because the first part of the year was concentrated on learning about their own family history, where their ancestors had come from and why they had left their homelands. Then they had to share this knowledge with their history class through letters from relatives and any other ways they had learned about their families.

In their English class they had to write stories or poems or essays about what they had learned about their families and give speeches about at least two relatives they had been able to learn enough about to share with their class members. And they also read stories, poetry, and even novels written by or about people who had come

264

as pioneers to a new land, leaving behind their native countries, customs, culture and even, in many cases, their language.

The first few days were a bit hectic, especially with the 10th graders, as Jack and Ella approached the stories of their family history very differently from teaching out of a textbook. Jack motivated his 10th graders to get involved in real life history lessons as they tried to trace where their ancestors came from and why they left their homelands, along with where they first settled in the New World and how one or more of them ended up in Myrna.

Ella focused on grammar and writing exercises and speaking before a group, assigning them to write about their family stories and histories and then present these to the class. Since they were more or less creating their own textbooks, Ella and Jack had more freedom with the 10th graders and could more easily make up the lost time. All their older students adapted to the changes quickly since, for all except the 10th graders, it was what they had grown accustomed to before the new principal had taken over.

The students in the top two grades that concentrated on American History in the 11th and World History in the 12th had to do some extra reading at first to catch up, but Jack and Ella worked hard at helping them cover the main points of the first two chapters that would prepare them for more in-depth study as they moved further into their textbooks.

Since both Jack and Ella emphasized their students' personal contacts with the history they were studying and how their families' lives had been affected by what was happening in their country of origin as well as in their new country, and in the world around them, the great majority of their students caught up quickly and maintained the interest and curiosity that had grown in them over time as they had explored how they and their families had become Americans.

Jack and Ella met after school with those few students who were having problems catching up, sometimes working with a student one-on-one and other times walking through the subject matter with them, discussing problem areas, and letting them work together in pairs. Within two weeks of extra classes, Ella and Jack both felt these students had caught up well enough to be expected to keep up with their classmates, yet still encouraging them to study and to be willing to ask for additional help when they needed it.

However, it had become a matter of pride to show their fellow students the little extra time they had needed had enabled them to catch up and stay caught up. While these students had generally been C students, Jack and Ella were delighted and praised them when they made a B and even occasionally an A. One of the 10th-grade D students actually grew to love history and by the end of the year received an A- for the second semester from Jack.

4

One evening at Bible study Father Banks started the class by saying that he'd had a really good visit and conversation with Fred Benson a few days earlier. Fred had come by his office and asked if he had time to talk, and of course, he'd said yes.

"I don't intend to go into a lot of details about our conversation, but two weeks ago a sad thing happened during their Sunday morning church service. Fred's voice started shaking as he told me that Pastor James had preached on trusting in God, saying that true trust means God can do anything for those who have real faith in Him. And he finished his sermon saying he was going to demonstrate what real faith is—and he went to a cage he had behind the pulpit and took out a snake, which he then sort of wound around his left arm. Then he walked forward, talking all the time about trusting God to watch over this creature that He had created and would keep it from doing anything that would do harm to any person who had deep and true trust in God's power of love and goodness.

"Pastor James had been moving his left arm a bit along with his right arm, gesturing to make his point. Then suddenly, with no warning, the snake opened its mouth and dug its fangs into the upper part of Pastor James left arm. The Pastor gave out a sort of scream, took his good hand and started trying to get the snake to let go of his arm. The snake finally was unwound and fell to the floor and slithered off into a corner or somewhere.

"By this time the pastor was sweating and saying, 'I need to see a doctor. I need to see a doctor.' His wife had come down from the choir where she is a soprano. And she was holding his arm that was bleeding and saying, 'I've tried to tell you, Preston, that one day a snake would bite you. Now we've got to get you to the doctor's office, only it's Sunday, and what doctor is in his office on Sunday?'"

"Anyway, Fred had his car and it was parked close to the church. So he said he'd take him and his wife to find a doctor. He got his car, drove it up close to the front door where Mrs. James had her arm around her husband and was trying to hold him up. Fred got out and helped her get him into the back seat, and she got in beside him. Edith had followed them out the church and when she got in the front seat with Fred, they drove to the hospital, finding Dr. Anderson who had just come by after church to check on one of his patients. They helped Pastor James into his office and onto an examination table, but by this time the Pastor was really out of it, babbling, not making sense.

"They told Dr. Anderson what had happened, and he wanted to know what kind of snake had bitten him. Mrs. James said she was pretty sure it was a copperhead because her husband had found one down by the creek and brought it home just over a week ago. She made him keep all his snakes in a big box out in their shed because she didn't want them in the house. Anyway, the point is that the pastor died last night.

"Doc Anderson had tried to bleed him and get the poison out, but evidently he didn't get it all or it was too late to help him. Pastor James died about midnight."

John Banks sighed and said, "This was truly a sad tale, and I want us to be silent for a few minutes and offer prayers to God for Pastor James and his family and congregation, and also for Edith and Fred Benson, because Fred told me that Edith has taken Pastor

James's death to heart, and he fears she will no longer believe in God or any church. So let us pray for all those who have been hurt by this death."

After a good five minutes of silence, Father Banks closed the prayer time saying, "God of mercy and forgiveness, we pray for your presence with the members of Holiness Church, for Pastor James's wife and child and other family members.

"We ask that you lead us in kindness and understanding and give us light into your ways so we may know what it means and what it is like to live and grow in true understanding of faith in you. Help us to trust in your love for all of creation and for your presence with us, with Pastor James's family, and with the members of Holiness Church, even when we don't understand your ways or what you truly want from us. In Christ's holy name we pray. Amen."

The Bible study never really got underway that night as the group shared stories and memories of their own feelings of missing Fred and Edith as part of the Bible study group and what they might do to reach out to them and encourage them to return. Edith's mother had died a few months earlier and while some of the church members had been to see both Edith and her mother before her death, the visits had felt strained and uncomfortable, and they didn't quite know why. Father Banks had also gone by soon after they had left the group but, without having called first, arrived while Pastor James was there visiting. He'd felt a bit awkward and hadn't stayed long.

The evening ended without the group's never discussing the passage from Luke that had been planned. Father Banks encouraged the women in the group to try to make contact with Edith.

For his part, Father Banks had called Fred at work the next day, telling him that he would like to go by and visit Edith but wanted to know if Fred thought a visit from him would help or hurt her.

Fred had responded, "Oh, Father Banks, I don't know. I don't think it will hurt, but she is really confused right now. She was so sure Pastor James had all the answers. She has never been very sure of her own faith—thinks like her mother that God doesn't love her.

She has always been trying to figure out and do what she thinks will please God, and yet never feels she has succeeded. Now she says she doesn't believe in any church or any preacher, much less in God who's supposed to be so good and loving. I just don't know if she'll even see you. But I think she needs you, needs to hear from you, even if she doesn't realize it or can't admit it even to herself."

"What is the best time of day for me to go by, Fred?"

"Probably about 10:00 in the morning. She's been sleeping later than usual, but I think she'll be up, dressed, and will have had at least a cup of coffee by then. Actually, wait till about 10:30, just to be sure she'll be ready for 'company.'"

"I'll be there at 10:30 in the morning. It will probably be better if you don't warn her I'm coming because that might really upset her or make her angry. We'll just have to see if I can do anything to help her feel better about God, Pastor James, and herself. Truthfully, it's in God's hands, and maybe He'll use me to help Edith."

"Oh, Father Banks, I hope you can, I believe you can."

"Well, Fred, it'll be God working through me, not me by myself. Why don't we have some minutes of silent prayer as we pray for Pastor James, his family, his church, and for the two of you and all the church members who have been affected by Pastor James's death."

So they did.

* * *

Father Banks knocked on the door of the Benson home at 10:30 the next morning. Having spent time in prayer and then sharing his concerns with his wife Sarah, whose understanding, wisdom, and discretion he trusted completely, he still felt nervous about calling on Edith. But to his surprise she opened the door herself, and said, "Oh, Father Banks, you are truly an answer to my prayers. Please come in."

He followed her into the kitchen where she asked him to sit down at the table where she had been having a second cup of coffee and asked if she could pour him one. John Banks had already drunk two cups of coffee that morning, but thought quickly it would be better to drink at least a good part of another cup than to appear unwilling to let Edith serve him—and perhaps easier for her to talk if they were sipping a cup of coffee together.

"Oh, Father Banks, I've truly wanted to talk to you because I've been so upset by Pastor James's death and everything that has happened since at Holiness Church. But I was afraid you were still angry with us for leaving the Bible study group and wouldn't ever want to speak to us again. So I just didn't know what I should do. This whole thing has just really shaken my faith in God. Will God let Pastor James into heaven? Is there even a heaven? And then today, here you are at my front door and now sitting with me at my kitchen table. It's like God answered my prayers, and so maybe He does exist after all. I'm just so confused."

John Banks had just sat quietly and listened patiently, remembering how Edith could go on and on about something, but knowing she basically had a caring heart. When she paused to take a breath, he had reached out and taken her hand in his, saying, "Edith, my dear, I can understand and appreciate what a terrible and sad thing Pastor James's death has been to you and to the entire congregation. While I disagreed with Pastor James on some things, like handling snakes, I believe he was a sincere man of God. We so rarely know what goes on in a person's heart and mind that makes him or her think or believe the way they do.

"But we can trust that this God we worship and serve is a loving and caring God who does know and understand why we are the way we are and do the things we do. I am sorry I did not ever get to know Pastor James, but I believe him to be a sincere believer and follower of the same God I love and try to serve, and that the people at Holiness Church are trying to know and love and serve. I do not know what had gone on in his growing up years or during these past years to lead him to want to test his own faith and his congregation's faith as well as their lives by bringing live, poisonous snakes into worship. But I have no doubt of his sincerity in believing or thinking this was what God wanted him to do at this time."

"But, why did God let him die? Why didn't God do something to stop that venomous creature from biting him?" Edith started crying.

"I have no way of being certain of what was in God's mind any more than I do of what Pastor James was thinking, Edith. But perhaps God recognized Pastor James was driven by something that had happened to him earlier in his life, and his memories caused him to put God's love to the test. And while it probably didn't work out the way he had wanted or expected it to, I am sure God loved and still loves Pastor James and now he is with God and at peace from whatever drove him to use a deadly snake to prove God's love for him."

"Do you really think he is with God right now?"

"Edith, I truly believe the God I worship and preach about is a God of love and mercy. Therefore I trust this life here on earth is not all there is. And therefore, death is not just an end of this earthly life but also the beginning of a new and more wonderful life with God in eternity.

"Now don't ask me how I know that or exactly what it is like, because I am a mere mortal. But the Scriptures and my relationship with this God who is Father, Son, and Holy Spirit, leads me, helps me, trust that what I've just said to you is so—is true. And while I know many people who have the kind of faith in God I've just tried to describe, there are also many who don't believe, who don't live with that kind of faith.

"And I am sorry about that. So I do the best I can to live out my beliefs and share them with anyone who is interested or who is searching for what gives life a deeper and more far-reaching meaning than the few years we live on this earth. I am here with you right now, in hopes that by sharing what I believe, what gives my life meaning and hope for a future life beyond this one, will be of comfort to you and will provide you with hope and faith and love to help you move forward. Do you think that is possible?"

"Oh, Father Banks, I want it to be. I want to know and trust and love and serve the God you are talking about. I thought

Holiness Church would enable me to do that, but it really didn't. There were people there like me who were looking for something and thought they, or we, had found it in Pastor James's faith and teaching. But that Sunday with the snake, I saw him as a desperate man who was looking for proof of God's power by engaging with a deadly snake. And it didn't save him from the snake. So where do I, where can I, find this kind of faith?"

"Edith, Christianity is supposed to offer you a pathway, a road to that kind of faith. Some of us do a better job of helping people find the road and stay on it than others. The truth is all churches, all faith communities, are composed of imperfect human beings, some more imperfect, others more perfect, but none with no imperfections. I am an old man and do not serve a church any longer, but I still try to serve God. That is why I have the Bible study group that meets in a Presbyterian Church instead of an Episcopal one. But I like that our group has people from other churches, people who are Jewish, people who are open-minded and who are trying to know and serve the one God, in whatever ways we worship and by whatever name or names we call the Creator of all life.

"Edith, I beg you, do not give up on churches, and certainly do not give up on God, not for God's sake but for yours and for Fred's as well. There are no perfect churches, but keep searching until you find one where you can 'feel' God's love and mercy, feel it in the exchanges among its members, feel it in the worship, and also in the outreach to help others in the community regardless of their faith or church attendance.

"I've been here longer than I intended, Edith. I don't want to wear you out. Do you have any comments or questions for me?"

"Can Fred and I come back to our Bible class in Sunday School and the Bible Study you lead?"

"Of course! I cannot speak for the Sunday school class at the Episcopal Church because I'm not supposed to attend any church activities there since I'm the former minister. But both you and Fred will be truly welcomed, I know, by the Bible Study group.

272

We've added a few new people while you all have been away, but it's still a good group of 'searchers' just like you. We're still meeting the second and fourth Wednesdays of every month in the Fellowship Hall at First Presbyterian. I'll look for you there. Now let's have a prayer together."

And they did so with Father Banks praying that God had welcomed Brother James into heaven and given comfort to his wife, family, and congregation. And then he thanked God for His presence in Edith and Fred's marriage and prayed the Bible Study group would continue to grow in love and service to all those who wanted to know God better and serve as God's caring people in God's world.

5

The months seemed to speed by as football season ended with the final game on Thanksgiving Day. Myrna's fans were delighted when their team managed to make the winning touchdown with only three minutes left in the game.

Then the Christmas season was upon the town with everyone trying to figure out how to make gift-giving happen within a smaller budget than even that of the previous year. The teachers in the schools and the townspeople worked together to make gift buying possible by advertising and focusing on thoughtful and needed items as gifts, with emphasis perhaps on one special gift per person.

Ella grieved because they had realized it was too expensive to have Dan come home from the Naval Academy for such a brief time but was truly touched when Jonathan and Catherine Mackinley had him over for dinner on Christmas Eve. Then he went with them to midnight service at their Presbyterian Church and he even spent the night with them, sleeping on the sofa in the living room. Ella had mailed his gifts to the Mackinleys' house, along with some homemade candy and cookies for the family.

She and Jack were both touched because Dan called them long-distance from the Mackinleys' home on Christmas afternoon and told both his parents that in spite of missing being with them, he was having a good Christmas. Then both Jonathan and Catherine spoke briefly to Ella and then Jack, saying how much they had enjoyed the opportunity to get to know Dan.

Ella, of course, soon wrote a long and very sincere letter of thanks to the Mackinleys for taking their son in and giving him a home for Christmas!

Part IX

The War Draws Nearer to Home: 1940

1

All during this "waiting period" President Roosevelt was struggling with how to awaken the majority of Americans to the dangers of remaining neutral and uninvolved in what was happening in Europe. Yet 1940 was an election year, and Roosevelt was running for a third term, ignoring the precedent set by President George Washington of a limit of two terms. Franklin Roosevelt declared his motivation for running for reelection was that the threat of a world war demanded the United States be led by someone with an experienced and stable hand and not change horses in the middle of the stream.

While campaigning for re-election he promised American parents in a speech in Boston on October 10, 1940, "I have said this before, but I shall say it again and again and again: Your boys are not going to be sent into any foreign wars." He won the election handily. However, the challenge that immediately faced him was how to keep his word and still support the Allies.

The President needed and wanted to make it very clear the United States would provide the European democracies *with arms and war materiel but not its sons or husbands*. Roosevelt made it possible for the USA to extend its involvement in the war without directly involving its military while also being able to keep his promise to American parents—at least for the time being.

Jack and Ella decided to splurge by making the trip to Annapolis
for Dan's graduation from the Naval Academy. They really had
not planned on taking that long trip again, but in early spring
Dan had finally confessed he had been taking flying lessons for
the last three years and had been told that most likely he would
receive an assignment to Pearl Harbor in the Hawaiian Islands
immediately after graduation.

Dan had also written his family he had proposed to Lilly, who
would finish nursing school in Little Rock in mid-May, and she
had said *yes*. If possible, he planned to come home and marry Lilly
after his graduation and so would be able to send for her if he were
assigned to Pearl Harbor. But he feared he might not have time for
a trip home and hoped they would bring Lilly with them to
Annapolis if her family couldn't make the trip, and they would ask
Chaplain Mark McGinnis to marry them.

All of Dan's information and plans were hard for Ella to deal
with because she had not expected her son to be so "in charge" of
everything. She realized as never before that he was a grown man
now, and soon would be an officer in the United States Naval
Services. He had ignored her wishes and learned to fly an airplane
and might soon be flying one in battle against an enemy, probably
Hitler's German air force.

She wasn't sure how she would have dealt with this "blow" had
it not been for Jack and both Pastor Mitchell and Father Banks.
All three of them listened to her concerns and prayed with her
along with promising to keep her, Jack, Dan, and Lilly in their
prayers—and definitely not ignoring the world that was already
dealing with a war and the United States that seemed to be
growing closer and closer to entering one!

Dan had written each graduate would receive six tickets for
special seats at the graduation ceremony. Jack had already decided
that while it would be a bit costly to take the train to Annapolis,
sometimes money was worth spending, and since they weren't sure

where Dan was going to be stationed and Hawaii would obviously be a much more expensive trip for them to undertake, they would most certainly attend Dan's graduation.

The ceremony was scheduled for Saturday morning, June 8. When Dan heard from Lilly she would be coming to Annapolis alone, he wrote to his parents he'd like for Lilly to ride to Annapolis on the train with them. Ella replied they would be delighted to have Lilly come with them and would invite her immediately. Dan checked with Ella about their train and hotel reservations and then made the same reservations for Lilly, paying for them himself.

Lilly was actually relieved to be traveling with Ella and Jack. She wasn't really a shy person, but she was not at all knowledgeable about Navy protocol and did not want to embarrass herself or the man she planned to marry, much less his parents!

The three actually arrived on Thursday the 6th and spent Friday touring the grounds of the Academy on the 7th, getting to meet several of Dan's professors and classmates, as well as reconnecting with Chaplain Mark McGinnis, whom Ella thought of as a longtime friend. The Chaplain told Lilly he had hoped to perform their wedding but understood they wanted it held in her home church in Myrna. He was just glad he was able to meet Lilly and wish both her and Dan many, many years of happiness together.

Since they would have extra tickets for the graduation ceremony itself, Ella and Jack had invited Jonathan and Catherine Mackinley to be their guests. Never having attended a graduation ceremony at the Naval Academy, the Mackinleys were delighted to accept their invitation. Jonathan had first met Dan briefly during one of Dan's visits to see Jack at Walter Reed. The Mackinleys had kept up with him, enjoyed having him spend Christmas with them, and now felt he was almost a son.

On Graduation Day Ella, Jack, Lilly, and Jonathan and Catherine Mackinley had excellent seats near the front, facing the podium where the Academy officials and faculty sat facing the soon-to-be graduates seated in the middle section, their proud families and friends in rows on both sides of the midshipmen in their white dress uniforms.

Ella had to admit she had barely heard and remembered even less of what the speakers said that morning. She couldn't erase early memories of Dan as a baby, a boy, and now a grown man, and so the words of those speaking from the podium didn't penetrate. The singing by the Navy choir and the music of the Navy band touched her much more than the words that were spoken. She and Lilly both had tears in their eyes as Dan went forward to receive his diploma and his orders for the coming year, although they already knew what they were.

The graduation ceremony ended with the playing and singing of the Navy Hymn followed by the National Anthem, with probably everyone present wondering what lay ahead for this nation to which they, and now their sons, had pledged their allegiance and for which many of these young men participating in this ceremony might sacrifice their lives as well. Even the fathers present for this graduation ceremony found it difficult to keep the tears from forming in their own eyes as they stood and watched the rows of strong young bodies with eager expressions on their faces march out. When the last graduate had made it to the clearing at the end, they threw their hats into the air and cheered.

A reception followed in Bancroft Hall, and Ella and Jack were able to meet and speak to many of Dan's professors and friends. Dan had claimed Lilly and was taking her around to meet his friends. Ella worried Jonathan and Catherine might be bored but instead were amazed at how many people they knew and were chatting with. It turned out that several members of the faculty were Presbyterians and members of the church they attended. As the sun rose higher and the day began to grow warmer, the crowd began to scatter.

Jack and Ella found Dan and Lilly, having invited them to join them and Jonathan and Catherine for lunch. Dan said he was ready for anything now that he had his diploma in his hand and his wife-to-be with him. Jonathan and Catherine joined in Jack and Ella's laughter, but inside they were all wondering what the future held for these young people. Catherine was hoping it would all be over by the time Jonathan's and her boys would be old enough to serve in the armed forces, while Ella was struggling to curb her imagination of what the future could bring, holding back the tears that kept threatening to rise to the surface and spill over.

3

June seemed to fly by, mostly taken up by the preparations for Lilly and Dan's wedding to be held at the First Methodist Church where Lilly and her family were members. It bothered Ella a little that neither Father Banks nor Greg Mitchell would be officiating, although she liked and respected Pastor William Evans, the minister at First Methodist.

Lilly had picked a pattern for a square-neck dress with short capped sleeves and a fitted waist with a slim skirt that fell just below her knees. She was pleased with the way she looked in it when her mother had finished it. Her mother had also found a small white hat that fit the top of Lilly's head perfectly. She covered it with tiny white roses which she had learned to make in a ladies' craft group that met weekly at her church and had also made a veil she attached to the hat. It covered Lilly's face fully to her shoulders and yet looked lovely when it was lifted and left hanging down the back. Her younger sister Rose and Dan's sister Mary Beth were her only attendants while Dan had asked Jack to be his "best man" and Lilly's brother Philip to be his groomsman. Ella was glad to have Mary Beth, Patrick, and their two children as her support during the ceremony.

Dan and Lilly were married on Saturday, June 22, and would have almost two weeks together before Dan would leave for California and then go on to Hawaii. The Methodist ladies had prepared a lovely luncheon before they left for their honeymoon. Dan and Lilly had considered going to the MacPhersons' cottage that they had been offered, but when they realized it took almost an entire day to get there, they decided to go to Hot Springs because Michael had a friend who owned a cabin there and he had access to it as long as they weren't using it at the time. Normally the family would have been there over the 4th of July, but this particular year they would be in California because their son, who was also an Annapolis graduate but several years before Dan, had been living with his family on the Naval Base at San Diego and was getting ready to be shipped to Hawaii. His wife and son would soon follow. The Petersons wanted to spend whatever time he might have available with him and his family.

Dan and Lilly refused to tell anyone where they were going except Ella and Jack because they needed to know how to get in touch with Dan in case the Navy wanted to send a message to him. They hoped that would not happen since they had only this time together and then would be separated until Dan had landed in Hawaii and could get permission for Lilly to join him as soon as possible.

4

July 27, 1940 (telegram sent to Lilly Wood)
Lilly, I finally made some headway. You should receive telegram instructions for you to fly to San Diego where you will get information about your upcoming trip on ship with info you will need. All is classified and I cannot send it here. Love you, Dan

July 29, 1940
My Dearest Love,

Your telegram arrived yesterday and I have my airplane ticket to San Diego. My plane will be met by someone from the Navy who will escort me to the ship on which I will sail, soon to be in your arms. I am so excited and can hardly wait. Must start packing! Your wife! I hope I have been discreet enough.

282

August 26, 1940

Dear Mother and Papa Jack,

My beautiful wife arrived here on Friday, the 16th, and we had the whole weekend together to help her unpack and get settled into our small cottage and then explore the island. She is as captivated by its beauty and its climate as I am. What a truly gorgeous part of the world! And the Hawaiian people are absolutely lovely, so friendly and so happy.

There is music everywhere we go, or so it seems, and dancing, and the food is different but so delicious. Sometimes it is better not to ask what I am eating but just enjoy the taste.

Lilly was a bit hesitant to try the food and was shy about trying to speak to the Hawaiian people, but that didn't last long. She is actually doing better at learning to speak and understand the language than I am, and I've been here almost two months.

She will meet with the director of the hospital day after tomorrow and is hoping she will be hired as a nurse. That will give her something to do during the day when I'm at work and will be even better when we go out to sea because she will have made friends with other nurses. She is also beginning to meet and get to know some of the other wives. But the attention that is paid here to the man's rank is almost funny. Of course, as an Ensign I am far down the list, even as a recent graduate of the Naval Academy, though it does give me some respect, at least above an enlistee, who is often really green.

I'm grateful I had already learned some of the Navy lingo, traditions, and rules but have picked up a lot more since I've been here. I already knew how to translate their commands, recognize their insignias so I know their rank and how to salute and address them accordingly. Some of it is intimidating and other things about all of it makes me want to smile or laugh, but I keep myself from doing either—and so I am able to get along with and even have great respect for the officers and even more for the enlisted men who are here for a wide assortment of reasons.

But the enlistees mostly come across as good men who are looking for some kind of order in their lives and the opportunity to do something meaningful, even worthwhile, that will give them reasons to be proud of what they are doing and who they are. Some of them are so like the guys I knew in Myrna, especially the ones who lived out on the co-op farm. They are just really good people who didn't have the advantages of money and education I've had because of the two of you. But the truth is they really love our country and are ready to give their lives to protect it.

By the way, I finally found out where Larry Coleman works and actually got to see him. He is a shipman, is part of the crew of a destroyer and so is out to sea some of the time as they practice and learn what to do in case of war. He still hasn't married, and so we had him over to dinner a couple of nights ago. He and Lilly liked each other, and she had cooked an amazing dinner. It was good to reconnect with him, but since he's on a ship while I fly airplanes, we probably won't get to see each other as often as we might like.

I had been surprised that he wasn't still a pilot, but he told us he has had some problems with his ears and hearing that caused issues with his sense of balance, and so now he's on a ship. But if he continues to have problems on board ships, he'll end up in an office on shore. He's so smart, the Navy says they want to keep him, even if he's at a desk job.

The truth is he and I both love our country and realize we may be two of those who die trying to protect it, one way or another. But I want you to know I give thanks to God for you, Mother, and for my birth father whose life got cut short. And I'm so grateful for you, Mother, for your strength and wisdom, and especially for being smart enough to attract and marry Papa Jack!

284

There, I've gone on long enough. Lilly and I are getting ready to head to a movie, It's a Wonderful World *with Jimmy Stewart and Claudette Colbert. I think I remember you two saw this in Annapolis when you were able to walk and enjoy some life outside Healing House and after your physical therapy, Papa Jack! I have to say Hawaii is a bit behind in the entertainment world, but I hope we enjoy it.*

Love you both so much, Dan

Ella and Jack had to laugh at the idea that Dan and Lilly were going to see *It's a Wonderful World,* hoping they would be able to keep up with the crazy ups-and-downs in the story better than they had been. But they knew Dan and Lilly were so in love it didn't really matter! Just as it hadn't mattered to them!

Part X

The Waiting Game: 1940

1

Having become close friends with both Hank and Ruth Fredrick, Ella approached Ruth about coming to the class and sharing with them a little about her life in Bavaria, that part of Germany not in the news as frequently as Berlin and other cities. Ruth immediately said she would be delighted to come and share with the class one of the major festivals in her part of Germany, the Oktoberfest, the most famous of all Bavaria's holidays. She even remembered the dress she had worn as part of her dance class's presentation during the Oktoberfest when she was 16 years old. She could share the story of how and why the festival began and how long it had been occurring, and she thought she could even remember what their dresses looked like because they were typical of what peasant girls had worn for the Oktoberfest for many, many years.

Since it was nearing October, Eleanor thought Ruth would be a wonderful Friday program for her and Jack's 10th-grade English and history classes. Two Fridays a month, Ella and Jack often recruited a speaker to come and share some of his or her own family history with all the 10th-grade students, and that real-life flavor of human history inspired their young people to want to learn more about where they or their families had come from.

On Friday the 27th of September Ella and Jack gathered all the 10th graders into the library where the tables had been moved and 64 chairs had been placed. A small stage with a podium in the center had been brought in. Ella and Jack stood at the entrance to the library to greet the students as they entered and to welcome their speaker. They were both amazed when Ruth appeared in a red-and-white checked skirt with apron top over a white blouse with puffed sleeves. She was wearing long white stockings and black low-heel pumps, and she had a red bandana tied in the back around her shoulder-length black hair.

"You look about 16 dressed in your festival peasant-girl finery," Ella told her, leading her up to the podium. "Students, you have a treat this afternoon because we have with us a young woman who grew up in a beautiful part of Germany called Bavaria. She is wearing a native dress like the one she wore for a festival she is going to tell you about. So it is my great pleasure to introduce you to a relative newcomer to our town, but a person who has become a good friend of ours. Please welcome Ruth Fredrick."

As the students clapped, a few who had recognized the name *Fredrick*, turned and looked at her son Sam, who turned bright red and lowered his head.

Ruth began by saying, "I am sure you all are wondering what a grown woman is doing dressed like this. Well, I am dressed for a special occasion in the area of the country where I was born and grew up. That area is Bavaria, in the southern part of Germany.

"Over a hundred years ago, on October 12 in the year 1810, Crown Prince Ludwig of Bavaria married Princess Teresa, and they had a big party to celebrate their marriage in the capital city of Bavaria, which is Munich. Munich is where I grew up, but *many, many, many* years after Ludwig and Teresa's marriage. (The students laughed appropriately.) Munich's a city surrounded by mountains and castles, palaces, monuments, and a great number of beautiful buildings. And in October for many years except, during the war, Munich has held a two-week-long festival in honor of Ludwig and Teresa's marriage.

"When I was 14 years old my parents enrolled me in a dance class of young girls, where we learned some of the old dances the German people have been doing for several hundred years. Actually, I don't know for how long. There were 16 of us young girls in my dance class, and we learned different kinds of dancing, but when I was 16 we practiced and practiced doing folk dances until our teacher thought we were good enough to enter a contest—a special contest because dancers who were good enough would be asked to dance at the opening of the Munich Folk Festival in memory of Prince Ludwig and Princess Teresa. We would dance at the same time every day for the two weeks that the festival lasted. The festival always began on the first Sunday in October and ended two weeks later. During those two weeks many of Munich's citizens dress in *dirndl* and *lederhosen*. *Dirndl* is the kind of dress with an apron front like I have on and a scarf in their hair. *Lederhosen* are the long thick stockings that both men and women wore to protect their legs.

"The school librarian is kindly letting us use the school's Victrola so that I can play this recording of one of the songs we danced to, and if you don't mind, I will show you a few of the steps, although I don't have a partner. Mrs. MacLean is going to start the Victrola, and you will just have to pretend I have a "someone" I am dancing with."

Ella put the needle down onto the record, and immediately the room was filled with the joyful sound and rhythm of German *volkmusic*, and Ruth was clapping her hands and moving her feet and body to the rhythm of the music. Her dance lasted about five minutes but drew loud applause from the students.

"Did your group get a prize for being the best dancers?" Susie Morris asked.

"Actually, we did, and each of us girls received a charm engraved with the Munich City Hall on it and were told we had danced so well the city council wanted us to return the next year."

"Do you still have your charm? Did you bring it so we can see it?" Susie asked.

"I don't have it. So I'm sorry I can't show it to you." Ruth said.

"Did you dance the next year?" Betsy Adams asked.

"The group did, but I was told that I could not perform with the group any longer." Ruth said.

"Why were you told that? What did you do to be told that?" Susie asked, her indignation showing in her tone of voice.

"I didn't do anything except be born Jewish. I am a Jew. And in Germany in those days and even in these days, Jews are hated and are treated as though they are criminals, even if they have done nothing wrong."

Glen Mitchell raised his hand, and when Ella nodded, he said, "My parents were talking about that the other night after dinner. I had come out of my room to ask Daddy for some help with an algebra problem, and they were talking about Jews in Germany being treated like they were bad people or something, having to wear a big star on their clothing and not being allowed in some stores or other places. I don't understand why Jews are treated this way." Glen's voice displayed his puzzlement.

"Because they killed Jesus!" Marty Higgins called out.

"Actually, the Romans killed Jesus," Glen Mitchell said, "though some of the Jews wanted him to be killed. But all that happened almost 2,000 years ago. Why punish Jewish people today for something that was done some 2,000 years ago?"

"Because even Jews today don't believe in Jesus as God's Son," Marty Higgins answered.

"But suppose I said I'm not sure I believe that Jesus even lived or was the Son of God, would you want me to be killed too?" Glen asked.

"Your Daddy's a preacher. You have to believe Jesus was God's Son!" Marty exclaimed loudly.

"Yes, my Daddy's a preacher. But I don't think he'd want to kill *anyone* just because they don't believe what he believes," Glen said with conviction.

"Thank you, Glen," Jack MacLean said, as he walked up on the stage. "You are right. I know your Dad, and he would be shocked at the idea of harming by word or deed anyone just because he believed or thought differently. But I think this conversation has gone far enough.

"Instead, what I want each one of you here today to do is to think long and hard about this. Look at Ruth Fredrick, and imagine her as a girl just a little older than you are right now. Look at her even as a grown woman who has been gracious enough to offer to come here today and share with you something about her life and the city and the country where she lived when she was about your age.

"Imagine you are Ruth, and somebody comes into this room or knocks on the door of your house and tells you that because you don't like the President or believe what the President says—or you don't like your Preacher or believe what your Preacher says, then you can't go to or participate in any school or its activities or parades or groups in your town. You can't even leave your house to go anywhere unless you are wearing some emblem on your coat or dress that lets everybody know you are not to be treated as a person but as something bad. So it's okay to make fun of you and to call you ugly names and even throw rocks at you.

"Think about her children who are students in this school. Think about yourselves and what it would be like to be treated this way—and it could happen if a large enough group decided they weren't going to accept anybody who believed in Santa Claus or had green eyes or spoke with an accent different from those of you who have grown up in Myrna.

"I apologize for getting all heated up about this, but I had a small part in a war to try to keep this kind of cruelty and unfairness from happening again. And we failed. It's growing in Germany where Mrs. Fredrick came from. In fact, Germany has recently declared war on Poland, and now England and France have declared war on Germany. And so, now much of Europe is at war or soon will be. Mrs. Fredrick came here today knowing that the country she was born in has started another war, and who knows how or where it will end.

"She came here today to share something she had loved being part of until she was forbidden to participate any longer, not because of anything she did or didn't do, but because her family was of a different faith from the majority of the German people. And that's wrong thinking and wrong acting, or should be, to all

Americans who settled this country to find freedom—even freedom to believe about God in their own way.

"Do any of you have questions or anything you want to say?"

Several of the students raised their hands.

"I want to say how bad I feel that you were treated that way as a girl, Mrs. Fredrick. I can't imagine how awful it would be to live in a country that made you feel like you didn't belong. Is that why you and your family moved to the United States?" Paula Moore asked.

"That was a major part of the reason," Ruth replied.

"Are you glad you are here, even when something like today happens?" Jimmy Majors asked.

"Yes, I am, because I believe that most of the people here understand how important it is to be free to have your own religious beliefs and other kinds of beliefs as well, as long as you don't try to force people to think or believe as you do or punish them in some way if they don't," Ruth smiled at the group, and said, "I am happy all of you are here today. My family and I have been grateful for the welcome we have received from the people of Myrna. I hope people of all faiths and all skin colors will be welcomed in this country that we want to live in as its citizens. Thank *you* for welcoming me here today."

As Ruth turned to speak to Ella and Jack, someone stood and began clapping and soon the whole room was filled with students who were standing and applauding. Ella's eyes were filled with tears as were Ruth's, and Jack had to clear his throat a couple of times as he and Ella accompanied Ruth to the door.

"I think you have made a real difference here today, giving our young people a face, a person to visualize and think about when they hear or read about what is happening in Germany," Jack said as Ella nodded her head, saying,

"I realize some of our students are from homes that have swallowed Nazi prejudices and propaganda. We appreciate your courage and your willingness to expose yourself in coming here today, but by putting a face and a personality onto being Jewish, you have likely changed, or at least begun changing, some attitudes and ideas about Jews and even Judaism. Thank you for coming," Ella said, hugging Ruth again as they had reached the door to the outside and her car.

Ruth hugged her in return, got into her car and drove away, praying she truly had, in some way, made a difference in those who feared or resented Jews because of the few ways they differed from other groups and religions. But she also prayed that while there was still some dislike of or prejudice against her people, this war that had just begun with the conquest of Poland would not spread much further and draw in this country where she and her family now felt they belonged.

2

As a mother, Ella was probably not alone in hoping that, if and when war began, the United States would remain neutral, even though she hated to think of the Germans and Italians ruling over England, France, Poland, Holland, Belgium, Spain and other smaller countries in Europe. She prayed the French and the English might be strong enough to bring the war to a quick end, but that did not look likely to happen. She prayed her daughter Eleanor, her husband Ronald and his family, and her precious grandson Lee and new granddaughter Amy would be able to remain safe. She hoped Dan would be given a desk job some-where, but ultimately she had to accept that her *hopes* were unlikely to be realized.

* * *

But regardless of what Ella hoped and prayed for, life went on throughout the world. In early December Dan and Lilly wrote that getting ready for Christmas in Honolulu was as odd an experience as they had ever had. For one thing, the weather was so warm and the flowers and trees so beautiful a person found it hard to realize it was almost Christmas.

The stores and houses were decorated, but they looked more like they were decorated for a "fiesta" than for a "holy holiday"! Only at the few churches in Honolulu did Lilly and Dan get any kind of a "feeling of Christmas" because each one had a Manger Scene either inside or outside or both.

Inside one Catholic Church they actually experienced the Christian understanding and feeling of the meaning of Christmas as the gift of the Christ Child. And in the air in a few of the stores there was a feeling of love and kindness that gave its shoppers a glimpse or an echo of the gift whose real meaning was love offered to everyone, absolutely to *everyone*.

Meanwhile, Ella, Jack, and Mary Beth, Patrick, and their children Pat and Nora were finding all sorts of ways to make Christmas "merry" in spite of what was happening in other parts of the world. The members of First Presbyterian each year joined with three other churches in the town to "adopt families" who were in need, especially those with younger children. The Methodists, Baptists Episcopalians, and Presbyterians who participated every year took turns leading the planning. This particular year the Presbyterians were in charge. As was the custom, the elementary grade school teachers and principals had given a list of the families most in need of help to the pastor of whichever church was in charge of the project that year.

In this case, Presbyterian Minister Greg Mitchell then invited the ministers of the other three churches to a meeting at which each church would declare how many families had volunteered to fill a family's requests. Families had been asked to provide the names, sexes, sizes and likes for each child and make one request per child. They also could list one or two items of clothing needed in each child's size. Sometimes two families would offer to take on one large family. Smaller churches like the Presbyterians and Episcopalians usually limited themselves to choosing eight or 10 families who were on the list while the Baptists and Methodists generally volunteered for 12 to 18 each.

The churches rotated their choices in order, and this year the Presbyterians would have first choice of the families they wanted to help celebrate Christmas. Next would be the Baptists, then the Episcopalians, and then the Methodists. Next Christmas the Baptists would be first, and the Presbyterians would be last. The list rarely had more than 45 families on it. Many of the families who lived in the country were too proud to ask for help. Those who sharecropped on farms looked to the owners to provide gifts or money for the workers.

This year the Presbyterians had signed up to take responsibility for nine families. Ella and Jack along with Patrick and Mary Beth had signed up to get gifts and food for two families with young children about the same ages as Pat and Nora. The gifts would be given anonymously—all with cards from Santa, Mrs. Santa, the Elves, and so forth.

The MacLeans and the Carnahans had decided they would make their lists, shop and then get together to wrap and pack the boxes for each family. It took a bit of planning so that the family would receive a nice gift for each one, toy or game for the children, a sweater or shirt or jacket for parents or older children, and then groceries that would include a ham or roast, plus vegetables, fruit, and a dessert for Christmas Day.

Patrick and Mary Beth took their children with them to shop for their chosen family whose children happened to be two little boys, one six and the other four. When they had made it very clear to Pat and Nora that these were presents for children who might not get anything otherwise, they were pleased at how well both children entered into the idea of finding something they thought someone their own age would like too. Mary Beth and Patrick ended up choosing a wind- up train set with tracks and a village and some smaller toys to go in knitted stockings for the two little boys. They found a pretty pink sweater set for the mother and a pair of good outdoor gloves and a stocking cap for the man.

Jack and Ella filled their Saturday afternoon during the second week of December shopping for their family, amazed at how much they enjoyed buying for people they actually knew since the family they had chosen were two young people, now a married couple, whom they had taught the first year they tried their new system of 10th graders researching their family's history. As teen-agers they had seemed so young but both were good students. Now they had an almost-three-year-old daughter and 15-months-old twin boys. It gave Jack and Ella much pleasure to remember these young people and pick out something they were fairly sure they would like. They chose a pretty girl doll and a set of play dishes for the girl and push toys that made noises for the twins along with a rubber ball for each. They had also bought a blue sweater set for the mother and a flannel shirt for the daddy.

On that same Saturday evening, since both families had done all their shopping except for the food, Ella and Jack took wrapping paper and Christmas cards over to Patrick and Mary Beth's so that both families could enjoy seeing what the others had chosen for their families and then wrap them in Christmas paper and put them in separate piles to bag up for delivery. Pat and Nora made the wrapping like a party as they looked at and examined the children's gifts and even felt the gifts for the parents. Both children and adults felt like Santa had come to see them. Ella and Jack especially enjoyed watching Nora and Pat pick up the gifts they had chosen and then show them to Ella and Jack, saying "This is for Tim and this is for Tom. Do you like it, Gramma and Grampa?" And Ella and Jack would exclaim that it was a wonderful gift for whichever child would receive it.

Once the gifts were wrapped and bagged, only the food remained to be bought and that would wait until a day or two before Christmas so it would be fresh. Then early on the Sunday afternoon nearest Christmas Eve, the pastor who was in charge would put on a Santa Claus suit while members from the various churches who wanted to help with the deliveries would dress up as elves or clowns or whatever kind of costume they could come up with and drive around helping with the deliveries, singing carols, and spreading cheer.

When all the deliveries had been made, all the workers were invited to come to the host church for spiced tea and cookies and an opportunity to visit and then sing Christmas carols and even some non-religious tunes like "Jingle Bells." If Christmas Eve happened to fall on Sunday, the church in charge usually set the delivery date a day or two early.

This yearly event and all the preparations leading up to it had become Jack and Ella's favorite part of Christmas, along with the Christmas Eve service itself at 6:00. The Presbyterians had a family-style evening service with lots of carol singing and a Christmas story told or acted out by members and children. The service always ended with the Biblical account from Luke, the lighting of candles, and singing "Silent Night" in the darkened sanctuary.

Afterwards Mary Beth, Pat, and their children, John and Sarah Banks, Michael and Esther Lewis, Ruth and Hank Fredrick and their boys, the Mitchells and their four children would come to Jack and Ella's for a simple dinner or pot -luck supper that ended no later than 10:00. John and Sarah were the only ones who stayed up and attended the midnight service at St. Mark's. Jack and Ella held their own service of prayers for peace and for the safety and well-being of those they knew in England and all over Europe whose lives were in danger from the Germans and Italians and Russians who seemed to be taking over so much of that part of the world.

Part XI

Europe at War: 1940

1

The Russians took advantage of the time after the defeat of Poland to settle troupes in strategic locations in the small nations of Latvia, Lithuania, and Estonia, all three of which had declared their neutrality along with Denmark, Finland, Norway, and Sweden, should a war begin.

On April 9, 1940, Hitler's armies invaded Denmark and Norway, while Russia took control of Finland. The Phony War was over. The real war that had begun with the invasion and fall of Poland now began in earnest.

The Nazi-Soviet Pact of August 24, 1939, had given Stalin a free hand in the north. After the fall of Poland, he had wasted no time capitalizing on it by trying to turn the Gulf of Finland into a Soviet seaway. He had bullied Latvia, Estonia, and Lithuania into letting the Red Army be stationed at key points on their territory as he moved forward in his plans to take over Finland by the threat of force. When the Finns decided to fight rather than submit, the Russians bombed the capital Helsinki and invaded the country with 1.2 million soldiers. The Finns fought valiantly for 105 days before surrendering their country to the Soviets. As one Finn put it, "The Russians had more men than we had bullets."

Hitler's plan was to invade the Low Countries of Holland and Belgium and move into France. Although the French were equally prepared in troops and armor as the Germans, both the British and the French preparations were inadequate. The French preparation emphasized static defense and fortifications, while naval power continued to be the centerpiece of British military planning during this period. Britain had been reluctant during the intervening years between wars to invest heavily in its re-armament program, although it did devote money and other resources to the development of fighter aircraft and bombing capability to defend the island against attack from the continent.

The main problems facing the French were that the French Third Republic was lacking in political cohesion and its army lacked a unified command and therefore failed to respond speedily enough to Germany's *Blitzkrieg*. Anticipating the Germans would attack through Belgium, the French ignored intelligence that the German army was massing in the Ardennes Forest. Hitler's troops invaded, Holland and Belgium simultaneously in early May of 1940, cutting off the Allied forces in Belgium.

Then the German army raced across northern France and Belgium, easily establishing control of the area. However there were additional problems for the French and English because the French army lacked a unified command, and its divided leadership failed to respond speedily enough to the Nazi *Blitzkrieg*. The truth was the government of the French Third Republic lacked the political cohesion to deal with the Nazi forces—in the air or on the ground.

However, the most amazing action, or lack of it, was that Hitler ordered the advancing German forces to halt 15 miles from Dunkirk, where British forces were trapped, having been trying to stop the Germans' and Soviets' conquest of the northern countries. The rescue of 338,000 Allied soldiers by one Navy ship and trips by hundreds of English citizens in their fishing boats and motor boats across the channel between England and France from May 26 through June 4 was one of the miracles of the war.

Hitler's army then turned its attention to taking Paris and on June 10, the *Weygand Line* to the north of Paris collapsed, leaving the city unprotected. On that same day Mussolini's Italy declared war on France. On June 13 Nazi troops took control of Paris.

Under the terms of the armistice signed on June 16, Germany would occupy coastal and northern France while the Vichy Regime would administer the rest of the country. France would be allowed to retain its empire and its fleet. More important, Charles DeGaulle escaped to London, where he established a free French government.

With the western European countries now under Nazi Germany's control, Britain stood alone. The German *Luftwaffe* began bombing cities in England, all along the eastern and southern coast, with a concentration on London. Unknown to the Germans, however, some five years prior to the beginning of the war, a scientist had invented or discovered RDD (Radio Detection and Ranging) better known as *Radar*. The British Air Force had immediately installed Radar in their planes. They also set up a Radar protection system for the country itself, by installing a ring or a network of stations that transmitted generally accurate information about the position, numbers, height, and directions of German airplanes to the Royal Air Force (RAF) control stations. Once received, the fighter planes could be manned and air-born in minutes.

The WAAF or Women's Auxiliary Air Force, composed of the Dowding System of Radar operators, then kept the fighter plane pilots informed with reports they were receiving from their Radar posts on the ground. So the British pilots had the advantage of knowing where, when, which, or how many German planes were behind or around them.

The German air attacks on London and along the coasts came at all hours every day for months. In London no buildings were sacred or safe. In mid-September bombs fell on Buckingham Palace, the House of Lords, the Law Courts, and eight historic churches. The *Blitz* that began in August of 1940 continued long into 1941, moving into other parts of England, as far north as Coventry where bombs destroyed much of a beautiful Church of England Cathedral.

While a good many British fighters and civilians died during the *Blitz*, the total number of the dead was not as great as it might have been, had its people not had the courage and the will to endure the terror and the horror of the many months that the *Blitz* continued while they sheltered in basements and underground rail stations.

Yet during all the months of the *Blitzkrieg* the warnings Radar provided for those on land and the communication it sent to the British fighter pilots in the air instilled strength and courage, not only in those men in the planes but also in the English people living along the coast and in London and other cities, keeping the spirit of freedom alive at a great price but with the reward of its survival at the war's end.

Britain had depended primarily on its sea power but had begun devoting more resources to developing its air force than on its army. Yet the cold facts were that after the fall of France in 1940, Britain stood alone to face the Germans, Italians, and Russians. Germany had very easily become the dominant power in Europe. Hitler had given the order for the conquest of Britain by *Operation Sea Lion*, the crossing of the English Channel by the German army to take place in late summer or early fall.

The British believed strategic bombing of Germany was its best, if not its only, offensive option. Its other hopes lay in a naval blockade of Germany on the North Sea and support from anti-German resistance movements throughout Europe.

But Britain had incurred deep resentment from the French because it had destroyed the French navy from the air in July of 1940, to keep it from falling into German hands., and President Roosevelt in the United States had promised to send arms and weapons, but not men. At this point the truth was that England was standing alone. It could expect help of sorts from its Commonwealth nations and from the United States, but the future was daunting, to say the least.

In June of 1941, Roosevelt made it clear the United States would provide European democracies with arms, while the Lend Lease Plan would supply the Allied countries with war *materiels*. These actions allowed the USA to extend its involvement in the war without directly involving its military.

306

An added threat. along with Germany, Italy, and Russia, was Japan. It had begun to assume its own place as a warring country eager for territory in its own sphere of the world, forcing the western world to begin paying attention to its movements.

2

In early June of 1940, word went out all over Britain that the Royal Navy needed help in rescuing the more than 300,000 men who had been fighting to keep France from being conquered by Germany, but the British army was not succeeding in keeping France free. It looked certain that the French government would be forced to surrender to the Nazis, leaving all these British soldiers trapped on the coast near Dunkirk, right across the English Channel from home. In fact, on many days, if the weather was good, they could see the English coast. What mattered now was that these brave men be rescued off the beaches surrounding Dunkirk and returned to their homeland.

Eleanor was not at all happy when Ronald announced that he was going to take their motor boat which could hold up to eight people and join the effort to rescue the men stranded on the coast of France.

The Royal Air Force would help by providing some air cover, but the entrance to the harbor at Dunkirk was not large enough for the British warships to enter and there were not enough smaller ships to rescue all the men who were on the shore, hoping to escape capture or death. Small water craft would have a better chance of picking up the soldiers and returning them to their home shore. God only knew how many trips these small boats would have to make to complete their task, but Ronald said he was determined to do what he could to save as many lives as possible before returning home. He would be back before Monday, he promised, because he had classes to teach that day.

Eleanor understood that her husband felt guilty because he had failed his physical due to a heart murmur, and he saw this as one way he could play a part in the war-effort. She knew it would only upset Ronald if she begged him not to go or make him more determined if she got angry with him. He was a truly good man and a wonderful husband, and she didn't want to lose him, and so while she was afraid for him to take their water craft on such a dangerous mission, she never expressed her fears. She only nodded her acceptance of his decision and clung to him just a bit longer than necessary as she kissed him and said, "Do be as careful as possible, my love." He nodded and kissed her once more and left.

She never saw or heard from him again. Three weeks later, after the amazing rescue of the British forces trapped at Dunkirk, a British soldier showed up at her door and asked to speak with her. He told her he had been on Ronald's boat when it hit or was hit by something and quickly capsized. He, himself, had been knocked unconscious by something and pulled from the water by men in another boat. The boat he had been in had sunk quickly. Several other men on his boat had been saved but not the captain. At least he hadn't seen him after the boat sank. He had had a hard time, amid all the confusion, finding out the name of the man whose boat he had been in, but when he did, it had taken him a while to find out where he was from and if he had family so that he could come and thank her for her husband who had saved his life while losing his. He had tears in his eyes as he talked to Eleanor. She wanted to scream and sob, but she couldn't let herself do such a thing in front of this kind, thoughtful soldier who had made such an effort to find her and tell her how brave Ronald had been and how he wished he could thank him for coming to rescue them off the beaches at Dunkirk.

Instead she asked him to come into the house and meet her children Lee and Amy, and she fixed him a sandwich and a cup of tea and brought out a small plate of cookies. She asked him his name and what part of England he was from and learned that he was Freddie March and had grown up in London but had been living in Sussex when the war began. He was married, and was going back to Sussex to be with his wife as soon as he left Durham, but he had felt like he needed to find Ronald's widow first.

Eleanor thanked him for this kindness, this time letting him see her tears as she told him how hard it had been to keep going without knowing what had happened to her husband, the father of her children. Now she could explain, at least to her son, why their father had not returned, and he would understand why sometimes he found her crying, and he could even cry with her or alone if he wanted to. Their daughter was just over a year old and wouldn't understand why they were sad. She kept asking for "Da-Da" and she didn't know how to tell her that "Da-Da" would not be coming home. She well knew she was not the only mother in England who had to break this kind of news to her children. Freddie said his wife wanted to have a baby soon, but he wasn't sure it was fair to bring a child into the world right now. What did she think?

Eleanor sat looking at him and shaking her head. "I don't know. It's hard. But for your wife's sake, a child would be her reason for going on living, if something happens to you, though it's difficult to be both mother and father to a child. And money may be a problem, how you're going to feed and clothe them unless you have a good job. I don't know, Freddie. I've got a support system here. Does your wife have one where you all live?"

"She's got a good family—is living with them right now. I need to get on my way. There's a train leaving at 3:00 that'll put me home by 6:00. Thank you for the sandwich. I'll put you in my prayers, Mrs. Douglass." And he took her hand and shook it gently.

But after he left, Eleanor sat down and wept until Lee came in and asked her why she was crying, and she had to tell her son his dad would not be coming home. And they both cried together as she hugged her son close to her heart.

Part XII

Homecoming: 1940

1

But the war went on, and Eleanor, who had grieved with Ronald's family over his loss and had been visited by the priest from St. James Episcopal Church in Durham where Ronald and his family were members and she had joined before their wedding there. She had met with the rector of the Durham University Chapel and asked him to join with the priest from the St. James Episcopal to have a service of remembrance for Ronald since there was no corpse for a funeral. She continued to attend church services and sit with Ronald's family and to have them to dinner or more frequently take her children with her to their home after church on Sundays.

But after two months of living without Ronald, trying to go on as if nothing had changed, she realized she wanted to go home to Myrna because that was the only place she felt her children would be safe, especially now that the German *Blitzkrieg* of London had begun. She felt it would spread to other parts of England soon and she wanted to get her children back to middle America, far, far away from the bombs. She wrote to her parents that she wanted to come home and bring her children to a safe place, and Ella had wired her they had room for all three of them in Dan's large bedroom and bath upstairs. Dan and his new wife Lilly were safe in Hawaii, and she and Jack would be delighted to have Eleanor and Lee and Amy with them for as long as they liked.

The Douglasses, while they didn't want Eleanor to leave and take with her the most precious mementoes they had of their son's life, understood Eleanor's reasons for leaving Durham and Northern England. While Durham itself had not been bombed, Coventry and some other northern towns had been hit, and who knew when they might be next. The thought of their grandchildren being killed by German bombs or even having to live with the terror of bombs falling near or on them enabled them to accept and even encourage her to return to America. They would still have their other children and grandchildren near and would have them to worry about. In a way, as greatly as they would miss her, Lee, and Amy it would be a relief to know they were safe.

They wanted to help pay for their trip to America and insisted they fly if they could find an American airline that might get them out of the country safely and land them in New York. If she and the children could get out of England on an American plane, they felt they would be safer flying than going on a ship, since German warplanes would attack British planes and ships but most likely were not going to go after American ones and give that country more reasons to enter the war.

Mr. Douglass made a few telephone calls and found out that Pan-American Airlines still had one flight into Edinburgh every week, although that might not continue if the Nazis decided to stop them. It flew in on Monday with its return flight to New York on Wednesday. It was a passenger plane only and was a large plane that could carry 75 passengers and flew high enough to be safe from enemy ground fire. Its American markings were large enough to keep the enemy from daring to shoot at it because Germany faced enough problems in subduing Great Britain. He said the airport manager had told him he did not know how much longer Pan-American would continue its flight into Edinburgh because it really was not booking enough passengers to keep it going and who knew when the Germans might invade their part of the island.

Reginald asked Eleanor how soon she thought she could be ready to leave, and she said by the next Wednesday, which would give her almost a week to pack, let the landlord know they were leaving, and then have some time to tell all the people she had

314

grown to love good-bye, at least for now. She teared up, as did Mrs. Douglass, and they embraced and held onto each other until they were able to get control of their emotions. Tears had become second nature to all of them ever since they had learned Ronald had died at sea.

Eleanor wired Ella and Jack as soon as Mr. Douglass reserved three tickets on Pan-Am's Wednesday flight into New York, and she asked Jack to reserve tickets for them on whatever train would be headed to Memphis on Friday. As the flight left at 3:00 p.m. on Wednesday, Mr. Douglass made a reservation for them and would take the day off so he and Mrs. Douglass could drive them to Edinburgh. Then they would drive home so Mr. Douglass could go to work the next day and they would wait to hear from her that they had arrived in New York. The plane would arrive in New York at 5:00 a.m. the next morning due to the time differences. Their train to Memphis left at 8:00 a.m. By the time they deplaned, got all their luggage off the plane and loaded onto carts and then onto a bus that would take them into New York, Eleanor realized they might as well go straight to the train station. It would be a long night, but she hoped they might get some sleep on the plane, as well as on the train.

All of the Douglasses dreaded saying "good-bye" but understood this was best for both Eleanor and the children. Still that did not make the leave-taking easy for the adults who had grown to love one another and were still grieving over the loss of the one who had brought them together as family!

2

Ella and Jack had driven to Memphis and were planning to meet Eleanor and the children as the train unloaded its passengers at the Memphis station on July 9 at 7:00 p.m. but were running late. Ella was beginning to get upset when she saw at a distance a group where a black porter was helping a woman with two children. The black porter from the train was carrying Lee while Eleanor held Amy nestled on her shoulder, hoping all the commotion would not waken them. Another porter had the luggage on a cart and was signaling yet another porter to come to their aid by getting help from some others.

Eleanor was so grateful for their kindness, she managed to get the three dollar bills and the five she had stuffed in her jacket pocket and give it to the porters who had helped by corralling others and had been such a help to her. "This is not nearly enough to pay you all for your help and kindness to me," she said as she handed it to the porter who was carrying Lee. If you can share some of it with the others, I would really appreciate it."

"Ma'am, I don't need your money to thank me for helping you and your chil'ren. I heard how your husband died trying to save sailors from drowning at Dunkirk. I'm proud to be able to help you and your chil'ren."

"Oh, please take it and share it. It's so little. It can't begin to pay you for your help, your kindness to me and my children. But I do want you to have it as a remembrance of your help to this woman who needed it at this time." Eleanor held out her hand to clasp his. She had tears in her eyes, and when she looked at him, he had tears in his also. "Please tell me your name," she said.

"It's James," he said. "God bless you and your little ones," he said.

"Thank you, James, and God bless you too."

Ella had barely finished speaking when she heard her mother cry out, "Jack, here they are! Oh, my daughter, I'm so sorry we're a bit late. We couldn't find the right gate at first. My darling girl, I'm so glad to see you and the children." Ella said as she embraced her daughter and granddaughter, while Jack had taken Lee who had waked up and was asking where they were.

Both Ella and Eleanor were in tears as they hugged each other, and then Jack, who was having difficulty containing his own emotions, did his best to hug Eleanor with Lee in his arms. "How

316

was the trip over the ocean to New York and then the train ride here?" Jack asked, hoping he would be able to get control of himself if they talked about more ordinary things.

"It was long and hard at times, but it would have been really hard if there had not been so many kind people, the stewardesses on the plane, passengers on the plane and at the airport in New York. Somehow word seemed to have gotten around that my husband had died at Dunkirk, and so many people helped me with the children, helped me with my tickets and baggage, and in every way possible, to get inside and then find a taxi that would get us to the station to catch the train to Memphis.

"Strangers chatted with me about everything—where I was going, why I had been in England when I was an American—everything except asking me why I was traveling alone with two children. Somehow the word about Ronald and Dunkirk must have gotten around. I really don't know how, but it must have because so many people helped me with everything, even with the children when Lee and Amy would let them. I actually had to beg some people not to give them sweets because they had already eaten too many of them.

"I really don't think I could have made it to the train station to get the train for Memphis if I hadn't had so much help. You saw how the porter in Memphis made sure I had all our luggage and even helped me with Amy and Lee."

Eleanor couldn't seem to stop talking, partly from exhaustion, but mostly from the need to share the experiences she had had and the helpful people she had encountered on this trip that she had dreaded but also longed to make, *to be home and away from war.*

She kept talking as they walked, "It was the same in New York. It was almost like they had received word of this woman traveling with two little children, because they met me at the gate, had all our luggage on a cart and even let Lee ride on the cart a little ways before they asked him to walk with me and hold my hand because they would get in bad trouble if any of their bosses saw him riding on a cart because he might get hurt.

"Lee's old enough to understand rules and getting in trouble if you don't obey them. He thanked the man who had let him ride a little ways and told him he really hoped he wouldn't get punished and lose his job.

"The porter, who was black, smiled and said, 'Yes sir, I appreciate that. You are a fine young gentleman. I know you're gonna' take good care of your mama and your little sister.'

"Lee gave the man a big smile and said, 'Yes sir. I sure will— or maybe I should say that I will try hard to do that.' Mother and Papa Jack, I was so proud of my little man. I kept thinking if only Ronald could have been with us to hear him respond to the porter that way!"

"Maybe Ronald was there in some way we humans can't understand, Eleanor," Jack said. "Anyway, you were there, and Ella and I are so grateful you shared that with us."

By this time they had walked outside the airport. Jack was pushing the luggage cart while Ella held Lee's hand. Another black porter approached Jack saying, "Sir, may I help you with your cart and get you to a taxi?"

Jack said he had driven his car which was parked not more than a block from where they were standing and said he would need the porter's help and more once he drove his car back to where they were standing. He was certain from looking at all Eleanor's luggage he would not be able to get it into his car.

The porter smiled and said, "Sir, just looking at all of these suitcases and trunks, I understand what you're saying. You're going to need a taxi along with your car." And he whistled to a driver who had just driven up. "I'm going to tell him to take you to your car and then come back here and help you load both vehicles and then help drive you to wherever you're going."

The porter did just that, and Jack got into the taxi and drove away, leaving Eleanor and Ella standing there with two babies and a lot of baggage, hoping they would be back soon! And they were— Jack hopping out of the cab almost before it had fully stopped and saying, "I hope you weren't worried I wouldn't come back."

"Not really, but we're glad to see you anyway—just couldn't imagine how we'd get to the Gayoso alone—and with all this luggage!" Ella and Eleanor were smiling now, although they had had a few apprehensive moments in which neither had said a word except to answer Lee's question when he had asked where Papa Jack had gone.

Jack had told the cabdriver they were going to the Gayoso Hotel where they were going to spend the night. He had gone on to say, "Our daughter and grandchildren have crossed the Atlantic from England in a plane, ridden a train from New York for almost 12 hours, and are exhausted. We will drive to our home in Arkansas tomorrow when they've all had a little rest. So I do hope we can get their luggage in my car and your cab."

"Sir, if I can't, I will rent a small luggage carrier that will fit on the back of my taxi. It will cost you $2.00 to rent it, but seeing how valuable all your passengers are, I will let you have it for one."

"It's a deal," Jack said. "And if you get all of us and all their luggage to the Gayoso safely, I'll add a dollar to make it two. You will deserve it."

The taxi driver did have to rent the luggage carrier, and by the time he had gotten everything loaded, the children had fallen asleep, Amy in Eleanor's arms and Lee nestled against Ella.

While Jack was helping the cab driver with loading all the luggage, he found out his name was Dudley Mitchell, was from Forrest City but had moved to Memphis to find work during the Depression. He liked Memphis and just might stay there, unless the country went to war. Then he'd join the Army. Jack then said he had a son who was in the Navy in Hawaii.

"Now that's a good deal," Dudley said. "I wouldn't mind being in Hawaii! How'd he luck into that?"

Spent four years at the Naval Academy in Annapolis, learned to pilot airplanes, and then got stationed there after his graduation," Jack replied.

"He must be a smart young man. I hear the Academy is not an easy ride," Dudley said. "And it must have cost you all a pretty penny!"

"Well," Jack said quietly, "I guess you could say that's the good part. If you are smart enough and have recommendations from some people in your state who are senators or representatives, and the Academy accepts your grades and recommendations and you keep your grades up, it doesn't cost you anything to graduate, except serving your country in peace or in war after you graduate," Jack said quietly.

"I beg your pardon, Sir. I did sound rather like a *smart alec*. I hope he stays safe. I know we're living in a bad time right now and that it's more likely to get worse than better. I sure hope President Roosevelt knows what he's doing 'cause I don't see how he's going to keep us out of this war forever."

"I agree with you there, Dudley, as much as I hate to say it. England and France are in for it. I'm afraid France won't last long. She's already lost a good part of her land; and poor Poland has already fought to stay free and lost. Austria, Denmark and Finland had already fallen to Germany, along with Czechoslovakia. Hitler just keeps getting stronger and now has Russia fighting alongside him," Jack's voice displayed his concern over what was going on in the world around them.

"No, Sir. It's not a hopeful picture. And it's going to get a lot worse if our President doesn't step up to the plate. It's not that I want your son to have to go to war. It's just that I don't want to see our whole country taken over by Germans, Italians, and Russians! No Siree, I sure don't want that to happen."

Jack said he agreed with that, but since they had now finished loading both his car and the taxi with the luggage carrier, they needed to stop talking and head for the Gayoso. He hoped neither Eleanor nor Ella had heard any of their conversation, though they had spoken quietly. He did not want either of them to hear war-talk right now. They rode to the hotel, speaking quietly so as not to wake the children. Jack told the two women he had learned Dudley was from Forrest City and had come to Memphis to find work and liked his job as a Taxi driver because he was able to meet some interesting people that way. They spoke quietly, going without talking at all when the traffic grew heavier.

Jack was glad when they arrived at the Gayoso and was even happier when the first voices he heard were those of Michael and Esther Lewis, who were standing on the steps of the hotel as they drove up.

"What are you two doing here?" Jack exclaimed.

"We both figured you'd need an extra vehicle to get everything back to Myrna. We didn't see how Eleanor would be able to bring clothing for three plus extra things to make the adjustment for the children easier, not to mention things that mean a lot to her," Esther said.

"Oh, Esther, you both are so thoughtful. I've been wondering all the way from the airport how we were going to get everything and everybody in our car for an almost three-hour drive. I'm sure Jack has been thinking the same thing," Ella said, and Eleanor echoed her.

"Just thought you might like a little help and a little extra vehicle space," Michael said as he wasted no time in helping Jack and Dudley unload the little luggage carrier on the back of the taxi and then lifted the trunk out of the taxi itself. We knew you almost always stayed at the Gayoso when you came to Memphis. So I telephoned, found out you had reservations here for tonight, and then made a reservation for us also."

Esther was helping Ella and Eleanor with Lee and Amy and the purses and bags they had in the backseat. Lee was awake and wanted to know if they were home while Amy just sighed and nestled further down into Eleanor's shoulder. Neither Eleanor nor Ella spoke loudly because they didn't want to waken Amy, and Esther dropped to a whisper.

But Jack, Michael, and the driver, Dudley, were speaking loudly enough Lee wanted to join them and help with the suitcases and other pieces of luggage. Jack realized Lee just wanted be one of "the men" and handed him one of the smaller, lighter bags to carry, telling Lee he thought this was an important bag to carry because it must have some of Amy's things in it, and only a big brother should be taking care of it. So Lee carried the bag up to his mother, who was holding Amy, and said, "Mama, this is an important bag because it belongs to Amy, and I'm taking care of it!"

Eleanor smiled at Lee and said, "That's just what a good big brother does—takes care of his little sister."

Ella and Esther smiled at each other with tears in their eyes, glad Eleanor and the children were here, safe in the United States, but sad for the reason they were here alone.

Esther and Michael had arrived more than an hour before the taxi arrived with Jack and Ella and the travelers from England. They had ordered supper to be delivered on trays to their bedroom which also had a sitting area, and they invited Jack and Ella and the exhausted travelers in for a light supper before they went to bed. The adults and Lee were hungry while Amy continued to sleep, but this time in the middle of a bed with pillows surrounding her in case she awoke and tried to get up without the adults noticing.

However, none of the adults lingered over their food because it was obvious how exhausted Eleanor and the children were. They had spent part of the first day and all of that night on the airplane, getting to New York at 7:00 in the morning. Then they had taken a taxi to the train station and had spent a long day on the train getting from New York to Memphis.

Eleanor mostly wanted to get her children into the bed and asleep so that then she could take a long bath, not only to get clean but also to relax and let go not only of the tension she had felt building up as she prepared for this journey but also the emotions that would not stop roiling through her as she realized she was leaving behind such a good life lived with a loving husband and his family.

She managed to hold back her tears until Lee had also fallen asleep in the bed beside Amy, and she at last was in the bathtub with the door to the room open so she would be able to hear the children if they wakened. She let the warm, clean water and soap work at erasing the strain not only from the grief she had felt during the weeks of packing but also from the long flight to New York, followed by another long train ride.

Now all she had to do was begin a new life as a widow, mother of two young children, find some kind of job that would help her earn some money, although she knew she had room and board with her parents as long as she needed it. She smiled sardonically as these thoughts rolled through her mind.

But she was not yet 30, and she hoped her life was not completely over. She didn't want to be just another war widow with nothing ahead but watching her children grow up, though God knows, she loved them more than life itself. But—but—the truth was they *would* grow up and deserved to have a life of their own.

Her mother and step-father had allowed her that privilege. They had not stopped her from going to England, getting her Master's degree in English literature and history, marrying an Englishman, even beginning to work toward getting a Doctorate, and even spending the rest of her life there until this horrible war started. She still felt a kind of anger at Ronald for taking the boat to go rescue those soldiers stranded on the beaches at Dunkirk, but there was also a bit of pride in his bravery and self-sacrifice she felt after meeting and getting a first-hand account from Freddie about what had happened on that horrible day.

The truth was that Ronald, a smart, honorable, caring man, the man she had loved deeply and lived with so happily until the damn war started, was gone from her life, leaving her with two precious children who would barely remember their father. Her life wasn't over. Her children's life was only just beginning. She wanted them to know and love and be so very proud of their daddy's sacrifice of his life in order to save the lives of soldiers who were trying to protect democracy and freedom at home and in other countries. But at the same time, her life wasn't over—she still had some good years ahead of her, years she wanted to be productive, to do something that would make a difference.

Oh, she knew she had made a difference in giving birth to these two precious children who were part of Ronald and who would be his legacy in the world. But she didn't want that to be all she accomplished, as happy as she had been in giving birth to both of them.

In that tub of warm water, she vowed to herself and to God she would always be as good to and supportive of them as Ella had been of her. She wanted them to succeed and to be people they could be proud of being, people who is some way would make the world a better place, and God knew, the world needed that now and would continue to need it once this horrible war ended.

The water in the tub was beginning to cool, and Eleanor realized again how exhausted she was from the emotional strain and physical labor of the last month. She removed the plug from the water in the tub, stood and wrapped the soft white towel around her to help it soak the water off her tired body. She hung the towel on the rack and slipped on the fresh nightgown and her house-slippers. Embarrassed by the ring of grime the water was leaving as it went down the drain, she then knelt by the tub and washed away the dirt from her long trip, grateful for her parents and for this opportunity to start a new life in a former setting. She turned off the light switch in the bathroom, left a night light burning, crawled into bed between her son and her daughter, and fell asleep quickly from exhaustion and gratitude to be home where bombs were not falling on any cities!

Part XIII

At Home in Myrna: 1940

1

During the first couple of weeks after arriving home in Myrna, Eleanor almost felt like a visitor from a foreign land. She had exchanged much of what life in a small town in middle America was like for life in a much older country and culture where everyday language was spoken with a different accent. While the people were every bit as interesting, kind, and friendly as they had been in Myrna, they expressed their friendship, kindness, and interests in different ways from the people she had known in Arkansas or even at Southwestern in Memphis, Tennessee. She had lived in northern England for almost eight years and hadn't realized how greatly she had acclimated to British ways until she was back in Arkansas. People had difficulty understanding what she was saying, while she had to make an effort to speak—and understand, the Arkansas dialect and its Southern accent so that she would "fit in" again.

She and her "little" sister Mary Beth had some good laughs over Eleanor's difficulties. Lots of people wanted to call her "Nellie" since that was the name she had grown up with until she went to live in England and decided to become *Eleanor*. Actually, that was her birth name, from her mother's given name of *Mary Eleanor*. However, her parents had named her just "Eleanor" but then nick-named her "Nellie" because they thought "Eleanor" was a long name for a little girl. She was the first-born, and by the time Mary Beth was born, her parents had chosen *Mary* for the baby and then added the *Beth* from her father's grandmother, "Elizabeth."

Both sisters were delighted their four children seemed to make friends with each other immediately. Actually, Amy was still a bit young to play, so they treated her as a doll, and Eleanor and Mary Beth had to be sure Nora, Pat, and Lee were careful with her and not let her put things in her mouth or try to crawl too far. Amy had been crawling for over three months before they left England, and was now pulling herself up on anything she could grab hold of. All three of the older children were taken with her and what she was learning or trying to learn to do, not remembering when they had been that same age. They made good baby watchers, often making Amy mad because they kept interrupting her efforts to stand up by holding onto a table leg or a chair seat because they were afraid she'd fall and hurt herself. Eleanor had to explain to them that all three of them had learned how to stand and then walk the very same way—by holding onto something. They had rarely hurt themselves by falling because they weren't far from the floor when they tried to pull themselves up. So it was good for them to watch Amy try, and then comfort her if she hurt herself or got mad because she had failed.

Eleanor was relieved when she began to feel more at home in Myrna, recognized people from the past and now even remembered most of their names. Since Ella and Jack had become members of the Presbyterian Church, she went to Sunday school and church with them, but missed the formality and quietness of the Episcopal Church she had joined when she had married Ronald and then attended with other members of his family. After all, she had grown up in the Episcopal Church in Myrna with Father John Banks as her priest for years.

However, Eleanor really liked the Presbyterian minister, Greg Mitchell, who preached excellent sermons and whose worship leadership was formal and worshipful, although she missed kneeling for prayer. Yet even in England, when kneeling had become extremely difficult toward the end of each of her pregnancies, she believed God heard people's prayers from whatever position they were offered.

For Eleanor, being back in Myrna away from the war that was always in one's mind, even though it might not be mentioned in conversation, offered relief. She realized after being back a month the war was not always in her thoughts and there were even a few days when she realized she had not been thinking "Ronald is dead. I am a single parent and have to start a new life on my own!"

Instead she had become absorbed with the realization she needed to start looking for a job. Ella and Jack had the high school English and history classes under their control and were obviously so popular and highly respected that, while history and English had been her joint majors and she had finished her Master's degree, she had to look somewhere else for that kind of teaching position.

Eleanor had begun to make some new friends in Myrna and particularly liked Ruth Fredrick. In late July Ruth had come by to see her at Eleanor and Jack's house and after some initial chitchat, said, "I know you are looking for a teaching job. Hank says there may be a vacancy in the English Department at Arkansas State and thought you might be interested in applying there. I know it's a fairly long commute to and from the college because Hank makes it every day, and I'm fairly sure we'll move there once the boys are through high school. But this has been such a good place for them, we really haven't wanted to make them go through another change."

"Arkansas State sounds interesting, though a bit challenging to be so far from Amy and Lee," Eleanor said thoughtfully. "They have adjusted amazingly well to our move. They've even stopped talking about their dad except for every now-and-then when Lee will ask, 'Mama, is daddy going to come here to see us?' Of course, that breaks my heart. I'm glad they are happy here, and I don't want to leave them, although I know I have to go to work soon."

"I understand what you are dealing with," Ruth said. "My boys are happy here, and we've moved them around so much we don't want them to have to make another adjustment until they decide where they want to go to college. Since Hank's settled and satisfied enough at Arkansas State, they may want to go there, although because their daddy is there, they may choose somewhere else. Life does get a bit more complicated when you add children to it, doesn't it?" Ruth smiled as she shrugged her shoulders.

"Yes, it definitely does. It was hard for me to decide to move them here, but I truly was afraid the Nazis would start dropping bombs on Durham where we lived. I didn't think I could stand having to worry about losing my children who were all I had left of Ronald. Yet they adjust to loss and change more easily than adults do, certainly better than I do. They have accepted that their daddy is dead, or at least Lee seems to have done so most of the time.

"Amy still looks at me and says, 'DaDa' like a question, and my heart breaks every time she does that because I don't know what to say other than 'I don't know.'"

"That has to be so hard, Eleanor! I can't even imagine what that must feel like to you—or to her. Do you think she understands what you are saying?"

"I know she misses her daddy and wonders where he is, and I don't know when I need to say more than 'I don't know.' She's just over a year old, too young, I think, to talk about death.

"Lee understands his daddy drowned trying to save our soldiers, and that he is a kind of hero. He asked me once, 'Is Daddy with God?' and I told him 'Yes, Daddy is with God.' Then he wanted to know, 'Does Daddy miss us?' and I assured him Daddy misses us a lot but he is happy with God because one day he will see us again when we die and go to be with God.

"Yet not long ago he asked me if his daddy was going to come and visit us in Arkansas. I have no idea what he understands about death and war or any of that, but it seems to help him deal with the absence of his daddy in his life, our life. I wish it had been that easy for me to deal with losing Ronald in my—our lives."

"I know how awful this time we're living in is," Ruth said. "My parents were under a kind of house arrest in Munich for months simply because of being Jewish. If they left the house they had to wear a big 'Star of David' on their coat or jacket or whatever. And they might hear ugly things said about Jews or be stopped and interrogated in the street about where they were going and why.

But at least, so far as I know, they are still living in their house, though I can't help feeling they are in danger because Adolph Hitler despises all Jews and wants to eliminate all of them.

"I have not had a letter from my mother or father in ages, and I don't know what to do. I am afraid of drawing attention to them if I make inquiries to the people in power in Munich because now they are all Nazis. I haven't been in Munich in so long I don't even know if any of our Jewish friends are still there or how to get in touch with them if they are. The last time I heard from my parents was four months ago, and they were still living in their house, and only rarely left it. All their servants but two, a husband and wife, had resigned. The two who were left would do the grocery shopping for my parents so they did not have to deal with the rudeness of the soldiers and even of some of the citizens of our city."

Eleanor, who had sat listening to Ruth with tears in her eyes, put her arms around her, saying, "Oh, Ruth, how horrible to be so far away and afraid for your parents! I know you and Hank left Germany because of fear of what Hitler and his Nazis would or could do to you if you had stayed. You told me soon after I met you that Hank had tried to convince your mother and father to move to England with you all, and they refused, feeling they would be safe if they stayed quietly at home and did not draw attention to themselves. Maybe they are still there," Eleanor said.

"Oh, I pray you are right and I will hear from them soon. But I know how evil Hitler is and that he hates us Jews. I honestly don't understand why he hates the Jews so much, but he does. I think he really wants to eliminate us from the face of the earth. There, I didn't mean to get so emotional but this is a hard time for our world."

"That it is, Ruth, that it is!" Eleanor said with a sigh. "I am fairly sure that this country cannot remain out of this war forever. I can't believe we will sit back and watch Hitler and Mussolini or even the Japanese take over the world. I think the Japanese are getting active in the Pacific Ocean. My brother and his wife are in Honolulu, though they should be safe. Those islands are a long way from Japan.

"The England I learned to love during those years I lived there, along with France, will have to be really strong until the USA decides, as it surely will at some point, to step in and fight to save the world for democracy. Doesn't that sound like we are superior, and maybe we are, but it certainly doesn't feel or look that way at the moment, does it?"

"It's safer than Bavaria where Munich is, which at the moment doesn't feel at all safe to me, even if there is no fighting going on there as far as I know. But I hope you are right about this country's strength and the strength of England and France for the sake, no— rather our hope—for the future.

"There, that's enough about fear and hope. I need to go home, see what my sons are up to, decide what I'm going to cook for supper and begin to put something together. It's what I do every day, but oh, I'm so grateful to be here safe and able to do this for my family without fearing the Nazi police will come and take all of us and lock us up somewhere.

"Pray for my parents, Eleanor, and for all Jews and for our world, Eleanor, and hope God is listening and cares! I know I sound like a disbeliever when I say that, and I admit right now I am struggling with my faith."

"Oh, Ruth, I do understand. I have fought against my anger at Ronald for taking our boat to rescue the army at Dunkirk and especially at God for letting him die doing it. Most of the time I win my battle, but sometimes I lose, and my grief and fear for the future win it.

"But, my dear friend, that doesn't last because I am surrounded by love. Even in England, Ronald's family who were grieving just as much as I was gave me and my children love and support as did the church and other friends. We are not alone, Ruth. We are never really alone despite what it feels like at the time. God in all kinds of ways is with us. Even our friendship is proof of that."

The two women stood and held each other with tears running down their faces, finding comfort and strength in each other and their trust in the God they dared believe in was really in charge of the world and its future.

2

Hank gave Eleanor the name and college address of the head of the Language and Arts department at Arkansas State College and encouraged her to send in a resume and a copy of her transcript and diploma from the university and the college in Durham where she had received degrees, along with the college where she had taught. He knew the freshman English professor at Arkansas State was afraid he was going to be drafted into the army if the United States entered the war; so he was going to join the Navy before he received a draft notice. Eleanor followed through with an application as soon as she told her parents and her sister what she was thinking about doing, and Mary Beth had immediately said she would be happy to take care of Lee and Amy during the day if and when Eleanor found a job. Eleanor's tears flowed as she hugged her sister and thanked her for her offer, saying she knew Lee and Amy not only would be well-cared for but they were already 'in awe of' and 'in love with' their older cousins.

Eleanor had already begun working on the first draft of her letter to Dean James Atkinson in the Department of Language and Arts at Arkansas State, telling him a bit about her college experience at Southwestern in Memphis, her courses at the University of Durham in northern England from which she had received her Master's Degree, and her early experience as a teacher of seniors and juniors in high school, along with taking several courses that would apply toward her doctorate in British literature. After reworking her letter several times and providing addresses for Southwestern in Memphis and the University of Durham and the names of professors at both who would be able to provide opinions of her scholarship and of her probable teaching ability, she mailed it to Dean Atkinson, mentioning as a reference her friend Dr. Hank Fredrick who had encouraged her to apply and who would be able to give the Dean additional information about her.

Eleanor had mulled over whether to go into any detail about her personal life, but didn't want it to look like she was looking to be hired out of sympathy over her husband's loss. If the Dean wanted to ask Hank anything about her and Hank filled in those details, that would be fine, as long as he added she was not looking for sympathy or expecting any special treatment because of her husband's death. She said those exact words when she told Hank she had sent her letter to the Dean and he might or might not ask Hank about her. Hank laughed and said he was pretty sure the Dean would bring it up because they frequently ate lunch together in the school's cafeteria, and the Dean liked to talk.

Ten days later Eleanor received a letter from Dean Atkinson saying he had received her letter, had wired the University of Durham asking for her transcript and had not only received her grades but a long letter from the Dean of the University with an excellent recommendation of Eleanor's scholarship and personality. He had also had a most positive conversation with Hank Fredrick about her. He hoped she would be able to come to his office on Wednesday, August 15, for an in-person interview. Delighted with the speed of his reply, Ella telephoned his office, spoke with his secretary, and set up the interview for 10:00 a.m. on the 15th.

The interview went even better than Eleanor had hoped. Dean Atkinson was delighted with her British accent and told her not to lose it, especially when she was teaching Arkansas students who would mostly be entranced with someone who didn't sound like them. Eleanor laughed and said she would try her best not to lose it completely, but after all she had grown up in Myrna and was doing her best not to sound too foreign and therefore "stuck up" when she went shopping downtown there. However, she had really worked at mimicking the British accent while she lived there because she didn't want to sound like a "foreigner" to her English classmates and students. She knew how easy it would be to begin sounding like an Arkansan again, but she would try not to lose all her accent because the truth was she enjoyed sounding like a Brit. And she wanted her children to keep their bit of an accent also. It was good for Arkansans to get some exposure to the larger world. The Dean said he agreed completely.

334

The outcome of the interview was that at far as he was concerned she was hired to begin teaching as soon as the college students returned to class on September 9. There would, of course, be some faculty meetings and a faculty get-together toward the end of August, but she would receive information about all of that as soon as the President and Board acted on his recommendation, and that should be after the board met at the end of the week.

Eleanor went home with a pile of books she would be using in her classes on *American Literature after 1865, Shakespeare's Trajedies,* and *British Poetry during the Age of Wordsworth and Coleridge.* She could hardly wait to get started but wondered what her students would be like and could she get them interested in what she had to teach them!

But at least she had a job teaching in a college. She hoped she would be pleasantly surprised by the level of education her students would have attained, but mostly she hoped they would accept and like her and be willing to study and learn what she could teach them. She hoped she would not come across as too British, so different they couldn't identify with her or want to learn from her. And she also hoped to be thought of as a kind of friend, one they could ask questions of, seek help from when they needed it, someone they could trust to be "on their side" but not let them get by with poor work habits or just poor work! She knew she was not much older than some of them would be, and she didn't want them to think she was "one of them." Instead she wanted them to respect her and look up to her, but not be afraid to come to her for help if they needed it.

When she called Ruth and Hank to tell them she had been hired to start teaching in September, Hank said he'd be glad to give her a ride to Jonesboro every day so she wouldn't need to worry about transportation, and Eleanor accepted with gratitude. She hoped one day, perhaps within the next year, she would be able to find a used car, but for now she was delighted not to have to worry about that and would enjoy riding with Hank.

Filled with excitement over what lay ahead and just a bit of apprehension about her ability to meet all the demands of this new position, Eleanor walked over to Mary Beth's to get her two children, fully aware they too posed questions for her. She wanted not only to be a good teacher but an equally good, if not better, mother to Amy and Lee who were as dear to her as life itself and her only tangible tie to the man she had so dearly loved and with whom she had expected to lead a long and full life. She closed her eyes and whispered to God, "Holy One, be with me and give me wisdom, knowledge, skill, and patience to be mother and teacher to my two children by birth and to all these almost completely grown children I will try to teach. In the name of your Son who received and lived by your teachings to Him, I make my prayer. Amen."

3

As August, 1940, bore down upon them in heat and dry weather, Michael and Esther Lewis received a letter from Eddie Carnes saying he had a week of vacation coming up the second week in September, and he would like to spend his vacation in Myrna, staying with them part of the time and the other part with Lee and Suzanna Jones. Would they be willing to put him up for three days and nights?

Esther immediately wrote him that they would be delighted to have him stay with them any time of his week of vacation that suited him, but the first part of the week would work out a little better for them, if that was all right with him.

Eddie had to smile when he read Esther's letter because it was so like her to offer all of something but then to throw in a "but" to let the reader or hearer know which alternative she preferred. He wrote back and said he would be arriving by bus the first week in September and looked forward to staying with them Tuesday, Wednesday, and Thursday nights. Then he would go to Lee and Suzanna's for Friday, Saturday and Sunday, heading back to North Carolina on Monday.

When Esther mentioned to Ella one day that Eddie Carnes was coming to Myrna the second week in September and planned to spend three nights with them, then going to Lee and Suzanna's on Friday night, Ella's first thought was "Eddie can be our first speaker of the year for our 10th-grade classes." She and Jack had been discussing whom they could ask who would be able to give the students the kind of personal information that would motivate them to want to do something with their own lives, learning more about themselves and their own families. When Ella spoke to Jack about Eddie's coming and her idea of making him their first speaker, Jack was hesitant at first until Ella told him how well Eddie was doing in the Civilian Conservation Corps and that Esther was actually excited about having him come "home" for a few days.

That convinced Jack. If Esther was really happy about having Eddie come visit, the CCC had helped him grow up from being a "trouble maker" and become a man. But he suggested she share her idea about having Eddie address their class with Esther, and if she thought it would be a good idea, he was for it.

Ella broached it with Esther the next day and Esther said she was for it if Eddie was willing to do it. She gave Ella his mailing address and suggested she write to Eddie to see if he would speak to their joint-10th-grade classes.

Ella and Jack sat down together that night and wrote a long letter to Eddie explaining how they liked to invite guest speakers during the school year who would share with their 10th-grade students a bit about their life, what was important to them, and what they wanted to accomplish. They knew how proud both Esther and Michael Lewis were of what a difference the CCC was making in Eddie's life and hoped he would be willing to share some of that with their students. He would be addressing the class on Friday afternoon, September 14. They put the letter in the next day's mail and then waited anxiously for Eddie's reply. The truth was they had been wracking their brains about who to get for their first speaker of the year, and if Eddie turned them down they weren't sure what they were going to do.

They were both relieved when Eddie answered back immediately that he would be "honored" to speak to the class. He was arriving on Tuesday, September 11, and would come prepared to talk to their class on Friday. Actually, he telephone the MacLeans Tuesday evening after he had arrived at the Lewises and asked if he might drop by about 7:00 on Wednesday night to talk with them a little bit about what he planned to say about himself and see also how long he would be expected to talk and so forth. Ella wrote back they would be delighted to have him come by on Wednesday, but 7:30 would be more convenient for them. She explained their daughter Eleanor and her two children were living with them at the moment, but they would have finished eating and gone upstairs by 7:30 for their nightly baths before bed.

Both Ella and Jack almost didn't recognize Eddie when this tall, well-built, nicely dressed young man knocked on their front door three weeks later. They invited him in to have a seat in the living and offered him a class of iced tea and a piece of cake. He accepted the tea and refused the cake, saying he'd had dessert with Mr. and Mrs. Lewis. They chatted a bit about his life in the Civilian Conservation Corps with Eddie saying it was hard work but he liked being outdoors and also had become good friends with other young men in the CCC and even with some of the officers.

He wanted to know whether Mr. and Mrs. MacLean had any special things they wanted him to say about his life in the CCC. Jack answered, "Not really. Actually we just hope you'll say a bit about what kind of work you and the Corps do, what your life there is like, and what you are learning that you can take with you into ordinary life when you leave the Corps. If you're willing, you can tell them how you happened to go into the CCC and maybe even what you want to do when you leave it, that is if you know. We don't have any kind of script you must follow. It's important you be honest with them if they ask you any questions, and we're pretty sure you will get some questions. Does what I've said help you know what we want you to do?"

Ella spoke up, "We just want you to be who you are now, perhaps share what has influenced your life, what has helped you become the young man you are right now. I hope that helps you understand what we are hoping you will share with our students."

338

"Yes, ma'am. I think you can see I'm certainly not the same person I was. I will do the best I can to show the class who I am today."

"We believe you will succeed in doing that, Eddie," Jack said. "We appreciate your coming by to give us a glimpse of what to expect on Friday." As Eddie rose to leave, Ella asked, "I know you are with Michael and Esther until Friday, but where are you going after that?"

"To spend the weekend with Lee and Suzanna Jones. They are also like family to me. Mr. and Mrs. Lewis are sort of my parents. Suzanna and Lee are my sister and brother. I can hardly believe there was a time I thought I was better than black people because I have white skin. Now I don't even see the difference in the color of our skin. They are just people I love and they love me too." Eddie's voice had a bit of a catch in it as he said those last few words.

Ella, who had never paid much attention to a person's skin color, said, "They are good people, good teachers." And Jack added, "You've come a long way. I think we need to change your name a bit. No more *Eddie*. Instead you are now *Ed* because you are a man." They shook hands and Ed left, already feeling more mature than when he had arrived.

On Friday Ed arrived at the school at 1:45 dressed in his khaki CCC uniform, his shirt ironed perfectly and his pants also pressed with a crease down the front of each leg. As tall and filled-out as he had grown, Ed made quite an impression on the 10th-grade boys and girls who had entered the library where the two rows of chairs were now filled with students.

Jack made the introduction to the class, saying, "Class, it is a pleasure for me to introduce Ed Carnes to you. We used to know him as 'Eddie' but that is a boy's name. This is a fully grown and a very mature young man who has spent the last two years working for the government in the Civilian Conservation Corps. I'm going to let him tell you his story. Please welcome Ed Carnes!"

The class clapped appropriately, the girls making more noise than the boys, as Ed stepped forward. "I really appreciate Mr. McLean's using my real name. I have been 'Ed' ever since I went into the CCC, although when I was living here everybody knew me as *Eddie*. I guess the first thing I want to tell you about me is that Eddie wasn't a very smart or a very nice boy; so I'm really glad now to be known as 'Ed' and that's what I hope you will remember me by.

"You see, I was kind of a 'smart alec' kid when I was growing up. I was the youngest in my family, and my parents didn't act like they cared much about me or were interested in how I turned out. So I figured I really wasn't worth much, and it didn't much matter if I did some bad things, more stupid than really bad, but bad enough at times to get me into trouble with the law. I spent a few days in jail a couple of times.

"I might have spent more if a man in this town hadn't taken an interest in me. This was an important man. You will recognize his name when I tell you. He is Michael Lewis, the owner of First National Bank and half-owner of Lewis Brothers Department Store.

"I was arrested and put in jail after I had talked some boys, who were kind of trouble-makers like me, into dressing up like Ku Klux Klan members and going to Mr. Lewis' house where he was having a dinner party. Mr. and Mrs. MacLean were guests, but what had gotten under my skin was that they'd invited a Negro couple to their dinner party. That's why I came up with the idea of acting like Klan members. I don't think I would have been brave enough to really do anything to the Negro couple and certainly not to the Lewises or MacLeans, but I wanted to scare them all and show them we didn't think white people and black people should be socializing together.

"Well, Mr. Lewis and Mr. MacLean came out to meet us as about 10 of us stood there with our burning torches. I didn't have any more sense than to speak up. But after all, I was the leader and this had been my plan, and I had talked the rest of the boys into going with me. What I hadn't counted on was that Mr. Lewis would recognize my voice. I don't know how he knew who I was, but he did, and he called me by name. He also figured out who a few of the others might be since he knew the kind of boys who were my friends. He called some of their names, and as soon as they realized he knew they were in on this with me they began to disappear. Pretty soon everybody had slipped away, and I was standing there alone.

"On top of that, Mrs. Lewis had called the chief of police, and he drove up, arrested me and carried me off to jail. But before he did, Mr. Lewis said something to me that took me completely by surprise. He said he thought I was too smart to be doing such stupid pranks like this. And he said he was going to come by the jail the next day to see about me or something like that.

"I want you all to know my own daddy never would have said that or come by the jail to talk to me like Mr. Lewis did. My daddy never cared about me or about what I was doing. But Mr. Lewis did. He talked to me like he thought I was worth something and could make something good of my life. I was almost 17 years old, had dropped out of high school, and had nothing going for me, had nobody who acted like I was worth anything, and this man who owned a bank and a department store treated me like I could amount to something.

"He and his wife took me out of jail and let me into their own home where they treated me like I was a good person. I had my own bedroom. I had to help Mrs. Lewis around the house if she asked me to, and she didn't ask for much. I had good meals and two people who made me feel like I could make something of myself.

"Another thing they did for me that changed my life was to take me out to meet the Negro man and his wife, the very ones I'd tried to threaten and scare with my Ku Klux Klan robes and torches.

"Lee was almost finished building a nice house for himself and his new wife out in the country. They were both school teachers. Mr. Lewis had arranged for me to help Mr. and Mrs. Jones put the finishing touches on their house. I ended up living with them for a couple of weeks. By the end of the first week, I never noticed or thought about the color of their skin. They were two of the smartest and nicest people I'd ever met. And they accepted me even though I am white, appreciated whatever work I did to help finish the house, and made me feel welcomed to be there with them, just like Mr. and Mrs. Lewis had made me feel.

"When school started, I went back to the Lewis' house. Mr. Lewis told me that he had found a place for me to go to get away from Myrna for a while. I thought for a minute he was going to send me to prison, but I should have known by then he wasn't that kind of man.

"What he was talking about was the Civilian Conservation Corps, and there was a camp in North Carolina where I could go and live with a lot of other young men who needed a job and were willing to work outdoors and learn how to do all sorts of things. They would feed me three meals a day, furnish the clothes I needed to live and work there, and give me a bed to sleep in. I would get paid a dollar a day, and at the end of the month they would take five dollars of the $30 or $31 I had earned, and give it to me to spend at the camp for a soda or a candy bar or whatever I wanted. They would send the rest of the money to my family or whoever I wanted it sent to. It was a good place for me to go to and grow up.

"The best thing is that I started taking correspondence courses, and I now have a high school certificate of graduation. I just got that before I came here for vacation. I've spent the first three days here with Mr. and Mrs. Lewis and then after I leave here I'm going out to stay with Lee and Suzanna through the weekend.

"I have to tell you that I am truly grateful for people like Mr. and Mrs. Lewis, Lee and Suzanna Jones, and Mr. and Mrs. MacLean who have made me feel like I can make something good of my life. I'm willing to be open for questions if it's all right with Mr. and Mrs. MacLean." And he looked toward Ella and Jack who nodded their heads in approval.

Ricky Palmer asked the first question: "I notice you call white people like the Lewises and the Macleans 'Mr. and Mrs.' But you call the black people by their first names. Is that a sign that you don't have respect for Negroes and so you can call them by their first names?"

"Absolutely not!" Ed replied with feeling. "When I was helping them finish their house, I started out calling them Mr. and Mrs.

Jones, but that ended after my first week there when I had started spending the nights in their guest bedroom. You see, they live 10 miles out in the country, too far to expect Mr. Lewis or Lee to drive me out there or take me back to town every night. One night at supper Suzanna and Lee said they had something they wanted to ask me, maybe invite me to do if I felt comfortable doing so.

"Lee said, 'We'd like for you to call us by our given names of Lee and Suzanna. How would you feel about doing that?'

"I was surprised, but I liked them both so much and thought so much of both of them, it had felt right to address them both as Mr. and Mrs. I said as much. Suzanna spoke up then and said they had both begun to think of me as being their younger brother, despite the color of my skin.

"Then she said, 'Brothers and sisters call each other by their first name. How about that for a reason?'

"I actually choked up. Nobody in my family, in my life, had ever made me feel like they wanted to be kin to me. I said that I was really proud they could think of me as a younger brother, and I would try to be worthy of them."By this time all three of us were a bit emotional. Suzanna had gotten up from the table, and she came over to me and asked me to get up so that she could give me a sisterly hug. Then Lee came. I'm choking up just remembering how much it meant to me. Y'all, please excuse me a minute while I blow my nose."

Ed turned away, blew his nose, using his handkerchief. Then he turned back to the class and asked, "Does anyone else have a question?"

Susie Jacobson said, "I do. Wasn't it hard for you to do the lessons for your correspondence course after you had worked outside all day?"

"Yes, it was. Some nights I was so bone tired I just couldn't make myself do it, especially if it was an English assignment. I didn't grow up in a house where people spoke good English. I had a lot of trouble with using correct grammar, but my memory is good and I got so I was being able to underline the right verb form or pronoun in assignments.

"But writing essays was the worst. Then I got lucky because one of the CCC leaders saw how hard I was struggling with a writing assignment one night, and he came over and said, 'Carnes, I can see you're actually sweating over this assignment. One of the guys told me it's an essay. My mother used to teach high school English before they closed the high school in my town because of the Depression. She helped me learn how to write essays, and I'll be glad to see if I can help you with that.'

"I was so willing to be helped we started that night. I have to say nobody's ever going to publish anything I write, but I did learn how to write decent sentences with a subject and a predicate that said something appropriate about the topic of the essay. He made me aware of sentence structure and correct grammar, especially verb usage. Nobody's ever going to pay to read what I've written, but I made a B in my English correspondence course, and I'll be grateful to Corporal Evans for the rest of my life.

"Anybody else have a question?"

"Yes sir, I do." Bobby Felton had his hand up. "How long do you think you'll stay in the CCC?"

"That's a good question, and I am not sure what to answer. I'll certainly be working there a while longer. This Depression is not over yet, and I'm grateful to have a job, even though it doesn't pay much. We just make a dollar a day and at the end of the month, after giving us a little money to spend at the canteen, they send the rest to our family or to whoever we want them to send it to. It's not much, but it helps the family a bit. I send mine to Lee and Suzanna because they're my family.

"But the truth is that I think we're headed toward a war. So I'm thinking about joining the Army. I have learned how to do a lot of things in the CCC I think I could do in the army like build bridges or cut paths through brush or even build buildings. I don't really know what they'd have me doing, but I think I'm being trained in some skills that ordinary recruits probably won't have. So my plan is to volunteer before we enter the war and let the Army decide how it can use me."

"Wow, Mr. Carnes. You really think we'll be going to war even though we live in the United States and nobody has attacked us here?" Bobby asked.

"I do think there's a good chance we are going to end up fighting in this war. I certainly hope we won't be attacked. But I don't think if it comes right down to it we'll let Hitler and the Germans take over the world. Now that's enough today about war, and I hope I'm wrong."

Before Ed asked for other questions, Jack broke in and said the bell to end the school day would ring soon and they needed to thank Ed Carnes for his time with them.

Immediately the whole class stood up and applauded him. The bell rang as they were clapping. Several of the boys and even a few girls stayed and thanked Ed personally. The girls told him how impressed they were with him for joining the CCC. The boys wanted to ask more questions about the possibility of war. Ed had immediately felt bad about getting into the threat of war and answered the boys saying he had no inside knowledge about the possibility of war. It just seemed smart for the country to be prepared if it should occur. Nobody could disagree with that and the remaining boys again thanked Ed for his time and his words.

Ella and Jack were both so proud of the man he had become and told him so in different ways several times until he began to be embarrassed by their praise. He told them he needed to leave and get back to the Lewises because Lee and Suzanna were picking him up to take him to their house at 4:00. They hugged him and asked him to please stay in touch with them, and as he left they said at almost the same time what a fine young man he had become.

4

That night after dinner when Eleanor and the kids had gone upstairs Eleanor and Jack were still talking about Ed. "Who do you think made the real difference or the most difference—the Lewises or Suzanna and Lee?" Eleanor asked.

Jack said, "I think they both were important but in sort of different ways. Michael and Esther treated him like he was a worthwhile human being who had something to offer the world in which he lives. Boys, probably all boys, but boys who grow up in families like Ed's need that kind of encouragement to feel not only worthy but that it's possible to make something good of their lives.

"But what Lee and especially Suzanna gave him was love, a feeling of being wanted, of simply being appreciated for who he is and of belonging within a family that cares about him. That was something he'd not ever had.

"Both of those things are important, are necessary for a male, probably just as necessary for a female, but since I'm not one I'll leave that for you to comment on, my Ella."

"I agree with you about both of these needs and say they are necessary for both females and males. I lean toward thinking that being loved is maybe a tad more important to females, maybe because we grow up feeling it is our responsibility to provide love for the family members while it is generally the man's responsibility to provide for the physical comfort and well-being. I know I certainly have leaned toward making my husband and children feel loved, but after Daniel's death I became much more aware of the need for me to be able to contribute financially. Then you came into my life and eased that burden so that we share it, though you take care of it more than I, and I am grateful for that."

"Ella, did you feel loved when you were growing up? You are so loving now and have been as long as I've known you, so I'm guessing you were loved."

"I did receive love from my mother and her parents, my grandparents, when I went to visit them sometimes in the summer. I hardly remember my father, but the memories I do have are not of a loving parent. He was strict and stern. But he was killed when I was so young, I probably am not being fair to him. What about you, Jack? Did you grow up being loved?"

"Only by my nanny. I think she started taking care of me when I was a baby. Actually I don't remember a time when she was not there. She had a room of her own in Mother's house in Richmond. My daddy never lived with us, and I really didn't get to know him until I went off to prep school in Massachusetts. The only reason I know anything at all about loving and being loved was because of Nanny Alice. She was my real parent.

"Then when I was old enough to start high school Daddy insisted I come live with him in Massachusetts. He got me into Groton, a well-respected prep school where I learned how to fit in. Daddy would get me on holidays and take me around with him 'to show me off' because by then I was doing well at Groton, had friends whose fathers were well-known so that he could mention them in a conversation as though they were his friends too. I realized my father was simply using me for his own benefit and if he actually had any affection for me, I rarely, if ever, saw it or felt it.

"Then after the war I made a disastrous marriage to a woman who simply was trying to escape her own family and then her marriages—first to me and then to the Frenchman, and you know all about that and how it turned out. You know that your love and support were the only reason I made it through that horrible time. I'll never be able really to express to you how you enabled me to get through all of that.

"So the truth is I've only known real love from Nanny Alice, you, and from your children after they got to know me and really accepted me, and from deep friendships with people I have met here in Myrna like Molly Wainwright, Michael and Esther, John and Sarah Banks, and to a slightly lesser extent, with the MacPhersons, and now the Mitchells.

"However, I also have to confess I would never have made it through my early adult years without getting to know and love and want to be a child of this amazing God who has been with me all along, even when I was not aware of the love that was holding me and keeping me going. So finally it's to God that I give thanks for bringing me through all those years before He brought you and this family into my life, my Ella. Through you, I have experienced real, human love for these past 10 years, and I hope you know how grateful to God and to you I am."

Ella said she also was aware of God's loving presence in her life and in their lives as a family, and how that love had enabled her to get through Daniel's murder that left her as a single mother trying to hold her family together, especially when her 10-year-old was filled with so much anger. She snuggled closer after kissing him tenderly, and then they went to bed and expressed their love and gratitude for each other in delightful ways.

5

The fall days seemed to pass quickly so that it was Thanksgiving before they knew it. And then Christmas was upon them with all its memories and traditions. Eleanor was especially aware of Ronald's absence, while the presence of Eleanor and her children filled the gap in Ella and Jack's life that Daniel had left when he entered the Naval Academy in Annapolis. Then he and Lilly were sent to Hawaii, too far to come home for the holidays, even though Lilly had been hoping they could get leave time. Daniel knew better than to expect to go home for the holidays because they hadn't been in Honolulu long enough to accumulate vacation time.

Christmas arrived with its lights and decorated trees and carols being sung in the schools for the Christmas programs and in homes with or without piano accompaniment. The giving of gifts to families in need had become a tradition in Myrna, having begun soon after it was obvious the Depression was going to continue for some time.

Yet more jobs were beginning to open up as England and France needed help in manufacturing necessities for war but also in supplying more ordinary items for daily life. Even though the United States was still holding back from offering manpower to help England and France fight the Germans and the Italians, the necessary items for carrying on a war demanded other kinds of aid as well.

Consequently, a new factory that made tents that could be used in war moved to Myrna and provided steady work for many of the men who had not been making enough money trying to keep their cotton farms going. It also attracted workers from the surrounding area, and the town began to grow a bit as workers decided to move their families there. When finding decent housing became a problem, a new business began that bought land on the outskirts of Myrna and began building small and medium sized houses that were sold with long-term loans to families.

The idea of getting involved in the war was still unpleasant, but it was obvious that in some ways it was creating new life in Myrna. It was bringing in shoppers for the stores, new students in the schools and even new members in some of the churches, and a new energy throughout the town. Some people welcomed the newcomers and the atmosphere they created. Others resented having people they didn't know, people who hadn't grown up in the town and then stayed there to become leaders. Most people weren't bothered by the town's growth either way. They simply accepted it and went on about their lives, more worried about the possibility of the country's getting involved in the war in Europe than in having to get to know and accept people they hadn't grown up knowing.

The end of 1940 came with little fanfare. A lot of the young people and even a few of the older ones shot off a few fire crackers and bottle rockets at midnight. The Episcopal Church held a midnight prayer service for peace in the new year. Yet most people simply stayed at home wondering what 1941 had in store for them, hoping it was peace and prosperity, a time when it seemed the horrible Depression that had been burdening the country, actually the world, for more than 10 years was finally ending, and life would provide opportunities for every man willing to work hard to make a good living for his wife and family. Nobody was really sorry to see 1940 end. Everybody just wanted 1941 to bring in better times!

Part XIV

Waiting: 1941

1

School re-opened on the 6th, the first Monday in January. It didn't stay open long because the first snow storm of the season arrived a week later with one of the heaviest snows northeast Arkansas had received in years. Schools were closed for an entire week. Mail trucks didn't deliver. Grocery stores ran low on, and even ran out of, some of their most common items—like bread, milk, eggs, and even flour and sugar. Children actually got tired of sledding and playing outside, coming home complaining of how cold it was.

Finally after an entire week of icy cold and more snow than many of them had ever seen and certainly ever tried to play in, the rains came, warm enough to melt the snow and ice and create their own messiness. But school did begin again, including Arkansas State College in Jonesboro. The roads, even the road between Myrna and Jonesboro, were in such bad shape that Hank Fredrick telephoned the MacLeans' house and told Eleanor that while he thought they could make it in to Jonesboro and the college, they might need to leave an hour earlier since he had no idea how long it would take them to drive there.

On the way home from Jonesboro that afternoon Hank said, "In a way I have my own ulterior motive for hoping you would be willing to take a chance on the roads with me. The week before the storm hit Ruth received a letter from her parents' housekeeper that informed her they were both dead. She wouldn't even let me read the letter, and so I don't know any of the details because she wouldn't or couldn't bring herself to tell me what had happened. The whole week we were at home together with the boys she tried to act as though everything was all right, but she wasn't her usual self.

"Our sons found her crying in our bedroom one afternoon, but she wouldn't tell them what was wrong, just that she was tired and not feeling well. She had made me promise I wouldn't say anything to the boys until she was ready to tell them herself. But, Eleanor, I don't know when that's going to happen. She's not at all like her usual self, and I truly don't know what to do to make her better because right now she doesn't seem to want me near her. It's breaking my heart because we've always been so close, and I'm at my wits' end.

"I know how much she likes, even respects, you because of what you have had to deal with in the loss of your husband. Is there any way you think you might be able to see her, find out what's going on with her, and help her get past her parents' death. I have this feeling that maybe they committed suicide, but I'm scared even to broach the topic because I don't know how I'd deal with that if it were my mother and father. If this is more than you feel you can handle, I will certainly understand since that's my problem too. So please be honest with me."

Eleanor had sat in total silence, absorbing everything Hank had said to her and feeling grief for both of them. Ruth had told her back in the fall how concerned she was about her parents and that it had been four months since she had received a letter from them. She could imagine what a terrible shock it would be to receive such a letter from their housekeeper. After a few minutes she said, "Hank, I love Ruth pretty much like I love my sister. I need to pray a bit about what to do, how I can help her deal with whatever has happened to her mother and father. I'm already wondering if I were in her place, how I would feel, wondering what I'd do. I went through that when I realized Ronald had drowned and I would never see him again in this world. It was horrible, but I had to keep going for the sake of my children.

354

"Ruth has that same feeling, I'm sure. But she needs somebody she can cry with, express all of her feelings to. I'm a bit surprised she hasn't been able to do that with you—unless, unless this is something so bad she is fearful a strong man like you are could not understand and accept, or help her accept, what happened to her parents. So suicide is a real possibility.

"In a way I felt Ronald had committed suicide by going down with his boat, and I was angry with him. I had to work through it pretty much on my own because I couldn't tell his parents how I felt. They were grieving just as I was. I spent a good bit of time being angry with God, and I'm really not sure what got me past that.

"However, one day one of the young men who had been on Ronald's boat when it started taking on water knocked on my door. He had come because he thought I would want to know what had happened from someone who had been there. Of course, I invited him in after he told who he was and why he had come. He told me that when he got home he started trying to find out whose boat he had been in and finally read something in the paper about Ronald's death and realized he must be the one. He came to see me and described to me what it had been like that day, how once he'd made it into another boat, he looked for the boat he'd been on and realized Ronald's boat had disappeared into the water. He thanked me for Ronald's efforts, for his bravery in taking his boat out to rescue stranded soldiers on the shore at Dunkirk.

"I don't really understand why, but his visit ended my anger at Ronald for going, and especially for dying, trying to help rescue those thousands of stranded British soldiers.

"And I don't know what any of that has to do with what Ruth is going through, what she's feeling about her parents. But somehow I think there's a connection. Let me sleep on this, and I'll tell you in the morning if I feel there's anything I can do to help Ruth get through this, whatever it is. Will that work for you?"

"Eleanor, I just appreciate the fact you've listened to me and have the desire to help my wife, and of course, I hope you will be willing to try. That's all I'm asking, really all I'm hoping for." Hank looked so hopeful and yet so forlorn Eleanor had tears in her eyes when he let her out at Mary Beth's to pick up her children. She had to wipe them away before she went in to visit a few minutes and then walk back to Ella and Jack's with Lee and Amy. Sharing Hank's request with Mary Beth crossed her mind, but she pushed it away immediately, realizing she had no right to share his concern with anyone, not even her sister.

That night after she had read her children a bedtime story, tucked them in and kissed them goodnight, she went into the study room next door and went over her preparations for tomorrow's classes. Then she turned Hank's request over to the God she had learned to trust and let guide her in decision-making. Lying in bed, Eleanor let her thoughts wander, but they kept coming back to Ruth and what she was dealing with, what she most probably was feeling.

Suddenly it struck her Ruth might not just be struggling with the idea her parents had committed suicide but how they had died might also be troubling her. While she had never known anyone who had killed himself and certainly not a couple who had done so, she thought she could imagine how difficult it would be to deal with if your parents who had given you birth and raised you and loved you throughout your life had done this to themselves, having decided this was the better choice than what life was offering.

After she had thought this idea through thoroughly, she began to feel God was nudging her to accept Hank's plea and offer to visit with Ruth and see if she might help her get through this awful grief.

The next morning on their way to Jonesboro Eleanor told Hank she was willing to try to get Ruth to share her feelings with her. They decided Hank would go with the boys to the basketball game at the high school that night, giving Eleanor time to go by and see if Ruth would talk with her.

Ruth had been glad to send her males to the high school basketball game. They had left the house at 6:45 to get there before the junior high team's game started at 7. She felt relieved not to have to act peppy and happy around her family. This was an attitude, really an emotion, she had been dealing with ever since she had received the letter from the Schneiders telling her why and how her parents had died.

When there was a knock at her front door, she almost didn't answer. Having to deal with anyone was the last thing she wanted to do while she had the house to herself and could cry or grieve as much as she liked. But she went to the door and was surprised to find Eleanor Douglass standing there.

"May I come in, Ruth? I'll stay only as long as you want me to, but I do want to visit with you a bit if you are up to it."

"Why wouldn't I be up to it? You're acting as though I'm sick or something is wrong with me, Eleanor." Ruth's voice displayed her irritation and her emotional state. Eleanor almost turned and left but instead stood her ground and said, "Ruth, my dear friend, you are dealing with the deaths of your mother and father, and something about your loss is troubling you to the point you are not quite like the Ruth we all know and love.

"I don't know what it is or why you feel you can't talk about it, but I don't think you can come to terms with it and find peace until you let it out by talking to someone you can trust. I hope that someone is me because I love you as my true friend here in Myrna. Grief needs to be shared and brought out into the open. I'm here to help you do that—share your grief, let the wounds it has caused you bleed, and so free you to heal. Will you let me do that with you?"

Ruth burst into tears, sobbing as she said, "Oh, Ruth, I don't know if I can talk about this or not, but I am hurting so much inside I'm afraid if I don't get some of it outside of me, I might do something as awful to myself as my parents have done. Come in, please, and let's sit down and I'll try to explain why their deaths have made me like this."

After Ruth stopped by her bedroom to get a handkerchief, they sat down side by side on the sofa. Ruth said, "The Nazis who control Bavaria and Munich now are intent on ridding the area of all Jews. The talk around town, according the couple who had remained loyal housekeepers to my parents even after all the other servants left out of fear of being arrested by the Nazis, was that even the once-wealthy, highly respected Jews like my parents were going to be arrested and sent to a prison camp, in their case probably to Dachau, because it is nearby, where they would be separated from each other and probably never see each other again alive.

"Mrs. Schneider wrote me she thought that is what drove them to commit suicide. They had been together so long and still loved each other so deeply they couldn't bear the idea of being parted, or killed without each other. Mrs. Schneider wrote she had suspected they were thinking about, maybe even planning, to die together at home although they never mentioned it in front of her or her husband. They simply continued to be the kind and thoughtful, even caring, people they had always been to them.

"So although the idea of their committing suicide had become like a real possibility, she had no idea how or when it would occur. She and her husband were both shocked and grieved by the way they did it."

As she spoke these words, Ruth started sobbing again. Eleanor put her arms around Ruth and let her cry until she shook her head, took her hand-kerchief she had wadded into a ball, smoothed it out a bit and then wiped her eyes and blew her nose. "I truly cannot imagine how my father found the strength and the courage to do what he did. He used an old pistol he'd had since before the first war. I didn't know he had any kind of weapon in the house. He never showed it to me or even mentioned he had it. But he did, and he got it out from wherever he had it hidden, evidently cleaned it, pulled out the box of bullets it used and I think fired it once to make sure it still worked. Then the two of them lay down together on their bed. I don't know they said anything to each other, but I like to imagine they said they loved each other, maybe even asked God to forgive them for what they were about to do. It comforts me a little to think they did that anyway. Then Father shot Mother in the heart, and after that he put the gun into his mouth, pointed it upward, and shot himself.

Ruth began to weep again, and Ruth simply held her and let her cry until she stopped. "I cannot stand to think about my father doing this, but I realize he felt a quick death for both of them would be better than Dachau.

"The Schneiders found them the next morning. They had left a letter to me all nicely addressed to us here in Arkansas, and they had left a letter to the Schneiders with a rather large amount of money my Father must had kept hidden away in case of emergencies. He was always afraid something would happen, and he wouldn't be able to get his money out of the bank.

"I know all of this because I eventually received the suicide note in a rather long letter from Mrs. Schneider telling me all this, giving me the details which were hard to read and are still hard to think about and accept, though I suppose in a way I wanted, even needed, to know what happened to them."

With those words spoken, Ruth's tears flowed again but the sobbing was less. Eleanor simply held her and let her cry until she stopped.

"But that's not the end of the story. The Nazis came to arrest my father and mother and were furious they were already dead. The Schneiders had left the house and had tried to remove their fingerprints and leave as little of themselves behind as possible, though they realized the Gestapo would know they had been my family's servants. They know everything!

The Schneiders had taken the letter my father and mother had written to me and the letter he had written to them. They were afraid the Nazis would come to arrest them and find the letters. I guess they destroyed my father's letter to them. But his letter to me, they managed to mail to Mrs. Schneider's sister who had left Germany before Hitler came to power and moved to Switzerland where she had married and now lives in Bern. Afraid the German secret police watched all mail going out of Germany, they had carefully written the first few pages in German telling news of the country with kind words about the Nazi government and then had written about a cousin's new baby and other very common place things hoping the readers would get bored and quit reading. That's when they hid my father's letter to me in between pages of nothing important.

"When Mrs. Schneider's sister received the letter, she thought her sister had lost of mind, but when she came to the letter to me, she caught on because my father had included my address in America and had slipped in a bit of money that would pay for the stamps to send it.

"I think I really needed to tell someone this, especially the part about how my parents killed themselves, especially how my father died. It's so awful I have had real problems dealing with it. I have waked up in the middle of the night seeing his head with no top to it. I would start sobbing and Hank would just hold me. He thought I was just crying because they were dead. Of course, some of it was that, but how my father died was the worst part for me, and I just couldn't talk about it.

"But, you know, Eleanor, now that I've said it, talked about it to you, gotten it out in the open so to speak, I feel like a big weight has been lifted off me. I think that maybe I can deal with it now and even tell Hank. I understand why they died, and I will always hate the Nazis and all they stand for, but I can understand my parents decision to die by their own hands, or rather my Father's hands, than be separated in some camp and die by the torture the camp would mete out. And I know Hank can understand that too, though I really don't think I need share how he died with my boys. They are too young, and I don't want them ever to have to deal with anything like this!" Ruth took several deep breaths as though she were cleansing some inner part of her body.

360

"Thank you, Eleanor, for coming and helping me talk this out, deal with my own grief, and my anger toward the people who did this to my parents. I would write the Schneiders and thank them, but I am afraid that if the Nazis read their mail, they would punish them in some awful way."

"You know, Ruth, if you really wanted to let them know how grateful you are for letting you read the truth about your parents' deaths and for caring for them all those years, you might go through the sister in Switzerland, write her and depend on her to manage to get the message of your gratitude to Mrs. Schneider, that is if you saved her letter and it has her address on it."

"That's a wonderful idea, Eleanor. I did save the letter and the envelope because I wanted to thank her for getting the Schneiders' letter to me. I hadn't even thought about her being able to write to them and let them know how greatly I appreciate their care of my parents during all those years of faithful service to them after all the other servants had left them.

"And thank you for coming and helping me get this grief and anger outside of me. I realize I was punishing my husband and children without meaning to just because I had all these emotions inside I didn't know what to do with. They wanted to help me, but I didn't know how to let them, and they really didn't know what to do with or for me either."

"Well, you thank Hank because if he hadn't shared his concern and love for you, I never would have known about all you were dealing with. I was sorry about your parents dying, but had no idea of the circumstances. So you really owe your husband, because he loves you dearly and has obviously been terribly worried about you and that he couldn't seem to help you deal with this, whatever *this* was. Life is horribly tough and strange sometimes. We really do need one another. So just know that I'm here when you want a listening ear or a shoulder to cry on."

With these words Eleanor and Ruth stood and hugged each other, standing with their arms around each other, grateful for their friendship, knowing it had deepened greatly because of what they had meant to each other on this night.

The next morning when Hank picked Eleanor up for the drive to school he was smiling and immediately thanked her for whatever she had done to help Ruth make progress in getting past her grief. Ruth had shared a good bit of her and Eleanor's conversation with him, but he'd realized it was not only Eleanor's words but her obvious compassion and understanding of what Ruth was feeling that had made the real difference. They both expressed their gratitude for the friendship the three of them shared.

3

The winter months dragged on as they plowed through January, letting the upcoming Valentine's Day bring a bit of brightness into their lives. Since Valentine's Day occurred on a Friday, Mary Beth and Pat decided to have a small dinner party of people in their age group, inviting Eleanor to be a co-hostess if she would like to do so. Eleanor was delighted to accept. She hadn't entertained or been invited to a party in all the months she had been in Myrna. Although her year of mourning was not quite over, Ella and Jack both encouraged her to go, knowing Mary Beth could use an extra set of hands since Pat was not accustomed to giving parties. He had grown up in such a large family his mother had never had the time or the money to entertain. Ella and Jack offered to keep all four children over night, and that was immediately accepted by both sisters with gratitude.

Mary Beth and Eleanor began their planning on Saturday morning, February 1, two weeks before Valentine's on Friday, the 14th. The guest list was not long: Ruth and Hank Fredrick, Lynne and Morgan Thompson from their church, and David Masterson, who was a math professor and a friend of Hank's and a new friend, or really more a new acquaintance, of Eleanor's. Since they had decided on eight because Mary Beth and Pat's dining room table could comfortably seat that number, the two women began planning how they could carry out the Valentine theme with both food and entertainment.

For dinner Eleanor and Mary Beth had both thought of Ella's marinated pot roast she had served at large family gatherings and had always been a hit. Add a potato, onion, and cheese casserole, red beet salad, corn pudding, and homemade rolls and butter with strawberry jelly—and you had a hearty meal. But what about dessert. You simply had to have dessert at a Valentine's Party! They both said at the same time—"Mother's Valentine cake!"

"Do you suppose she still has the heart shaped pan?" Mary Beth asked.

"She never had a heart-shaped pan. She made a cake in a square pan and then miraculously managed to cut a heart out of the cake, which she then carefully and generously covered with icing—sometimes white with pink decorations, sometime chocolate with red decorations. The cake itself was almost always a white cake with something in it to give it body so she could cut it," Eleanor said. "I do not volunteer to make that cake."

"Neither do I, and I really don't think it's right to ask her to make it since she and Jack are taking on all four of our children. You know, let's just go with Valentine cookies and homemade ice cream. After all, we're planning a pretty heavy meal. What do you think, Eleanor? Will that do?"

"It should. After all, during these winter days just to be invited to somebody's house to eat would be a treat, at least for the woman. And Mother's iced-sugar cookies are yummy. I'm guessing you have the recipe. I'm sorry, but I left all my recipes back in England. I just didn't have space to bring everything, though I did mean to bring my recipe box but forgot it because of everything else I was trying to remember to pack," Eleanor said.

"Of course, I have it. It's my 'go-to' cookie whenever I'm too tired to make the effort to cook something sweet that's more demanding. I have to confess sometimes I don't bother to do cutouts or anything. I just put all the dough in a pan, smooth it out 'til it's flat, and make a cookie cake. I ice it and cut it in squares, and nobody seems to mind. At least, my children certainly don't." Eleanor and Mary Beth both laughed.

"Having little children certainly has compelled me to take an easy route out at times too, "Eleanor said, still laughing. "When does it get easier? Or does it?" she asked.

"I think it gets easier in some ways, like when they can dress themselves and don't have to wear diapers any longer. But then there are other things that still are hard. They start asking questions or want to do things you don't want them to do, even though some other children are doing them. We haven't quite gotten there yet, but I hear other mothers talk, and I know it's coming."

"Yours will get there before mine do, Mary Beth, and I'm going to count on you to help guide me through the parenting issues we both know are going to come up. But—back to the party. What are some games we can play or topics for conversation to sort of break the ice?" Eleanor asked.

"Well," Mary Beth paused. "Since it's Valentine's, what about love questions and answers, like 'Who was the first girl you kissed? How old were you and how old was she? Where were you two when you kissed her? Was that the beginning of you two as a couple?' And then we ask the same questions to the women."

"Good ideas, Sister. And then we could ask them to share when they knew they had found the 'right woman or right man' and ask the men when or how did they propose and the females how they accepted." Eleanor then added. "You know, this will be a fun way for us to get to know one another better. But I just had a thought: I wonder if David Masterson has been married. Well, I guess this is one way to find out. Do you need to share these ideas with Patrick, Mary Beth?"

"No. Well, maybe. He won't like them if I tell him about them. Truth is, he's not much of a 'game player' unless it's some kind of physical game. But he's a good husband who's pretty patient with me and my ideas, and he'll be a good sport and go along once we get started. Just thinking about it, maybe we ought to start with

364

the women. We're more ready to answer questions like that than men usually are. But if we break the ice and then sort of tease them if they won't share since we've shared with them, I think they'll all go along. Actually I think we'll end up laughing, especially over the first set of questions and it'll be fun." Mary Beth paused.

Eleanor said, "Maybe we should stop with the first set. Or at least, just see if the conversation can naturally move toward how the couples at the table met and fell in love. Since we really don't know anything about David and whether he's ever been married or what happened to his wife, and then I'm a recent widow, it may be better not to go further," Eleanor said.

Mary Beth responded, "Just the first part will be a fun way to warm up and a great way for us to get to know one another—much better than if we just sat around and talked about what's going on in Myrna or the world, especially since it looks more and more like we will end up going to war."

"Now that's a conversation that could kill the spirit of this or any party! I say that if anybody even tries to bring up the subject of war, we both say immediately the topic is off-limits during this special evening." Eleanor said emphatically. "Do you agree, Mary Beth?"

"One hundred percent! I don't think anybody will dare disobey the Wood sisters!" Then they both burst into laughter.

"We certainly sound tough, don't we? But what about decorations, Mary Beth? Do you have any ideas?"

"I've got those covered. I've been collecting Valentine decorations ever since Pat got old enough to have some idea of what Valentine's was all about, and so I've got place cards covered and even some stuff to hang on the doors of put on the table or wherever.

"Do you suppose you could get Hank to come back to Myrna early that day so you could come over and help me decorate and do any of the cooking we need to do here that afternoon?" Mary Beth asked. "And if we can get Mother to take the children as soon as she gets home from school, that will help too."

"All of that sounds possible, Mary Beth. And maybe we'd be smart to make the invitations for guests to arrive at 7:00 p.m. I'm counting on you to do the grocery shopping because I get home from Jonesboro so late every day. But I'm willing to come over Thursday night and help with any food preparations that can be done the day before."

"I will shop Thursday morning and will be delighted to have help with whatever we can get prepared that night. We also might set the dining room table and put up some of the decorations. Patrick and the children could even help us do that."

The two young women put their plans in a check list on paper with the days they planned on getting each thing done. First on the list were three invitations they put together that morning, having them ready for the mailman who usually arrived around 11:30. They had asked that the invited guests respond to the invitation by telephoning Mary Beth at #482 no later than February 7. They hoped everyone on their list would be able to come!

Also on that same Saturday morning they went over the menu and the grocery list, which Mary Beth had said she would be willing to buy on the Friday before the party, although she was going to call Callaway's Grocery early in the week to order the pot roast early on Monday to be sure the store would have it by Friday morning.

Eleanor said she would find a sitter to keep the children busy for part of Valentine's day so Mary Beth could spend the day getting everything ready for the party that night with Ella coming over to help as soon as she came home from school.

Ella had asked Hank during their drive home from Arkansas State on the Thursday after the invitations should have arrived that Monday if he had heard anything from David Masterson, and he said David had told him about the invitation and was planning to accept. Actually, Mary Beth should receive his acceptance note in today's mail, and when she drove her parents' car to Mary Beth's to pick up Lee and Amy, Mary Beth showed her David's accept-ance note, saying he was looking forward to the party. Eleanor was impressed at how nicely he had expressed his pleasure in accepting the invitation and what good penmanship he had. She wasn't interested in finding a new husband, certainly not yet, but it would be nice to have an occasional outing with someone who was literate! However, he was a mathematician and that did not raise her expectations he would be a reader, at least of the sort of literature that interested her.

Valentine's Day arrived with some sunshine and temperature in the 50s, a good bit warmer than the early part of the week had been. Mary Beth and Eleanor had stayed up the night before working on decorations and had the table set with Valentine place cards on which she had carefully printed the names of those who would be sitting at the table, with Patrick at the head and her at the end. Then she had placed each couple across from each other, one side seating man, woman, man and the opposite side woman, man, woman. During that week leading up to the party she had carefully written out the questions dealing with the "first kiss" with one set for the men and the other set for the women.

4

But by Valentine's night the cold weather had returned, and the five guests arrived wrapped in coats, scarves, and gloves. Patrick opened the door and led the guests to his and Mary Beth's bedroom where they piled their outer wear on the bed and hurried to the fire roaring in the fireplace. Mary Beth and Eleanor brought in trays with cups of hot spiced tea that were eagerly taken and held with both hands around the cup for its warmth. The fireplace blazed at the end of the living room, giving off welcomed warmth, and everyone gathered around it except for Mary Beth and Eleanor who were in the kitchen preparing to bring out the food and place it on the lowboy from which the guests would serve themselves.

Once the food was ready and on the lowboy, they held hands around the table while Patrick prayed God would bless the food, the hands that had prepared it, and all those who partook of it.

They easily found their places at the table, since each place had a Valentine with a name on it. Of course, Patrick was at the head and Mary Beth at the end nearest the kitchen. Eleanor and David were in the middle seats on each side, facing each other. David was sitting between Ruth and Lynne while Eleanor had Hank and Morgan sitting on either side of her, facing their wives.

Once they were all seated and had begun eating, the awkward moment Eleanor and Mary Beth had worried about when someone would need to initiate the conversation was broken to their surprise by David, who said. "I cannot express how much I appreciate being invited to this party. It's been a while since I have even eaten with anyone except family. The only party I've been to was the faculty Christmas party, and it was pretty quiet. And the truth is I don't ever remember being invited to a Valentine party."

Everybody at the table laughed and agreed they couldn't remember how long it had been since they had actually been to a Valentine's Party for adults, if ever. How had Mary Beth and Eleanor come up with the idea? And with that the conversation flowed easily around the table.

After they had finished with dessert Mary Beth said, "One of the reasons we thought about hosting this kind of party was we thought it would be a fun way to get to know each other better. And so we've come up with a few questions that will, we hope, bring out some information about one another we probably haven't even shared with our spouses. So we're going to begin asking the women first because I think we are probably more open to sharing those experiences than men are, but don't worry, gentlemen, your chance will come. So I'm going to start with my sister. Eleanor, who was the first boy who kissed you and did you kiss him back?"

"It was Tony Nichols, a 10th-grade boy who had invited me, a ninth grader to go to the school dance after a football game. We left the dance at 11:30 because I had to be home by midnight. He didn't drive me straight home but went out toward Jonesboro and stopped on the side of the road. I got nervous because I wasn't quite sure what to expect. I wasn't exactly scared, but I was nervous. Then he said, 'Eleanor, I have enjoyed our date, and I would like to kiss you. Would you mind?'

"Well, I had never been kissed by a boy, but I thought I might like it, so I said that I wouldn't mind. So he kissed me very gently once and then said, 'That was nice. May I kiss you again?' And I said he could. So he did. This kiss lasted a bit longer but was still gentle. Then he said, 'I like kissing you, but I think I better take you home now.' And he did.

"But when Mother wanted to hear all about the date, I told her we'd had fun and that he was a perfect gentleman. She seemed relieved to hear that, and I never told her he'd given me my first kiss. I confess I had a hard time going to sleep that night and kept remembering what it had been like to be kissed by a boy and liking it."

"Did you tell anyone you had received your first kiss?" And Eleanor answered that she hadn't.

"Why not?"

"Because I didn't want to be teased or even to talk about it. I just kept it to myself and treasured it. Actually, this is the first time I've told anyone."

"You didn't tell your husband?"

"The truth is I had forgotten about it. I hadn't thought about that kiss for years until Mary Beth and I started planning this party. Now it's not a secret anymore because seven people know about it."

"Maybe he told some of his friends."

"Maybe, but nobody ever mentioned it in front of me or teased me about it, so I imagine he kept it to himself."

"Did you all date after that?"

"Not really because his daddy was already really sick with something, I don't remember what. Anyway, his family moved to Alabama where they had parents. To be truthful, I never heard from him again after they moved away. Now it's your turn, Ruth."

"I'll be honest and tell you I lived a very sheltered life in Munich. Because we were Jews, my parents didn't socialize much and then only with other Jews who were close friends. They were shocked and concerned when I started dating Hank because he was a Christian, but he was so open with them about who he was and that he was not going to do anything to hurt me or get me or them in trouble with the Nazis they began thinking it was a good thing for me to be seen with a Gentile.

"The best kiss I ever received was on my 20th birthday when Hank took me to a nice restaurant where he had invited two other couples, friends of ours, to join us. We had champagne and a lovely dinner, followed by a birthday cake and ice cream.

"Then he gave me a box and within it was this ring, my engagement ring, and he kissed me right there in the restaurant and asked me to marry him. I had led a very sheltered life, and while Hank had kissed me before, this is the kiss I remember most because I kissed him back and told him I loved him and would marry him." And she held her left hand up and displayed it along with her wedding band.

"Now that's a beautiful story!"

"What a romantic you are, Hank Fredrick! I'm impressed!"

"No one can beat that, but it's my turn," Lynne Thompson spoke up. "I had just turned 'sweet 16' and had never been kissed, not really. But I was invited to go to the Senior Prom by the handsomest boy in our high school. When he came to pick me up, he brought me this beautiful corsage of pink roses. He was driving his father's Pontiac, and I felt like Cinderella going to the ball. We had such a wonderful time that night, and he kissed me so sweetly on the mouth when he brought me home I went to bed thinking, 'This is the man I'm going to marry.' And I did!"

"Okay, Morgan! You did well, old Man!"

"Hey, that's one way to make points!"

"You've got a big night waiting for you at home tonight, Morgan."

The men were having a great time.

"Mary Beth, it's your turn. What was your first kiss like?"

"I was 14 and had a huge crush on a boy who was a year older than I was. He was in the 10th grade and played football. We had

370

'Sadie Hawkins Day' back then. It was always on a Friday when there was a home football game that night. In the pep rally during our assembly on Friday, the players were 'auctioned off' to the highest bidder, and they would be the date to the Sadie Hawkins dance that night of whichever girl 'bought' them.

"Well, 10th-grade players didn't get 'sold' for much, but Lenny was cute even if he wasn't on first team. I used to baby sit for a few neighbors' children from time to time and worked on Saturdays at Lewis' Department Store, so I had saved up almost $5.00 for the auction. A couple of 10th-grade girls were bidding on him too, but I stuck with it and bought Lenny.

"That night I wore my Daisy Mae outfit that Mother had made for Eleanor when she was my age. She now thought she was too old to be interested in Sadie Hawkins' Day. That's how I got to wear it, and I felt so cute when Daddy drove me to pick Lenny up at his house after the ball game and then dropped us off at the high school gym for the dance.

"We had a pretty good time at the dance, but he wasn't really much of a dancer. When the dance ended, Daddy picked us up and drove us to his house. I got out of the car to walk him to the door, but he leaned down and grabbed me and kissed me hard on the mouth, then turned and ran to his door. I just stood there stunned. My first kiss! And it had hurt. My lip was bleeding. Daddy, who was a doctor looked at it when he got home, assured me it would heal, and said not all kisses would be like that."

"Okay, Patrick, let's see what the doctor has to say about his wife being kissed by a young stud"

"Yeah, bruising her lips!"

"Did you know this kid?"

"Actually Patrick, we women have done enough sharing. What we want to know is who was the first girl you ever kissed and what was that like?" Eleanor asked the question.

"That's been so long ago, Eleanor, I don't remember." Patrick was shaking his head as he spoke.

"Now don't give us that kind of lame excuse. Everybody remembers his or her first kiss to or from a member of the opposite sex, certainly whether it was a good, so-so, or bad experience," Eleanor was laughing as she pushed him to answer.

"All right, all right! The first kiss I ever gave a girl was to Polly Malone in the third grade. I thought she was the prettiest girl in our class. So one day during recess I asked her if she wanted to do something daring, and when she said she didn't think so, I just grabbed her anyway and kissed her on the mouth.

"She started crying and went and told the teacher on me, who took me to the Principal's office. He told me we couldn't have that sort of behavior going on and he was going to let my mother hear about this. He said if I was smart I'd tell my mother myself before she received a letter from him.

"Of course, I told my mother the minute I got to the house. She gave me a good paddling and told me much worse would happen to me if she ever received another letter from the Principal about my behavior.

"My mother didn't say things she didn't mean or wouldn't do if she said it. So I didn't kiss another girl until I left home to go to college. Even then I always made sure the girl wanted me to kiss her!"

"Did she ever mention getting the letter from the principal?" David asked.

"No, she never did. After a while I quit thinking about it, but by the time I was in junior high I realized he had never written my mother. He'd just counted on scaring me enough about writing her I'd be sure to tell Mother myself. He'd already had three of my older siblings in his school and knew Mother ran a tight ship. He also knew Mother could put the fear of God in us and so was 99 per cent sure I'd tell her. And he was right!

"I never dared asked Mother if she'd heard from him. In fact, I was careful to stay out of her way for a good while. When I asked her about it after I'd finished medical school, she didn't remember anything about it. After all, she had seven of us kids to keep on a straight path, and so far as I know, we're all still on it! Wouldn't you agree, Wife?"

"I most certainly would," Mary Beth said with a giggle. "So who wants to go next? Hank?"

"Well, you've already heard about me from my wonderful wife!"

"Yes, and that's her story about you. But don't try to make us believe that in all those years before you met Ruth you never once kissed another girl because no one will believe you!" Eleanor said laughing.

"All right. But my first kiss wasn't very exciting. I was in the seventh grade in Germany. Herr Hitler was already making a name for himself, and Germany was already leaning toward the kind of strictness Hitler was soon to make the rule of law.

"There was a pretty girl a year younger than I was in my neighborhood. We had more or less grown up together, although we didn't go to the same school. That year I learned why. She was Jewish.

"One day I was out in the street in front of my house kicking a soccer ball in the street, just fooling around really, and I saw her come out of her house. She was crying. We were pretty good friends so I went over to ask Helga what was the matter.

"She told me her father had been taken away to an internment camp. The men who had come to get him had the Nazi symbol on their arms. They said they'd be back soon to pick up her mother and her and take them to a camp too.

"That's when I put my arms around her and just held her while she cried. And then I kissed a girl for the first time, kissed her on the mouth—not hard but a real kiss, even though by then I was crying too."

"The Nazis did come the next day while I was at school. I never saw Helga again. But when I met Ruth I was determined the same thing would not happen to her or to her parents. She was willing to marry me, leave her homeland to go with me to England. Her parents were not. They said they were too old to start over in a new place where they did not know the language. They thought they would be safe if they just stayed in their house and did not draw attention to themselves.

"We were afraid for them, but we could understand why they didn't want to leave. We hoped rather than believed that they would be safe from the Nazis. But of course, they weren't. Anyway I didn't intend to throw a cloud over this delightful evening." Hank looked truly regretful, while Ruth had tears in her eyes which she tried to dab away with her napkin without letting anyone see.

"This has been such a delightful evening, we can't end it on such a sad note," David Masterson spoke up to everyone's relief. They'd all been sitting there, caught up in the tragedy of Hank's story, feeling the pall of war and cruelty hanging over them. "My first kiss, a real kiss not from my mother or any family members, came when I was 14 and had fallen in love—or so I thought—with a girl in my ninth grade class. She was not really beautiful, but one of those girls who exudes personality and fun. I sat behind her in my English class, and we'd pass notes to each other occasionally about something or other to do with class.

"When I found out she lived fairly near me, we started walking home together on afternoons when neither of us had to stay late for a meeting or ball practice or whatever. We became friends—not romantic friends, but just friends who liked each other and had fun talking and kind of fooling around, laughing—that kind of relationship.

"Then one day when we were walking home she told me they were moving. Her dad had been offered a job, a good job in Pennsylvania, and he was moving to Philadelphia in a couple of weeks and would send for his wife, and her little sister and her as soon as he found a house, or even better, had sold theirs. Then she teared up because she said she really didn't want to move. She liked living in Jonesboro. And that's when I put my arms around her and kissed her. It was my first time to kiss a girl. I cared about this girl, realized even that I loved her, though I don't think it was romantic love so much as deep friendship for a person I liked, more than just casually. I don't have any siblings; so in a way she had become like the sister I had never had.

374

"We still stay in touch at Christmas and on each other's birthday. She's married and has three children. I wish we lived closer, but our lives have gone in different directions. Still, it is really a wonderful blessing to have friendships that extend over long periods of time and don't just end because someone moves far away. So here's to friendships—those far away and those near at hand!"

"Hear! Hear!" Patrick said. "We still have some cider warming on the stove. Mary Beth and I will bring it in here with cups we can fill." They both left and quickly returned with mugs and cider to pour into them. Then Patrick said, " "Let's have a toast of gratitude for friends—both old and new! Happy Valentine's Day to all!"

The guests left soon after with laughter and with feelings of gratitude for new friendships formed and old ones deepened.

As they emptied the table of dishes and silverware, with Patrick washing and the sisters drying and putting the dishes away, they chatted about everything from the food to the guests. Both Mary Beth, Eleanor, and Patrick agreed that it had been a good evening and could not have gone better.

All three of them had liked David very much and were glad Hank had suggested they invite him. He had seemed to fit right in with the three couples, and Eleanor said she had not once felt like a spare tire, thanks to having David there as a sort of partner. Eleanor said while she and David had not had any time to talk one-on-one, she had not felt awkward with him as a kind of partner. And she hoped he had felt the same way. He certainly seemed at ease and to enjoy the evening.

As soon as they had washed all the dishes and pots and pans and put everything away, Patrick drove Eleanor back to Jack and Ella's where she was relieved to find her parents had been able to get all four children in bed and asleep. They were sitting in the living room where Jack had the fire going and wanted to hear all about the party. Eleanor was happy to share the experience with her parents, thanking them again for taking care of the children and making the evening possible for her to enjoy!

As she lay in the bed with the two little girls beside her, she realized this was the first time in 10 months she remembered laughing and talking without constantly being reminded that Ronald was dead. She certainly didn't want to forget him and knew she wouldn't, but it was nice every once in a while to have had this much time when she hadn't been constantly made aware he was gone from her life. She said a silent prayer of thanks to God and then turned on her side and went to sleep.

Part XV

David and Eleanor: 1941

1

David Masterson drove back to his rooms in Jonesboro thinking over the evening and realizing he couldn't remember having been in a group he had enjoyed this much in the three years since his wife's death. It wasn't that he had lived immersed in grief for these past three years. It was more like laughter and fun had been on leave from his life. Was it possible life could once again feel like it was worth living? God knows, he had loved Gloria and had been thrilled when she told him she was pregnant. He really didn't care whether she was carrying a boy or a girl, just as long as this one was healthy.

They had both grieved the first time she was pregnant when she had miscarried at three months. The doctor had told them he couldn't tell what sex the baby was because there had been some abnormalities, and it was a blessing the fetus had died. That had been a tough time for both of them.

They spent many hours discussing whether they should try again. But they both wanted children and they both wanted to believe Dr. Peterson when he told them one damaged fetus did not mean the next one would be that way. So when Gloria told him she was three months pregnant and had been examined by Dr. Peterson, who had said everything appeared normal and both she and the baby were healthy, they had celebrated. They had gone out for dinner and then come home and telephoned both sets of parents who were eager for grandchildren since both he and Gloria were only children.

The pregnancy appeared to be going well with normal side effects on Gloria—some morning sickness, more tired at the end of the day than usual, but she was cheerful and happy.

And then when Gloria was five months pregnant, the unthinkable had occurred. He was driving her to her regular monthly doctor's appointment when a truck, a very large delivery truck approaching them, blew a tire, swerved across the center line and smashed into the side of the car where Gloria was sitting. The impact had knocked the door off its hinges throwing Gloria against the dashboard where one side of the truck had her penned. The fire department sent a truck and the firemen used tools to cut the truck away. An ambulance had come immediately and taken Gloria to the hospital where she was barely alive. David had ridden with her and was holding her hand in the emergency area when she died. The baby girl had died first, but Gloria didn't know it, and the last words she'd whispered to David were "Take care of our baby."

David himself had a bruised chest from hitting the steering wheel, a sore foot from hitting the brake, but he had hardly been aware of physical pain because his emotional pain was so much greater.

He'd felt anger—toward the truck driver, whom he understood was not at fault for his brakes going out, but more toward God who most certainly could have stopped this accident from occurring and taking from him his beloved wife and the little girl he'd never had the chance of knowing, of holding her, of watching her grow up.

David could barely remember that first year after the accident. The funeral service for his wife and daughter was the hardest thing he'd ever gone through because he was still so angry at God he found himself resenting all the people who came to comfort him because they were alive and whole and happy. And he felt, actually was sure, he could never be really happy again.

He had spent the first year after the funeral living off the insurance money he'd received from the trucking company, drinking whiskey to dull his emotions, and feeling sorry for himself. His parents tried to help him, but he didn't want their help. They couldn't bring his wife and unborn child back to life. He was angry at God who hadn't kept his sweet, wonderful wife who was carrying their little girl from being killed. God either was not the powerful God religion made him out to be or God was uncaring. Either way, God was no help and certainly didn't deserve to be worshipped. That's how he'd spent the first year.

2

The second year David had pulled himself together a bit and had re-applied for a job teaching mathematics at Arkansas State College in Jonesboro. The Dean of the college had known David's family and watched him grow up. He had hired David to teach after he had graduated from the University of Arkansas with a Master's Degree in mathematics and had been proud of the grades he'd made there and of his work as a teacher until the accident. Then he had accepted David's resignation after his wife's death and hoped he'd get past his loss. He had kept up with David's slide into alcoholism, wondering if he could regain control of himself and of his life, hoping that would happen though not at all certain it would.

When David had reapplied, Dean Atkinson hired him on a part-time basis for the first semester, and gave him freshman classes to teach, figuring if David could stay sober and get freshmen to learn how to study and care about learning and if he could serve in a way as their friend and counselor, he would be worth his salary. He said as much to David, who accepted this trial period, determined to pull himself out of his grief and get back some sort of life. At least, he could perhaps have something to give to freshmen math students.

It was during his first semester back that he had met and made friends with Hank Fredrick. Hank understood better than most how difficult life could be as he was married to a wife who was a Jew and who had experienced what prejudice and hatred could do to her people and the danger that always hid just beneath the surface of ordinary daily life.

David passed his first year back at Arkansas State with flying colors. The Dean was delighted he had made the right decision in giving David the opportunity to come back to life. He had maintained sobriety, but even more important he had regained interest in living. He had thrown himself into his teaching and into building relationships with his students. He became a kind of surrogate older brother, friend, and counselor. His students not only came with questions about the mathematics course they were taking but also about relationships and ordinary problems of daily living.

His second year he had moved onto the campus as a resident-head in the men's dorm. Even the residential students who were not the least interested in math loved him and sought him out as a counselor on all sorts of topics. They appreciated his frankness when he would tell them they needed to talk to a professional who had more knowledge about the subject than he had. They came to him when they just needed a kind friend or one with an understanding heart.

3

It was Hank who had told David about Eleanor and how she had lost her husband and then asked if he'd be interested in attending the Valentine's party she and her sister Mary Beth were planning. Hank would tell Eleanor if he were because he drove her to and from the college every day. David had said he was interested, and now, after having truly enjoyed the evening, he was so glad he had done so.

David realized Eleanor was nowhere near ready for any sort of relationship beyond friendship. He understood that because he was not at all sure he would ever be ready to marry and take the chance of losing a wife and a child again. But he had been impressed she had talked about her first kiss and had been able to do so without tearing up and mentioning or thinking about the kisses she was not getting from the man she had married and who had given her two children.

The trouble was he never saw her when she was on campus. She either was in class teaching or somewhere grading papers or preparing for her next class, and not even Hank knew where she did that.

* * *

The first week she had started working at Arkansas State College Eleanor had gone to the library, met the head librarian, and explained to him her need for a quiet space where she could study between classes because she lived in Myrna and rode to and from the college with Hank Fredrick. Paul Smithers, who had heard Eleanor's story from several sources on the faculty and was impressed with her courage in trying to rear two children on her own while pursuing a new job, was eager to help her.

He led her to a room reserved for faculty usage on the second floor of the library which was, he told her, rarely in use, and he gave her a key that would enable her to enter the room any time the library itself was open. Ella expressed her gratitude for his help and assured him it was just what she wanted when she was between classes and needed time to go over her lesson plans or prepare for the next day.

Hank usually wanted to leave the campus at 3:30 and three days a week she didn't have a class in the afternoon. The other two days her classes ended at 3:00 and even when a student wanted to talk with her, she could be done by 3:20 and walk to Hank's car without keeping him waiting. The space in the library was just perfect for her needs. She had told Mr. Smithers she would appreciate it if he didn't make it known she was using this room or what her schedule was because she truly needed time alone to prepare lessons for her classes. She told him she had two young children at home who wanted and needed all the time and energy she could give them, and so it was important she use this time to prepare herself for teaching the next day's classes.

Eleanor's manners and her sincerity had completely won over Paul Smithers, who had also noticed her beauty. He promised her if she would give him the schedule when she planned to use the office, he would make certain no one else would be there at the same time. He said he had a comfortable chair for reading he would have the library's custodian move into the space along with a desk and chair, and a lamp that would give her more light. The room was so rarely used he kept these items in storage so students wouldn't bother them. On rare occasions a couple might come up to the second floor and try to enter the room for things they were not supposed to be doing on campus. He hoped she understood.

Ella said she did understand, and was grateful for his offer to provide the desk, chair, and lamp to make her work easier. She told him she most often would be there from 1:00 to about 3:20 on Mondays, Wednesdays, and Fridays, and would also likely be there Tuesday and Thursday mornings from 8:30 or 9:00 until 11:30. At least, that was her schedule for the first semester. It very likely could change for the second semester.

She and Hank enjoyed each other's company on the ride to and from Myrna, chatting about students, college gossip, campus politics. As they became more comfortable with each other, they sometimes talked about the war and what they thought it would take to get Roosevelt to lead the United States into it or what Prime Minister Churchill was doing to keep England's spirits up when the country was being bombarded day and night by the Nazi air force.

Hank worried it wouldn't end before his sons became old enough to have to fight, and he dreaded that because he knew what it would do to Ruth—and to him too—if anything happened to either son.

Eleanor said her mother had been worrying about Dan ever since he had graduated from the Naval Academy, and she didn't know how she would deal with it if he had to fly and bomb people or if his plane were hit by ammunition while he was in the air.

Because they usually ended their conversations on as positive a note as possible, on the ride home on Wednesday after the

Valentine's Day dinner, Hank said again that the Valentine's dinner had been a big success, but he had a sort of question for her.

"My friend David Masterson really enjoyed the evening and had asked me if he thought you would be willing to go to dinner with him sometime. He understands how recently you lost your husband, and this would simply be an evening between friends who know what it is like to lose the one you loved, but he hoped you might still be able to enjoy occasionally being with someone of the opposite sex just for companionship. Eleanor, you can be totally honest with me if you want me to tell him you're not interested or maybe 'not ready' would be kinder."

Eleanor took a deep breath and said, "When I told Mary Beth I'd co-host the dinner with her on Valentine's and a single man would sort of be 'my partner' I was aware something like this could happen. Mary Beth and I had a long talk about when I might be ready, if ever, to see, spend time with other men. I liked David. His loss in some ways is greater than mine because his wife was expecting a baby, a much wanted baby.

"Lee and Amy have been my reason for moving ahead, of trying to put my grief over Ronald's death behind me, or at least, not letting myself dwell on it constantly. I'm definitely not ready at all to fall in love again, or marry again. But I do miss having a man in my life. If David can be satisfied with friendship that most likely will never be more than friendship, I'm willing to have dinner with him.

"At least, I think I am. If I'm honest, Hank, I both want to fall in love again and I don't want to fall in love again. It hurts too much to lose the one you loved with all your heart and looked forward to spending the rest of your life with. I'm truly not sure I'll ever want to take that chance again."

"If anybody knows what that's like, Eleanor, it's David. He lost his wife three years ago, and this is the first time since I've known him he has even thought about a woman, at least as far as I'm aware. And we've become good enough friends I think I would have heard about it if he had. So do you want me to tell him 'yes' or 'no'?"

385

"Tell him 'yes' but also tell him I am not over grieving for my husband. He needs to know that."

"I will tell him, because if anyone will understand that, he will." Hank said softly. "Thank you, Eleanor, for being so honest with me about where you are. God knows, how, where, and when Ronald died is still incredible to me, and I'm sure even more so to you. Yet you've moved forward with your life, and you have not let your grief keep you from being an actively involved and loving mother."

"I've had to because of Lee and Amy. They're too young to understand what this kind of grief is like. They miss their daddy, but while they've been told how and why he died, they still sometimes ask when he'll be coming home. They are blessed with having Papa Jack nearby who adores them and will entertain them when he has the time, and can answer those kinds of questions far better than I can, if he is asked. And I am blessed with having Mary Beth and Patrick nearby, especially Mary Beth because she keeps them during the day and treats them with the same kind of love she shows Pat and Nora.

"I think a part of me is so satisfied with the loving family I, we, have that I don't want to complicate it by adding someone else to the mixture. So that's one reason for my hesitation about adding David to the list. But I also know nothing stays the same for very long, and I did like David. Am I making any sense to you, Hank?"

"All kinds of sense, Eleanor. I've moved Ruth and even our boys around so many times since we married I totally understand your feelings, your hesitation to get involved in someone else's life when you've not been here that long.

"After we left Germany, we moved to England, and then left England and moved to New York, and while we didn't stay long in New York, once we arrived here and she, we, were welcomed by Michael and Esther and then your parents and others, I promised her we were here to stay, at least until our sons were grown and had decided where they were going to settle down. I'm not even sure we'd move then because they need the chance to make their own lives. If we live long enough to need their help, then we might,

386

just might, move closer to one of them. But that's not anything we've even mentioned or much less talked about yet."

"I understand what you're saying, Hank. Ruth was so grieved over her parents' death it's truly good you all are here now where you have Esther and Michael as family along with all the friends you've made here. Thanks for sharing all of this with me and letting me share back. You are a bit like an elder brother, something I never had, though I adore my younger one."

That ended their conversation for the day, and they rode the last few miles in silence, each lost in thoughts, mostly of gratitude for a friendship that frequently makes life more enjoyable but is equally important when it helps it become bearable.

4

The war continued to rage in Europe. England refused to surrender even though the German warplanes had continued their *blitzkrieg*. Yet Hitler felt certain the continued bombing of England had left the island unable to wage war on the continent.

Instead Hitler's attention was drawn elsewhere as he turned his attention toward Operation Barbarossa, his plan for the invasion of Russia in the late spring. Hitler had used Molotov to establish a relationship with Stalin that he'd used to invade and conquer Poland, but he did not like Russia's continued advances in the Baltic. So Hitler had started planning to take on Stalin and Russia and then set his attack to begin in the spring of 1941.

Hitler had decided the goal should not be the capture of Moscow or other major cities but instead would focus on the destruction of the Red Army which he and his generals felt sure had been weakened during the winter. He questioned the army's leadership, organization, and morale and focused on destroying it, feeling certain that without the army, Russia would easily fall under Nazi rule. Hitler had planned for the invasion to begin on May 15, but due to unusually wet weather all during the spring, it was postponed until the end of June.

Stalin, who had allied himself and his army with Hitler for the invasion and conquest of Poland along with Denmark, Norway, and various other conquests of smaller Baltic countries, discounted intelligence reports of Hitler's plans to invade his country. Instead he believed Churchill was putting out false information in order to foment trouble between Germany and Russia.

When the Germans began the invasion on June 22, they took the totally unprepared Russian army by surprise. In the first 24 hours the Germans inflicted tens of thousands of casualties, took almost 10,000 prisoners, and destroyed 1,200 Soviet aircraft, almost all of it on the ground.

The German army—not the Nazi party—issued directives to its troops that all "Jewish sub-humanity" should be destroyed without regard to the Geneva accords. In the meantime Europe waited and waited for the United States to made the decision to join the war.

5

March had melted into April and still Eleanor had not heard from or even run into David Masterson on campus. She couldn't help wondering if Hank had relayed any of their conversation to David. Maybe he had and it had discouraged David from contacting her. If so, that was all right with her since she wasn't at all sure she was ready even to have dinner with a man, any man, even one as nice as David had seemed to be.

The college had spring break the first week of April. Eleanor was delighted to have the week off and not have to get out of bed at 5:30, get Lee and Amy out of bed at 6, then dressed and fed and ready for Jack and Ella to drop them off at Mary Beth's at 7:15 on their way to school.

She was grateful her children generally did not complain about having to get up and they wore what she had ready for them to put on without an argument. She couldn't help wondering how long that would last, probably not for much longer because Amy was already showing signs of wanting to wear certain things, whether they matched or not.

At least they were just going to Mary Beth's, and she'd already watched her sister deal with Nora's stubbornness in selecting her own outfit for the day. She and Mary Beth had both laughed over it, remembering how they had often balked at wearing whatever outfit Ella had picked out for them.

But today she would let them sleep as long as they wanted and wear whatever they pleased. Eleanor was looking forward to being able to work in the garden when the sun warmed up the temperature enough to do so. She loved planting flower beds and after breakfasting with her parents and getting Lee and Amy involved with their toys, she sat down with a catalogue of spring plants and flowers the local hardware store sent out to its customers in the middle of February every year. She had barely found the page she was interested in when the phone rang and Ella had answered it and then called, "Eleanor, it's for you."

"Eleanor, this is David, and I'm sure you have been wondering why I haven't called before. But my dad's been ill, and I've been trying to help Mother with him and also take her to the grocery store and that kind of thing." He had said all of this without taking a breath.

"I hope your father is better now," Eleanor said. "And the truth is I have wondered a bit why I hadn't heard from you. It's also amazing our paths haven't even crossed on campus."

"Dad is better, and thanks for asking. I have to confess I've hoped we would run into each other somewhere. I finally did learn you have a study room in the library where you go during the day when you don't have class. I certainly understand why you need that time alone when you have two young children who want your attention once you get home.

"But the real reason I'm calling is to see if I might take you and your children on an outing today. I'll bring a picnic lunch for us and then we might explore one of my favorite places. Do you think that might work for all of you?"

"Truly, that sounds like a wonderful idea, David. It's so nice to have a day of sunshine, and I'm sure by noon it will warm up a bit more. Lee and Amy love to be outside, and when I tell them we're going on a picnic and an adventure they'll be even more excited. But are you sure you really want my children? They can be a handful sometimes—actually much of the time!"

"Yes, I want your children to go with us. They need this kind of time with you. I need it too! And they'll just make the day easier for both of us. If it's all right with you, I thought I'd pick the three of you up about 11:30. We'll see how the day goes after that!"

Eleanor thanked him, then went into the living room where her mother was doing her Saturday cleaning and asked her to stop while she filled her in on what the telephone conversation had been about.

Eleanor had heard a good bit about David from Mary Beth, but she had only mentioned him as one of the guests at the Valentine's party to Ella and Jack. And so she was amazed he had wanted to include the children on their "first date" but thought it was a good idea.

Eleanor went upstairs to tell her children they would all be going on a picnic and an adventure with a friend of hers, a man who also taught at the college where she worked. They both were excited at the idea of going on a picnic and wanted to know the man's name. When she told them "David Masterson," Lee said, "That's a long name. What do we call him?"

Eleanor said, "I don't know. Why don't you ask him what he'd like for you to call him when he comes to pick us up?"

Lee thought that was a good idea. Amy, who had turned two in March, was also a big talker, though sometimes she was hard to understand because she wanted to sound like her big brother but would often get her words and sounds all mixed up.

The morning passed quickly. Eleanor had showered and washed her hair, which she normally did on Saturday night. She picked out warm play clothes for Lee and Amy and put them in the bathtub together, drawing comments from Lee who complained they usually bathed on Saturday night, and Ella saying if they got too dirty playing, they would get a second bath that night in order to be clean to go to Sunday school and church the next day.

David was right on time, getting out of the car to come in to meet Ella and Jack and help get jackets on Lee and Amy and even hold Amy's hand on the way to the car. He had such an easy way with children both Ella and Eleanor were amazed and wondered how he had developed that since he was an only child, and his wife and the child she was carrying had been killed in the accident.

He even had special seats in the back for Amy and Lee, and he insisted they sit in them to be safe. When Lee, who was going on five, asked, "Aren't you a good driver?" David had quietly answered, "I try to be, but sometimes the other people are not, and sometimes something can happen to whatever vehicle they're driving that can cause them to hit a car that hasn't done anything wrong. So I try to be careful, especially when my passengers are special people, like you are."

Eleanor was amazed he had fixed his car with safety precautions for her children. Even though she remembered what Hank had told her about how his wife had died, it had never occurred to her that he might create safety measures in his own car for her children. She said as much, and David replied, "Well, I've been trying to think of some way to make the front seat safe for adults. So far, nothing I've tried has really worked, but I haven't given up."

They had driven out of Myrna and were headed for the mountains in the distance. "We are going to eat lunch soon, at a picnic place I've found in a grove of trees. A friend of mine owns it, or actually his father owns it, but I have permission to picnic there whenever I like. My friend and I went to high school together. He's married now and lives in Memphis, but his dad died not long ago, and his mother has moved to Memphis to be near her son. They still own the land, though I don't know how much longer they'll keep it, but until they sell it, I can use it and bring my friends out here for a picnic."

The land was fenced and one part of it was kept mowed. A picnic table with benches around it sat in the middle of a grove of trees. David had brought a table cloth and napkins which he and Eleanor spread over the table. He had even brought some cushions to sit on, so Amy and Lee would be tall enough to eat from the table. He had two thermos bottles, one filled with lemonade and the other with sweet tea. The sandwiches to choose from were peanut butter and jelly or ham and cheese, and he had made enough for two apiece. He had also brought celery and carrots that had been scraped and cut into pieces big enough for little hands as well as for bigger hands. And he had even come with chocolate chip cookies which he said he had made himself.

Eleanor was amazed at how much thought he had put into making this outing about her children's wants and needs. She asked him where he had learned so much about little children.

"I have always liked children. Because I was an only child, I loved getting to play with other children, and by the time I started to school I had begun paying attention to how their parents treated them when I would be invited to play and sometimes spend the night and even once or twice go someplace with them if they had only a couple of boys and would let each take a friend along. I really enjoyed seeing how other families lived, how they dealt with their children. Some were so much better, so much more loving and fun than others I began to decide which ones I wanted to be like and which ones I didn't. Because I was an only child, I decided early on I wanted to have several children. I wanted my children to have brothers and sisters, not too many but at least one of each if possible."

As he told her all of this, she watched in amazement how he helped Lee cut his sandwich and poured Amy more lemonade when she was ready for more, and never stopped telling her about his liking for children. His actions spoke even louder than his words. She found herself hoping, even wishing, she might be able to fall in love with him.

Ronald's death was still too fresh in her memory so she knew it was far too soon even to be considering this man or any other for her life partner. While it was wonderful to see his attentiveness to her children, she needed someone who would meet her needs as well. After all, children grow up and go off to live their own lives.

She had known she and Ronald were a great fit, with or without children. She had recognized the "chemistry" between them early on. She did not feel any of that for David, although she sincerely liked him, especially the way he was with Amy and Lee. But a marriage, at least the one she wanted, needed more, much more, than that.

After they had finished their picnic lunch and gathered the left-overs and put all the bits and pieces in a trash bag David had brought with him, they got in his car again and drove up one of the mountains where they found a roadside parking area with a path that led further up the mountain. Both Eleanor and David realized the children would only be able to go a short way before they became tired or bored or both, but the day was still beautiful and they each took a child's hand and started up the trail. David had Lee's hand and could tell Lee the names of trees and bushes and how to recognize them. At one point they came across a tree with a hole in the trunk where squirrels had built a home, and Lee wanted to know how they had done it. David had been able to tell him a little about what went into the building of it, enough that Lee was satisfied.

Amy began to get whiny, indicating it was time for her nap, so they started back down the hill, with David carrying Amy and Lee holding Eleanor's hand. She had to pretend she needed him to help her go down the trail and was so glad to have his strong hand holding hers.

Once they had returned to the car, Eleanor and David were amazed at how quickly they both fell asleep. Eleanor immediately said, "This has been a wonderful outing for both my children, David, and for me also. Thank you! I realize how much I need to do this kind of thing with them, but I so rarely make the time. For one thing, they're at an age where it's hard to keep up with both of them. And actually, I loved the way they both responded to you. Lee adored his daddy and Amy did too. Both of them had a terribly difficult time accepting he was never coming home again. Any time Amy would see a man, she would say, 'DaDa?' And I would have to say 'No. That's not DaDa.' After a while she quit asking, but I know she doesn't understand what happened to him.

"The truth is that a part of me doesn't understand it either. What made his boat come apart like that? What happened to it to cause him to drown? Why didn't he try to get into one of the other boats the way the men who were with him did? He was a good swimmer. Some part of me keeps thinking he is still alive somewhere. But that's crazy, I know. He loved me, loved his children, and he would never have deserted us.

"I'm sorry for telling you all this. You've given all three of us a lovely outing, and here I go talking about my dead husband. Please forgive me!"

"Eleanor, there's nothing to forgive. That entire first year after my wife was killed, I was a basket case. I tried to drown my grief in liquor, and that didn't help, not really, even though sometimes it just put me so out of it, I couldn't or didn't remember what had happened. But that loss of memory did not last. It came back when I least expected it to.

"I would think I was getting better and then something would trigger a memory of Gloria pinned in our car and obviously not going to survive the accident, death taking our unborn child along with her. I remember railing at 'death' as if it were an actual person, in this case a villain who had destroyed my wife, my life, my happiness as if it didn't matter a bit to anybody in the world but me. It was an awful time.

"You are amazing because you have had the strength to pack up, leave England, and bring your children home where you are making a new life for yourself and for them. How did...how do you do it?"

"Because of the two who are now sound asleep in your back seat. Believe me, there were days at first when I thought I couldn't go on. Waiting and waiting to hear something from him, daring to hope he'd been picked up by another boat and would show up at our door. Not really knowing what had happened to him."

Eleanor took a deep breath and then continued, "Then one day, a few weeks after 'the miracle of Dunkirk' as it was often referred to in England, a young soldier turned up at my door. He told me he had been on Ronald's boat when it had hit something and had begun to come apart, but he had not known Ronald's name. He joined the rest of the men on the boat, jumped into the water, and swam to another boat full of soldiers. They had seen what was happening and pulled him in. Once he had gotten in their boat, he'd looked back, but Ronald's boat and Ronald had both disappeared. However, the boat he was in made it back to England's shore.

"After his boat had landed and he'd gotten home to Sussex where his wife was, he started trying to find out the name of the boat and the man who was driving it. One day he ran across an article in a newspaper about what had happened, and it had the name of the man who was driving the motor boat. He looked up Ronald's address and came to find me and tell me what a brave and good man Ronald was.

"I wept when he told me all of that, and he apologized for making me cry, and I told him how grateful I was to him for coming and telling me, so that at least I could sort of know what had happened to him.

"The young man was just an ordinary British soldier, but he had the heart of a hero as far as I was concerned. With an army made up of other men like him, I felt sure we would eventually win this war."

By this time Ella had tears running down her cheeks and was feeling in her purse for a handkerchief when David held out his.

"It's not completely clean because I wiped Amy's mouth and hands with half of it, but the other half is still okay, more or less."

Eleanor wiped her eyes. blew her nose, and said, "Thank you, David. You are an amazing man, and I am glad to have you for a friend. That's as far as I can go right now."

"Eleanor, no one understands that better than I do. It has taken me over three years to even think about dating a woman, and even now I am spending time with your children to try, in a way, to heal my own heart from the deaths of my two who died before they were born.

"But the truth is that while that's a part of the reason I invited you and Lee and Amy to go on a picnic today, that's only a part. I can feel inside that I am actually getting better because a part of me, a bigger part than I had even realized when I invited the three of you, is that I just like children. I really enjoyed having Amy and Lee around and being able to take a walk with them and you, play with them, help them at lunch, and simply enjoy watching them with each other in the outdoors.

"I think it would be easy to fall in love with you simply because of Amy and Lee, but that would hardly be fair to a woman who has as much to offer a man as you do. I simply hope we can be friends who enjoy each other's company once in a while—and that you will allow me to be like an uncle or something to your precious children and maybe even take them with me to a playground or something like that. You can come along or just trust me to take good care of them, just treat me like any baby-sitter, but one you don't have to pay because I would be doing it for me, for my pleasure. Is that a possibility?"

"Of course! Papa Jack enjoys my two and is good about reading to or playing with them in the house before they go to bed, but he says he's too old to be a playmate. He's happy just being their grandfather. So just let me know ahead of time when you want them, and I'll have them ready and be grateful for a little 'home' time by myself."

Eleanor and David rode the rest of the way back into Myrna with easy silences broken only when something along the road caught their interest or when one of them thought of something he or she wanted to say.

When they arrived at Jack and Ella's house, David carried Lee and Eleanor carried Amy inside since both children were still sleeping after all of their walking and playing during the outing. Both Jack and Ella greeted them quietly, so as not to wake the children, but as soon as the adults put them down on their beds, Lee woke up, asking how they'd gotten home and in their beds. David laughed and said the good fairies had brought them, but Lee wasn't believing that and said to David, "You carried us in, didn't you?"

"Well, only one of you. Your mother carried Amy."

Eleanor had slipped out as soon as she put Amy in the bed and saw that she was still asleep.

"Can we go on another picnic sometime?" Lee asked.

"You know something, we will! Sometime soon. Or we'll do something else, maybe—like go fishing. And it might just be you and me. Would that be okay with you?"

"Yes, sir!" And Lee gave David a big smile. "I've wanted to go fishing for a long time!"

"Well, we'll be sure that happens—as soon as the weather warms up a bit more. We'll go some Saturday afternoon to a place I know, and then maybe we'll come back and get Amy and your mom, and we'll all go have supper somewhere. How about that, Lee?"

"That sounds fun! You won't forget, will you? I don't want you to get lost like my daddy did!"

"The best I can promise is that I won't forget. And I'll certainly do all I can not to get lost!"

6

The weather did stay warm so that the spring became more beautiful every day with more flowers blooming, the trees gaining leaves, and the air filled with fragrances. Finally on a beautiful Friday evening, David called for Eleanor to ask if he could take Lee fishing the next afternoon. Then he'd like to come by for her and Amy, and they would all go out for supper.

"That's a lovely idea. What time do you want to pick up Lee?"

"How about 2:00 or 2:30. I figure that unless the fish are biting and he's getting to pull some in, he will get bored with it after a couple of hours. Of course, I hope they're biting at least a bit because I want him to have a good time. If I pick him up at 2:00, we should be in the boat on the lake by 2:30. If we fish till 4:30 or 5:00 at the latest, we should be back at your parents' house no later than 5:30. Will that work?

"It works for Amy and me."

"I have a feeling both Lee and I may need a little washing up before we go out to eat anywhere. We may smell too much like fish for you or anyone else to want to be in close contact with us. Will your parents mind if we use your bathroom?"

"We have a guest bathroom downstairs with a shower for you to use and one upstairs where I can get Lee cleaned up in a jiffy. Will that work for you?"

"Sounds perfect if you're sure your parents won't mind. I promise we will be at your house as close to 5:30 as possible, and maybe a bit before if the fish aren't biting at all."

"That sounds good to me. I'll have Lee ready to go by 2:00. He's been talking about going fishing with you and will be excited about Saturday. Thanks so much for doing this for him, David. You're truly a good friend." Ella hung up the phone and went to tell her son

David was right on time to pick Lee up, to Eleanor's delight because Lee had been ready for an hour and was about to drive her crazy asking every few minutes "Is it time yet?" and she would say how many more minutes it would be before he arrived. "You've made points with me as a baby-sitter because you got here when you said you would," Eleanor said, smiling.

David just laughed and said, "So let's go catch some fish, Lee. Tell your mom we'll see her and Amy at 5:30."

"Bye, Mama; we'll be back at 5:30." Lee was so excited, he didn't even kiss her good-bye, but took David's hand and headed for the car where he could see two fishing poles in the back seat.

Ella had let Amy stay up until Lee left with David, and then she enticed her to bed to take a nap so that she could go with Lee, David, and her to supper that night. Amy fell asleep quickly, giving Eleanor two hours to work on preparing for her Monday classes. The time flew by because Eleanor became completely engrossed in doing some reading and planning how to engage her students in studying *Hamlet* for her Shakespeare class.

7

David and Lee drove up to the house a bit before 5:30 bringing with them the five fish he and Lee had caught. David said he would take them home with him that night and clean them and then give them to Eleanor on Monday to bring home and cook for the family. Lee was so excited and proud he'd caught three of the fish, he couldn't stop talking about how much he liked fishing. And he had started calling David "Uncle." David whispered to Eleanor he hoped she approved, and she mouthed, "Absolutely."

Amy, who had waked up feeling a bit jealous because Lee was home from his outing with David, said, "I want to go fishing like Lee. When can I go fishing?"

"When *may* I go fishing?" Eleanor corrected her.

"Do you want go fishing too, Mama?" Amy asked, getting a laugh from both David and Eleanor.

"Not really, sweet girl. It's just more polite to say 'May I?' than 'Can I?'" Eleanor said in her school teacher voice.

Lee, who had been listening to them, said, "Mother, we aren't in school. Why are you talking like we are?"

Eleanor gave a deep sigh and said, "All right. I'm not your school teacher, but I am your mother, and it's my job to help you learn how to be polite and ask things in a polite way. Now that's enough or David may be sorry he asked us out to dinner." She shook her head and looked at David who was having difficulty not grinning at their exchange.

"Are you sure you want children?" Eleanor mouthed at David.

"If I could be sure they'd be like your two, I'd say 'absolutely!'" he whispered back.

Lee and Amy who had rarely ever eaten at a restaurant had promised Eleanor they would use their manners and act like this was something they did fairly often. Lee understood quickly, and Eleanor hoped Amy would copy him. The outing went smoothly with both Lee and Amy acting good and not making too big a mess with their food. They were both hungry and ate the children's meals that were sat before them, allowing Eleanor and David time for conversation.

"How did you spend your afternoon with only Amy for company?" David asked after they had ordered."

"Being grateful Amy took a good long nap, giving me time to work on my plans for teaching *Hamlet* next week."

"Ah, 'To be or not to be, that is the question!'"

"I'm impressed that you can quote from *Hamlet*!" Eleanor said, "And you a mathematician at that!"

"Actually, I can't quote much of the play, but I for some reason remembered those words from having read them in Freshman English. It came to mind after Gloria's death when at one point I was contemplating committing suicide. I really was asking myself was life worth going on with. I was drinking a lot during this period, and that didn't enable me to deal any better with the grief I was feeling, which was also very much about the loss of the baby she was carrying. I've told you it was a really low time for me. I apologize for bringing it up."

"Please don't apologize for that, though I'm glad you were speaking softly and the children were so busy eating they didn't hear our conversation. What helped you through that awful time?"

"I'm not sure. I suppose I could say it was God or the Holy Spirit, though I didn't have a religious experience or anything like that. Funny thing is that I did go back and re-read *Hamlet*. It's a powerful play, a sad play with a sad ending. Reading it again, however, did make me realize I really didn't want to die, at least not yet.

"As I think about it now, it was a sort of turning point for me because I knew deep down I wanted to live. I wanted to believe life still had a purpose for me, and for the first time since the accident, I wanted to find out what that purpose was."

"And have you found it in teaching?" Eleanor asked.

"Well, yes and no. It's not that I don't enjoy teaching, but what has really made a huge difference is the kind of relationships I have developed with a lot of the boys in the dorm where I'm the Resident Head. But I shouldn't call them boys—because they are young men who are trying to figure out who they are and what they want for their lives and often need someone older with a little experience with life and pain who will listen to them.

"I don't try to solve their problems or tell them what they should do. Instead I just ask questions and listen and sometimes ask more questions and listen, but they know, they feel, that I care about them, and I do.

"Sometimes I recommend they go talk to a real counselor or to their pastor or priest. And then I am amazed when they do and then often come back and tell me what they've been told.

"Occasionally, they'll even say the minister or the counselor has asked them about something I said that they've told the counselor or priest, and he'll have told them that what I've been quoted as saying was good or 'right on target.' I admit that makes me feel good."

"It should, David! Have you given any thought to going back to school to take classes and get certified as a counselor?"

"Not really. I've just been sober a couple of years, and I'm happy being at Arkansas State. I guess I've just really started to feel I've gotten my life back on track."

"That's really great, David. But you sound genuinely happy about being able to listen to and talk with the young men in the dorm where you are living. Since I'm assuming that not all of them are or have been your students and you seem to enjoy this part of your life more than you do teaching, I'm wondering why you don't at least think about going to graduate school somewhere and getting a Master's or a Doctorate as a counselor or even a therapist."

"I don't know, Eleanor. I like feeling that I am 'one of them' and not an expert on anything. These past months have helped me feel I have something to give these young men. Maybe it's just friendship and a willingness to listen. Maybe that's enough for me and for them.

"But I'll think about what you have said, and I thank you for seeing possibilities for my life I've really not thought about, certainly not seriously thought about anyway."

Lee and Amy had finished their meal and were beginning to get restless. David said, "Eleanor, what about if we shared a couple of bowls of ice cream? Would you be up for that? And if you would be okay with that, do you think Lee and Amy would be?"

Eleanor shook her head, laughing. "Just look at their faces! You've mentioned the magic words—ICE CREAM! That is a huge treat where we live! All right, David! I hope our waitress will bring several extra napkins. Amy and Lee, what kind of ice cream do you want?"

"Chocolate!" they both said at the same time.

"Chocolate it is for Lee and Amy!" David said. "What about you, Eleanor?"

"Might we share a bowl too? I really just want a bite or two, and I'm happy to let you choose what you like because I'm not particular," Eleanor said, looking at David and waiting for his answer.

"Do you like caramel ice cream., Eleanor?" he asked.

"Very much!" she replied.

So David ordered two bowls of ice cream with four spoons—and extra napkins. Their waitress, whose name was Susie, came back shortly with two ice creams, four spoons, six napkins, and a bowl of warm water.

Eleanor said, "Now here's a young lady who knows what mothers need when their children eat ice cream! Thank you, Susie." She tried to help Amy use her spoon to get some ice cream on it and then put it into her mouth. But Amy was, at barely two, a child who liked to feed herself—or rather try to feed herself, and she said, "I do it, Mama. I'm a big girl!" So Eleanor put the napkin around her and under her chin and said, "Okay, Big Girl, try not to spill it."

By the time Amy got one spoonful in her mouth, Lee had eaten two big ones. "Go easy, Lee," Eleanor said, "and give Amy time to get some on her spoon and into her mouth."

"Mama, I'm always having to wait on Amy to do *something* before I can do it. It's not fair!"

"Well, Son, it may not be fair, but it's just what you do when you have a younger sister or brother. The truth is when you were Amy's age I was the one who had to wait on you to do things. So turn-about is fair play!"

David was getting a big kick out of watching Eleanor deal with her two children. He said, "Eleanor, if you don't stop taking care of others, I'm going to eat all this delicious ice cream, and you won't have even had your two bites. Now David and Amy, you don't want *your mother* to miss out on her two bites of ice cream, do you?"

"No, Sir," Lee said, sincerely, while Amy said, "You can have some of my ice cream, Mama." Then Lee said, "It's my ice cream too, Amy, and I'll let Mama have some of mine."

"Children, that's very sweet of you both, but David and I are going to share our ice cream, and all I, *we*, want is for the two of you to share, and I do mean *share*, yours! David, where's my spoon?" Eleanor asked, looking around the table.

"It's right here, Eleanor. I was afraid it was going to fall off the table with all the activity going on, and I moved it out of the way a bit. So have your two bites, and there's plenty here if you decide you want more than two."

She ended up eating four bites, with David offering her more she wouldn't accept. The two bowls of ice cream soon were empty. Eleanor took the wet napkin that the waitress Susie had left for them and washed both children's faces with one half of the napkin and then washed their hands as best she could. She ended up going to the ladies' room, rinsing the napkin, and then bringing it back for another go on their hands. David had enjoyed watching the entire episode and was smiling broadly as he paid the bill at the counter and then took Amy in his arms and carried her to the car while Eleanor followed with Lee.

David drove them home, helped Eleanor get both of them in the house, and said with a huge smile, "Thank you, all three of you, for a lovely day."

"Can we go fishing again soon, Uncle David?" Lee asked.

"I don't know how soon it will be, but we will go fishing again. Good night, Lee, my buddy, and to you too, Amy. Sleep tight! And thank you, Eleanor, for sharing your family with me."

Both Ella and Jack had heard them come in and came to the door to help with the children and to tell David good night.

"He is a good man, Eleanor," Jack said as he picked Amy up to carry her upstairs to her bed, followed by Lee who said, "I've had a busy day, and I'm really sleepy." He sounded so grown up Eleanor almost laughed out loud.

"Well, let's get you two into bed," Eleanor said and then turned her head and said to Ella, "and then I'll come back down and visit with Mother and you, Papa Jack."

"Daughter, David is truly a good man, but I don't want you to rush into a serious relationship until you are really ready," Ella was smiling as she said these words to her oldest child who had come back downstairs after putting Amy and Lee to bed. They had both fallen asleep almost as soon as their heads hit their pillows. Eleanor had stood a few minutes at the end of the bed watching them, loving them, and making sure they were really asleep before she went back downstairs. She had been fooled before and found herself climbing back up the stairs before she had even sat down to talk with her parents.

"You two needn't worry. He's not quite ready for a serious relationship either. He's wonderful with the children and I like him. He is a good man, just as you both said, but I'm not at all sure he's really over losing his wife and the baby she miscarried and the one that died with

404

her in the accident. He's come a long way, but he's not completely over those losses and may never be, just as I am not close to being over losing Ronald and am not at all sure I will ever be.

"Sometimes I'm still so mad at him for taking our boat and trying to rescue soldiers stuck at Dunkirk with no way to get back to England except for the Englishmen who came with whatever they owned that could ferry all those stranded men back home. But then I'm proud of him for trying to help even while I'm angry he died. My feelings have me so messed up inside I am not at all sure I'll ever be able to love and marry anyone else.

"David is as messed up as I am, and while I really like him and respect him, I'm not in love with him. So we're both still in love with the spouse who died or was killed or whatever you want to call it.

"But I do think David has some real gifts for listening to and even advising young people about life and where their gifts and interests lie, and I mentioned that to him at dinner tonight and recommended he find a school where he could get the kind of training or education to become a counselor or therapist. But I'm not sure he's ready to take that kind of step. He certainly didn't seem interested in pursuing my idea when I talked about it tonight. He's come a long way since his wife's death and that of the baby girl she was carrying, but he doesn't sound ready to move forward in any way," Eleanor said.

8

Eleanor was wrong. Little did she suspect her suggestion to David that he think about going back to school for training as a counselor or going beyond that to become a therapist had rooted itself in David's mind, and after a week of mulling it over he had gone in to see the Dean to get his thoughts.

To his amazement, Dean Atkinson was very positive in his belief that David should pursue this matter. He recommended

David should begin looking into universities that offered courses and training in counseling and then if he felt he was on the right path and wanted to go further, he might look for a medical school to get an MD. He said that in fact, he had a good friend who was a professor at Vanderbilt, and he would telephone him and tell him about David and ask what Vandy might have to offer him. He was pretty sure his friend would be interested in hearing about and even talking with David about his future.

David thanked him profusely for taking this kind of interest in him. "But Dean Atkinson, you need to know it was Eleanor Douglass who listened to me talk about my experiences with the young men in the dorm and then broached the subject of my moving beyond being a kind of advisor to getting some training so that I might become a licensed counselor or go even further and get a doctorate in psychology. I told her I'd had never thought about any of this and right now was satisfied with befriending young men in the dorm and providing a listening ear when they had something they wanted to talk with me about.

"While I've known how much I not only liked getting to know the men as friends, I've also realized that a few of them had some deep problems they were sharing with me but needed someone with more education and training than I had in order to be able to help them and give them sound advice. I was always ready to listen and even empathize when I felt I knew what to say, but sometimes I just told the young man he needed more help and advice than I could provide.

"Sometimes after that, I never heard from the young man again, and that left me feeling not only had I failed, but I'd worry about where and from whom he might be getting help, and just hoping he had gone to a doctor or someone who could actually provide what he needed."

The Dean then said, "Thank you, David, for sharing all that you have just told me. Your care of and concern for these young men have given me more reason to think you have gifts for psychology and mental health beyond teaching freshman mathematics. I will call my friend today, and as soon as I have been able to talk with him, I will telephone you and we'll go from there."

9

In early May David invited Eleanor to go out for dinner, just the two of them, explaining when he invited her he had something he wanted to tell her, and it would be easier if the children weren't there. She couldn't refuse because he had taken her and the children on several outings, though only once for supper, while the four of them had gone on at least four picnics together. Yet the fact he had something he wanted to tell her made her a bit nervous, even though he had given no indication on the other occasions he was going to propose. She hoped this wasn't going to lead into a proposal because as much as she liked him and appreciated the time he spent with the children and her, she was still not in love with him or anybody for that matter, and doubted she would ever be in love again.

David suggested she just stay late in her library room at Arkansas State on that Friday afternoon so that he wouldn't have to come to her parents' house and upset Lee and Amy who had become so accustomed to going places with the two of them he didn't want to begin the evening on a sour note. He would drive her back to Myrna after their dinner together if that would be all right with her.

Although she agreed with David it would be easier on everybody if she just told the children she would be late getting home that day, and she was sure her mother and father would be fine with it, Eleanor was even more nervous about the evening. While he had done nothing at all to make her think he had marriage on his mind, she couldn't imagine why he wanted to take her to dinner in Jonesboro, other than the larger town had more and nicer restaurants, certainly nicer than the two in Myrna.

She had told Mr. Smithers, the librarian, she had an appointment on Friday, and could she use her study room in the library until almost 6:00 when a friend would pick her up and then take her back to Myrna. Because the library stayed open until 9:00 on Friday nights, Mr. Smithers saw no reason for that to be a problem. He was dying to find out who her friend was, although practically the entire faculty knew she had been seeing a good bit of David Masterson, but with some difficulty he refrained himself from asking.

She and David had arranged to meet at the entrance to the campus at 6:00, fairly sure that it would be clear at that time in the evening, and David was glad to see that it was when he pulled up to the curb at 6:00 on the dot and found Eleanor standing there, looking very professional with her book satchel in one hand and purse on the other. They both were aware they were "sort of an item" of campus gossip, although they actually saw very little of each other during the week. Eleanor had suggested he not get out of the car when he picked her up because it would look too much like they were on a date if anyone saw them. Instead David leaned across the seat and pushed the door open for her to get in, glad there were no passers-by at the moment.

"I can't believe you look this fresh and lovely after a long, warm day of teaching," David said as she slid into the seat and pulled the door closed.

"I have to confess, I did bring a change of clothes in my brief-case this morning, along with a toothbrush and make-up in my purse. I'm so grateful for my 'office' in the library because I can go there and lock the door and nobody knows I'm there most of the time except Mr. Jamison, the custodian and he's my friend. So where are we going for dinner?" Eleanor asked as they appeared to be headed out of town.

"There is a little place near Jonesboro I've discovered and like because it has really good food, and there are tables outside as long as the weather's nice and the mosquitos don't get bad. Truthfully, they have several fans outside that keep the insects away. It's generally not busy until after 9:00 because they have some live musicians that start playing then and a small dance floor for anybody who wants to dance. Don't tell me you've never heard of Billy Watkins and his Hillbilly Boys?"

Eleanor laughed and said, "Of course, I've heard the name. I've just never been fortunate enough to hear them play!"

"Well, you probably won't hear them tonight unless we decide to stay that long. Truthfully, I doubt we will because—well because, I don't know how you're going to respond to what I have to tell you. But before we get into that, we probably need to get there and order. *Buster's* does have good food."

After they had been seated on the stone "patio" with a lovely view of the hills, Eleanor looked at the menu that had been hand-printed on a large piece of cardboard and decorated around the sides with hand-painted flowers and plants that were quite pretty. "Somebody has some talent," Eleanor said as she looked at the menu. "But what do you recommend, Mr. Masterson, since this is obviously a place you are familiar with?"

"They have a chicken casserole that is truly delicious in my opinion. I don't know what all it has in it, and when the waitress brings it to the table you'll think you'll never be able to eat it all, but you do—or at least, I do. It comes with homemade biscuits and a tossed salad that is not too big but is also delicious. And you'll want to save room for their desserts.

"Now if you don't want the chicken casserole, you can have fried chicken, or pork chops, or beef cooked almost any way you want it, though it may take a little more time because they don't have it already prepared. I guess you can tell, this is one of my favorite places to eat, not just in Jonesboro but in the state of Arkansas!"

Eleanor chose the chicken casserole with the salad, as did David. And both were amazed at how quickly it arrived with big glasses of iced tea they always served with lunch and dinner unless the guest ordered something else.

David had not exaggerated about the tastiness of the food or the amount of it. Eleanor had to ask for a little box to take home, not just because she couldn't eat all of it but also because she wanted Ella and Jack to taste a little of it. She wondered if they had ever heard of *Buster's*.

As they finished eating, with Eleanor getting a spoonful or two of David's banana pudding, Eleanor asked David, "At some point, you really are going to get around to telling me what this evening is all about, aren't you?"

David smiled and said, "Well, yes, but I wanted to make sure you had eaten before I tell you because I think you're going to be surprised, although you were the one who suggested I do this."

Eleanor did look surprised but waited quietly until he continued.

"After you helped me realize how much I care about and enjoy listening to the men in my dorm and making an effort to hear and respond to the things they talk to me about, I went into see Dean Atkinson. We had a really good conversation, and he was very supportive of the idea that I investigate what it might mean to get some more education in this area.

"He has a good friend at Vanderbilt in Nashville who is a professor in this area. I took a train up there two weeks ago and met with people in his department, and I've signed up for summer courses in psychology and counseling. I will also sit in on some of the other more advanced courses and even have my own counselor along with taking a battery of tests to see whether this is an area I would want to dedicate my life to pursuing and have the intellect and personality to do so."

"Wow, David, this is amazing! I didn't think you were the least bit interested in pursuing anything like this after our talk. But I'm so proud of you for trying this and seeing where it may lead. When do you start?"

"June 2, Eleanor, but I'll move there on May 31 and get settled in a dorm. I think there is a special section of this dorm that has little apartments that are for psychology, mental health, psychiatry students. All of them are supposed to have a regular degree, preferably not in psychology or something like that.

"And if this pans out, if I have the abilities it will call for, I will owe you a lot of thanks because you made me start searching myself to see if this might be my 'calling'—so to speak. What do you think?"

"I think this is wonderful. I'm really proud of you for deciding to look into this to see if you 'fit' although I will be very surprised if this is not what you should be doing, and I truly am so pleased you are going ahead and pursuing it to see if this is your calling. How many years will it take you?"

"I guess it depends on how far I want to go with it. There will be some medical school involved I imagine if I go beyond being a high school counselor or teaching psychology or something in a college. The truth is that I don't know how long it will take or how far I will go with it. That's sort of the scary part of this, but this much of it feels right to me.

"The truth is that I don't know enough about myself, about who I am, what I want, what I need, or what I'm capable of to make any long-term decision about my future.

"But I do hope we can continue to be friends with no strings attached. Do you think that's possible?"

"Of course, it's not just possible, it's already a done deal. I like you, I respect you, I'm proud of you and not only for coming through a terrible time of loss in your own life during which you not only suffered, but because you made it back, you overcame it. You have succeeded and come out a stronger, better person who now wants to find out how you can help others who are dealing with hard things in their own lives. Wherever this takes you, David Masterson, you are going to succeed in helping people, in making a difference, making their lives healthier, happier, more beneficial for humankind and the world!"

David started laughing. "Goodness, Eleanor, you make me sound so wonderful I have to laugh at you and at me for letting you go on and on about me and what I'm going to accomplish!"

Eleanor started laughing too. "You're right, David. That's me! I just get carried away sometimes. But, and I'm serious now, you are amazing because you have dealt with sadness, with abusing alcohol and then cutting it out of your life, with getting a position in a college where you have already touched the lives of young people in who knows how many ways, and you have made discoveries about yourself and are following through on using those learnings to explore what you will do with them in this next phase of your life.

"I am glad to call you my friend, David. And I'm going to try to follow your example and explore what I need to be doing with mine, besides trying to help two children to grow up and become what I think God intended them to be when he gave them life."

"Eleanor, I have no idea how you and I or our relationship will turn out, but I am so grateful I have gotten to know you, and I hope we can maintain our friendship over the next weeks, months, maybe even years! Can we shake on that?"

"Of course. I think we might even hug on it!" And they did.

10

David did leave for Vanderbilt at the end of the spring semester. He had come by to tell Eleanor, Lee, and Amy good-bye the day before he left to drive to Nashville. He hugged each of the children who clung to him, asking him not to go. Amy started crying, saying "Please don't go, Uncle David. I love you. I don't want you to go!" when David had answered Amy by saying, "I'm sorry, sweet girl, but I have to go." And even Lee asked, "But why do you have to go?"

David looked so upset and sad that Eleanor took pity on him and said, "Children, sometimes adults just know when it is time to do something else. It's hard to leave. Do you remember when I decided we needed to leave England and come here? How hard it was to say good-bye to the people we loved, to Grandpapa and Grandmama? We were all sad, but they understood why we needed to come here, and they drove us to the airport to get the airplane that brought us to New York. You see, they understood that coming here was the right thing for us to do at that time. It doesn't mean that we will never go back to England and see Grandmama and Grandpapa again. But right now we are better off here."

"Because there is no war going on here. Isn't that right, Mama?" Lee said. And when Eleanor told him that he was right, he asked, "Is that why you're going to Nashville, Uncle David?"

Giving Lee a hug and smiling, David replied, "No, thank goodness, there's no war here. I'm going to go back to school to learn some things I am interested in and would like to do, but I need to read about and study them. I am not going away forever. I'll be back here in a year or two, and by then you will be older and bigger and probably will have forgotten who I am!"

"No, Uncle David. We won't have forgotten you. And we will be so glad to see you!" Lee said. And Amy held out her arms and said, "Hug me, please!" And so he did.

As Eleanor walked to the car with him, holding each child by the hand, she said, "Do write and keep me posted on how you're doing and what you are learning. I will write back as soon as I hear from you and have a post office box or an address where I can send a letter."

David hugged all of them again and then left in his car without looking back at them because he didn't want them to see the tears in his own eyes. He would miss all three of them badly because they had truly filled a void in his life, a void that had needed filling and that he hoped and prayed would be filled again at some point.

David did write as soon as he had gotten settled into his small apartment and had an address to give to those who had expressed hope of hearing from him once he was settled in. Eleanor was the first recipient, and she answered him immediately, to his joy.

June 14, 1941

Dear David,

I have to be honest and say that we have all missed you. The children at first almost drove me crazy asking "When will Uncle David come home?" sometimes two or three times a day until I told them, "He won't come back until you stop asking that question and maybe even forget about him." I don't really know why that stopped them, but it did.

I miss you too, but I feel so good about you, for what you are doing as you seek to learn more about human psychology and what role you want to take in using it, not only for your own life but also to help others make sense about who they are and what they want to be, do, become…in life.

I also wanted to share with you a conversation we had in my English class after we finished reading Hamlet. I told my students that one of my favorite quotations from the play was the last sentence in Polonius' rather simplistic advice to Hamlet on how to live. But these are his final words and are not simplistic at all: "This above all, to thine own self be true. And it must follow as the night the day, thou canst not then be false to any man" (or woman—my addition). Obviously, what you are doing is "being true to yourself" as you enter this new stage of life.

"But what happened that day in class is really what I want to tell you. I asked my students "What does 'being true to oneself mean? What is your 'self' and how do you know what being 'true to yourself' means and how do you go about being 'true' to it? And why does that matter? Why might that be important?"

And I was amazed at their answers and their questions and the entire discussion that this led to. First, they got into a discussion about what the "self" is and had some of these responses:

"the inner me,"

"the real me that I often hide from people,"

"I don't think I really know or like my "inner self, and I'm not even sure anybody else would like it either,"

414

"I don't know what 'self' means, what it involves. Is 'self' my personality, my wishes and wants, my hopes and dreams, my interests and pleasures? I honestly don't have a clue about 'my inner self'!"

"I think maybe my inner self is my soul, that part of me that is God within me or that God has given me to be His agent in the world. Since neither the self nor the soul is an actual thing like our body or our brain, perhaps they refer to the same 'God-thing' even though I have no proof that either exists."

"I realize that I often am not true to my real self. I tend to go along with the crowd even when I'm really not comfortable doing so."

"It's pretty obvious to me that a lot of us don't have any idea about what being true to ourselves means."

"I wonder about what I'm doing here in college. Maybe it's to deal with questions like what it means to be true to myself or true to God or true to my family and those I love. I just don't know. Wonder if there's some kind of class that teaches you how to be true to yourself?"

These are not all the comments or questions I jotted down that day. Many of them were more or less repetitions of what someone else had already said, but I was amazed as I've thought about them at their honesty and even their self-awareness and most of all of their need for people like you who are being trained to help people sort out things like who they really are, what their values are and perhaps what they wish they were and how to go about becoming the self they would like to be.

Then it struck me that this is exactly what you are doing for yourself, and that as you grow in understanding why and how you are doing this for you, you will be able to help other people do it for themselves.

This a long letter, but I kept thinking about my students' responses and how that applied to you and to what you are doing and I just had to get it down on paper and send it to you.

On more ordinary subjects, I will tell you that I am enjoying being out of school this summer, at least for the first term, and having lots of time with Lee and Amy and with Mary Beth and her two. And I have had dinner with Hank and Ruth once with another couple and me as their guests—people you don't know but who were nice. There have also been a couple of family dinners at Mother and Jack's or at Mary Beth and Pat's with all the children included.

I've written about "my social life" so that you 1) won't feel sorry for me and 2) will understand why I've missed you. I do hope you are getting to meet and know other people in and not in your field of study.

And I hope I'm going to receive more than one letter from you while you are making Nashville and Vandy your home. Lee and Amy send their love. They still miss you and I do too.

Eleanor

Within a few days after she had mailed her letter to David, Eleanor received this reply:

Eleanor, you cannot imagine how glad I was to receive you long, newsy letter, and I will soon reply with one I hope will be as long and equally as interesting. But I was most taken by the comments you included that your students had made in your discussion of Polonius' "advice" that "above all one must be true to oneself." I particularly was taken by, impressed by, the one that saw an identity of the "self" with the "soul" and the more I read it and thought about it, the more I began to think that this comment was not from a college student but was your own. It was too deep and thought-provoking to have come from a 20 year-old student, certainly not a usual one anyway. I have never made a connection between the "soul" and the "self" but it made so much sense to me that I had to write you immediately to see if I am correct that it came from you, and if you threw that out for your students to

416

think about, how did they react or respond? More later—about me and my life here when I have time. Right now I'm still just trying to get my bearings. But please do keep writing me.

David

Eleanor had written back:

You know me better than I realized you did. I did write about the possible connection of the self and the soul. It was something I had never thought about when I read Hamlet in college, but it struck me this time, now that I'm older and dealing with my own life as a mother, a widow, a woman who is trying to find my own way into an unknown future that will most likely include more blows and challenges to my personhood, my faith in God or goodness or in life itself than I have already experienced, that I really want to be true to myself, my soul or whatever that means, and like my students, I'm not always sure how to do that! Wow! That was a far too-long sentence. But I am hoping you are going to find out some answers, helpful answers, in your study of our human psychology.

Eleanor

Part XVI

Summer: 1941

1

In mid-June Ella and Jack received a letter from Dan that was really addressed to the whole family, telling them that as he was almost at the end of his first year of service in the Navy, he was getting a week's leave at the end of July, and he and Lilly would be flying to the States for the week. They would let both sets of parents know when they would arrive as soon as they knew the actual date. They were really looking forward to seeing everybody, for even though they loved Hawaii, they missed their families. They would be staying with Lilly's family because they realized that with Eleanor and her children at Ella and Jack's, it would be easier for everyone if they stayed with the Simpsons. But they would spend time with the MacLeans every day and even into the evening sometimes. They were truly looking forward to being there and having lots of time to spend with family!

Ella could hardly wait to see her son, for as much as she loved her daughters and was grateful to have them and their children in Myrna with her and Jack, she looked forward to seeing her only son, her third child she had longed for while Daniel had been serving as a doctor with the Army in France. She and Daniel had both been delighted when she became pregnant not long after his return when the war had ended.

Her joy and excitement over having Dan and Lilly home was equal to Lilly's mother's, who was as eager to see her daughter, now Mrs. Dan Wood, as Ella was to see her son. Ella had telephoned Betty Simpson as soon as she had read Dan's letter, sure that Betty had her own letter from Lilly in hand. Both women spent almost half an hour talking about how wonderful it was going to be to have their children in town, even if only for a week. They also discussed an idea Ella had of co-hosting an open house at the MacLeans' and inviting the couple's friends, both young and old, to drop-by for light refreshments and a visit with Lilly and Dan.

Betty though that was a great idea and she would be glad to work with her if Lilly and Dan were willing for their mothers to have this kind of party for them. Ella had immediately wired Dan and Lilly about the possibility of having a sort of "open house" for them and was glad when they replied immediately that both of them liked the idea and would be grateful for a party where they would be able to visit with lots of people without having to find the time to go around town to see them individually. They would send their mothers the list of friends they particularly wanted invited. This way while they could see and briefly visit with many of those they liked, they would have a bit more time to visit with their closest friends besides being able to spend most of their time with family.

Ella was determined to make it an easy party to host because she and Betty would split up calling those on the guest list and any others they felt needed to be added to it. And they would share preparing light refreshments. Betty was willing to bring all her glasses and small plates to the MacLeans' since neither woman had enough for 30 or 40 people or even more since they really had no idea how many would be invited and then come. Ella said she would ask Doris, who worked for her during the week, if she would come the night of the party and keep the plates and glasses washed so they would not run out. They had agreed for the refreshments to be finger food and lemonade, sweet tea, and water so they wouldn't even need any forks or spoons.

While both Ella and Betty were so eager to see their children they couldn't wait for them to arrive, right now they just wanted to know the date Lilly and Dan were arriving because they planned to have the open house the next night after they arrived. That way they would then be free to enjoy their children the remainder of the week without worrying or even thinking about the party. Now all they had to do was hear from their children what their schedule would be, and get their guest list!

2

Both Ella and Betty received letters from Dan and Lilly informing them they were booked on a Navy plane flying into San Diego on Friday, July 25, and they had tickets to fly on an American Airlines plane into Little Rock that was supposed to arrive at 2:15 p.m. on Saturday. They hoped one family would meet them and drive them home to Myrna that afternoon. Then the other family could be responsible for getting them to Little Rock to take their plane back to San Diego on Saturday, August 2. They would stay overnight at the Naval Base there and then fly back to Honolulu the next day.

After discussing it, Betty and Ella decided they would plan the open house for Sunday night, and Betty and her husband would meet Dan and Lilly's plane in Little Rock and then drive them to Myrna where they would stop at Jack and Ella's house to see them and Eleanor, Mary Beth, and their families for light refreshments and a short visit before going on to their house where Lilly and Dan would be staying. If Dan wanted to come back by after supper, he could drive their car or even walk since they lived only a few blocks apart.

Since both mothers would be busy on Sunday afternoon preparing for the party on Sunday night, Ella and Betty felt it would be a good day for Dan and Lilly either to go to church together or split up and go to their own church with their own parents. Then they could spend Sunday afternoon with their siblings and any really close friends who were available, and they might even be around to help their mothers if they were needed.

Having come to an agreement on who would meet their plane in Little Rock and who would drive them back to Little Rock for their plane trip to San Diego and then on to Honolulu, Ella and Betty felt good about their plans for the visit and hoped Lilly and Dan would also!

3

The days seemed to crawl by for Ella and Betty who were both eager to see their son and daughter. Although it had been only a year since their wedding, it seemed much longer to their mothers. Both wondered if their child had changed, and if so, how much and in what ways. Their letters home had been eagerly read and re-read, and they were interesting and positive, although both hinted in places about the possibility of the war in the Pacific reaching Hawaii at some point. The idea of war in Hawaii was extremely troubling to both families. Living in the middle of the United States tended to make them feel safe from both Germany and Italy while Japan was so far away, a war with them seemed unimaginable, at least to Betty and Ella.

Yet Dan and Jack had some long discussions about the war in Europe as well as Japan during their time together on Sunday afternoon while Ella was in the midst of preparations for the open house that night, and Lilly had chosen to stay at home with her own family. Both Jack and Dan were amazed the Nazis had broken their peace treaty with Stalin and the Germans had begun an attack on Russia.

Japan was another matter entirely. Although few people in the United States were paying very close attention to the Far East, the Japanese, who had emerged as the dominant power in that part of the world at the end of the first War, continued to increase their influence and strength. By as early as 1931 the Sino-Japanese conflict had established Japan as the leading power in the Far East. Japan had seized and was now in control of the Marshall, Mariana, and Caroline Islands in the Pacific, all of which had been Germany's possessions.

Then at the Versailles Conference after the Great War had ended, Japan was awarded former German concessions in China, even though both China and the United States had protested. Consequently, many of the officers in the Japanese naval and armed forces had become convinced that Japan's hope of becoming a major player lay in expanding its territory, particularly on the Asian mainland. They sought access to food, oil, and other raw materials through military conquest, especially in China and also in Manchuria, which was rich in natural resources that appeared ready and easy for the taking.

Japan's major problem lay with Russia, as influence in Manchuria had been split between Japan and Russia since 1905. But in 1931 the Japanese seized control of Manchuria and then created the Japanese puppet state of Manchukuo, although Japan had withdrawn from the takeover in 1932 when the League of Nations had condemned it.

Japan's withdrawal from seeking power in the region ended in 1937 when Japan entered into a full blown war with China. While the Soviets and the Chinese Communists announced their intentions to support China's Chiang Kai-shek and his forces who were fighting to protect Nanking, the Chinese capital, their support did not stop the Japanese from taking control of Nanking on December 12. The "Rape of Nanking" drew widespread condemnation of Japan, especially in the United States Congress where support for China and Chiang Kai-shek was strong.

Jack, who subscribed to both the *New York Times* and the *Washington Post* on Sundays, was more aware of what was going on in the East than most people in Myrna. But it was Dan who was really on top of what was happening in the islands and countries in the Pacific Ocean.

Dan said it was pretty clear there was going to be war with the Japanese sooner rather than later, and the United States would have to be drawn into it because the Japanese resented the USA's support of Chiang Kai-shek in China. Germany's conquest of much of Europe had impelled the Japanese to replace its cabinet with more aggressive members who were eager to crush China, silence domestic opposition, and push on into Southeast Asia.

Dan had more or less sworn Jack to silence about repeating their conversations to anyone, not even to Ella, but he said that the United States' relations with Japan were deteriorating, and he felt certain that in the near future war would very likely be declared between the States and Japan. And if that happened, a declaration of war against the Germans and Italians would follow. Dan said he never shared any of this kind of information with Lilly. In fact, he'd likely be court-martialed if it were ever known he'd talked with Jack about it, but he knew Jack had been in the last war and that he would keep silent about what Dan had told him. He just needed to know that somebody in the U.S.A. was going to be expecting war.

Jack assured Dan he wouldn't say a word to anybody about what he had told him. But Jack also told Dan that columnists in the *Times* and the *Post* were writing about some of the same things Dan had told him, though maybe *hinting* would be a better choice of words. He imagined they had some sources who were providing them with information the people in the States needed to know in order not to be taken completely by surprise when war came, since it definitely appeared to be on the horizon.

4

The open house was a huge success! Betty had created a guest book she brought for people to sign or even write messages in, if they chose to do so, along with two fountain pens, making sure they were filled with ink. Ella set the guest book on the hall table with a sign asking all guests to please sign the book for Lilly and Dan to take back to Hawaii with them. By the time the evening ended, some 60-plus guests had signed, many writing a little note to go along with their signature so that every page had something written on it.

Doris and Ella had been busy in the kitchen all night, though Ella also was making the rounds to be sure everyone had had some refreshments. She and Betty had both taken turns helping Doris keep up with washing the plates and glasses by drying them and returning them to the dining room table, keeping it covered both with food, lemonade, tea, and water plus clean plates and glasses. They were grateful the evening had become cooler after the sun went down, and the ceiling fans on the porch and in the living and dining rooms were working, as well as the one in the kitchen.

Both young and older people attended the party. Michael and Esther Lewis, Father John Banks and his wife Sarah, Principal Doug Adams and his wife, Pastor Greg Mitchell and his wife Ginny with their four children had come early, along with Hank and Ruth Fredrick and their two sons. Few of the older group stayed long, as Ella had suspected would be the case.

Lee and Suzanna Jones were there, pleasing both Ella and Jack. After they had visited with both Dan and Lilly, Michael and Esther had immediately drawn them into their conversation group. Yet Lee and Suzanna had become so well-known and had made such good reputations for themselves by their work as teachers at Morton High, with Lee also a coach and Suzanna as a counselor, they fit in easily so that many of the guests made a point of stopping to chat with them. They ended up having conversations with all sorts of people, old and young.

Doris and her two children were passing back and forth between the kitchen and the dining room. Doris was working at keeping the plates and glasses washed, dried, and back on the table ready for guests to use. Her two daughters were helping by taking plates and glasses from guests who were finished with them or bringing in platters from the table that needed to be replenished. All of Ella's friends knew Doris and many spoke to her by name when she had brought more of something into the dining room while some went into the kitchen to speak to her.

Ella knew how glad Dan was that Lee and Suzanna had come. She hoped at some point people would never even notice anything unusual about people of different colors socializing together.

The Pastor of First Methodist, William Edwards, who had performed Lilly and Dan's wedding ceremony, and his wife June had also dropped by. In fact, there were several pastors present. Somewhat to Ella's surprise, the pastor at St. Mark's Episcopal, Brian Chandler came with his wife, Nancy, and Ella made a point of welcoming them and telling them how pleased she was they had come. Ella knew she had caused some hard feelings when she married Jack and left St. Mark's to join the Presbyterian Church and was touched that Brian and his wife had come by. Brian actually told Dan how much he and Nancy had enjoyed getting to know him through Sunday school and youth fellowship. Finally Ella quit even trying to remember everyone, especially all the friends in Dan's and Lilly's age-group who were there.

Dan was asked several times what his title as an officer in the Navy was so that they could address him "properly" and each questioner was a bit surprised when Dan answered "Ensign." "What kind of title is that for an officer?" they would want to know.

"It's just what the officers who are the lowest on the totem pole in the Navy are called," Dan would answer.

"Well, we didn't expect you to be an Admiral," one guest said, "but I have to say I'm a bit disappointed in 'Ensign' and hope you move up in the ranks quickly."

Dan laughed and said, "Well, I'm afraid I will be an Ensign for some time because you pass through several levels of 'Ensign' before you earn another title."

Guests had been invited to come anytime between 7:00 and 10:00, and both Ella and Betty were glad that by 10:00 the last of them had gone. Dan and Lilly also left then to meet with some of their friends at somebody's house to visit further, promising Betty they'd be home by midnight. By 10:30, Doris and her children had finished in the kitchen and Jack and Frank had gone to drive them home. The two women separated Betty's plates and glasses from Ella's and packed them in the boxes they had come in and put all of Ella's back in their cabinet. And then giving a sigh of relief and exhaustion, they hugged each other because the evening had been everything they had wanted it to be. Jack was driving his car into the driveway as Ella and Betty hugged. The men loaded Betty's boxes of glassware into the Simpsons' car, and Jack and Ella watched them drive away.

"You two did it, my Ella. You gave Dan and Lilly a lovely 'welcome home' party, and lots of people came. I know you were preparing for 50, but I estimated around 60 were here, though I may have counted some twice. Anyway, it was well attended and everybody seemed to enjoy getting together, even though not everybody was here at the same time, thank goodness, since while we don't have a small house, it's really not large enough for 50 or more people at one time.

"Actually I was glad the evening was not too warm and there was a little breeze so that people could go out on the porch if the ceiling fans weren't doing enough to keep the inside cool. Anyway, my wife, you and Betty outdid yourselves and I know it meant a lot to Dan and Lilly to be able to see and even visit with so many of the people whose lives have touched theirs."

With those words Jack took her hand and led her into their bedroom. Eleanor had taken her children to spend the night at Mary Beth's, and tired as Ella and Jack were, they looked forward to sleeping a bit later in the morning without Amy and Lee there to wake them up!

5

The week passed quickly, too quickly in many ways. The first two nights after the open house Dan and Lilly ate dinner on Monday at the Simpsons and on Tuesday at the MacLeans. The third night Lilly ate at her parents' house with her mother, father, and brother while Dan ate at home with Ella and Papa Jack, Eleanor and her two. The fourth night Jack and Lilly, along with Eleanor and her two children and Ella and Jack had dinner at Mary Beth and Patrick's with all four children present. The fifth night Ella and Jack were invited for dinner at the Simpsons because it was Dan and Lilly's last night in Myrna since they would fly out of Little Rock the next day to San Diego.

Ella hoped it had been a good week for her son and for his wife too. She'd had a little time alone with Lilly and liked her more every time they were together. Lilly had talked freely about working as a nurse in the hospital on the base, which was not far from where she and Jack lived. She had a bicycle she had bought with her first paycheck and that she rode to and from the base hospital unless the weather was bad, which it seldom was. Even when it rained, it was not a cold rain, and a raincoat and rainhat kept her dry enough to go from their house to the hospital. Dan had to be at work on the base by 7:00 each morning, and he would take the car because it was too far to walk to his work.

Lilly talked freely to Ella, who was an excellent listener, about her work and some of what she was learning about caring for men who sometimes were injured on their jobs. These were enlisted men, not officers like Dan, but she liked them because they were always so grateful to the doctors and nurses who took care of them, trying to keep them out of pain and help them heal as quickly as possible.

Lilly had talked about the friends she had made—some of them nurses who were single and some of her friends who were married to Navy officers like Dan or of even higher rank. Most of the younger wives weren't as conscious of their husbands' rank as those who were older. Lilly had realized after being in Honolulu a while that one's husband's rank made a great deal of difference in the perks he received in housing, assignments, pay, social standing, and respect shown. She knew that none of those things meant that much to Dan, and she would try not to let them become important to her either.

She told Ella that at first she had thought she wanted to join the Navy herself and become a Navy nurse, but the longer she was there the more she had started thinking what she really wanted was to have a baby so that if Dan were sent to sea or something, she would have a part of him with her. So she had been trying to get PG for the last few months and nothing had happened. But she had missed her period which had been supposed to start right before they came home, and she had felt a bit queasy a couple of mornings, so maybe she was pregnant. She hadn't told anyone, not even Dan, but she just had to tell someone and Ella was a really good listener, much better than her own mother, though she loved her mother dearly. But would Ella please not tell anyone until she was sure and had told Dan and then her mother. Ella promised to keep her secret but hoped it would not have to be for long!

Ella, who was grateful Lily had found her easy to talk to and had told her more, and in more detail, than either of her own daughters usually did, realized she could honestly say she loved her daughter-in-law! She was equally delighted when Lilly told her she'd like to write Ella letters. She wrote her mother once a week, and although her mother wrote her once a week too, her letters weren't long or very interesting. She hoped Ella would tell her more about what was going on in Myrna or school or anything Ella thought was interesting. And if Ella just wanted to include her in the letters she wrote to Dan, that would be fine because she was always excited when Dan had a letter from his mother and shared it with her because Ella's letters were fun to read. Ella assured her that now they had become friends as well as mother-and-daughter in-law, she would definitely include Lilly in her letters, maybe even adding a paragraph or two especially for Lilly when she knew of something that might interest Lilly but probably not Dan. That way Lilly would know the letter really was meant for her too.

Ella and Jack drove Dan and Lilly to the airport in Little Rock early Saturday morning because their plane to San Diego was leaving at 10:00. Both Ella and Jack found it difficult to say good-bye at the terminal where Dan's and Lilly's plane had already landed and passengers would shortly be boarding, Jack because he felt war with Japan was imminent and feared what it would mean for Dan, and Ella because she realized how much she would now miss not just Dan but also her daughter-in-law.

Part XVII

The War Comes Home: 1941

Fall

1

After Dan and Lilly's visit, the rest of the summer seemed anti-climactic. Ella had been saddened when she had received a letter from Lilly and Dan in mid-August telling them Lilly had miscarried. While they were disappointed, they would try again as soon as Lilly had completely recovered from the miscarriage. Actually, it had not been too painful even with the obstetrician's work to curette her, and they didn't expect to have to wait long.

Jack and Ella had already started preparing themselves to face a new class of 10th graders, while Eleanor also was ready to go back to work. As much as she loved her two pre-schoolers and had enjoyed all the time she'd had with them, she had also missed teaching—not just the students but the actual work of preparing for classes, the reading and thinking she had to do to come up with ways to engage these young adults.

Whenever she'd had a spare hour or so she had opened her textbooks and jotted down ideas of how to pull them into the readings, not just as an assignment but as a way to open their minds to the content and also to the characters and their development in the story or drama. She wanted them not just to understand or get the facts about what they were reading in a novel or story but to have feelings about them, feelings that made the characters seem real and likeable but also to acknowledge what their feelings were that made some of the characters unknowable or people they simply couldn't understand or like.

435

She also wanted them to be able to appreciate the writing itself and to let the good writing help them write more intelligently, recognizing their own gifts as well as those places where they needed to improve. She wanted her students to learn how to write, and even speak, in ways that challenged readers or hearers to see or consider new ideas about life and love.

Even more she also wanted them to think about their values and the values of America. She wanted them to recognize the threats to those values and consider how to keep them alive and important in the world they were already living in and, even more necessary, how to deal with what might threaten or change those values in case of war.

Eleanor and David had continued to exchange letters throughout the summer. She had hoped he might come to Myrna during the brief summer break before the fall classes began again, but he'd been invited to participate in a seminar with a visiting psychologist the week of the break, and it was such a good opportunity to meet and listen to Dr. Van Epps he couldn't pass it up. He promised to share with her anything he learned that might be something she could use in her own teaching.

Eleanor was also well aware that her two were getting older. Lee had one more year with Mary Beth before he would start school. And Pat would start school this year. Nora still had two more years at home and Amy three. Mary Beth said her life was getting easier each year, and she was planning to go back to work at the clinic with Patrick and Jeffrey in two years if they could find some place for Amy. However, there was no reason to worry about that yet. Who knew what their world would be like in two years?

2

As September drew nearer, Jack and Ella starting wondering whom they might invite to be their 10th graders' first speaker, someone who might help set the tone for their joint class in family history and learning to write and speak about that history with well-written papers and in oral presentations that would grab and hold their listeners' interest.

That problem was solved when Esther told Ella in mid-August that Edward Carnes had left the Civilian Conservation Corps to join the army and would be coming to Myrna for a few days before he had to report for Basic Training at Fort Sam Houston in Texas on September 20. Ed was more certain than ever the next war would be starting soon, and he wanted to be ready when it did.

Jack and Ella wasted no time in writing to ask, invite, Ed to speak to their 10th graders about what he had learned from serving in the CCC, and what had led him to leave it and join the Army. Most of the older students at Myrna High remembered Ed from when he had spoken to the 10th graders two years before. They had no doubt some of them would want to see and speak to him this time. They were both relieved when Ed replied that he would be pleased to address their 10th-grade class when he came to Myrna. He wouldn't have much time because he was arriving on September 14, a Sunday, and would have to leave Myrna early on Friday, the 19th, to report to Fort Sam Houston the next day.

Jack immediately called Principal Doug Adams to see if they might have Ed speak to the class on Tuesday afternoon, September 16, and he immediately said "yes" providing he could stand in the back and hear what Eddie, now Ed, had to say. He had realized what an impact Ed had made on the 10th graders who now were seniors and wondered if they might not just make it an all school assembly, or at least for the top three grades. Jack said he and Ella would talk it over and get back to him on the senior high assembly idea.

Ella and Jack quickly accepted the idea of having Ed speak at an assembly of the entire student body. And when he and Ella were talking about the plan, Ella said, "I think it would be good if Ed could speak to Lee's classes too. Do you think Ed would be willing to do so?"

"I honestly don't know—don't even know if Lee would be willing to have him come. It could stir up a hornets' nest. Let's invite Lee and Suzanna to dinner soon and see what they think, though the truth is we need to see whether Ed would be willing to speak to Negro students."

Eleanor agreed and they put the letter to Ed in the next day's mail. Ed answered immediately saying that he would be honored to speak not only to the students at Myrna's high school but also to those at Morton High School. He thought of himself as a member of Lee and Suzanna's family since they had made him their unofficial younger brother. Both Ella and Jack drove out to Lee and Suzanna's home later that same afternoon to see how they would feel about having Ed speak to their students. Eddie Carnes had come a long way from the boy who had gathered up his cronies and brought them dressed as KKK members to Michael and Esther's house, demanding Lee be turned over to them.

But the really amazing part was that Michael had gotten Eddie out of jail, brought him home to spend a few weeks with him and Esther where they treated him more like a son than a juvenile delinquent. Eddie had even spent a few weeks helping Lee and Suzanna finish the house they were building. There Lee and Suzanna had put additional touches on Eddie's young manhood by treating and loving Eddie like a younger brother and a good man.

The CCC had added the finishing touches on Eddie by opening his mind and heart to other young men from various backgrounds and places he'd never heard of, just as none of them had ever heard of Myrna, Arkansas. He had become Ed there as he learned from the men in charge of his CCC camp what it means not only to be a good man but an American man, so he had just resigned from the CCC to become a soldier in the US Army Corps. While he would begin his service by going through basic training at Fort Sam Houston in Texas, he had no idea where he would be sent after that.

Lee and Suzanna thought it would be good for all their students, especially their young men at Morton to hear Ed's story, to realize it wasn't just Negro boys who had a hard time, and to understand that even as Eddie had overcome his past and become

Ed and a soon-to-be private in the U.S. Army, they could do the same thing. It might be a big more difficult for them, but it had also been hard going for Eddie, and yet he had succeeded.

At least, their Negro students in general had families that loved, encouraged, and supported them, the kind of family Eddie had not had. He had received that kind of support from one white couple and from a black couple. Lee told the students that Eddie had worked for him, helping him finish the house where he and Suzanna lived and had become like their younger brother, which shows that race and color do not have to make it impossible for black, brown, and white people to respect, love, and care about one another.

Lee talked with the rest of the staff about inviting Ed Carnes to come and speak at a special assembly, tell his life story and about his time working with the Civilian Conservation Corps and why he had made his decision to enlist in the Army. The Negro teachers all realized if the United States entered the war, it might not be long before their young men would be called up for service. They enthusiastically approved Lee's idea to invite Ed Carnes to speak to their student body in a special assembly.

Ed did speak to both sets of students: to the Myrna students on Tuesday and the Morton students on Wednesday. He did so well in sharing his story and in describing life in the CCC and then explaining why he had left the CCC to join the US Army that both places he addressed gave him standing ovations.

Truth be told, the one that touched him the most came from the Morton students who didn't know him but who understood from his speech that life had not been easy for him but that he had, with help, put the bad times behind him and had become a man, a real man, a good man in spite of what he had been as a boy.

He had received help, help that hadn't come from his family but from people who had seen something good in him, something worth helping him to develop and become. Now he had joined the Armed Forces because he believed his country would soon enter the war, and he wanted to do what he could to preserve the ideals and promises on which it had been founded.

The Negro teachers and young people who heard Ed's talk realized while Ed had not had an easy life, he had one advantage they did not have, that of being *white*. And while many of the young black men who heard Ed's speech would also end up fighting to preserve the United States, it often would not be easy to overcome the prejudices against people of color so many white people continued to hold.

3

While life continued to move forward not only in Myrna but throughout the rest of the United States, the average citizen was barely aware of what was happening in Europe or even Russia and certainly not in parts of the world like Japan.

Ordinary people in the United States, and most likely many of those in government positions, did not know that on April 13, 1941, Japan had signed a non-aggression pact with the Soviet Union, an agreement that freed both countries from a war on two fronts.

Japan was already involved in an aggressive war against China, a war that concerned Franklin Roosevelt's administration because it was obvious Japan wanted to dominate the Far East by force. Consequently on July 24, 1941, both Britain and the United States froze Japanese assets in their countries as a protest against Japan's extending its power by occupying French Indo-China, which Japan had done in September of 1940.

President Roosevelt assumed Japan would respond rationally to this act, but Japan's government ignored FDR's move. Instead of modifying its actions, Japan sought alternative energy supplies and turned to other colonial empires in South East Asia like oil-rich Burma and the Netherlands' East Indies. After Cordell Hull, the US Secretary of State, spent over a 100 hours negotiating with the Japanese Ambassador at the State Department, the President warned Japan publicly on August 17 that any further actions like those by Japan would cause America to take measures to safeguard her interests in that part of the world. As a sign America meant what it said, the Pacific Fleet was moved from California to Pearl Harbor, while the US government was also providing financial aid to General Chiang Kai-shek's Chinese Nationalists in their fight against Japan's invasion of Chinese soil.

But FDR and his Administration underestimated the pride of the Showa Dynasty of Japan who took America's actions of deterrence as unacceptable provocations. The hard truth was that many Americans in power did not take the Japanese seriously and had some very prejudiced ideas about their fighting ability and courage. For example, one mistaken and racist belief held by some senior American politicians was that the slanted eyes of Japanese pilots meant that they could not make long flights from their homeland and so were no danger to the Hawaiian islands.

Yet after Lieutenant-General Hideki Tojo, nicknamed "Razor," came to power in Tokyo in mid-October, within three weeks the Imperial General Headquarters had finalized plans to attack Pearl Harbor and to invade the Philippines, Malaysia, the Dutch East Indies, Thailand, and Burma. The Japanese would soon surprise the United States with its attack on Pearl Harbor.

4

Halloween came with its carnival at the high school and then before they could believe it Thanksgiving had come and gone. In their last letter home that Lilly and Dan had written together on Thanksgiving Day, their big news was Lilly was six weeks pregnant and so far was doing fine, and that was their main reason for giving thanks this year. Ella had immediately written back that both their families had been delighted with their news and had also added it to their "thanksgiving" lists.

Dan and Lilly were still in bed on the morning of December 7 when the bombs began to fall. They were taking advantage of its being Sunday when neither of them had to be at their jobs by

7:00 a.m. Lilly actually had been up because morning sickness had sent her to the bathroom and she had barely gone back to sleep before the explosions awakened her. Dan had already bounded out of bed and was out on the stoop looking up at the planes as the bombs fell. Some of the planes came close enough he could see the red circles on them.

He tore himself away to go back inside and took Lilly in his arms, saying, "Well, this is it. It's the Japanese! The President and Congress will have to declare war after today. I've got to get into my uniform and go to the office, if it's still standing. I'm sorry, my darling, but this is really it. Stay here, stay inside. We don't know what's going on in the town. Most likely there are spies among the Hawaiian people, and so we need to be careful right now.

"I'm sure our parents are going to be frantic with worry about us. I'll try to send a wire that we're okay, but I may not be able to send anything. We may have closed everything down to keep the Japs from getting into our network for communication. Honey, I just don't know what I'm going to find. I'll let you know something as soon as I can."

"Oh, Dan, I wish I could beg you to stay, but I can't. I know you have to go. But please be careful. Please don't get killed now!" Lilly was crying as she held onto him, but after kissing him, she let him go. "Dan, I know you may not be able to telephone, but do try to keep me informed about where you are and what's going on as best you can. This is so awful, but I don't want to miscarry again. I have our son or daughter inside me, and I will be careful, but I want her or him to have a Daddy!"

* * *

In Arkansas where it was a quiet Sunday afternoon, Jack was sitting on the sofa reading the newspaper with the radio on low when the classical music playing was silenced by these words: "We interrupt this program to bring you this news bulletin from Hawaii. Pearl Harbor is being attacked by Japanese bombers. At this time we do not know the extent of the damage or of the loss of life. Again I repeat, Pearl Harbor is under attack by the Japanese Air Force. We will break in again as soon as more information is available."

Jack took a deep breath, then got up to find Ella and break the news to her. He knew she had been dreading something like this would happen just as he had, and they both knew this meant the United States would declare war on Japan. Jack also had serious doubts the war would be limited to the Japanese, even though he hoped that might be the case.

He held Ella close while she wept in fear her son and pregnant daughter-in-law had been killed. The telephone rang, and he let go of Ella so he could answer it. It was Lilly's mother, Betty, who was almost hysterical as she asked if they had heard the news. Ella was talking to her when Eleanor came down the stairs asking what was going on. As Jack was explaining the situation to her, Mary Beth, Patrick and their two children came in. Mary Beth was saying, "I just can't believe this! Have you heard from Dan? Are they all right? Does this mean we are in the war?"

Jack said, "Slow down, Honey. We haven't heard from Dan, and I doubt he'll be able to get through to us anytime soon. So we don't know. And while we're not at war right now because this attack was obviously a surprise to everyone on the island, as well as to those of us living in the States, probably even to the President, only the President and Congress can declare war. Yet I imagine that will happen soon, probably tomorrow. We may just declare war on the Japanese, though I think that will lead us into the war in Europe also. What do you think, Patrick?"

"I can't imagine we'll be able to get by with just fighting Japan. Hitler and the Germans and even the Italians and Mussolini are doing so well, they may be eager to take on the Japanese too—or make them allies.

"But I can't see us letting Hitler rule Europe and I know the English won't let go of their country—or even their Empire— without a fight to the bitter end. After all, England does have some members of the Empire who are fighting on her side. They might not like being under British rule, but I am pretty sure they would prefer it to Hitler's, Mussolini's, or the Japanese Emperor's."

"I agree with you, Patrick," Jack said. "I think we've all feared this was going to come, that we'd be drawn into it at some point. Roosevelt has kept us out of it far longer than I'd expected. But this it. He can't just brush this off. I'd be surprised if he doesn't declare war on Japan by tomorrow and no later than Tuesday. Of course, he's got to get the Congress to vote for it, but I don't doubt that will happen, and happen soon."

The next day, December 8, 1941, Ella and Jack and the Simpsons received telegrams from Dan and Lilly that said, "WE ARE SAFE. DON'T WORRY. WILL WRITE SOON." They did write soon, or at least Lilly did—a long letter describing what that day had been like while Dan was at the Naval offices and she was busy at the hospital taking care of men and even some women who had been hurt by the bombs that had fallen.

Lilly had heard some amazing stories from people who had been outside when the bombs began falling. One civilian American pilot was in the air giving flying lessons to a young man when they saw airplanes, a lot of airplanes with the Red Circle of Japan, flying toward the islands. The pilot had grabbed the controls from the young man and headed toward the civilian landing field, managing to land it safely.

The saddest, actually the worst story, was that of a young Navy officer who was manning the Westinghouse radar system early that morning. He saw the blips on the radar, but since it was a Sunday morning, he decided they were nothing to worry about—that is until they had gotten close enough for him to tell the blips were most likely Japanese bombers. But by then it was too late. Lilly wrote she feared his career in the Navy might not end well.

Truly, she and Dan were grateful to have lived through the bombing, although the targets had been the ships in the harbor and not the houses on the base.

While the damage was terrible, it was not as bad as it could have been. Dan had told her the Navy had been fortunate because three of America's aircraft carriers and seven heavy cruisers were at sea that morning. But the human toll of 2,403 servicemen and civilians killed and another 1,178 wounded was heavy. While the actual numbers were not known or posted until later, Lilly's experiences as a nurse at the hospital were as demanding and difficult as Dan's on the ground.

On December 8, Congress voted 470 to 1 to declare war on Japan. The only "no" vote came from Pacifist Jeannette Rankin of Montana.

President Roosevelt addressed the nation, rallying its citizens with his words: "Yesterday, December 7, 1941—a date that will live in infamy—the United States of America was suddenly and deliberately attacked by naval and air forces of the Empire of Japan." The President went on to say that while a number of American lives had been lost at Pearl Harbor, Japan had also attacked Malaya, Hong Kong, Guam, the Philippines, and Wake and Midway Islands. He concluded his brief statement by saying, "No matter how long it may take us to overcome this premeditated invasion, the American people in their righteous might, will win through to absolute victory."

The President's speech to Congress was only 25 sentences long, but he was interrupted so often by applause from the Congress that it lasted 10 minutes.

5

Three days later Hitler declared war on the United States, even though he was already in the middle of a war with Stalin's Russia. America was an uninvadable land mass, and Russia was practically so. While Hitler's army had begun its invasion of Russia six months earlier, it would soon realize its failure in succeeding.

President Roosevelt was finally ready to lead his nation in joining the British, the French, and at last, the Russians in their war against the Germans, the Italians, and the Japanese in order to prevent the conquest of the western world. Yet none of these nations knew what the cost would be or that this war would finally end with the dropping of two atomic bombs—one on Hiroshima and the other on Nagasaki—causing such death and destruction as had never been seen!

And the world would never again be the same.

The End

Afterword

Most likely to everyone in the United States and the rest of the world, the air attack on Pearl Harbor on December 7, 1941, came as a surprise and even a shock. Although the Japanese Ambassadors Nomura and Kurusu had requested a special meeting with Cordell Hull, the U.S. Secretary of State, set for the exact time in Washington the bombing of Pearl Harbor was to begin, neither Hull nor anyone else in the government had expected the attack when it actually occurred.

The State Department knew from intercepted Japanese messages that Japan was planning to break off all negotiations with the United States, but since the message from Tokyo didn't mention either war or Pearl Harbor, Washington was taken as much by surprise as the Navy officers and all the people of Hawaii who were awakened by bombs falling at 8:00 on that Sunday morning. The fighter planes attacked in two waves. The first wave was undetected, and so the Japanese aircraft were able to attack the ships and planes docked at Pearl Harbor from the west. Only three American patrol aircraft were in the air that morning, and none of them detected either the first or second wave of the Japanese air and sea forces until it was too late.

The Japanese pilots found seven American battleships moored in a row while another, the *Pennsylvania*, was in dry dock close by. The ships had been packed close together to make them easier to guard, but they were also much easier for the Japanese bombers to hit. Only one quarter of the Navy's machine guns were manned that morning while one third of the ships' captains were ashore since, after all, it was a Sunday.

By 10:00 a.m. it was over. Of the eight American battleships in port, three were sunk. The Oklahoma was capsized and the other four were damaged. Three light cruisers, three destroyers and some other vessels were sunk or badly damaged. The good news was that no submarines had been affected except for the five midget submarines near or inside the harbor, all five of which were sunk. Only 54 out of 250 Navy and Marine planes either survived the bombing intact or could be repaired. But 166 out of the 231 Air Force planes were safe.

The American death toll came to 2,403 servicemen and civilians killed with 1,178 wounded, while the Japanese lost only 29 planes and 100 lives.

A third wave of bombers had been planned, but the Japanese withheld it because they feared a counter attack from the American aircraft carriers that were not in the harbor. This third wave of bombers were meant to destroy the oil depots and repair yards the Pacific Fleet would need to rebuild itself, and it actually would do so in six months after the attack. So even as the Japanese airmen celebrated, its leaders understood they had not accomplished all they had needed to do. As it was, all the ships except two destroyers would be repaired for service in the war effort. Only the *Arizona* would lie in its watery grave, still able to be seen by visitors to this day.

Neither the American people or the people of Hawaii would know all the above facts about the bombing until after World War II ended. It was the Hawaiians themselves, along with the American Naval and Air Force officers and servicemen, who lived through that surprise attack. They understood and grieved over their losses and feared others, if not to the Hawaiian Islands themselves, then to other islands in the Pacific and throughout the entire world.

Obviously most of the facts listed here were not made public until after the war, but they should not be forgotten. I am grateful for information provided by those who were alive at the time or had resources from the time. I especially thank the Reverend Don Campbell who connected me with Wendy Cole and Grace Height who in turn provided the incidents about the flying lesson pilot and the Naval officer who didn't sound the alarm about the approaching Japanese aircraft.

Sally Stockley Johnson

Acknowledgments

As this will most likely be my last novel, I want to acknowledge three important people. The first is my brother, **Grif Stockley**, who began as writer of the *Gideon Page* mysteries about a lawyer/detective who solves murder cases.

Grif then moved on to write about true-life situations as in *Blood in Their Eyes: The Elaine Massacre of 1919* and *Black Boys Burning: The 1959 Fire at the Arkansas Negro Boys Industrial School* that took the lives of 21 of the 69 boys locked in at night in the burning building where they were housed. At least 48 did escape after help arrived to break open the locked doors.

Grif's history *Ruled by Race: Black/White Relations in Arkansas from Slavery to the Present* has been used as a textbook in colleges and high schools.

His biograph of *Daisy Bates* gives us insight into the life of this amazing woman, while his autobiography, *Hypogrif in Bubbaville: A Memoir of Race, Class and Ego*, lets us get to know the real Grif Stockley. Grif died in 2022 to my sorrow and that of his daughter and three granddaughters and his many friends.

My second acknowledgment is to my editor, publisher, book designer, dear friend, and spiritual guide, **H. K. Stewart**. He recommended changes that improved the writing and the story and encouraged me when I've needed it. I owe him more than I can say.

My last acknowledgment is to the memory of my beloved husband, **Carlos Alberto Lopez**, who brought so much love and joy into my life during the 22 years of our marriage.

For Further Reading

The Storm of War: a New History of the Second World War, by Andrew Roberts, published by Harper, 2011, 2012.

World War II: A Military and Social History, A course Guidebook with written information along with lectures on DVDs by Professor Thomas Childers of the University of Pennsylvania, published by *Great Courses*, 1998.

V Was For Victory: Politics and American Culture During World War II by John Morton Blum, published by Harcourt Brace Jovanovich, 1976.

The Great Depression: America, 1929-1941 by Robert S. McElvaine, published by The Three Rivers Press, New York, 1984.

The Oxford History of the American People by Samuel Eliot Morrison, published by the Oxford University Press, New York.

Obviously the facts listed here were not made public until after the war, but they should not be forgotten. The writer is grateful for information provided by others who were alive at the time or had resources from that time.

About the Author

Sally Stockley Johnson was born in 1937 in Memphis, Tennessee, and spent her early years on her daddy's farms in Arkansas and Mississippi until the family moved to Marianna, Arkansas, where she and her brother, Grif, and sister, Harriet, finished high school. In 1955, she received a scholarship to Southwestern at Memphis (now Rhodes College), from which she graduated with distinction in 1958.

In June of 1957, she married her high school algebra teacher Voris Johnson, who was also the basketball coach, and after graduation, returned to Marianna to teach English and Spanish and give birth to Julie in 1962 and Charlie in 1965. When Voris was offered the position of head basketball coach at Hot Springs High, they moved there in 1966. Sally taught Spanish at Hot Springs and then stayed home with their young children and gave birth to Voris, Jr., in 1970. She taught Spanish and English at Lakeside High School from 1972 to 1976 when she was offered the opportunity to become the first church educator at Westminster Presbyterian Church, where she remained for 11 years.

During that time, she and Voris divorced and she was encouraged to answer God's call to ministry. She moved to Austin, Texas, in June of 1987 to attend Austin Presbyterian Theological Seminary. After graduating two years later, she accepted a call to be associate pastor at Northwood Presbyterian Church in San Antonio. In 1993, she met Carlos Alberto Lopez, a Cuban and a retired Presbyterian pastor, and after a "truly whirlwind courtship" they were married in 1994.

During their 23 years together, she worked briefly at Mo-Ranch Presbyterian Camp and Conference Center, and then served as interim minister at churches in Temple, Texas, and Houston before she was called to pastor Beacon Hill Presbyterian Church in San Antonio. She retired in 2005, and she and Carlos moved to Little Rock, Arkansas, three years later. He died in January of 2017. Today, she enjoys their children and grandchildren and writing and serving wherever she can.

www.ingramcontent.com/pod-product-compliance
Lightning Source LLC
Chambersburg PA
CBHW020502020726
47493CB00001B/141